E. L. Doctorow

18 II 22

E. L. Doctorow

A Reconsideration

Edited by Michael Wutz and
Julian Murphet

EDINBURGH
University Press

Edinburgh University Press is one of the leading university presses in the UK. We publish academic books and journals in our selected subject areas across the humanities and social sciences, combining cutting-edge scholarship with high editorial and production values to produce academic works of lasting importance. For more information visit our website: edinburghuniversitypress.com

Edinburgh University Press Ltd
The Tun – Holyrood Road, 12(2f) Jackson's Entry, Edinburgh EH8 8PJ

First published in hardback by Edinburgh University Press 2020

Typeset in Sabon and Futura
by R. J. Footring Ltd, Derby, UK

A CIP record for this book is available from the British Library

ISBN 978 1 4744 5883 2 (hardback)
ISBN 978 1 4744 5884 9 (paperback)
ISBN 978 1 4744 5885 6 (webready PDF)
ISBN 978 1 4744 5886 3 (epub)

Contents

Acknowledgments

The editors would like to thank their respective institutions for their support which made this volume happen. Michael Wutz is grateful to Scott Sprenger, Dean of the Telitha E. Lindquist College of Arts and Humanities at Weber State University, for a sabbatical, which allowed for the space and time to move this project forward at a critical juncture. He would also like to thank WSU's Master of Arts in English Program for receiving the 2016 Robert M. Hogge Faculty Teaching Award, which enabled him to develop a seminar on E. L. Doctorow into a laboratory of ideas. Bob Hogge was a devoted Americanist and a cherished colleague, who kindly endowed this award before his retirement. I dedicate this book to him.

Julian Murphet organized a symposium on the late Mr. Doctorow's work in Sydney, the year that he died, where some of the papers collected in this volume first had a trial outing. He is grateful to Dr. Mark Byron of the Department of English, University of Sydney, for hosting that symposium, and to all who attended and delivered such outstanding papers, including John Frow, Diana Shahinyan, Mark Steven, Kate Montague, and Alys Moody. The event was publicized and co-run through the no longer extant Centre for Modernism Studies in Australia, based at UNSW Sydney, where James Donald, the then Dean of Arts and Social Sciences, was a firm supporter of all our initiatives, including this one.

A sincere thank you is also due to Dr. Samuel Dickson, who was part of our original editorial troika but who saw himself forced to look for greener pastures—that is, full-time employment and a living wage—outside the academy. (That he felt he had to do so is an indicator of the precarious state of the humanities.) The reviews of two anonymous manuscript readers were as a constructive as they were encouraging and helped us refine and enrich our thinking.

Even clean and solid manuscripts undergo a makeover during the various stages of acquisition and copy-editing. To that end, we and all of our contributors would like to offer a sincere thanks to Michelle Houston, Commissioning Editor of Literary Studies, and Ersev Ersoy, Assistant Commissioning Editor of Literary Studies, at Edinburgh University Press for their help, especially during the review and permissions process. We are also deeply grateful to Ralph Footring, who copy-edited our manuscript with the utmost care and diligence. The professionalism, expertise, and acumen of Edinburgh University Press's editorial team is visible on most very page of our book.

As is almost always the case when scholarly passion brushes up against family and friends, the ones closest to us deserve a special and most heartfelt thanks. This book was in the making for several years and inevitably took its toll on time spent with family and friends. We owe them our profound gratitude for their patience and understanding.

Finally, Michael Wutz would like to acknowledge his long-standing relationship with Edgar Doctorow, which began in April 1993, when Edgar was the featured speaker at the National Undergraduate Literature Conference (NULC) held annually on the campus of Weber State University. Over the years, and punctuated by visits when Edgar and his wife, Helen, received us at their summer home in Sag Harbor, and at Edgar's office on Bleecker Street in New York's Greenwich Village, this acquaintance ripened into a warm friendship. A not infrequent letter exchange, about all things literary and not, further deepened our rapport and culminated in Edgar's second visit to our campus in 2011, when we were, finally, able to reciprocate his and Helen's hospitality at our home. Assembling this volume in the wake of his passing in July 2015 is, in that sense, a personal as much as a professional tribute to one of the most gifted men of letters mapping the American landscape. Thank you, Edgar.

Contributors

Stephen Arch is Professor of English at Michigan State University. He is the author of two monographs on early American literature, and the associate lead editor of "The Writings of James Fenimore Cooper" (SUNY Press). His essay on the gothic in Elizabeth Stoddard's *The Morgesons* (1862) appeared in the collection *Haunting Realities: Naturalist Gothic and American Realism* (edited by Monika Elbert and Wendy Ryden, 2017).

Tamlyn Avery was awarded her Ph.D. in literary studies from UNSW Sydney, where she teaches in English and media studies. Her most recent publications look at representations of women's labor, racial characterization, and the mediatic unconscious in American modernist literature. She is currently writing a book on the history of the American *Bildungsroman*.

Mark Azzopardi is Assistant Professor of Intellectual Heritage and Modern Literature at Temple University, Japan Campus. He completed his Ph.D. in the Department of English at the University of Sydney in 2015 with a dissertation exploring the mid-century American novel's national and international dimensions.

Don DeLillo is among the most widely read American novelists of his generation. He is the author of fifteen novels, including *Zero K*, *Underworld*, *Falling Man*, *White Noise*, and *Libra*. He has won the U.S. National Book Award, the PEN/Faulkner Award for Fiction, the Jerusalem Prize for his complete body of work, and the William Dean Howells Medal from the American Academy of Arts and Letters. In 2010, he was awarded the PEN/Saul Bellow Prize. His story collection *The Angel Esmeralda* was a finalist for the 2011 Story Prize and the PEN/Faulkner Award for Fiction.

Jennifer Egan is the author of several novels and a short-story collection. Her 2017 novel *Manhattan Beach* was a *New York Times* bestseller and was awarded the 2018 Andrew Carnegie Medal for Excellence in Fiction. Her previous novel, *A Visit From the Goon Squad* (2010), won the 2011 Pulitzer Prize, the National Book Critics Circle Award, and the *Los Angeles Times* book prize. She has written for *New York Times Magazine* and currently serves as President of PEN America and Artist-in-Residence at the University of Pennsylvania.

Nathan D. Frank is a doctoral candidate at the University of Virginia. His work appears in the *Rocky Mountain Review*, *Biblical Interpretation*, *Kudzu Quarterly*, and *Humanities*, and in several edited collections. His dissertation explores how the work of novelists such as E. L. Doctorow, Toni Morrison, Joshua Ferris, Salman Rushdie, and Adam Levin invokes, reimagines, and emulates scriptural modes of textuality. Forthcoming is a Karen Barad-driven project that seeks to read U2's most recent albums diffractively.

Alexander Howard is Lecturer in Writing Studies at the University of Sydney. His research focuses on modern and contemporary literature and film. He is the author of *Charles Henri Ford: Between Modernism and Postmodernism* (2017).

Jieun Kwon is Associate Professor of British/American Literature and Culture at Hankuk University of Foreign Studies, Seoul, Korea. Her research explores intersections between 9/11, affect, and the possibility of a new form of community. An essay reexamining the problematic of "white male crisis" in Bret Easton Ellis's works appears in *The Explicator* (vol. 77, issue 2, 2019, pp. 63–7).

Nicholas Murgatroyd studied English literature at the University of Cambridge before teaching in the Czech Republic, Spain, and Mexico. He then completed a Ph.D. in creative writing at the University of Manchester, during which he undertook a study of democratic narrative form in E. L. Doctorow's works. He works at the University of Sheffield and has recently completed a novel loosely inspired by his visit to the Doctorow archive.

Julian Murphet is Scientia Professor of English and Film Studies at UNSW Sydney. He is the author of *Literature and Race in Los Angeles* (2001), *Multimedia Modernism* (2009), *Faulkner's Media Romance* (2017), and *Todd Solondz* (2019). He has co-edited a number of collections, including, with Natalya Lusty, *Modernism and Masculinity* (2014) and, with Helen Groth and Penelope Hone, *Sounding Modernism* (2017). With Sean Pryor he edits *Affirmations: of the modern*, an open-access online journal.

Victor S. Navasky is editor, publisher, and now publisher emeritus of *The Nation*, and is the George T. Delacorte Professor Emeritus of Professional Practice in Magazine Journalism at Columbia University.

His books include *Kennedy Justice* (1971) and, in collaboration with Christopher Cerf, *The Experts Speak: The Definitive Guide to Authoritative Misinformation* (1984) and *Mission Accomplished! Or How We Won the War in Iraq* (2008). *A Matter of Opinion* (2005) won the 2005 George Polk Book Award and the 2006 Ann M. Sperber Prize, and *Naming Names* (1980)—widely considered a definitive take on the Hollywood blacklist—a National Book Award for Nonfiction in 1982.

Michael Wutz is a Rodney H. Brady Presidential Distinguished Professor in the Department of English at Weber State University and the editor of the journal *Weber—The Contemporary West*. He is the co-editor of *Reading Matters: Narrative in the New Media Ecology* (1997), the co-translator of the late Friedrich Kittler's *Gramophone, Film, Typewriter* (1999), and the co-editor of *Conversations with W. S. Merwin* (2015). He is also the author of *Enduring Words—Narrative in a Changing Media Ecology* (2009) and is currently collaborating on a volume of Kittler essays entitled *Operation Valhalla* (forthcoming).

Introduction

Michael Wutz and Julian Murphet

The passing of Edgar Lawrence Doctorow in 2015, at age eighty-four, robbed American literature of one of its twentieth-century titans, still near the peak of his considerable powers, and still awaiting his proper critical due. After the flurry of interest in his postmodernism in the mid-1980s, and corollary reflections on his prowess at blending fictional and real-world characters, critical attention shifted elsewhere in the 1990s and the body of work as a whole has been treated to only a small handful of more or less descriptive studies. The decline in attention to this remarkable oeuvre—surely one of the more significant bodies of world fiction after World War II—is a testament to the crisis in literary studies today, which seems so uncertain of both its object and its raison d'être. While Doctorow cemented his post-*Ragtime* career with such mature masterpieces as *Billy Bathgate* (1989), *City of God* (2000), and *The March* (2005), it was often easier to find fully developed critical studies of the uneven likes of Bret Easton Ellis and David Foster Wallace than of this elder statesman of the art of the novel. His intelligence, so intransigent and yet so timely and precise, never waned, and neither did his often experimental approach to form and voice. If *The March* feels like a *summa doctorowica*, a magnificent demonstration of the artist's full powers and presiding concerns, then *Homer & Langley* (2009) and *Andrew's Brain* (2014) seem impish and playful by contrast, bags full of a younger man's tricks and frolics, opening up new horizons of possibility for the form. The truth is that Doctorow's body of work vastly exceeds its critical legacy, in scope, ambition, and conceptual richness, and this remains a challenge to literary criticism today, when both the novel as a form and the presumptions of critical practice are in such severe crisis. Doctorow's death in 2015 has had the inevitable result of completing his oeuvre and bestowing upon it a retrospective aura of total accomplishment with few equals in his, or any other, generation. It is to that total accomplishment that this volume is oriented, in an effort to begin a serious reconsideration of a body of work that asks so much of us, as critics, as readers, and as citizens.

Doctorow's achievement is multifaceted, but arguably it turns around a number of prevailing concerns: concerns with the fate of the American republic, with the political ramifications of literary fiction, with the novel as a critical humanistic instrument of thought and public intervention, with history as a series of manipulable inscriptions, with the criminal dynamics of fame and fortune in the evolving framework of monopoly capitalism, with the fate of the working poor under those same conditions, and with outsiders and losers in general, those whose minor fortunes and cruel destinies are the flipside of a glossy celebrity culture. But Doctorow was also a major Jewish artist, however secular, and the proud son of Russian immigrants, who took his not always comfortable (or wanted) place in the front rank of Jewish-American authors, alongside Philip Roth, Cynthia Ozick, Saul Bellow, Allen Ginsberg, Adrienne Rich, and, before them, Gertrude Stein and Louis Zukofsky, among many others. His depictions, especially in *The Book of Daniel*, *World's Fair*, and *Billy Bathgate*, of Jewish life in the Bronx and Brooklyn in the 1930s rank with the best evocations of that lost world of cultural, intellectual, and political commitments specific to a certain Eastern-European immigrant milieu between the wars, and his work negotiated a series of compelling relationships between, for instance, Jewish identity and African-American identity in *Ragtime*, or the Christian and Jewish dimensions of a certain modern American spirituality in *City of God*. Unlike some of his more orthodox Jewish contemporaries, however, he was more philosophically capacious in spirit and practice, drawing on what he called a "spiritual sort of alternating current" that structured his creativity early on:

> As the son of my fathers I am nonobservant, a celebrant of the humanism that has no patience for a religious imagination that asks me to abandon my intellect. But as the son of my mothers, I am unable to discard reverence, however unattached to an object, in recognition that a spontaneously felt sense of the sacred engages the whole human being as the intellect alone cannot.[1]

More than that, Doctorow can be considered a chameleonic adept in the varied arts of genre fiction, having tried his hands at the Western (*Welcome to Hard Times*), the gangster saga (*Billy Bathgate*), the *Bildungsroman* (*The Book of Daniel*, *Loon Lake*), detective fiction (*The Waterworks*), the science-fiction novel (*Big as Life*), and the war novel (*The March*), and even arguably the musical (*City of God*). And even such a catalogue, exhaustive as it already is, leaves out Doctorow's recrafting of such genres as the gothic, the historical romance, and the various Hollywood genres he inhabited as a one-time script reader (which is why his capacious reach into generic plenitude is not unlike that of Robert Altman and Stanley Kubrick in the world of cinema). This side of Doctorow's achievement is, on reflection, more sizable and more durable than might have been expected from such a serious exponent of the craft of literary fiction; for, unlike, say, Thomas Pynchon or Kurt Vonnegut, Doctorow's approach was not the indiscriminate blending and leveling of generic and subgeneric materials, but always the elevation or dignification of a hitherto spurned species of pulp fiction into something substantial and august, by virtue of a thoroughly non-condescending immersion in the form. And there are other dimensions to Doctorow's achievement that call out for a more searching and serious consideration today, not least his powerful attitudes toward sex and sexuality, toward the "desiring machines" of human consciousness and unconsciousness, and toward the darker reaches of the psyche's appetites, its tendencies toward chaos, and its often willing subjection to external control. The picture of the human animal that emerges from a thorough reading of Doctorow's oeuvre is far from the rosy portrait one might expect of a genial liberal humanist of the sort he tended to project in public appearances; it is significantly crueller, uglier, and queerer than first appearances might suggest.

But perhaps more significant still is the flickering evidence, thrown off by all his work, of a consistent and fully articulated fictional world, in which certain recurrent themes, characters, and situations, not to mention patterns, motifs, and symbols, reappear and modulate before our eyes into something grander and more imposing, or at any rate more obsessive and symptomatic, than any single work can encompass. This is the feeling that any thorough immersion in his oeuvre can trigger, that we are witnesses to the steady unfurling of a very grand project indeed, not without correspondence to the lifelong efforts of a Balzac, a Faulkner, or even a Bolaño, where each work finds its place in relation to all the others, and a plane of immanence is established wherein nothing is truly extrinsic or arbitrary, and everything finally belongs. Whether or not this was a fully conscious or explicitly developed horizon of the novels' meaning, it cannot be disavowed or avoided once detected, and calls into question many of the critically established divisions and distinctions between the works that make up the Doctorow canon. For if a character in *The March* can turn out to be the progenitor of a major character in *Ragtime*, or can have an unexpected afterlife on the pages of *The Waterworks*, and if certain luminous percepts and affects that blaze across the pages of *The Book of Daniel* can reappear in scarcely altered form in *Billy Bathgate*, or then again in *World's Fair*, then what Doctorow once called his "repertory company of characters" might be part and parcel of a significantly larger traveling operation, of continuous reinscription and recycling, where the sad waste and entropy that affect so many of his depicted lives in individual texts is transfigured in the cosmic light of the whole, via a species of literary eternity and transmigration. Such speculation is at least invited by the evidence to hand, and yet scarcely developed in the critical literature to date.

What we want this collection to do, then, is to begin a conversation along these lines; to provoke the literary critical community to re-engage with a body of work that not only has yet to be exhausted, but has yet, really, to be properly encountered, in all its strange and compelling richness. In what remains of this Introduction, we will first account for the major and durable findings of a previous generation of Doctorow scholars, and then turn to a scene-setting exercise for the essays that follow, which we will then summarize in brief synopses. In their entirety, these essays will help us map in broad outline what we perceive to be the most urgent tasks ahead in the critical reappraisal of Doctorow's total accomplishment, as a younger generation turns to encounter it for the first time. Mindful as we are that our volume does not feature dedicated essays on Doctorow's final three novels, *The March*, *Homer & Langley*, and *Andrew's Brain*—which is itself symptomatic of Doctorow's academic neglect—we invite scholars not only to take a second and third look at Doctorow's early-career achievements, but also to engage with these extraordinary late-phase works, which are part and parcel of an artistic arc that spans more than five decades of almost unequalled narrative production in the history of American letters.

Doctorow Studies—Taking Stock

The one brief moment when the critical-theoretical community engaged with Doctorow's work at a level commensurate with his—already, even then, significant—achievement was during the heyday of postmodernism, a term as amorphous, mutinous, and mutant then as it is now that it has lost some of its currency and been historicized in its own right. Years (and sometimes decades) before Doctorow entered a second sustained and productive phase that would yield such masterpieces as *The Waterworks*, *City of God*, and *The March*—and which have suffered from critical benign neglect to date, to put it mildly—scholars briefly put his work on the front burner of their enterprise. These were the years when professional readers were beginning to be attentive to

Doctorow's genesis as a publisher's reader of film scripts, as well as to the interactions between film and fiction more generally. As is well known, Doctorow's first novel, *Welcome to Hard Times* (1960), not only makes a nod to Charles Dickens, whose narratives of social justice would find a worthy successor in Doctorow's fictions a century later, but also proposes itself as a parody of the generic Western and analogous film scripts. *Ragtime* (1975) would carry this dialogue with film to the level of narrative theme and form, prompting one early critic to observe that the novel's use of "photography and motion pictures" illustrates "the human need to preserve and replicate experience so that it can be analyzed and understood; film becomes a means for characters bewildered by the seeming mutability and formlessness of reality to subject time to rational control."[2] What is more, the novel's "almost hypnotic repetition of short, standard English sentences" approximates "the mysterious opacity of the photographed image"; that is, *Ragtime*'s prose reflects the surface impenetrability of photography, to put the burden of interpretive depth onto the reader.[3] The novel's style, in that sense, could be seen to be equivalent to the signifying emptiness of the image, what Roland Barthes memorably called *"a message without a code."*[4]

Critics then began to extend Doctorow's self-conscious interest in media and machinery, especially as they regard the production of narrative and self, into a more generalized "technology of narrative." Geoffrey Galt Harpham traces the arc of Doctorow's development in the 1970s and 1980s from "a critique of the coercive power of the textual and ideological regime to a celebration of the powers of imaginative freedom," by demonstrating how compositional principles in Doctorow's early mid-career novels are coupled with a technology of (re)production specific to the historical moment they portray.[5] In *The Book of Daniel* (1971), which ends with the electrocution of Paul and Rochelle Isaacson, electricity operates, according to Harpham, as a "master principle of narrative" that "unifies all elements of theme and technique" and is "indigenous to the events themselves."[6] Subsuming other technologies of turn-of-the-century America, Henry Ford's assembly line in *Ragtime* encapsulates the processual nature of the novel's seemingly incessant self-propulsion, the speed and nimbleness with which some characters—most prominently, Tateh and Mother—morph into successive self-generations, and the way the novel's "perspectiveless perspective" gives the appearance of "having been produced by a narratological assembly line."[7] And *Loon Lake* (1980)—while chronologically following *Ragtime* into the 1930s—leaps into the digital age by telling a rags-to-riches story that, never quite clearly by whom, is composed on a word processor and allows for a montage of character fully in sync with the novel's scene of writing. Much like Gatsby remaking himself in the classical American myth of self-fashioning, the novel's protagonist, Joe of Paterson, is being fabricated through cut-and-paste and digital bricolage.[8]

Then, Doctorow's impish way of populating his fictions with historical figures, as in *Ragtime*, or the novelization of historical events, such as the Rosenberg case in *The Book of Daniel*, too began to flash on the radar of literary criticism. Linda Hutcheon famously described Doctorow's work of the 1970s and 1980s as "historiographic meta-fiction," a category of popular novel that includes Salmon Rushdie's *Midnight's Children*, A. S. Byatt's *Possession*, and Michael Ondaatje's *The English Patient* and that are "both intensely self-reflexive and yet paradoxically also lay claim to historical events and personages." According to Hutcheon, such works display "a theoretical self-awareness of history and fiction as human constructs . . . [that] made the grounds for [a] rethinking and reworking of the forms and contents of the past."[9] If Doctorow wouldn't quite put it that way, he certainly anticipated this slippage of fact and truth in his essay "False Documents," a declaration of narrative independence that is acutely mindful of the tension between presumed full linguistic representation and the always-already fiction-alized, that is, invented, artifice of any narrative. Paralleling similar thoughts in a climate framed by deconstructive practice, but largely bypassing the French fraternity in favor of Nietzsche and Benjamin, Doctorow staked a province for the novelist that exceeds the primacy of any fact-based reality:

> history is a kind of fiction in which we live and hope to survive, and fiction is a kind of speculative history, perhaps a superhistory, by which the available data for the composition are seen to be greater and more various in their sources than the historian supposes.[10]

This claim for the fluidity of often interpenetrating discourses, and often of various historical moments, became a point of entry for what may well be the most canonical discussion of Doctorow's oeuvre to date. For Fredric Jameson, *Ragtime* is a quintessential "postmodern artifact" because it advances a form of history that is an essentially empty pastiche of clichés.[11] While Jameson wants to acknowledge Doctorow as "the epic poet of the disappearance of the American radical past," he appears to do a critical-theoretical about-face when claiming that the novel's accumulation of stereotypes—by definition flat, reductive, and devoid of felt authenticity—yields nothing more than a pop history of modernist American ideas and ideals, emptied of deep political meaning or impact. *Ragtime*, in his view, stands as "the most peculiar and stunning monument to the aesthetic situation engendered by the disappearance of the historical referent," and hence diminishes literary narrative to the nostalgic recycling of vapid iconographies fundamentally unable to truly represent the historical past.[12]

If Jameson's statement oscillates between acknowledging Doctorow's political sympathies and the condition of the work of art in the age of postmodern vacuity, Christopher Morris is unequivocally admiring of Doctorow's achievement. The only single-author monograph on Doctorow published by a university press to date, *Models of Misrepresentation* (1991), is informed by the linguistic turn in literary-critical theory that evolved out of postmodernism's critique of hermeneutics and the deconstructionist slippage in signification.[13] Citing Friedrich Nietzsche, Jacques Derrida, J. Hillis Miller, and Martin Heidegger and Paul de Man (before the latter two compromised their standing within the industry for their ties to Nazi Germany), Morris draws attention to the way Doctorow's novels stage a crisis in articulation, or, to put it differently, the way language—as the tool of the novelist—brushes up against its always-inherent representational limits. For Morris, misrepresentation as one hallmark of Doctorow's richly textured fictions is not a sign of inaccuracy, but of "an incapacity to represent." If Doctorow's novels "at first seem to teem with rendered life," they "eventually disclose the artifice that created this first false impression of plenitude" in the first place.[14] Writing literary narrative, while seeking to construct imaginary worlds that allow for empathetic identification, social awareness, and perhaps political mobilization, is thus also always already a self-reflexive exercise about its representational blind spots.

At this juncture, it may be time to invoke Doctorow's caveat against any form of pigeonholing. Aware that slots and boxes can't help but squeeze a writer—and especially a writer with such imaginative capaciousness—into a prescriptive straitjacket, Doctorow has refused any label that might even remotely assign him to a particular camp. Growing out of a postwar sensibility, with substantive training in literature and philosophy (at Kenyon College, especially French existentialism and Continental thought), and graduate work in theater (at Columbia University), and with an unbounded intellectual curiosity, Doctorow has claimed much of the imaginable world for the province of fiction. With regard to the postmodern, he has observed on more than one occasion:

I'm not sure I'm interested in situating myself in that way. I mean, certainly, I have used certain postmodern techniques, but for what I think of as entirely traditional story telling purposes. What does that make me—a post-post-modernist?[15]

To the question whether his interrogation of key moments of American history and myth-making make him a "historical novelist," he has similarly observed—and with a similar twinkle in his eyes—that he prefers the simple term "novelist," without additional qualifiers, because it is all-encompassing and goes clean to the heart of the narrative enterprise.[16]

What this moment of "postmodern" exposure certainly did for Doctorow was to make him, momentarily, into a premier exponent of contemporary American literature on the (Western) world's stage. His literary currency at home was matched by an equal interest in countries such as Germany and Japan—two Axis powers on the losing end of World War II which, more than most other nations, felt the effects of America's postwar political and economic imperialism. Being dead center within the sphere of U.S. influence in the wake of the Cold War world order, such countries were, de facto, "Americanized," in an ideological and informational sense, and hence particularly receptive to the work of a writer known for holding up the mirror to his own country's nature. The Heidelberg German American Institute, for example (with the support of the U.S. embassy), held a prominent Doctorow symposium in 1985, with Doctorow himself in attendance, which was subsequently published, in a major series on American literature and American studies, as an early international volume, tellingly entitled *E. L. Doctorow: A Democracy of Perception* (1988). Similarly, Doctorow's well known lament that novelists should grapple with "the big political and social issues of [their] time," but have instead "pulled inward and miniaturized the significance of their lives,"[17] became a touchstone for a generation of Japanese writers and critics, because it seemed to capture accurately much of the state of twentieth-century Japanese fiction. Chia-Ning Chang observes that Doctorow's comments, while aimed at contemporary American literature

> resonate with a haunting ring to students of modern Japanese literary criticism *vis-à-vis* the twentieth century Japanese novel . . . . Certainly, many postwar Japanese critics have long been profoundly disturbed by what they consider to have been a conspicuous lack of a tangible social dimension in modern Japanese fiction.[18]

Even to professional readers and writers abroad, Doctorow seems to have been a transnational beacon of authorial integrity and social conscience at the time.[19]

That centrality at the forefront of the American narrative canon was, however, short-lived. While some of Doctorow's contemporaries equally benefited from the updraft of the postmodern thermal, his work, while not altogether falling out of favor with the professoriate, and certainly not with a broad-based readership, did not sustain itself within the larger critical and theoretical community. Adam Kelly has recently noted, correctly, that "if the MLA International Bibliography is to be believed, only one monograph or essay collection on Doctorow has been published since the turn of the 21st century," presumably *E. L. Doctorow* (2001) and *E. L. Doctorow's Ragtime* (2001)—two introductory volumes that serve a beginning readership but don't advance critical inquiry in a serious way.[20] At the same time, and despite receiving the highest imprimatur from much of the U.S. literary world—the National Book Award, two National Critics Circle Awards, the PEN/Faulkner Award, and the National Humanities Medal, to name just a few— Doctorow's work has been critically side-stepped, if not altogether muted, while an entire critical industry has accrued, and continues to accrue, around the work of Thomas Pynchon and Philip Roth, Toni Morrison and Don DeLillo, as well as Cormac McCarthy, long after the postmodern moment has passed.[21] The relative critical silence surrounding his work is certainly far out of sync with Doctorow's extraordinary output after the postmodern turn, just as it is with his wide readership and the acknowledgments his contemporaries have bestowed upon him. What is more, much of what little work has been done on Doctorow seems, almost inevitably, to circle back onto *Ragtime*, as if to suggest that Doctorow got stuck in his tracks, while in reality it appears to be the critical community that is unable to overcome its self-enclosing loop and recognize the creative evolution of a writer long after he had made, not just one, but several, first major marks.[22]

That early, almost autopoietic and inadvertent, canonization of a "landmark" novel, with its effects of sealing off and foreclosure, may be one reason for the critical neglect of Doctorow's work. It narrows the academic lens to one "exemplary" text, but shuts out a much wider, and often more challenging, body of work. Another reason, and an equally important one, may be the subdued, protean quality of Doctorow's oeuvre. Unlike other writers among his peers, whose stylistic signature (in a reprise of the modernist genius) is sustained and immediately apparent, Doctorow's novels are marked by an idiosyncratic and non-self-referential singularity—a quality of writing allowing his materials to seek their own voice rather than (en)forcing authorial control; or, to put it differently, a beguiling and disarming artlessness that is, in fact, carefully—and, hence, artfully—crafted without being flashy. Doctorow has often noted that each of his books proposes itself in terms of its own evolving style, and, thus, in the aggregate, don't allow for any formal unity and continuity, much as the themes of his fiction are bound by common core concerns. "I don't have a style, but the books do," he observed,[23] just as it has been observed by others.[24] What sets Doctorow apart from fellow writers of his generation, according to George Saunders, is that he is "first and foremost, a master stylist," a writer for whom "each book created and sustained its own unique and necessary language."[25] Translated into scholarly terms, such stylistic diversity may not offer itself up for ready-made critical-theoretical analysis and may at best be a moving target for particular "approaches" often defined by a specific, and sometimes myopic, lens. Cookie-cutter scholarship, in that sense, may finally be ill-equipped to savor the smorgasbord, the fine cuisine that is Doctorow's fiction, and indeed point to what Kelly has identified as one of "the present prejudices of literary scholarship": the continued preference for "the modernist figure of the demiurge-creator"—for which read: Pynchon & Co.—compared with "postmodern exponents of genre writing and less attention-grabbing forms of stylistic experimentation" such as Doctorow.[26]

Doctorow's creative work with what he called "disreputable genres" may, similarly, have compromised his standing within the academy. At the time when, at least in theory, the culture industry was to dismantle what Andreas Huyssen famously called "the great divide," the division between popular culture and its corresponding forms in elite practices may in fact still partly define the conversations within the communities of professional readers. Doctorow has noted that "popular genres are meaningful and a source of analysis of who we are and what we're doing," and that popular culture plays as "a kind of ground music" in readers' heads, against which writers can compose "some counterpoint."[27] Certainly, as we have already intimated, Doctorow's deft manipulations of genre fictions are not a matter of slumming in the sub-literary realm of pulp—the way *Ragtime*'s high society stages "poverty balls" to ridicule the poor[28]—but rather of infusing, and elevating, mass cultural forms with a presumption of honesty and import. Rather than being indiscriminate mash-ups of the high and low, Doctorow's transforms the Western, the sci-fi novel, and the gothic into sincerely ambitious narratives without undue gestures of mockery and play.[29] Academic readers, by and large, have not adequately acknowledged this dimension of his writing, even as they praise a younger generation of writers, who often acknowledge Doctorow's influence, precisely for overcoming that canonical binary.[30]

But whatever the reasons—and others suggest themselves as well— it is time to fully acknowledge, finally and if only for the first time,

Doctorow's lifetime achievement and to give his remarkable writings the scholarly attention they deserve—and which a large U.S. and international reading public has, in fact, already bestowed on him.

The Field of Engagement

If literary scholarship since about 1990 has seemed to desert Doctorow as a useful target for the calibration of its sophisticated ballistics, so too has the field itself been irreversibly transformed by a number of overlapping dynamics since the end of the millennium, the final result of which is an oft-noted and less often carefully defined sense of "crisis" around criticism's standard operating procedures. It is less certain than ever that literary studies even has a future, let alone a stable object; and absolutely unclear that what we had formerly taken to be the "guiding questions" (of power, ideology, imperialism, sexism, Western metaphysics, psychoanalysis, and so forth) continue to offer the most fertile ground for critical analysis in the neoliberal academy. Even less does it seem possible to toil in the furrows of that time-honored practical humanism of the sort that Doctorow himself liked to practice when he undertook his periodical, always enlightening, forays into literary criticism. Criticism has been subject to a series of catastrophic reversals of its former fortunes near the center of the humanities, and forced ever further toward an imperiling confrontation with its likely future as a marginal mode of antiquarianism—a Classics for the new age. The concomitant rises of an aggressive empiricism, of the "digital humanities," of the incontestable hegemony of the hard sciences in the domain of academic expertise, of a febrile and forever fragmenting identity politics, of a philistine skepticism, and of the welter of market forces and lowest common denominators that keep all these phenomena buoyant, has occasioned a collapse in the twin fortunes of literature as the primary lodestar of cultural value, and of Theory as the crystal ball best equipped to demystify it.

All of this works contradictorily to refashion our collective imago of Doctorow himself at the end of this second decade of the new millennium. On the one hand, clearly, the very public figure he once cut—the tweedy New York Brahmin Jewish intellectual, with one foot squarely planted in the austerities of the 1930s, and the other in the permissive Bacchanalia of the latter half of the 1960s, one wry eyebrow cocked at the ruinous absurdities of the American way of life, the other leveled severely at the crooks who maintain their existence—seems already Jurassic in outline. The public intellectual as such, and the literary intellectual in particular, no longer exists in the way that Doctorow so effortlessly embodied. Instead, a shrill and witless commentariat, thumbs drumming out their latest Twitter tirades, hawk for attention on the marketplace of sensations and recirculate the limpest of clichés rather than fashion even a single memorable sentence. The collapse of literature's fortunes as our prime cultural arbiter and distinction-maker exposes Doctorow's extant public profile today as always-already extinct, and prejudges his output as the anachronistic and verbose effusions of a well meaning but superannuated elder, stranded on the verge of the teeming information superhighway. On the other hand, however, that very obsolescence of the usual signs and portents of the literary system reveals a Doctorow much more securely in touch with the actual lines of force structuring our social and historical moment. The tales of *Sweet Land Stories*, the historical bricolage of *City of God*, the cognitive frissons of *Andrew's Brain* all seem to gather together a working theory of the contemporary social order that, when amalgamated with his acute sensitivity to semantic exhaustion in the late-capitalist semiosphere, the role of corporate media and mediation in the consolidation and intensification of capitalist social relations, and the ubiquitous critical eye cast on the economic elite of the "1%" in all his work, surcharge an image of Doctorow uniquely positioned to make sense of our pressing historical situation—and better placed, certainly, than the generally privileged white male sages of our moment: Philip Roth, Cormac McCarthy, even Jonathan Franzen, seem either too nostalgic or too hysterical to make comparable contributions. Only Pynchon, at that kind of level, seems to have been better able to bend the machinery of fiction to a more sustaining cognitive engagement with the present. And only Rachel Kushner, among a handful of younger novelists, appears poised to offer the kind of narrative illumination of the contemporary American scene by, significantly, resurrecting a brand of historical fiction that brings Doctorow's privileged narrative forms up to date. In such novels as *The Flamethrowers*, which "constantly entwines the invented with the real" and in which Kushner "often uses the power of invention to give her fiction the authenticity of the reportorial, the solidity of the historical," she gives Doctorow's narrative amalgamations a new lease on life that is as formally innovative and politically resonant as Doctorow's was at the time.[31]

A Doctorow for our time will be enriched and extended, too, by the rise in critical fortunes of certain other theoretical and political coordinates. Queer studies will help to disclose a stubborn fixation with, and recurrent deviations from, certain heteronormative functions and roles within the distribution of patriarchal power across capitalist space in his body of work. Doctorow has populated a fertile valley of deviancy in the folds between the institutional structures of heterosexual power and the limited sexual personae available to operate them. That valley needs to be charted, as will the terrain of social reproduction with regard to the role of women, the importance of family, and the domestic labor visible but often unacknowledged hands perform in his fiction. Ecocriticism will help to discern a pervasive interest in the "natural" limits to human endeavor and industry in Doctorow's typically, but never exclusively, urban landscapes. Indeed, *Loon Lake, Welcome to Hard Times, The March*, the geographical extremes of *Ragtime* (the North Pole, for instance), the sustained oscillation between city and nature in *The Waterworks*, and intermittent moments scattered here and there across the entire oeuvre, remind us that, for this author, the ecology sustaining his fictional worlds is an urgent concern. Cognitive science and evolutionary biology, and their take-up in the humanities, should also help to clarify the extent to which Doctorow had never fully accepted the Freudian subject as his privileged vessel, but tarried instead with more makeshift and provisional narrative entities, more distributed agential and actantial domains, whose structure and license might better be understood in terms of branching dendritic trees and complexly layered evolutionary functions than of the exhausted modern paradigms of ego and id.[32] Object-oriented ontology and actor network theory will discover in his works a rich seam of semi-autonomous "things" and quasi-agents, the flotsam and jetsam of the modern itself, whose densely marbled relations across the pages of *Homer & Langley*, *Ragtime*, and *City of God* cast into relief a world only partly defined by human activity, and sustained instead by largely inhuman networks into which the human is woven as one element among others. Above all, perhaps, contemporary media theory and history should engage anew with this incredibly media-sensitive writer, for whom writing was never just writing, but one technology nested among so many others— from photography to flicker-books, typewriters to word processors, the Nickelodeon to the multiplex, ticker-tape to the daily newspaper, tele- graphs to emails, radio to the eight-track tape player, television to the home computer screen—to the extent that, properly read, it may even amount to an original theory of the evolving media system itself. Not even Pynchon, it seems to us, has, finally, such an astute and reflexive account of the extent to which literature has been made and remade by the total transformation of the corporate media system since the end of the nineteenth century.

Virtually all of the essays in our collection fall within these more recent, innovative paradigms or can be accommodated within their fluid conceptual maps. While the titles to the parts of our volume reflect clusters of thought around which Doctorow's work can be seen to aggregate, from "Generic Border Crossings" to "Narrative, Media, and Cognition—The Case of *City of God*," these newer models afford a reconceptualization of Doctorow's writings and furthermore do due diligence to the plasticity of a body of work that often eludes clear demarcations. What is more, these models are arguably even more permeable than the loose assembly of the four parts of the book— themselves, of course, no more than a heuristic device—and are, hence, ideally suited to throw into relief the capacious elasticity of Doctorow's novels. Thus, most contributions are embedded within a fabric of disciplinary overlays and offer several perspectives at once.

Nathan D. Frank's essay (Chapter 8) is equally at home in digital media culture and in cognitive science, with punctual forays into quantum mechanics and evolutionary biology, arguing at heart that literary neutrinos become a multi-vectored (not to say charged) trope in *City of God* capable of "transgressing and reconfiguring boundaries" by "democratiz[ing]" the terrain within which it operates (not unlike what Doctorow at one point called a "democracy of perception"[33]). Drawing on a nucleus of theorists, Frank observes that "the quality of a neutrino" obtains when "information technologies, digital media, or the narrative technologies of print media" render "ontological difference between incompatible objects irrelevant, or even nonexistent," eventually urging a consideration of the novel as "a textual mind" that— traveling, neutrino-like, as it does through readers' minds—induces a cognitive operation broadly analogous to what it itself models: bridging informational gaps by assembling distinct representations into an (at least momentary) continuity, much like the supplementary functioning of a modular mind.

Michael Wutz's essay (Chapter 9) on Doctorow's millennial novel is similarly grounded in a mix of cognitive theory and evolutionary biology, science and religion, and, especially, information theory. If Frank understands neutrinos as a kind of universal metaphoric transmission channel, Wutz maps the various signs and signals—material and spiritual, linguistic and electric, biologic and electronic—circulating within *City of God's* narrative space, and how the novel negotiates the slippery terrain distinguishing sense from nonsense, signal from noise. He argues that Doctorow locates his metafictional reflections on meaning-making within the human system of language by juxtaposing how Ludwig Wittgenstein and Albert Einstein, two of the novel's key players, think about the fundamentals of communication— and while one ends in silence over despair at the infinitely regressive metaphoricity of speech, the other (much in the spirit of Doctorow) embraces the sonorous noise of signs to reconcile modern physics with metaphysics. Wutz also suggests that Doctorow translates the novel's attention to sound into the domain of media culture by crafting a text that proposes itself as a noise maker and, at the same time, in an information-theoretical way, as a noise processor, translating the larger cultural disorder into its own, however tenuous and tentative, system of order. He dissolves the aesthetic constraints of the (traditional) novel to foreground the proliferation of codes unprocessable in any single contemporary medium, instead favoring an appropriately inchoate textual assembly that is embedded within the sound cloud of the present and that forever resists closure and coherence.

Codes and cognition, media and materiality have, indeed, been crucial preoccupations for Doctorow, beginning in the 1990s, the twin final frontiers along which much of his later, mature work locates itself. *The Waterworks*, for example, fully partakes in the late nineteenth-century rhetoric of skulls and brains, and—in the notorious Dr. Sartorius (who reappears in *The March*)—features a singularly gifted but ethically compromised scientist working on the cutting edge of brain research and developing futuristic apparatus for measuring electro-encephalic output. Similarly, the novel advances an essentially gappy and distributed mode of cognition that is close to contemporary models of modularity whereby knowledge is necessarily fragmentary and contingent, and produced by a consciousness—clustered rhizomes of synaptic networks—filling elliptical voids. When Daniel Dennett, with the flair of a phenomenologist, observes that "at any point in time, there are multiple drafts of narrative fragments at various stages of editing in various places in the brain," he might also describe the nested fractals of Doctorow's late complex novels, composed as they often are of competing and complementary voices vying for authority and validation.[34]

Doctorow certainly was cognizant of the momentous changes in cognitive science, and in fact acknowledged "a cognitive turn" in the work of, roughly, his last two decades. Behind the characters suffering from cognitive deficits and memory lapses, as some do in *The Waterworks*, *The March*, *Homer & Langley*, and *Andrew's Brain*, is the knowledge that "neuroscientists have revised the standard model of the brain. The old idea was intransigent localization, whereas now it is understood the brain has plasticity and different areas can be retrained, or remapped, and made compensatory for areas that no longer work, as in a stroke."[35] The search for spiritual fulfillment and the soul, and for the very emergence of consciousness—so central to the neo-Augustinian

City of God—is similarly grounded in Doctorow's understanding of the battle lines that have defined an entire field. For a writer trained in Continental philosophy and with a particular penchant for French thought, the debate between biological materiality and a transcendent Cartesian ego was of particular fascination as the field of cognitive science defined itself. As he said in interview:

> The materialists who say there is no such thing as a soul claim that Descartes was wrong. It's the brain we are talking about, and when the brain's not working, nothing else happens. There is no thought, there is no feeling, there is no emotion, there are no ideas and there's no self-consciousness. So that's the central issue: the dispute with Cartesian dualism. I've been reading Antonio Damasio's *Descartes' Error*, and the work of others, who are attacking the Cartesians of whatever version. And then somebody says: yes, you materialists may be right, but how do we get from the brain to the mind—to the most abstract thought with the subtlest emotion, how does that occur? That's what the cognitive scientists are trying to figure out.[36]

A cognitive scientist, in fact, is at the center of Doctorow's last novel, *Andrew's Brain*, which, as its telling title suggests, revolves around the synaptic firings of a convoluted mind, and may—on the assumption that Andrew suffers from schizophrenia or a similar disorder—in fact unfold within the folds of his heavy brain. Shuttling back and forth between an unidentified interlocutor who might, or might not, be a self-correcting part of Andrew's dissociated self—call it Andrew's right brain—and his free associations, which range from literature to politics, cognitive science to machine learning—the virtuosity of his left brain—the novel may be seen to orchestrate the hemispheric communication taking place within a singular, embodied brain, diseased and burdened as that brain may be. Questions of the mind masquerading as a soul, the efficiency of distributed cognition—already touched upon in *City of God*—and the illusion of human agency when cognitive science suggests that "the brain can come to a decision seconds before we are conscious of it,"[37] all surface repeatedly and point toward a kind of neurochemical a priori that may redefine human being, even as it redefines the scope of Doctorow's fiction. If his early critical work had illuminated key moments in American history, often by giving voice to the unheard, his later works retain that laser focus but are more deliberately filtered through the flashy quicksilver meanderings of a fractured narrating consciousness. The cognitive turn thus puts this postmodernist writer in the company of such like-minded contemporaries as David Lodge (*Thinks . . .*) and John Barth (*On With the Story*) and a younger generation of "truly" postmodern writers such as Richard Powers (*Galatea 2.2*) and Jonathan Safran Foer (*Extremely Loud & Incredibly Close*), who all in their own ways have engaged this final frontier of the embodied brain.[38] At the same time, Doctorow's reach into the crazed and possibly delirious noggin of his last protagonist straddles the, well, cognitive gap between cutting-edge neuroscience and the psychodramas of his nineteenth-century namesake, for whom he was named: Edgar Allan Poe.

Poe's narrative grotesqueries connect Doctorow's later fictions to the genre of the gothic, the arch-romantic mode of storytelling—often from a perspective that is askew or possessed—beginning with *The Waterworks*. In Chapter 2, Stephen Arch sketches this tradition in Doctorow by tracing an arc in his narrative practice that morphs from the classically gothic space, as in the Collyer brothers' mansion in *Homer & Langley*, to the more constricting, because unreservedly conceiving and capacious, space of the mind. If one, as in *Homer & Langley*, becomes an index of material surfeit and of a modernist culture obsessed with commodification and consumerism (and is furthermore inextricably linked to the military-industrial complex), the cognitive recesses of the various narrators, as in *The Waterworks*, *City of God*, and *Andrew's Brain*, produce visions of the human condition as being absurd and a coincidence of evolution. Langley explicitly questions the "ontological distinction between outside and inside,"[39] and points to the wide open space between the external world of material objects and internal visions and projections. Both inform, as Arch puts it, Doctorow's "logic of representation" and "edge toward allegory while at the same time resisting a full-scale identification as allegory." Instead, they suggestively hover in what Homi Bhabha, in a different context, famously called a "third space" that articulates a more general political and cultural critique while allowing that critique to emerge from (within) an associative and at times delirious consciousness.[40] The personal and political are thus inextricably intertwined in Doctorow's fiction, as are his narrative forms and thematic concerns. Arch's essay, which we have placed under the rubric "Generic Border Crossings," might thus equally have found a (non-gothic) home in Part II, "Politics, Allegory, Difference," and suggests the indivisible interpenetration of Doctorow's work, and the inadequacy of any heuristic structure of a collection such as ours.

That is also true of Nicholas Murgatroyd's contribution (Chapter 4), on *The Waterworks*, which ranges from politics and literary heritage to the surmounting of generic constraints, in that it identifies (as does Arch) Hawthorne and Melville as the usual suspects, allowing Doctorow to provide a proto-allegorical critique of the Reagan–Bush era.[41]

Suggestively entitled "Submerged Politics and the Artist"—thus already echoing Doctorow's doctoring with "sub-literary" forms—Murgartroyd is the first to draw on the as-yet-unexplored Doctorow papers housed at New York University and to demonstrate that the novel's original design (then still called *The Soul*) morphed from "a gothic fantasy" with multiple narrators and largely theological concerns to a submerged political fiction with McIlvaine as a single narrator-journalist exposing the political machinations of the Tweed Ring. Murgartroyd teases out further parallels between draft versions of some of Doctorow's political essays at the time, and their eventual appearance in print form, and how they resonate with Doctorow's concerns about deregulation, the dismantling of social legislation, and the empowerment of corporate culture that typify both the Gilded Age and the Reagan–Bush years. What is more, he also suggests that this novel does double duty as a suggestive *Künstlerroman* written for and in an era when the arts were, and still are, under siege. In McIlvaine, who finds his fictional voice late in life, but above all in the painter Harry Wheelwright, who might come off as little more than a thirsty sidekick to Martin Pemberton, Doctorow has created a model of the "socially responsible artist in society" walking a fine line between commerce and culture, capital and craft. If Pemberton is unrelenting in his book reviews, only to maneuver himself into a literary offside, Wheelwright is a society painter with (secret) ambitions to do justice to the social reality surrounding him. Caught between the rock of making a living with his skill—hence his flattering paintings of the rich—and the hard place of postbellum America—studio portraits of disabled veterans—he makes visible the not-so-hidden cost of the war (with bosses amassing fortunes from "shoddy" goods) while performing a balancing act to make a precarious living. Untrue and true paintings, embellished art and its opposite—affluenced idealism and social realism, in short—are held in abeyance in his work, fearful as he is that too much grime might jeopardize his living, while not enough might compromise his integrity. Artists working in whatever medium, in both the late nineteenth and the twentieth centuries, *The Waterworks* suggests, are at the mercy of a culture industry within whose orbit they must create and sell, criticize and survive.[42]

Life on the margins is also at the center of Julian Murphet's essay (Chapter 6), on "freaks"—those malformed social misfits populating Doctorow's work who often congregate into communities of mutual support on the outskirts of the social structure and, while perhaps exploited, generate among themselves at least a uniquely ethical compact in the face of marginalization and abuse. As with Murgatroyd, Murphet demonstrates the allegorical significance of this recurring figure, arguing that the larger principle at stake in these figurations is the very principle of movement itself—the unrooted, drifting way of life that carneys and their freak shows have always embraced—of which Doctorow turns out to have been something like the epic poet in the twentieth century. Identifying a molar dialectic or structural antagonism between two dominant principles—the way of property, and the way of drift—Murphet probes Doctorow's canon for evidence of the imaginative fluctuations and patterns thrown off by its constitutive friction. From novel to novel, we see that structures of landedness and fixity are undone by the principle of flight and movement and impermanence, and *The March* here receives its due as perhaps the quintessential masterpiece of movement in Doctorow's oeuvre. Finally turning to the "cosmic" or ontological resonance of this persistent interest in impermanence, Murphet also attends to the molecular dimension of Doctorow's art: his interest in the swarming, protean, buzzing atomic world beneath perception, at which level all is flux anyway. There, in this "infrastructure of layered subversion," Doctorow sows the seeds for a revolution to come.

Perception and the dialectic of groundedness and drift, and of flux and fixity, also inform the essays by Tamlyn Avery (Chapter 1) and Jieun Kwon (Chapter 5), both centering on *The Book of Daniel* as Doctorow's first chef-d'oeuvre before it was eclipsed by the now-canonical *Ragtime*. Kwon reappraises the extent to which Doctorow gave rein in that book to a certain conspiratorial imagination of the left, allowing the author to get closer to a particular political truth by way of fantasized projections of government cabals and deals made behind closed doors. The witch-hunts of communists in the 1950s were, to be sure, all too real; but the specific version of events offered by Doctorow as a deep background to the Rosenberg case (in the guise of the novel's Isaacson family) is crafted to provide certain kinds of psychological pressure on the novel's protagonist, Daniel, and not as a web of historical facts. It is this very fracture line, between Daniel's more and more individuated, paranoid response to the tragedy, and the novel's own canny awareness of more abiding, structural norms and processes, that brings out the political salience readers have come to admire in Doctorow's most fully engaged political text.

Avery is similarly interested in a structure of vacillation evident in *The Book of Daniel*, but occurring with noticeable regularity in much of Doctorow's corpus: the *Bildungsroman* and its numerous diffractions, particularly the tactical formal ways in which the author deploys its generic conventions in order to let their larger ideological implications falter and fail. Turning to a concept first hazarded by Theodor Adorno, she rehabilitates the notion of *Halbbildung* (both "half-education" and "pseudo-culture") to account for Doctorow's interest in the structural blockages and frustrations that pursue any attempt at subjective "self-formation" in the context of monopoly capitalism. Arguing that Doctorow's efforts in the form should properly be construed as a varietal mode best labeled the *Halbbildungsroman*, Avery deftly shows how Doctorow practiced two versions of this mode: the quasi-sentimental recreation of a Bronx boyhood in the nondevelopmental idiom specific to it; and the exploration of a more fractured, distributed subject-formation across determinate material breakages in media, ideological functionality, and tone. Focusing her discussion on the formally complex warp and woof of *The Book of Daniel*, she draws nutrients from that text's distinctive lack of closure and teleological certainty for a theory of *Halbbildung* as, in part, a critical resistance to capitalism's coercive inscriptions of repressive subjectivity. "The end product of Daniel's self-formation," she argues, "is not meant to be a singular character development, or narrative fulfillment, but to feel the novel of the individual dissolving into the larger chain of human social development." This is the consummation devoutly to be wished for by the New Left, of which Daniel is such an ambivalent member, but it is also an effect of postwar capitalism's shift to full consumerism and the dissolution of longstanding patriarchal familial norms. Such ambivalence lies at the heart of the *Halbbildungsroman*'s formal compact with its readers in Doctorow's hands: disappointing the abiding expectations of the *Bildungsroman* form in ways that simultaneously portend collective liberation *and* stunted captivation.

If Avery shows self-formation as, ultimately, being illusory and diffractive, Alexander Howard in Chapter 7 extends that argument into the relationship between conceptions of sexuality, intimations and representations of erotic yearning, and geographically specific forms of political radicalism. Probing once more the allegorical flush of Doctorow's oeuvre, Howard works in particular to bear down critically on moments such as Billy Bathgate's eroticized perceptions of Bo Weinberg, and of Emma Goldman's erotic massage of Evelyn Nesbit, because these passages hint at the presence of what Howard describes as a queerly radical—and radically queer—current that pulses almost undetected through many, if not all, of Doctorow's celebrated works. Doctorow's work consistently demonstrates the pertinence of the axiom that radicalism will be queer, or it will not be at all, with corresponding overtones of, not so much stabilizing and grounding, as much as distributed selfhood and agency.

In Chapter 3, Mark Azzopardi, too, spotlights one of the most neglected (albeit not invisible) of Doctorow's enduring commitments:

his short fiction. Taking the posthumously published *Collected Stories* as a timely occasion, he probes the peculiarities of Doctorow's approach to the form—his reluctance to indulge the epiphanic mode, his avoidance of story cycles, his tendency to plot in minutiae—only to demonstrate his more abiding concerns: with moments of narrative time plucked out of context and suspended episodically alongside one another in a kind of radiant void; with the dialectic of a two-character dynamic; and with the overriding political sociality of alienated life. Considering Doctorow's specific relationship to two American masters of the form, who often emerge in profile from his narrative carpet—Poe and Hawthorne—Azzopardi demonstrates the degree to which inherited tactics of "estrangement" haunt the sixteen short stories published over his career; and considers how this may have affected our occasional dissatisfactions with his contributions to the art.

In Part IV, tributes by three close friends and fellow narrative practitioners reprise the probing assessments offered in these scholarly essays and reaffirm what has been the major contention of this collection: recognizing and securing, (if only) at long last, Doctorow's place within the American narrative canon. Speaking for a younger generation of writers (including Michael Chabon and Ta-Nehisi Coates) who have variously acknowledged their indebtedness to Doctorow, Jennifer Egan highlights the levels of historical sensibility that have defined Doctorow's oeuvre and become the benchmark for ambitious writing. Exceeding exhausting period-specific research that is, then, seamlessly integrated into a narrative's fabric, she identifies a "third level of achievement" that is purely Doctorow: "In that realm, a writer has such knowledge and authority about the period he's taken on, AND its historical context, that he can revel in his research and have it STILL feel essential." It is for that very same reason, she continues, that Doctorow has had such a wide appeal, allowing his stories to lodge themselves into the public imagination: "Doctorow's novels do more than occupy an historical moment; they own it, manipulate it, frolic with it, and become intertwined with it in our memories." His fiction, in that sense, is thus at least triply historical, in that it reimagines moments of (largely) American history; it preserves the nuanced iconography of those moments for future generations; and it advances a notion of fiction, as he himself insisted, as a form of "superhistory" that captures the *Zeitgeist*, sensibilities, and material culture of a historical moment far in excess of any fact-based account.

Drawing attention to Doctorow's mastery of style, Don DeLillo echoes these observations, noting (as George Saunders did in his obituary[43]) that "in Doctorow we find prose that has a kind of architectural integrity. It belongs to this book, not another." With a gesture back to Balzac and the epic swath of Victorian novelists, DeLillo locates Doctorow at the American forefront of that "great and shaky institution, the social novel"—in "the grain of American possibility, in the clash of voices and forces, and in the way in which plain lives can take on the cadences of history." For DeLillo, those cadences are grounded in Doctorow's language as "a kind of democratic experiment," an orchestrated cacophony of generational dissonance that records individual voices over and against "the monolith, the monotone of history, the single uninflected voice of the state, the corporate entity." Enriching and complicating this collective drone with particularized accents and tones is thus always a kind of narrative politics in action, whereby, in Doctorow's own words, the novelist counteracts the state's coercive *"power of the regime"* with his or her own imaginative *"power of freedom."*[44]

Gleaning insights from over a half century of friendship, Victor S. Navasky, a former editor of *The Nation*, offers a kind of personal and professional capstone to the collection. He not only provides glimpses of Doctorow the novelist, but also Doctorow the raconteur and editor, script writer and essayist, private citizen and public intellectual, and a congenial fellow traveler profoundly invested in the betterment of the world. Peppered with at times little-known anecdotes, his character mosaic reveals a writer deeply committed to the craft of fiction and for whom the act of writing was, fundamentally, an act of asserting integrity. Most importantly, perhaps, while writing out of deeply felt—for which read humane—convictions, he resisted charges of pushing a political agenda. As he put it to Navasky:

> It seems to me more of a comment on our time than on anything I have written that a novel that contains concern for our society is seen to be unusual. *Moby-Dick* is a political novel. *The Scarlet Letter* is a political novel. Dostoyevsky and Conrad wrote political novels . . . [T]o think that I'm writing to advance a political program misses the point. To call a novel political today is to label it, and to label it is to refuse to deal with what it does.

What grounds this belief in fiction as a discourse of engagement is of course Doctorow's belief, equally important, that print is up to the task. Media in virtually all their forms are close associates in his work and merge into one of his master narratives: print culture's engagement with the post-print world, and the manipulative power of the mass media that make up that very culture industry which artists are often called upon to resist. In turn, both of these nodal points branch out (inevitably, as they must) into Doctorow's parallel interests in social critique and cognition. "No one can out shout him because no one has as many microphones, TV screens, headlines at his disposal as a president" is the archived draft of a passage that appears, in modified form, in his essay "The Character of Presidents." Meant as a critique of George Bush Senior, it might as well serve as a kind of proleptic déjà vu of the current media-political situation in the United States now supplemented with, and outfoxed by, an ever-ready Twitter feed consumed instantaneously by millions. Similarly, as Doctorow puts it elsewhere, media both create and partake in an ideological bubble—as theorists from Adorno and Paul Virilio to Friedrich Kittler have observed—by "conglomerating all forms of communication, books and magazines and newspapers and radio stations and cable TV channels, movies, and music into one smooth reality-laundering revenue stream that is in fact a ready-made highly suggestive simulacrum of state-controlled media."[45]

Ambitious fiction can, of course, to a degree resist such homogeneity and streamlining, but finds a challenge in the visual short-cuts of film as a more easily consumable medium. If Pemberton in *City of God* acknowledges the epistemological a priori "that no writer can reproduce the actual texture of living life,"[46] film is even less equipped to do so:

> The term *film language* is an oxymoron. The literary experience extends impression into discourse. It flowers to thought with nouns, verbs, objects. It thinks. Film implodes discourse, it de-literates thought, it shrinks it to the compacted meaning of the preverbal impression or intuition or understanding. . . . In the profoundest sense, films are illiterate events.[47]

What is more, even as literary narrative is cognizant of its limits, a cognitive science perspective suggests that brain plasticity, as Doctorow put it, may "conform over time to the visually dominant culture so that the nature of thinking will change. Reading may not be necessary except for scholars, and someday they may be decoding our novels as scholars today pore over the cuneiform tablets of Sumer."[48] For a writer as deeply committed to the gifts of the literary enterprise as Doctorow, the devolution of reading and writing as among the highest expressions of the human genome, at least the way we currently conceive of it, is a most dire prospect and goes to the very heart of what it means to be human. If this dynamic threatens to make print artifacts into cryptic archeological finds of interest only to learned fossil hunters of the future, our hope is that this collection will demonstrate the urgent need and continued relevance of Doctorow's impressive artifacts for our own historical moment and beyond.

Notes

1. E. L. Doctorow, "Deism," in *Reporting the Universe* (Cambridge, MA: Harvard University Press, 2003), 67. The chapter delineates the complexities of Doctorow's religious and secular thinking. He also observes that when first reading Franz Kafka, I. B. Singer, or Saul Bellow, "it was never the case of any sort of ethnic bonding with them—they were too spectacularly themselves" (68).
2. Angela Hague, "Ragtime and the Movies," in Ben Siegel, ed., *Critical Essays on E. L. Doctorow* (New York: G. K. Hall & Co., 2000), 167.
3. Ibid., 174. For a related essay that is characteristic of such early investigations of film and fiction in Doctorow's work see Anthony B. Dawson, "*Ragtime* and the Movies: The Aura of the Duplicable," *Mosaic: An Interdisciplinary Critical Journal*,16.1/2, *Film/Literature* (winter/spring 1983): 205–14.
4. Roland Barthes, "The Photographic Message," in *Image—Music—Text*, trans. Stephen Heath (London: Fontana, 1977), 17; original emphasis.
5. Geoffrey Galt Harpham, "E. L. Doctorow and the Technology of Narrative," *PMLA*, 100 (1985): 82; 81–95. As a marker of Doctorow's currency on the stock market of literary-critical analysis at the time, Harpham's essay appeared in one of the profession's most respected journals, the *Publications of the Modern Language Association*, soon to be repeated by a second *PMLA* essay, Clayton Koelb's intertextual study between *Ragtime* and Heinrich von Kleist's novella *Michael Kohlhaas*. Such attention, at the highest level of professional and professorial reputation, was, however, short-lived. Clayton Koelb, "Incorporating the Text: Kleist's 'Michael Kohlhaas.'" *PMLA*, 105.5 (1990): 1098–107.
6. Harpham, "E. L. Doctorow and the Technology of Narrative," 88. Mark Seltzer traces the imaginary of the electric current as cultural currency—including the "rapid adoption of the electric chair . . . as the socially acceptable form of legal execution"—back to its beginnings in the late nineteenth century. He observes: "The electric switch, ready to hand, promises to reconnect the interrupted links between conception and execution, agency and expression. Such a violent immediacy posits an identity between signal and act and an identity between communication and execution—'execution' in its several senses." Mark Seltzer, *Bodies and Machines* (New York: Routledge, 1992), 11. These relays are at work in Mark Twain's *A Connecticut Yankee in King Arthur's Court* (1889) and are fully continuous in *The Book of Daniel*. Twain, not coincidentally, was one of Doctorow's favorite writers and of course prominently features in *Andrew's Brain*, among others.
7. Harpham, "E. L. Doctorow and the Technology of Narrative," 89.
8. For the evolution of Doctorow's mode of composition from

handwriting and manual typewriting to an electric typewriter and, eventually, a computer keyboard—in part to keep up with "the speed of thought"— see Michael Wutz, *Enduring Words: Literary Narrative in a Changing Media Ecology* (Tuscaloosa: University of Alabama Press, 2009), esp. 17. Doctorow would not begin composing on a computer until *Billy Bathgate* (1989), long after the publication of *Loon Lake*.

9. Linda Hutcheon, *A Poetics of Postmodernism: History, Theory, Fiction* (New York: Routledge, 1988), 5.

10. E. L. Doctorow, "False Documents," in *Jack London, Hemingway, and the Constitution: Selected Essays 1977–1992* (New York: Random House, 1993), 162.

11. Fredric Jameson, *Postmodernism, or, the Cultural Logic of Late Capitalism* (Durham: Duke University Press, 1991), 22.

12. Ibid., 24–5. Jameson's (conflicted) landmark assessment of *Ragtime* evolved in stages, such as in his 1984 essay "Postmodernism and Consumer Society," which preceded the publication of *Postmodernism* by a number of years. Doctorow, too, was confused by Jameson's statements, though he does not appear to have read Jameson himself: "I find it hard to believe that a reasonably attentive reader, let alone a professional critic, would misconstrue the irreverent spirit of that book . . . In *The Book of Daniel*, written previous to *Ragtime*, I offered much the same critique of nostalgia with Daniel's analysis of Disneyland—that is, the uses to which history is put in terms of replacing the felt life with a few reproductive images, or lies of nostalgia, that rob the past of its true meanings. But I would have to read the material you're citing to speak with certainty." Christopher D. Morris, ed., *Conversations with E. L. Doctorow* (Jackson: University of Mississippi, 1999), 192.

13. Previous introductions to Doctorow during this period include Richard Trenner, *E. L. Doctorow: Essays and Conversations* (New York: Persea Books, 1983); Carol C. Harter and James R. Thompson, *E. L. Doctorow* (Woodbridge: Twayne's United States Author Series, 1990); and John G. Parks, *E. L. Doctorow: Literature and Life* (New York: Continuum International, 1991). Christopher Morris's scholarly *Models of Misrepresentation: On the Fiction of E. L. Doctorow* (Jackson: University Press of Mississippi, 1991) was followed a year later by a general-interest work, Douglas Fowler's *Understanding E. L. Doctorow* (Charleston: University of South Carolina Press, Understanding Contemporary American Literature, 1992).

14. Morris, *Models of Misrepresentation*, 3.

15. Morris, *Conversations*, 193.

16. See the related comment by Tim O'Brien, who finds the "Vietnam-writer" label most irritating and reductive, much as his deployment in Vietnam has shaped his sensibilities: "It's like calling Toni Morrison a black writer, or Melville a whale writer, or Shakespeare a king writer. Or saying that John Updike is a writer for the suburbs, which he isn't in the

slightest . . . . I don't write about bombs and bullets, after all. I write about the human heart." Patrick A. Smith, ed., *Conversations with Tim O'Brien* (Jackson: University Press of Mississippi, 2012), 146.

17. Morris, *Conversations*, 105.

18. Chia-Ning Chang, "The Socialization of Literature: The Ideas and Prototypes of the Mid-Meiji Social Novel," in Adriana Boscaro, et al., *Rethinking Japan: Literature, Visual Arts and Linguistics*, 2 vols. (Folkestone: Japan Library, 1991), 31.

19. Doctorow notes that this inward turn in American fiction may be related to the "bomb" as "another reason for the quiet," and he suggests further that such a retreat "may also be necessary in order to psychically survive." Morris, *Conversations*, 106. Needless to say, such an observation is even more true of a country suffering from the nuclear trauma of World War II. Almost proleptically, one might say—and as part of his own grand narrative of discrimination and exclusion— Doctorow would years later feature the Japanese couple Mr. and Mrs. Hoshiyama in *Homer & Langley* (New York: Random House, 2009), who will be rounded up for internment in the wake of Pearl Harbor (82–91).

20. Adam Kelly, "E. L. Doctorow's Postmodernist Style," *Los Angeles Review of Books* (October 9, 2015) <https://lareviewofbooks.org/article/e-l-doctorows-postmodernist-style#> (accessed October 12, 2015).

21. The obituaries of Doctorow's contemporary Philip Roth are also indicative of this critical neglect: "Mr. Roth was the last of the great white males: the triumvirate of writers—Saul Bellow and John Updike were the others—who towered over American letters in the second half of the 20th century." Charles McGrath, *New York Times*, May 22, 2018.

22. See, for example, Christian Moraru, "Romanticism Reincorporated: E. L. Doctorow and the (Re)Production of America," in *Rewriting Postmodern Narrative and Cultural Critique in the Age of Cloning* (Albany: State University of New York Press, 2001), 41–53; and John McGowan, "Ways of Worldmaking: Hannah Arendt and E. L. Doctorow Respond to Modernity," *College Literature*, 38.1 (2011): 150–75.

23. Sarah Crown, "E. L. Doctorow. 'I don't have a style, but the books do'," *Guardian*, January 22, 2010 <https://www.theguardian.com/books/2010/jan/23/el-doctorow-homer-and-lamgley> (accessed February 7, 2010).

24. See Morris, *Conversations*, 173–7.

25. George Saunders, "The Bravery of E. L. Doctorow," *New Yorker*, July 23, 2015 <https://www.newyorker.com/books/page-turner/the-bravery-of-e-l-doctorow> (accessed July 24, 2015). Together with Don DeLillo and Jennifer Egan, who are both represented in this volume, Saunders in 2012 named Doctorow as the recipient for the PEN/Saul Bellow Award, an award which is meant "to honor a lifetime of *intense, sustained*

and *escalating* achievement" in American fiction (Saunders' emphasis). This phrasing seems, ironically, to map precisely the disproportion between Doctorow's literary achievement and critical neglect.

26. Kelly, "E. L. Doctorow's Postmodernist Style."
27. Morris, *Conversations*, 193.
28. E. L. Doctorow, *Ragtime* (New York: Random House, 1975), 34.
29. On the level of image, this genuine investment in "low" popular forms—including their association with labor and class—is perhaps nowhere more visible than in Doctorow's notion of rags, which runs like a master trope through a substantial portion of his oeuvre, most prominently *Ragtime*, *The Waterworks*, and *City of God*, but others as well. As he put it: a rag suggests "the impoverishment of the writer. The image of the writer as a ragpicker wandering through the streets, his disreputability and insecurity—I like that, in the sense that the materials of all novels are the lives the writer has lived or observed or heard about, these materials of rags, bits and pieces of thread, notions of stuff that he puts together." Morris, *Conversations*, 198 (see also 216). For the modernist, sartorial overtones of rags in Doctorow, see Wutz, *Enduring Words*, 137–41.
30. Citing Andrew Hoberek's work on post-postmodern American writing, Kelly lists Michael Chabon, Jonathan Lethem, and Colson Whitehead among a cadre of younger American writers who have resisted, and in effect redefined, "the widespread and persistent prejudice against genre fiction" still dominant in creative writing programs. Kelly, "E. L. Doctorow's Postmodernist Style." Growing up in a space infused with television, comics, Hollywood blockbusters, and what goes by the name of pop culture, such writers see no aesthetic contradiction between *The Odyssey* and Batman, or Mozart and *Star Trek*, but instead a field of productive cross-fertilization.
31. James Wood, "Youth in Revolt—Rachel Kushner's *The Flame-throwers*," *New Yorker*, April 8, 2013 <https://www.newyorker.com/magazine/2013/04/08/youth-in-revolt> (accessed February 10, 2019). Speaking of *The Flamethrowers*, Colum McCann observes that "DeLillo echoes here, as does Doctorow . . ." <https://www.barnesandnoble.com/review/colum-mccann> (accessed February 10, 2019). Significantly, Kushner echoes Doctorow's Hawthornian notion of romance when she observes: "Only a fool says writing isn't political. But the novel is a category of art, and art is something special, irreducible. It is not a vehicle for a message. Still, a good novel might prompt people to ask themselves questions that don't have easy answers, and to take a break from themselves and consider the lives of other people, and the mechanics of the world, and meet new streams of comedy and grief. There is always some surplus that isn't exactly political, but it cannot be clearly separated cleanly from the society one lives in." Amanda Demme, "Twenty Questions with Rachel Kushner," *Time Literary*

Supplement, September 18, 2018 <https://www.the-tls.co.uk/articles/public/twenty-questions-rachel-kushner> (accessed February 9, 2019).

32. Doctorow first took aim at Freud in the by now classic parody of the "German sexologist" aghast at the noise (and the lack of public bathrooms) in the New World in *Ragtime* (esp. 29–34). In *Andrew's Brain* (New York: Random House, 2014), Andrew repeatedly mocks his "Mr. Analyst" (13) and declares that the findings of cognitive science will soon render "your talking cure" obsolete (7).

33. Morris, *Conversations*, 113.

34. Daniel Dennett, *Consciousness Explained* (London, Penguin, 1991). For a full reading of *The Waterworks* along the lines of information processing and cognitive distribution, see chapter 7 of Wutz, *Enduring Words*, "Knowledge and Cognition in the Early Age of Data Storage," 156–80.

35. Michael Wutz, "On the Craft of Fiction—E. L. Doctorow at 80," *Weber—The Contemporary West*, 29.1 (fall 2012): 13; 2–15.

36. Ibid., 14.

37. Doctorow, *Andrew's Brain*, 34.

38. See, for example, Marco Roth's illuminating 2009 essay "The Rise of the Neuronovel," *n+1*, 8 (fall 2009) <https://nplusonemag.com/issue-8/essays/the-rise-of-the-neuronovel> (accessed April 20, 2018), or Alan Prince and Ian Carruthers, "An Interview with John Barth—Center for Cognitive Science" (Rutgers University), first published in *Prism* (1968): 42–62, now available through Yumpu <https://www.yumpu.com/en/document/ view/7511100/an-interview-with-john-barth-center-for-cognitive-science> (accessed April 20, 2018).

39. E. L. Doctorow, *Homer & Langley* (New York: Random House, 2009), 80.

40. Homi K. Bhabha, *The Location of Culture* (London: Routledge, 2004), 53.

41. As Doctorow put it (a sentiment he expressed on more than one occasion), "I particularly liked Hawthorne's definition of a romance: the idea of a sort of reality cured up into meaning, that you write a novel not from the accumulation of data the way the realists do but from structuring your story and using selective imagery. Well that's poeticism. One begins to turn out something that pushes in the direction of metaphor—or when you're not doing it absolutely correctly it falls into allegory, which Hawthorne lapsed into." Morris, *Conversations*, 214.

42. As an academically trained painter hovering between idealized portraits and urban poverty, prettified images of the well-heeled and realist images of metropolitan squalor, Wheelwright could be seen as an offshoot of the Ashcan School, centered around Robert Henri, making their mark(s) in turn-of-the-century New York. Like Wheelwright, these artists were torn between their social commitment and their desire to make a living with their craft. See, for example, Bennard B.

Perlman, *Painters of the Ashcan School: The Immortal Eight* (New York: Dover, 1979), esp. 15–16. Doctorow's relationship to the, especially nonliterary, artists in his work is still awaiting full scholarly exploration.

43. Saunders, "The Bravery of E. L. Doctorow."
44. Doctorow, *Jack London*, 152; original emphasis.
45. Doctorow, *Reporting the Universe*, 105. See Kittler's dramatic opening of *Gramophone, Film, Typewriter*: "*Optical fiber networks*. People will be hooked to an information channel that can be used for any medium—for the first time in history, or for its end. Once movies and music, phone calls and text reach households via optical fiber cables, the formerly distinct media of television, radio, telephone, and mail converge, standardized by transmission frequencies and bit format . . . Instead of wiring people and technologies, absolute knowledge will run as an endless loop." *Gramophone, Film, Typewriter*, trans. and with an Introduction, Geoffrey Winthrop-Young and Michael Wutz (Stanford: Stanford University Press, 1999), 1–2.
46. E. L. Doctorow, *City of God* (New York: Random House, 2000), 47.
47 E. L. Doctorow, *City of God* (New York: Random House, 2000), 214. Doctorow published many of these ruminations verbatim in an essay for the *New York Times*. Discussing prominent cinematic codes, he notes, "In some of today's film dramas 95 percent of a scene's meaning is conveyed before a word is uttered; 98 percent if you add music." "Quick Cuts: The Novel Follows Film Into a World of Fewer Words," *New York Times*, March 15, 1999, E1+.
48. Wutz, "On the Craft of Fiction," 13.

Part I

Generic Border Crossings

Chapter 1

Doctorow and the *Halbbildungsroman*

Tamlyn Avery

If man is ever to solve the problem of politics in practice he will have to approach it through the problem of the aesthetic, because it is only through Beauty that man makes his way to Freedom.
Schiller, *On the Aesthetic Education of Man*

It is as if human beings, as punishment for betraying the hopes of their youth and accommodating themselves to the world, are marked by premature decay.
Adorno and Horkheimer, *The Dialectic of Enlightenment*

A reading of E. L. Doctorow's novels discloses (at least) two versions of the author presiding over the words as they appear on the page. First, we sense the presence of a leftist critic and theoretician, whose progressive politics inevitably color the way we consume his nonfiction and fiction alike. And then, we observe the hallmarking of a professionalized aesthete, self-consciously working within the "system of knowledge" that is fiction,[1] the inheritor to its traditions, technologies, and marketplace. Ideology, in Roland Barthes's sense, constitutes operations that are "repeated and *consistent*"; *ipso facto*, counter-ideology must somehow disrupt those sequences which constitute the object of its critique. The role of the aesthetic in our society, as far as Barthes is concerned, must therefore be "to provide the rules of an *indirect and transitive* discourse (it can transform language, but does not display its domination, its good conscience)."[2] In a similar spirit, this essay treats Doctorow's interpenetration of form and politics to the consideration of a particular genre to which Doctorow often returns. That genre, what the narrator of *The Book of Daniel* might refer to as one "monstrous sequence" of bourgeois ideologies, is the *Bildungsroman*, here and for the moment translating to "the novel of self-formation."

When an interviewer inquired why Doctorow's novels so often take the perspective of a boy or young man as their premise, the author conceded that "the *Bildungsroman* is a very suitable container," and "a very useful way to go about things" as a writer.[3] The novel of self-formation allows authors plausibly to indulge in their "capacity for wonder" and to "find language for it that pleases" them by magnifying the wonderment for ordinary things which a child or young adult naturally expresses. But this genre also provides a "built-in kind of dramatic advantage," Doctorow adds; it capitalizes upon the reader's "presumption of innocence," which allows a writer to "impute to the narrator certain observations and feelings that sets up the entire dynamic for the book." In crafting the plausible vessel of innocence, the author may "go on to the corruption of it," he shrewdly concludes.[4] Doctorow elsewhere suggests how this tradition of corrupted boyhood novels began in American letters with Twain, forged in the parallax between the perceptions made available to a child reader to whom the boyhood books' juvenile voices market themselves, and the reception of the adult reader to whom Twain's books politically address themselves.[5] Doctorow's interest in Samuel Clemens's pragmatic turn as a mature writer to his own "usable past" echoes in the content and style of novels such as *World's Fair* or *Billy Bathgate*, in which Doctorow uses settings familiar to his own youth in order to fashion a remarkably similar effect.[6]

In this sense, Doctorow's works corrupt the prospect of the "aesthetic education" known as *Bildung*. Yet, the generic definition rehearsed above begins to fray as we turn to assess more complex *Bildungsroman* variants through this lens, such as *The Book of Daniel* or even *Loon Lake*, illuminating the need for us to sharpen our understanding of the *Bildungsroman* as a literary genre in order to make sense of Doctorow's statement. We must then prise open the Pandora's box lodged at the genre's core by isolating its philosophical root, *Bildung*, a term which abjures any neat translation. For, when Doctorow uses the corruption of the innocent as a narrative device, he sets in motion the formal corruption of the genre itself into which that subject is integrated lens and lever, a breaking down of the genre's implicit teleology to bring a subject into harmonious formation within his society. As Marc Redfield contends, the *Bildungsroman* which formalized out of this philosophical concept constitutes *the* fully "aesthetic" literary genre, with all its implicit ideological furnishings, in that the form projects the linear self-production of the self as an aesthetic construct. The *Bildungsroman*, in theory, forms a "trope for the aspirations of aesthetic humanism."[7] By going on to the "corruption of" the apotheosis of *Bildung*—that is, a subject who realizes his society's highest pitch of moral fiber by sacrificing his individuation to his nobler, social character—Doctorow sets up an "entire dynamic" in his novels written against the genre's natural idealism.

The Book of Daniel presents a failed initiation or formation of the subject as such; but more importantly it presents a clear case of the failure of the form itself (a novel which simulates Daniel's university dissertation) to cathartically accommodate the genre's aesthetic representation of the self-formation of the self. The ideal of *Bildung* depends upon the realization of rational autonomy, guided by both the personal and the cultural maturation of an individual; however, if the culture itself fails to realize its ennobling function in this process, if that culture succumbs to irrationality, the possibility for genuine individuation disintegrates. By this logic, the *Bildungsroman*, that novel form which tasks itself with reflecting *Bildung*, must in turn reflect the failure of *Bildung* if those preconditions for its realization are no longer possible. As in the case of *The Book of Daniel*, that formal disappointment abides by the logic of Theodor Adorno's revised theory of *Halbbildung*,[8] a term that refers to the pseudo-education resulting from the relapse of Enlightenment culture into barbarism in the twentieth century (in the German: "Symptome des Verfalls von Bildung"). When culture (*Kultur*) broadly fails in the face of mass culture, the edification of subjectivity (*Bildung*), which should reflect larger cultural ideals, instead falters and so testifies to this failure. Adorno's interlocutor, Thomas Mann, had in 1908 expressed how, if only a "century ago, idealism was supreme; half a century ago it had still not been dethroned; today its place has been taken by materialism," a delayed cardiac arrest to the idea of *Bildung* that literature was in turn absorbing.[9] *Halbbildung*, which translates as both half-education and pseudo-culture (Adorno oscillates between these two etymological emphases of the term), supplants the idealism of classical *Bildung* (culture; education) as society transitions from the internalization of conscious individual reflection and decision-making to unconscious socialization through mass mediation. This theory clarifies the stakes of many twentieth-century texts, particularly those published after World War II, which commonly feature the arrested development of a protagonist who fails to integrate. To follow Fredric Jameson's lead,[10] to participate in the *Bildungsroman* genre entails inheriting its political unconscious, grounded in the rationalist ideological logic of the Enlightenment which organizes that aesthetic reproduction; but the shift into administered barbarism from the mid-twentieth century transforms that political unconscious from within.

The example of *The Book of Daniel* puts renewed pressure on isolating and clearly articulating the evolution of that "indefinable," "phantom" genre,[11] which has led scholars to speak of the "failed" or "incomplete" *Bildungsroman* to make sense of the increasing disintegration of the genre over the course of the twentieth century. What Doctorow does not expand upon in the aforementioned interview, but which coils itself around the more formally complex variants of his boyhood novels, is the idea that the corruption of form goes hand in hand with the author's corruption of the aesthetic subject at the center of the *Bildungsroman* form. This gives sufficient grounds for laying down a theory of *Habbildungsroman* to complement his statement. In its late modernist guise, the "organismic logic" of the *Bildungsroman* may be turned "against itself, by autonomizing youth into a trope with no fixed destination," exposing the modernist critique of development as the "eternal logic of deferral."[12] A politics more suitable to a leftist *Bildungsroman* sprang from this aesthetic autonomization. While *Bildungsroman* scholars of all leanings can only generally concur that the characteristic structure of the genre privileges the articulation of bourgeois individuality, even without arriving at a central definition, twentieth-century left-wing novelists often attempted to transfigure the *Bildungsroman* from within, to critique capitalism's ideologies embedded in that generic mainframe; practical theories such as Barbara Foley's taxonomy of proletarian *Bildungsromane* give us an option to circumvent the genre's bourgeois centrism.[13] Nevertheless, as Foley notes, a wholesale theory of proletarian *Bildungsroman* does not necessarily apply to all left-wing fiction. We cannot argue, for instance, that Doctorow's *Bildungsromane* are proletarian *Bildungsromane*, despite their peripheral sympathies for the working class (*Loon Lake*, for example), and their often overt leftist tracts (*The Book of Daniel*).

Twentieth-century *Bildungsromane* often encode "capitalism's endless transitions within the trope of pure youthfulness, leaving the *Bildungsroman* stripped of the moralizing and dignifying rhetoric of national progress, civilizing mission, or even human rights," Jed Esty has argued, which may prove a useful lens for assessing Doctorow's works.[14] However, compared with a more general theory of failed or incomplete or anti-*Bildungsroman* common in contemporary studies of the genre, the term *Halbbildungsroman* offers additional advantages. It precisely articulates how an author writing under the auspices of late capitalism might use the novelized form to preserve the homological relationship between character and culture to hand in the *Bildungsroman* genre; the shift in emphasis merely advises that the rise of pseudo-culture alienates culture's exemplary character, a cause and effect reflected in novels which replace the achievement of individuation (*Bildung*) with a state of pseudo-individuation (*Halbbildung*). Adorno's theory of *Halbbildung* allows us the flexibility to interrogate the extent to which left-wing fiction can manipulate the *Bildungsroman* as the means to achieve its transformative political ends in other ways, without simply succumbing to a crude re-articulation of the individualistic bourgeois ideologies embedded in the form. All of Doctorow's *Bildungsromane*, in one way or another, attempt to break out of the teleological ideologies and sequences of self-production this genre demands by formally reflecting on what Adorno calls *Halbbildung*, the impossibility of self-formation through interiorized individuation, while reinstating the (only) basic premise of the form: to reflect the self-production of the self (even if the potential of that self remains unfulfilled). To formalize the dialectic between innocence and corruption which Doctorow sees lodged at the philosophical core of the *Bildungsroman*'s aesthetic program seems all the more useful for a writer who believes that we are "living inside a national ideology that's invisible to us because we're living inside it."

In the boyhood narratives of *Daniel*, *Loon Lake*, *Billy Bathgate*, and *World's Fair*, the result of the subject's development is a jaded acceptance of the bourgeois identity which inscribes them; however, the self-reflexive formalities allow Doctorow immanently to critique those ideologies. The issue, then, is identifying what the novelized genre of pseudo-self-formation could potentially look like as a "mode" (a generic modification) when formalized. The first mode of *Halbbildungsroman* could resemble Edgar Altschuler's subtle, but steady return to a childlike style of narration occurring within the limits of a memoir structure in *World's Fair*. The narratological mechanics of both *Billy Bathgate* and *World's Fair* give at least the appearance of chronotopic simplicity; that is, they follow a chronological first-person and largely preterite account of the formation of a self. In the latter work, Doctorow reframes his own "usable past," replicating his boyhood in the late 1930s Bronx, now reconstructed under the "illusion of a memoir."[15] This illusory structure, and its solipsistic first-person narration, does not consciously reveal its artifice to the reader. The childhood memories of Edgar, the narrator, subsume his language and thereby his character, facilitating a reversal of the aging process and violating the genre through form and syntax which reverses the development of the subject: "The voice gets younger. It's as if the narrator, in describing himself growing up, is growing down,"[16] which looks very much like a reformulation of the bourgeois politics of the development of the self in its reverse engineering of Joyce's feat in *Portrait of the Artist*.

The second category could look like the narrative of *Daniel*, with its nonlinear self-formation and constant interruptions from the heteroglossia grouping all the various dissonant voices of America's political melting pot. This second type of *Halbbildungsroman* could bear witness to the aestheticization of the self-formation of the subject, where, in *Loon Lake*, Joe's life becomes absorbed and taken over by the bourgeois circuit of desire which undergirds his existence, forming the aesthetic apotheosis of a rags-to-riches capitalist myth in the tradition of a Horatio Alger narrative.

In this regard, *The Book of Daniel* internally offers us the clearest "lit-er-ary map" of *Halbbildung* in form and content, and shall therefore bear the concentration of the forthcoming discussion. Doctorow argues that writers "can't ignore the conversation that goes on among works of art, every book, however original, replying to an earlier book—the artists of every genre responding not only to the life around them but to the work that has gone on before."[17] "Men make their own history," Marx argues, "but they do not make it just as they please; they do not make it under circumstances chosen by themselves, but under circumstances directly found, given and transmitted from the past."[18] Doctorow's novels work at "dissolving the pastiche by using all . . . substitutes for history," as Jameson argues of *Ragtime*.[19] Doctorow's *Halbbildungsromane* likewise exhibit a Marxist literary strategy which attempts to reveal the truth of deep structures (what "really is") by drawing attention to the superficiality of this mode of cultural expression; this negative dialectic breaks through the simulacrum which would instantiate itself as the authoritative image of the past or of culture. Jameson suggests that Doctorow cements his status as a novelist of the radical left by seizing the "whole apparatus of nostalgia art, pastiche, and postmodernism to work himself through them instead of attempting to resuscitate some older form of social realism, an alternative that would in itself become another pastiche."[20] In a novel such as *Ragtime*, or indeed as shall be argued of *Daniel*, the novelist insists upon "the very flatness and depthlessness of the thing which makes what isn't there very vivid" in order to dispel the limitations of a nostalgic reinvention of the past.[21] Daniel's *Halbbildung* forms an allegorical trope, certainly in line with Esty's assessment of the *Bildungsroman* as a tropological substitution for the historical spirit of a particular episteme, which rests upon the formation of the radical New Left born out of the tragic failure of the Old Left to realize its revolutionary potential.

The *Halbbildungsroman* of *Daniel*: Doctorow's Politics of Form

In all traditional *Bildungsromane*, Michael Minden has argued, the cooperation between the thematic motifs of incest (the pursuit of desire) and inheritance (instatement of masculine identity) plays a central role in formalizing the genre's narrative technique.[22] Subjectivity in post-Enlightenment Europe developed under a double-edged sword, requiring defense against a post-theological environment both liberating and disorienting, on the one hand, and, on the other, against modern scientific understandings of causality which nullified moral self-determinism(6). The *Bildungsroman* of a Hölderlin or a Novalis takes account of subjectivity in full knowledge that no accurate account may be given; but in doing so, the *Bildungsroman*'s "'unconscious' hero (a hero whose consciousness always lags behind his actions)" undertakes the process of "authoring or producing himself" (9), thereby redressing the aporias of the I's "attempts to unify itself in the face of the division of self-consciousness by turning away from thought to action" (8). To the fullest extent realized in Goethe, the *Bildungsroman*'s "closure or evident artificiality of the novel is *at once* organically pleasing *and* points beyond itself to truth to which it has no immediate access [. . .] Hence, a sense of infinite subjective potential—incest—can be played off against a closure or limit—inheritance—which it informs and transcends but does not disrupt" (10).

The Book of Daniel, true to this longstanding tradition, struggles against its dialectic between potentiality and inevitable closure from start to finish, a tension undergirded by the novel's focus upon an "I" who cannot turn thought, or reflection, into any decisive action. Here, perhaps, the generic association wavers. Still, the economic, technological, cultural, and indeed political crises which characterize the 1960s, the episteme which precipitates all the preconditions of postmodernity, brings *The Book of Daniel*'s eponymous narrator to a surprisingly similar brink of subjective crisis. Daniel Isaacson's inherited task, in the narrative's terms, is to register as an alternative, private history to dispute the official, public facts surrounding the trial of his parents, the Isaacsons, who in various ways represent thinly veiled substitutes of the real accused atom spies, the Rosenbergs. The narrative must bear witness to the historical transition from the Old Left, crippled by its betrayal of its own hopes in its proximity to Stalin, into the New Left, which must overcome the failures of its political ancestors, all while both combating the new and increasing threat in the form of the rise of late capitalist mass culture, and respecting the rise of new "minoritarian" counter-cultures taking form in feminism, Black Power, queer movements, and others. *The Book of Daniel* functions on several planes as a *Künstlerroman* (development-of-the-artist novel), a tradition where the form—well aware of its artificial nature—mirrors the fragmented stages which lead the individual to become the artist (in the vein of

Joyce's *Portrait*, or Fitzgerald's *This Side of Paradise*). However, this novel raises a serious formal paradox in terms of the genre: while the novel, taken as a whole, reflects the closed form of a rather disorienting historical dissertation submitted to Columbia University, the nonlinear development of its subject and the lack of closure as to his (and the New Left's) "liberation" at the novel's close reneges on any sense of finitude in terms of that self-formation of the subject.

Daniel's narrative hinges on his ability to decipher *das Bild* (picture; or form) of his parents, and to reproduce its essence through language, a gesture which reifies the etymological roots of the Bild*ungs*roman, and its "homology between character and culture."[23] The picture in question enframes an image of his parents, meaning Daniel's task to curate a portrait of their lives, in the literal and figurative senses, depends upon him developing his own individual portrait of the artist as the vehicle to tell this story. Both the "picture" and Daniel's central position as its keeper, in this sense, form an axis upon which the novel rotates, as both form and content work together to uncover the meaning enclosed within the portrait of Rochelle and Paul Isaacson. The narrative becomes a collage of different events and characters, memories and streams of consciousness, critical scholarship, all positioned as a not-so-carefully edited dissertation manuscript. Consider Daniel's conversation with his dying sister, Susan, in what could be considered a both literal and central figuration of incest within the *Bildungsroman*'s internal system: "'They are still fucking us,' she said, 'Goodbye Daniel. You get the picture.' He listened alertly. He was not sure if she said goodbye or good boy" (9; this motif also partially recurs on 16 and 159).[24] This narrative uses the image to force the outcome of the subject's formation, liberating him from his task as the inheritor to his parents' story and, by extension, the story of the failure of the Old Left they symbolize. The motif of "the picture" modulates into other dictions as a form of polyphony to replicate how other parties may be invested in this traumatic historical retelling. The instance where the narration assumes the following dialectical shift to Ebonics, for instance, indicates a rising in the text's racial unconsciousness, registering the betrayal of the African American interests by the Communist Party:

OH BABY, YOU KNOW IT NOW. WE DONE PLAYED enough games for you, ain't we. You smart lil fucker. You know where it's at now, don' you big daddy. You got the picture. This the story of a fucking, right? You pullin' out yo lit-er-ary map, mutha? You know where we goin', right muthafuck? (23)

These phrases also keep alive the genre's concern with incest, as centralized in the peculiar relationship between Daniel and his "starfish" sister, Susan, and precipitate an anticlimactic quest where Daniel never does "get the [full] picture." Whatever commissioned Daniel to write this text (in fulfillment of a tertiary dissertation, the radical left's most viable arsenal against historical erasure), this text refuses to remain a contiguous, subjective narrative of *one*, one person's collection of paraphernalia surrounding the case; in doing so, it also refuses its status as an objective account of his family's involvement in the McCarthy witch-hunts, where the generic framework might insist that politics should be divorced from feelings (and aesthetics).

The "picture" motif further enables Daniel to explicitly meditate on the idea of *Bildung* itself as an ideological reproductive organ (rather than genuine individuation), one human chain link in the sequence of humankind's existence, in which "the end of such apprenticeship consists in this, that the subject sows his wild oats, builds himself with his wishes and opinions into harmony with subsisting relationships and their rationality, enters the concatenation of the world and acquires for himself an appropriate attitude to it," as Hegel once quipped.[25] Daniel and his wife fornicate after standing before the "poster of the Isaacsons which is pasted on the kitchen wall," the same picture of the parents who "fucked" his sister and him into being, and "fucked" over the younger generation by signing themselves over to destructive Stalinist politics (175). Like Sterne's *Tristram Shandy*, the narrator who can never get past the sexual knot which produced him (his parents), Daniel expresses a desire to know "how education works":

> I wish I knew the secret workings in the soul of education. It has nothing to do with time as we measure it. Small secret chemical switches are thrown in the dark. Tiny courses are hung through the electric passages of tissues. Silken sequences of atoms which have no property other than self-knowledge. (175)

His first-person reflections devolve into a sad meditation on the trauma of human formation inevitably replicated through reproduction:

> leaning over her sleepy smiling eyes I could not find there the education recorded, no impression of the cruel thing, the cruel thing, and that it is always the cruel thing that mixes the tears of our eyes, the breath of our lungs, the creams of our comes . . . (175)

The end product of Daniel's self-formation is not meant to be singular character development, or narrative fulfillment, but to feel the novel of the individual dissolving into the larger chain of human social development. The form feels these underlying tensions chafing against the bourgeois ideology to which the novel is allied in its quest for circularity and closure (signified through the finalization of self-formation), which this mode of production renders impossible. *The Book of Daniel* consciously reflects on its own ambiguous ambitions to accurately convey reality by subverting and corrupting its realist apparatuses:

> In any event, my mother and father, standing in for them, went to their deaths for crimes they did not commit. Or maybe they did committ [*sic*] them. Or maybe my mother and father got away with false passports for crimes they didn't committ [*sic*]. How do you spell comit? Of one thing we are sure. Everything is elusive. God is elusive. Revolutionary morality is elusive. Justice is elusive. Human character. Quarters for the cigarette machine. You've got these two people in the poster Daniel, now how you going to get them out? And you've got a grandma you mention once or twice, but we don't know anything about her. And some colored man in the basement—what is that all about? What has that got to do with anything? (43–4)

Interestingly, this precise motif of the "colored man in the basement" Doctorow would in fact later return to and redevelop in *World's Fair*, as if that later, more conventional *Bildungsroman* means to round out some of the roughness, or in Daniel's words, the "elusiveness," of *Daniel* taken as a whole. Yet Daniel's concept of the elusive here reads as a rejection of the formal and historical absolute through a process of revisions, both literally in the misspelling of "commit," and conceptually drawing attention to the concept of totalistic idealized commitment: as a treatise of inherent contradictions within the formations of identity and realpolitik that do not harmoniously negate one another. If sequence is monstrous, then random intrusions to the order—such as misspelling—corrupt the regime of realism, or of ideological replication. The novel refuses to present any artificial aesthetic closure, and this refusal is wherein its political power lies.

When Marx wrote that the "tradition of all the dead generations weighs like a nightmare on the brain of the living,"[26] his "borrowed language" echoes in a line uttered by *The Book of Daniel's* eponymous narrator: "What is most monstrous is sequence" (252). Like Salinger's Holden Caulfield, to whom *Daniel* refers (98), or perhaps looking even earlier, to the more determined historic meanderings of narrators such as Melville's Ishmael, Daniel's narration prepares a long series of diversionary narratological tactics to resist assuming his role as the *Bildungsheld* (central character) of this narrative, including shifting into different dictions (colloquial, formal, first and third person) to create a dissociative effect. Daniel's meanderings undermine his authoritative rehearsal of the events leading up to the Isaacsons' deaths at the hand of the state, which is precisely the point they wish to effect: that any history, whether individual or collective, cannot be the authoritative or absolute truth. Daniel, referring to himself here in the first person and there in the third, self-reflexively casts himself in the role of the "monstrous writer who places one word after another. The monstrous magician," a writer forced to arbitrarily produce life, authoritative history, sequences, out of the illegible flux of phenomena ("one damn thing after another") all in the name of narrative, while paradoxically—as Marx estimated of all revolutionary acts—he can only "anxiously conjure up the spirits of the past" (252).

Doctorow's monstrous metaphor suggests how meaning is conveyed through the conduit of words arranged in this particular way on a sheet of paper, in an incantation which exhumes the dead and returns them to the world of the living. But this mystical language operates under smoke and mirrors; the writer conjures words not out of "nothing," but from within an existing matrix of speech genres in much the same manufacturing process as those sheets of paper themselves are produced from inert organic matter: all "made in USA by Long Island Paper Products, Inc." (3). "Every line of every novel of Henry James has been paid for. James knew this and was willing to accept the moral burden," Daniel elsewhere states (216), deviating from the historical subject to hand so as to question the chafing between implicit and explicit agendas of narrative and story-telling housed within this novel form. This logic extends to the figure of an academic *Bildungsheld*, who must "author" or "form" himself in order to achieve his professional use-value in society. Daniel's polemical position on the vocation of writing and self-writing, a position which he attempts to locate both here and throughout this novel, casts both the narrator and Doctorow himself in the role of Victor Frankenstein. The "monstrous" author (and the subject who authors and forms himself) stitches deadened ligaments together in the hope that, with the spark of an electrical current of progress, all organs of the literary corpse/corpus will come to life (as opposed to the novel's motif of the electric current which culminates in the actual electrocution of his parents):

> Reader, this is a note to you. If it seems to you elementary, if it seems after all this time elementary . . . If it *is* elementary and seems to you at this late date to be pathetically elementary, like picking up some torn bits of cloth and tearing them again . . . If it is elementary, then reader, I am reading you. And together we may rend our clothes in mourning. (56)

That corpus, as Daniel here evinces, is the complacent American *half*-culture (*Halbbildung*), which has turned rationality into irrationality, which sent his sister into catatonia and his parents to the chair, which suspends and threatens to dissolve all revolutionary politics.

Genres, the genealogy of words and the systematic arrangement of ideas, are the genetic sequences upon which every seme of human communication is built, granted that the law of genre, that shifting epistemological system, must be more or less knowable, transferable, enforceable, repeatable, and repetitive to convey its transmission. At one point, Daniel interrupts himself to ask the question, in a diction unlike his regular style of address, "You pullin' out yo lit-er-ary map, mutha? You know where we goin', right muthafuck?" (23). As the protean narrator here suggests, meaning and order can be created, conveyed, and evaluated only through recognizable, familiar coordinates which the receiver may interpret; but in *Daniel*, no neat sense of order is ever established. As Adorno might suggest (as he does of the lyric genre, for instance), putting the account of an alienated individual to paper, no matter how fragmented or isolated that individual appears, only ever suggests an *a priori* social act of understanding. By refusing to unify those coordinates through the *Bildungsroman* speech genre, the *Bildungsheld* assumes a resistant position in defiance of the ideologies which would inscribe him or her as the exceptionalized individual at the helm of this story, at the expense of using those same values (participating in this *Bildungsroman* genre) to achieve and maintain his or her distance from them.

"Printed words on a page," Hugh Kenner once argued, "—any words, any page—are so ambiguously related to each other that we collect sense only with the aid of a tradition: this means, helped by prior experience with a genre, and entails our knowing which genre is applicable."[27] If "[u]tterances and their types, that is, speech genres, are the drive belts from the history of society to the history of language,"[28] several of Doctorow's boyhood novels attempt to construct a history for which no appropriate speech genre exists; thus, they substitute a history of the individual for history. The novel (or perhaps, like Joyce himself, you prefer "epic," "encyclopaedia," or "*maledettisimo romanzaccione*") to which Kenner above refers, of course, is *Ulysses*. Yet, the statement could just as easily apply to *Daniel*, a text, like *Ulysses*, named to bring the modern text into "deliberate collision with a powerful predecessor."[29] The biblical allusion here speaks to the Judean visionary in the courts of the Babylonian kings Nebuchadnezzar and Belshazzar, and the Persian kings Darius and Cyrus, covering the period of the Exile of the Judeans. Daniel's messianic dossier reveals how the life of an individual, composed through various piecemeal retellings of episodes in his life and his holy visions, merge in order to paint a momentous portrait of a historical epoch, with prophetic undertones of revelation to come. His duty to receive and transmit the holy words of his God channels into the following order: "*Go thy way Daniel: for the words are closed up and sealed till the time of the end.*" The words transmitted by the biblical character Daniel are unknowable and beyond interpretation even to the prophet who utters them; they appear at the very end of Doctorow's *Book of Daniel* in reflexive summation of the text's polyphonic achievement.

A more conventional reading of Daniel might rationalize his style of narration as symptomatic of a traumatized, split subject, whose narrative strategy avoids reaching its painful climax, the trial and execution of the Isaacsons; without rejecting this line entirely, I suggest that the fractured form of *Daniel* furthermore suggests a detailed account of what a subject who becomes aware of his *Halbbildung* might look like. In writing *Daniel*, Doctorow claimed to be "attracted to formal experiments of the time in which writers sort of broke down the compact between reader and writer and intruded in ways to suggest to the reader that the material was totally unreliable and not to be trusted," but that the "presiding postmodern presence" at play in *Daniel* evokes the intrusive, transgressive, violations of Laurence Sterne.[30] Discussing the imbalance of objectivity and creativity which disturbs the writer-protagonist of Camus's *The Plague*, Doctorow illustrates how the character

> spends the entire book writing the first sentence of his novel and can never get past the first sentence because the critical factor is so strong for him that he is not released to take a chance, to the freedom to go on to the next line, and so he keeps changing the clauses in the sentence. He's trying this one sentence over and over in different ways because that objective quality is overdeveloped in him.[31]

In this sense, *Daniel* presents itself in a more obviously complex framework of speech genres than any of Doctorow's other boyhood novels, in that it does not want to *appear* to be a *Bildungsroman* at all. The text aggressively masks and reroutes its inner and outer generic function, sardonically unified in the following utterance which appears on the final page, which comes despite the fact that Daniel has already divulged to Linda Mindish that his Ph.D. has been conferred (272):

DANIEL'S BOOK: A Life Submitted in Partial Fulfillment of the Requirements for the Doctoral Degree in Social Biology, Gross Etymology,

Women's Anatomy, Children's Cacophony, Arch Demonology, Eschatology, and Thermal Pollution. (309)

The titular parody here doubly mocks the academic genre at its core, and subverts any attempt to bear witness to the congruous formation of the subject.

However, this split subjectivity signals some greater anti-formation at stake than the trauma of a single subject, certainly as in the instance where the narrator presents his lengthy discourse on the political implications of Disneyland as the "womb" of mass cultural reproduction (294). Here, Daniel echoes Adorno's concern about *Bildung* collapsing into mass culture as a substitute for genuine culture and education, what Adorno calls the *Bilderlosigkeit* (culturelessness) of the U.S. as the predominant bourgeois country after the war.[32] Consider the style of Daniel's experience of the event of visiting Disneyland to meet with his parents' old confidante turned betrayer, Selig Mindish:

> What Disneyland proposes is a technique of abbreviated shorthand culture for the masses, a mindless thrill, like an electric shock, that insists at the same time on the recipient's rich psychic relation to his country's history and language and literature. In a forthcoming time of highly governed masses in an overpopulated world, this technique may be extremely useful both as a substitute for education and, eventually, as a substitute for experience. (295)

The metaphor is clear: Daniel wants the reader to connect the sociological trauma of "culturelessness" to the trauma inflicted upon Selig Mindish, who is serving his own private death sentence, living on in this state of perpetual electric shock, frozen in a senile state of "mindless thrill." However, the narrative fluctuates between objective and subjective utterances, manifest not only is this particular chapter but throughout, where these sociological critiques of history, culture, and politics (stylistically characterized by observations such as, "One is struck by," or "One notices") dissolve into indicative first-hand accounts. Doctorow uses the same striking shorthand as what Louis Marin (*Utopic Degeneration: Disneyland*, 1977), Jean Baudrillard (*Simulacra and Simulation*, 1981), and Umberto Eco (*Travels in Hyperreality*, 1986) would all treat as the exemplary site of degenerate utopia and hyperreality. As Daniel turns to address his own cultural politics, to capture its essence and truth through critiquing its contradictions (a pseudo-culture masking itself as genuine culture), the novel calls upon Daniel to field a similar dilemma to Adorno's "psycho-dynamic question of how the subject is able to persevere in the face of a rationality which has itself become irrational."[33]

Daniel, as the eponymous hero of the book, must persevere in line with generic expectations; however, this is not to say that he is heroic, or even the central actor in the events it retells. Doctorow decentralizes the subject, giving him the outsider perspective of a Nick Carraway role rather than the role of a Gatsby, where the Gatsby under consideration is actually American culture itself rather than a single character. By telescoping outside of Daniel's interior life, the novel facilitates an awakening of its revolutionary collective consciousness from the anesthetizing dream-world of capitalism, even as Daniel's private quest for answers leads him to stumble into the very quintessence of the late capitalist behemoth in order to find truth, a truth that has, literally in the now degenerating mind of Selig Mindish, irreversibly devolved into a muted state of senility. The longer Daniel lingers in the Disneyworld dreamland, he, like Mindish, must succumb to a Benjamin Button-like reversion to the infantile state, the unravelling of *Bildung* as an anesthetized state of *Halbbildung* supplants it. The novel *Daniel* meditates on the *Bildungsroman*'s aesthetic humanistic aspirations directly through the recurring motif of the "picture" which the narrator must "get" in order to get out of—to liberate himself from this tragic generic framework. Transcendence, and catharsis, can only occur once he fulfills all the motions of a completed narrative of self-formation, the apotheosis of which is the death of his parents, which prematurely catalyzed his "young manhood."

To fortify this sense of subjective decentralization, to strengthen our sense of the *Halbbildung* taking the place of *Bildung*, Doctorow ensures that any last bastion of innocence is immediately corrupted through the novel, any personal development underscored with events of shocking cynicism and violence, reversing the dialectic between innocence and corruption, and harmony and disharmony. After briefly describing his parents' history for a paragraph, obliquely he interrupts himself:

> Let's see, what other David Copperfield kind of crap. So the Trustees of Ohio State were right in 1956 when they canned the English instructor for assigning *Catcher in the Rye* to his freshman class. They knew there is no qualitative difference between the kid who thinks it's funny to fart in chapel, and Che Guevara. They knew then Holden Caulfield would found SDS. (98)

Daniel refuses to satisfy the expectations of readerly fulfillment, interrupting himself with nonsequiturs; he defers from supplying cathartic facts to explain the significance of the grandmother, or the colored man in the basement, or any other intertextual "David Copperfield kind of crap" (98).

The same goes for Twain, from whom all American literature supposedly descends, whose familiarity spawns not from literature but from an amusement ride on an artificial Mississippi which winds through the late capitalist dream-work epicenter and electric commodity-playground, Disneyland. Twain is an atheist, and pornographer, Daniel's historical voice tells us, "whose great work . . . is a nightmare of childhood in confrontation with American social reality" (294). The bus at the Robeson concert, nearly overturned by a racist mob (51), as well as the disfigured body of a woman impaled on the fence of a school yard, her blood intermingled with the overflowing milk she just bought from the supermarket, bear witness to the trauma which Disneyland, as hyperreal shorthand for American culture (or lack thereof), insists upon repressing. Intermittently, Daniel willfully corrupts this neat order of the innocent *Bildungsheld* with shocking, graphic admissions of the most repulsive violence that he himself has enacted. He sexually degrades his wife and brands her with a cigarette lighter, and then provokes the reader: "Shall I continue? Do you want to know the effect of three concentric circles of heating element . . . upon the tender white girlflesh of my wife's ass? Who are you anyway? Who told you you could read this? Is nothing sacred?" (62). He rejects the sequence, cutting instead to an analysis of Dali and Buñuel's *Un Chien Andalou* and "the famous slicing open of the eyeball" as a symbolic demonstration of the torture he enacts (62–3) and that is enacted upon him by the pseudo-culture of simulation. Later, he challenges the reader again, accusing her or him of believing he cannot "do" the execution (302): that is, to narrate the murder of his parents by the state.

In one sense, the power of the *Bild* remains absolute: the two people in the picture remain there, without disclosing their objective meaning, their objective truth. However, the act of Daniel's book brings the significance of the indecipherable poster into a collective memory of collaged images, rather than allowing them to remain in objectivity. Rather than a quest of truth-seeking, Daniel must turn reflection into action, curating this portrait within a broader historical tableau, if only ever assembling fragments of narrative into a disordered, chaotic wreckage of history (a postmodern "flattening" of history). He must navigate this terrain to address the underlying question: what kind of politics is appropriate to *Halbbildung*? Daniel's political patchwork finds it metonymical signal within the text through the image of a collage on the wall to represent the standpoint of the radical New Left, as created by Daniel's comrade Artie Sternlicht. Artie's radical vision is one of aesthetic protest, to overthrow the Pentagon with saturation of images (145), rather than to transport images to the Soviet through Western televised technology:

> A collage of posters and real objects. Babe Ruth running around the bases, Marlon Brando on his bike, Shirley Temple in her dancing shoes, FDR, a bikini sprayed with gold paint, Marilyn Monroe on her calendar, Mickey Mouse, Gilbert Stuart's Washington with a moustache painted on . . . (140)

This work within the work is ironically entitled "Everything that Came Before is All The Same" (141). The reader, like Daniel, becomes stranded in a complex semiotic system of conspiracy, disorganization, and radical dissociation from reality, but also from the fictional reading event as we knew it. Rather than the genre's teleology which places the individual as the authoritative account of history, history and fictional negate one another in *Daniel*, dissolving the assurance of character upon which the reader relies, rather than bringing the reader to some condition of truth awareness. Borders are willfully collapsed between image and language, fact and fiction, innocence and guilt, and preservation and corruption.

Daniel leaves its reader to ruminate on the discomforting after-thought that history is pervasive, unpatterned, illogically unfolding, that this novel, and the events it contains, are only some small, alienated part of a much larger structure of meaning beyond comprehensibility. The chronotopic structure, framed around a narrative of self-formation or development which spirals out into an infinitely broader portrait of American culture and global history, emerges without a clear pattern or design. Like Walter Benjamin's discussion of Paul Klee's *Angelus Novus*, one must look beyond the wrecking pile of history if one wishes to be liberated from this novel's damning transmission. *The Book of Daniel* interlocks a multimodal framework of fiction, posing as a history, posing as a self-reflexive *Bildungsroman*, posing as dissertation, all of which bleed into one another, and, by definition, remain only ever "partially fulfilled" and stand in, metonymically, as the "fulfillment of a life" (309). The praxis, the revolutionary realization of the truth content, occurs outside of the book, which is rushed to a close, leaving the protagonist to wish "he had more time to speculate on some of the questions posed by this narrative" (309), presumably closing with Daniel going to join the Columbia revolt of 1968, finding out whether or not he "has been liberated," as the student who ushers him from the library suggests (309). As T. V. Reed concludes, "we can only proceed by giving up the illusion that we can get wholly outside the forms that narrate us."[34] Daniel "close[s] up and seal[s]" the words and disappears, along with the radical left, into the obscurity of our historical imagination.

After *Daniel*, Doctorow returns again and again to what F. Scott Fitzgerald once called the most "overworked art-form" in the modern American letters: the "history of the young man" genre,[35] otherwise known as the *Bildungsroman*. Each one of Doctorow's *Bildungsromane*, and in particular *Daniel*, demonstrates what John G. Parks has called Doctorow's "poetics of engagement,"[36] which looks much rather like disengagement from the fiction of the private life or self. Nevertheless, in their disengagement, most of Doctorow's *Bildungshelden* abandon and neglect the social and political dimensions of their enterprise (Joe in *Loon Lake* and, arguably, the narrator in *Daniel*). Doctorow's relationship to this *Bildungsroman* genre could be said to be modal, modes which—as John Frow has argued of genre—"start their life as genres but over time take on a more general force which is detached from particular structural embodiments."[37] Two types of *Bildungsromane* emerge accordingly in Doctorow's oeuvre: the first type is the more complex, fragmented texts which formally operate more obviously upon the basis of what I have defined as *Halbbildungsromane* (*The Book of Daniel* and *Loon Lake*); the second category, increasingly prevalent in his later career, remains openly prosaic in its generic narrative constructs of selfhood (*Billy Bathgate* and *World's Fair*). This is not to say that Doctorow's works lose their political charge; rather, the lens of *Halbbildung* allows us to detect Doctorow's shift away from formal varieties suitable to the New Left into a different, although no less newly avowed, forms of literary agitation. In spite of this chronology which casts Doctorow as increasingly relying upon a traditionally idealist genre which goes against his general politics, the theory of *Halbbildung* may assist analyses of these works by providing a method to discuss how Doctorow continually reworks the novel of the individual as a formal critique of capitalist ideology. For the subject of all these *Halbbildungsromane*, whose "proper" maturation is rendered impossible in various ways by the pseudo-culture that defines our mode of production, stands as a synecdoche for the late capitalist system that promotes this state of pseudo-individuation in the first place.

Notes

1. Quoted in Christopher D. Morris, ed., *Conversations with E. L. Doctorow* (Jackson: University of Mississippi, 1999), vii.

2. Roland Barthes, *Roland Barthes*, Richard Howard trans. (Berkeley: University of California Press, 1977), 104; original emphasis.
3. Quoted in Morris, *Conversations*, 140–1.
4. Quoted ibid.
5. E. L. Doctorow, *Creationists: Selected Essays, 1993–2006* (New York: Random House, 2006), 54.
6. Ibid.
7. Marc Redfield, *Phantom Formations: Aesthetic Ideology and the Bildungsroman* (Ithaca: Cornell University Press, 1996), 39.
8. Theodor W. Adorno, "Theory of Pseudo-Culture (1959)," *Telos*, 95 (March 1993): 15–38.
9. Quoted in W. H. Bruford, *The German Tradition of Self-Cultivation: "Bildung" from Humboldt to Thomas Mann* (Cambridge: Cambridge University Press, 1975), viii.
10. Fredric Jameson, *The Political Unconscious: Narrative as a Socially Symbolic Act* (London: Routledge, 2002).
11. Redfield, *Phantom Formations*, vii–viii.
12. Jed Esty, *Unseasonable Youth: Modernism, Colonialism, and the Fiction of Development* (Oxford: Oxford University Press, 2014), 210.
13. Barbara Foley, *Radical Representations: Politics and Form in U.S. Proletarian Fiction, 1929–1941* (Durham: Duke University Press, 1993), 322.
14. Esty, *Unseasonable Youth*, 210.
15. Quoted in Morris, *Conversations*, 103.
16. Ibid.
17. E. L. Doctorow, *Reporting the Universe* (Cambridge, MA: Harvard University Press, 2003), 5.
18. Karl Marx, "The Eighteenth Brumaire of Louis Bonaparte," in Robert C. Tucker, ed., *The Marx-Engels Reader* (2nd edition; New York: W. W. Norton & Company, 1978), 595.
19. Fredric Jameson, "Interview with Anders Stephanson," in *Jameson on Jameson: Conversations on Cultural Marxism*, ed. Ian Buchanan (Durham: Duke University Press, 2007), 61.
20. Ibid.
21. Ibid.
22. Michael Minden, *Incest and Inheritance: The German Bildungsroman* (Cambridge: Cambridge University Press, 1997), 1–2, and 4. Subsequent references to this source are cited parenthetically within the text.
23. Redfield, *Phantom Formations*, 38.
24. Parenthetical citations refer to E. L. Doctorow, *The Book of Daniel* (Reading: Picador, 1982).
25. G. W. F. Hegel, *Aesthetics: Lectures on Fine Art, Volume One*, trans. T. M. Knox (Oxford: Clarendon Press, 1988), 593.
26. Marx, "The Eighteenth Brumaire of Louis Bonaparte," 595.

27. Hugh Kenner, *Ulysses* (rev. edition; Baltimore: Johns Hopkins University Press, 1987), 3.

28. Mikhail M. Bakhtin, *Speech Genres and Other Late Essays*, ed. Caryl Emerson and Michael Holquist, trans. Vern W. McGee (Austin: University of Texas Press, 1986), 65.

29. Jennifer Levine, "*Ulysses*," in Derek Attridge, ed., *The Cambridge Companion to James Joyce* (Cambridge: Cambridge University Press, 1990), 131–2.

30. Quoted in Morris, *Conversations*, 134.

31. Ibid.

32. Adorno, "Theory of Pseudo-Culture," 27.

33. Ibid.

34. T. V. Reed, "Genealogy/Narrative/Power: Questions of Postmodernity in Doctorow's *The Book of Daniel*," *American Literary History*, 4.2 (1992): 302.

35. Quoted in J. D. Thomas, "F. Scott Fitzgerald: James Joyce's 'Most Devoted' Admirer," *The F. Scott Fitzgerald Review*, 5 (2006): 68.

36. John G. Parks, "The Politics of Polyphony: The Fiction of E. L. Doctorow," *Twentieth Century Literature*, 37.4 (Winter, 1991): 454.

37. John Frow, *Genre* (2nd edition; London: Routledge, 2015), 71.

Chapter 2

"The Dark Horrors of Consciousness": Doctorow and the Gothic

Stephen Arch

Throughout his career, E. L. Doctorow maintained an ambivalent relationship to popular narrative forms like the gangster novel and the detective novel. Repeatedly, he used such forms as scaffolding for what were, in effect, complex philosophical meditations on ethics, ontology, history, language, and aesthetics. His first novel, *Welcome to Hard Times* (1960), was ostensibly a Western; his second, *Big as Life* (1966), was ostensibly science fiction. These scaffoldings may have contributed to the sense that his novels were in some way ready-made for Hollywood, because to date at least six of them have been made into feature-length films. Hollywood for a long time resisted turning Pynchon's or DeLillo's novels into movies, but not Doctorow's.[1]

In fact, many of Doctorow's novels and stories are fundamentally antithetical to the style of Hollywood film. One of his own narrators, Everett (the writer/narrator of *City of God*), says with disdain that "[f]ilm is time-driven, it never ruminates, it shows the outside of life, it shows behavior. It tends to the simplest moral reasoning." Everett believes that the term "film language" is an oxymoron because films are visual and emotional; they work against the kind of verbal and written language that both reflects and enables complex, rational thought. Film, Everett says, "deliterates thought": it transforms thought into simple, emotional pictures. In what some readers have taken to be Doctorow's comment (not Everett's), he says that a film inspired by a book is always a "narrative simplification of a complex morally consequential reality."[2]

In contrast, Everett asserts, "novels can do anything in the dark horrors of consciousness" (214). Novels present us with morally consequential realities, functioning like a "printed circuit / for our lives to flow through, / A story told invokes our dim capacity / to be alive in bodies not our own" (181), as Everett himself puts it in a poetic meditation in *City of God*. They can move freely in space, time, and imagination.

At their best and most complex, novels can even "reproduce the actual texture of living life" (47).

In Doctorow's novels, that "texture" is very often articulated through the consciousness of a single narrator/character. Among his twelve novels, only *Big as Life* and *The March* are narrated in the third person, and to the end of his life Doctorow considered the former to be a failure. Persistently, Doctorow's fictions present us with a narrator who, as a character, is writing a text in order to make sense of his life: Joe in *Loon Lake*, the Little Boy in *Ragtime*, Billy in *Billy Bathgate*, Daniel in *The Book of Daniel*. In several novels that I wish to examine, those narrators remind us repeatedly that they are in the process of constructing the actual text we have at hand: Blue writing up to the moment of his death in *Welcome to Hard Times*; McIlvaine, the newspaperman, spilling after many years the story that "occupies" him, in *The Waterworks*;[3] Homer typing on a succession of typewriters the story of his and his brother's descent into madness; Everett first narrating into a tape recorder and then typing on a computer the thoughts that comprise *City of God*.

These narrators are haunted by memories and events, many of which happened to them and some of which happened to their acquaintances or to the culture at large. Within their narratives, memories bubble up, recur, persist. Fantasies become indistinguishable from reality. "After all these years in my head," McIlvaine writes, "my story occupies me, it has grown into the physical dimensions of my brain . . . so . . . however the mind works . . . as reporter, as dreamer . . . that is the way the story gets told" (219, ellipses in original). Significantly, they are *occupied* by their tales, or *possessed* by them as one might say in a gothic context. Similar to Coleridge's narrator in *The Rime of the Ancient Mariner*, Doctorow's narrators are often possessed of a "ghastly tale" they need to tell—or more accurately, perhaps, they are possessed by a tale they need to tell in order to understand just how ghastly it is. Insistently and persistently, those tales are grotesque, uncanny, abject, gothic.

I argue in this essay that the gothic mode is key to understanding E. L. Doctorow's fiction. While reviewers and critics have at times noted Doctorow's use of the gothic, especially in reference to *The Waterworks* and *The March*, we have not seen clearly enough just how gothic his narratives are. His narrators are uncannily possessed by stories that are simultaneously theirs and not theirs. And they perceive about them a world that is fundamentally grotesque in its perverse machinations: violent, occulted, inhuman, and inhumane. Yet strangely that inhospitable world is our home. To understand Doctorow this way is to align his work closely with the work of those nineteenth-century American writers who so strongly influenced him, especially Poe and Hawthorne.

But it is also to recognize that Doctorow ingeniously adapted the gothic mode to his own unique purposes in our postmodern world.

The Unhomely in *Homer & Langley*

In his 2009 novel, *Homer & Langley*, Doctorow re-imagined of the lives of Homer and Langley Collyer, real-life hoarders whose bizarre and compulsive behavior first came to the attention of the wider public in 1938 through articles in the *New York Times* and other national newspapers. The brothers died in 1947, Langley from asphyxiation after tripping a booby trap of his own devising and Homer from starvation and heart disease. Their deaths and the subsequent discovery by police and workmen of the tons of debris in the cluttered house were widely covered in the national press in the United States.

In Doctorow's novel, Homer is blind from a young age, while Langley is disabled from mustard gas poisoning in World War I. Their parents die in the flu pandemic of 1918–20, leaving the sons a small inheritance and a house already cluttered with objects collected on the parents' travels. These and many other elements of the novel deviate from the Collyer brothers' actual story. In reality, Homer went blind in the 1930s, at about the age of fifty, their parents did not die in the flu pandemic, and Langley did not fight in World War I. In conceiving the Collyer brothers, Doctorow uses some of the conventions of the gothic mode to remake their lives. The uncanny "sense of living with things assertively inanimate" was "our legacy,"[4] Homer writes, and the brothers extend that legacy to a kind of logical conclusion, stuffing their house with the abject odds and ends of the increasingly materialistic culture that surrounds them. Their house is unhomely. Both sons experience arrested emotional development in their late teens or early twenties. Langley retreats "into an iconoclastic life of the mind" because of his bitterness at the absurdity of the war (77). Having seen up close the dehumaniz-ation of men in the Great War, he comes to understand relationships with other people as absurd. He theorizes that human beings are simply objects in a succession of temporal moments, like molecules of water that are moved up or down by the action of a wave: Time "advances through us as we replace ourselves to fill the slots" (14). He distances himself emotionally from people, and collects objects as a way of re-assuring himself of his theory regarding the displacement of emotion in favor of the constant reassurance of things that are exchangeable and replaceable in their individual insignificance. On the other hand, Homer is fixated on women, seeing them both as sex objects and as idealized virgins; but he is never able to develop an emotional relationship with a woman. He was traumatized as a teenager by seeing a pornographic film: "I was rapt—horrified, but also thrilled to a level of unnatural feeling that was akin to nausea" (10–11). That moment in which he sees a brute sexual act is connected in his own mind to the death of his parents and to his brother's bitter response to war. He does not agree with Langley's theory, but he comes in his own way to replace people with things. "My sense of myself as damaged suggested the wiser course of seclusion as a means of avoiding pain, sorrow, and humiliation" (76). In a moment of insight late in the novel, Homer briefly realizes that, to the outside world, he and his brother had become "the ghosts who haunted the house we had once lived in" (198).

In conceiving the brothers' day-to-day existence in the house, Doctorow blurs the line between home and its uncanny or unhomely (*unheimlich*) opposite.[5] To outsiders, the Collyer house is unlivable, a nightmare space of worthless possessions stacked side to side and top to bottom in every room. It is evidence of an irrational behavior that only recently has been defined as a mental disorder,[6] just as it has also become an object of fascination in popular television documentary shows like *Hoarding: Buried Alive* and *Hoarders*. In effect, Doctorow traces an etiology of hoarding in *Homer & Langley*, demonstrating how the merely "cluttered" space of the parents' house becomes over time the bizarre, creepy, claustrophobic space of the sons' "home."

However, because Homer is writing the story and because he comes to inhabit that "unlivable" house almost imperceptibly over a long period of time, the novel feels less gothic than it is. Many gothic novels, from Horace Walpole's *The Castle of Otranto* to Alison Bechdel's *Fun Home*, emphasize the creepy or gloomy or uncanny atmosphere of the home, but in *Homer & Langley* the reader must in essence see what the narrator himself cannot always see. The Collyer mansion is "home" to Homer no matter what it seems to outsiders. He is "at home," as his name might suggest. Sometime after Armistice Day in 1918, Homer places Langley's Springfield rifle on the fireplace mantle, "and there it has stayed, almost the first piece in the collection of artifacts from our American life" (24). There are then books of poetry that Langley brings home to read to Homer, the several daily newspapers that Langley reads and refuses to discard, and eventually Langley's "full and uninhibited execution [of] whatever scheme or fancy occurred to him" (77), such as installing a Model T Ford in the dining room. When the family cook gently complains that "something made for the outside is inside" the house, Langley responds by questioning "ontological distinctions between outside and inside" (80). Though Homer cannot mark a precise moment when it happens, the brothers fail to maintain the boundary that separates the domestic life of the home from the wider world of nature and the public. Their behavior makes them abject, even as they continue to live within the city.

Doctorow's use of the gothic in *Homer & Langley* edges persistently toward allegory. Indeed, throughout his fiction Doctorow's gothic tales edge toward allegory while at the same time resisting a full-scale identification as allegory. This is, in a certain way, reminiscent of Hawthorne's method in his novels and stories, although, as I suggest below, Doctorow's motives differ from Hawthorne's.[7] For example, Homer's observation that the Springfield rifle is the first piece in "the collection of artifacts from *our American life*" (emphasis added) tells us that the objects in the house do not begin as detritus; they potentially signify something about America and about American life in the twentieth century. Throughout the narrative, Doctorow hints in these kinds of ways that the Collyer brothers' story has a broader allegorical significance, that it means something more than or different from a mere description of a psychological disorder.

Langley himself suggests that the brothers' story is "remarkably prophetic" (176). In their neighborhood, they are threatened and cursed for allowing pests to proliferate in their house, and Homer imagines that their house thus prefigures the city itself in its "deterioration in the civil order" (171).[8] Their accumulation of possessions tracks the increasing commodification of American culture before and after World War II. Their refusal to separate trash from assets, refuse from use, objects of waste from objects of value reproduces literally the "moral insufficiency" that, according to Langley, has "contaminated" humankind in the twentieth century (136): the reckless disregard of human life by dictators, the dehumanization of people by technology, the alienation of citizens by inhumane governments and nonhuman corporations.[9]

Coming from Langley, these claims might be seen simply as justifications for outlandish, anti-social behavior. But Homer also comes to see the brothers' story as prophetic. We learn late in the novel that Homer is writing the narrative for or to a French reporter whom he met, or more probably whom he invented in order to have a reason in his isolation to write his narrative (201). In talking about Central Park in New York City, the "reporter" says that its construction in the mid-nineteenth century "suggests what [its designers] may not have intended—a foretelling—this sequestered square of nature created for the time coming of the end of nature" (188). Like Doctorow's *Waterworks* and his *March*, Central Park in *Homer & Langley* is a nineteenth-century harbinger of the future; its meaning becomes clear only with the passing of time. Its designers could not have known that humankind would by the 1950s be able to destroy all of nature with nuclear weapons, but as a sequestered green space it foretold that future. That we *needed* such a green space foretells its eventual absence or loss, according to the "reporter." By analogy, Homer implies, the Collyer mansion, stuffed with its commodities and trash, is a "foretelling," perhaps of a time when commodities themselves must come to an end, when the planet is surfeited with objects and the "ultimate technological achievement will be escaping from the mess we've made" (136).

Indeed, by choosing to make Homer the narrator and to make him blind from a young age, Doctorow encourages us to consider the novel as a kind of epic. Like Homer and like Milton, Homer Collyer "sees" into and behind and beyond the things of this world. "The images of things are not the things in themselves," he writes at the end, even as he takes to feeling and touching things in order to reassure himself that the external world still exists. "There are moments when I cannot bear this unremitting consciousness," he says. "It knows only itself" (207). He wishes to become a thing himself, as he does at the very end, when he dies. But epic, like allegory, gestures beyond itself. Homer is well aware that his family story resonates with that of another famous fictional "house," the House of Usher: what was the point of the stories about us, he asks rhetorically, "except to indicate the decline of a House, the Fall of a reputable family, the shame of all that history in that it had led to us, the without-issue Collyer brothers lurking behind closed doors and coming out only at night?" (176–7). His own narrative of their lives in the mansion is shot through with the gothic: the house gradually becoming *unheimlich*; the queer behavior of both brothers; the vampiric night wandering of Langley outside the house; the past literally lying "upon the Present like a giant's dead body" in the form of commodities stacked throughout the house.[10]

Or, it might just house two tormented brothers who are not like us at all.

The Haunted Mind

In "The Face of the Tenant: A Theory of American Gothic," Eric Savoy argues that the American gothic operates in a "tropic field that approaches allegory": the American gothic is most "powerful, and most distinctly American, when it strains toward allegorical translucency."[11] For American writers responding to a particular set of historical and geographic forces, Savoy argues, allegory "provided a tropic of shadow, a kind of Hawthornian 'neutral territory' in which the actual is imbued with the darkly hypothetical." Novelists in the American tradition wrote a kind of gothic realism that strained "toward" allegory without becoming fully allegorical. For Savoy, a fiction like Poe's "The Fall of the House of Usher" is an allegory haunted "by a referentiality that struggles to return in a narrative mode . . . that is committed to repress what it is compelled to shadow forth" (9). In other words, Usher's house only hints at darker secrets, especially incest. The house suggests something about aristocracy, about the South, and about forbidden desire, but the narrator's account of it never coheres sharply into an allegory about any one of those things.

This is a helpful way to understand many of Doctorow's fictions, which are Hawthornian not simply in his borrowings (as in "Wakefield"[12]) but in their logic of representation. In *Homer & Langley* Doctorow uses the gothic, uncanny, *unheimlich* space of the Collyer mansion to suggest the larger fate of a world that has come to fetishize commodities, discarding one object for another in endless succession. At the same time, he refuses to make that novel a simple moral fable or allegory about that fate. As characters, both Homer and Langley retain a sense of being grounded in the specifics of their history and their place, rather than abstracted as allegorical figures. They do not even represent all hoarders; they are distinct and specific hoarders who died at a time of Doctorow's choosing (circa 1980) but who are nevertheless tied somehow to the real, historical Collyers who died in New York City in 1947. Their disorder develops from historically specific causes like World War I. Hawthorne used various concepts like "romance" or "legend" to distance his fictions from actual localities found on printed maps and from what he claimed was the realism of the novel.[13] Doctorow uses the fiction of the first-person narrator/character crafting the narrative we have in our hands to achieve a similar effect. On the one hand, Homer narrates a gothic story that implicates the reader in its realistic and then its allegorical reach: "our American life," our modern world, our alienation. The Collyers prophesy our fate. On the other hand, Homer can hardly be trusted; he is not really in his "right" mind.

Where *Homer & Langley* is a sort of tell-all memoir dominated by the gothic trope of the haunted house, Doctorow's 1994 novel, *The Waterworks*, is a city mystery that initially focuses our attention on the Croton Reservoir, a city-block-sized water reservoir, "an unnatural thing" designed in the early nineteenth century as a kind of Egyptian "temple" that marked "the geometrical absence of [the] city" itself (57).[14] It was near this reservoir that Martin Pemberton first glimpsed his father Augustus in March 1871, long after his father's supposed death, a sighting that triggers the events that follow in the novel. But Martin is later held captive at the distributing reservoir of the Croton Aqueduct in Westchester, twenty miles north of the city (208–9). Those "massive granite waterworks" house a Poe-like gothic nightmare: "a vast inner pool of roiling water . . . churning up a mineral mist, like a fifth element" (210, ellipsis in original). Lost inside the cavernous, confusing interior space, the narrator, McIlvaine, comes face to face with the absurd scene of wealthy old men dying, or dancing like automatons with nurses. It is surreal.

The "waterworks" of the title is thus not so much one gothic building as the complete system by which water was collected, purified, stored, and pumped to New Yorkers in the mid and late nineteenth century. Such waterworks, in tandem with the construction of subterranean sewers, tunnels, and subways, were crucial to the development of "a modern industrial city."[15] These complex systems or networks enabled the rise of modern urban cities. But in McIlvaine's vision the waterworks serve as a metaphor for the troubled modern world. They hide from view the dark secrets of the wealthy corporate titans who selfishly and ruthlessly finance the impersonal modern city. They monetize natural resources, thus enabling the social control of masses of people. In the narrative itself, the Croton Aqueduct serves as a laboratory for Sartorius's amoral experiments, some of which were inspired and prophetic (e.g. blood transfusions, heart transplants) but others of which verge in the narrator's mind on madness (e.g. using the "blood . . . the bone marrow . . . the glandular matter . . . of children" to prolong the lives of "elderly, fatally ill [rich] men" [233, ellipses in original]).

There is yet a third gothic building connected to the figure of the waterworks. In chapter 24, McIlvaine dreams about Sartorius.[16] In his dream, McIlvaine is standing on the embankment of another fantastic reservoir. He has tracked Sartorius, his "black-bearded captain" (217), to this location. Sartorius in turn is watching a child's toy boat rise and fall on the waves of the reservoir; suddenly, in the manner of dreams, both men are running to reach the interior structure of the waterworks. It is dimly lit, suffused with humidity and the "chill of entombed air" (218). Inside, they discover the body of a boy caught in the giant sluice-gates. Workers retrieve the body and Sartorius drives quickly away with it, smiling at McIlvaine "as at a complicitor" (219). McIlvaine intimates that the corpse will somehow be defiled.

He is haunted by this specific dream, and also by the dream-like events that he cannot control, but which he recounts at great length. His dream merges with reality and with fantasy into a story that possesses him: "After all these years in my head, my story occupies me, it has grown into the physical dimensions of my brain" (219). He is haunted by his sense of complicity with the powerful and amoral Sartorius, by his dream of the death of the working-class child, by his awareness of the thousands of children and women crushed by the impersonal forces of the city, by the figure of the waterworks: a complex man-made mechanism with a dark, cold interior, designed to control one of nature's life-giving forces but at the same time indifferent to the humans it is supposed to serve. It crushes the boy's body, infests the lungs of the workers, and invades McIlvaine's mind.

Indeed, McIlvaine tells us that the entire narrative is a report of his own mind's experience, "a true deposition of the events, and the state-ments, claims, protestations, and prayers of the souls whom I represent as seen or heard." Like those other Doctorovian narrators/writers who compose their texts, McIlvaine chooses and filters everything we see and hear. "This is not a ghost tale," McIlvaine insists in that same passage (64). And yet his narrative *is* a ghost tale, both in the sense that he is writing many years after the events and is thus populating the narrative with people who have long been dead, but also in the sense that McIlvaine is cut off from the people around him, "content to live alone with [his] feelings and judgments" (132). A confirmed bachelor, he is filled with queer desires that he does not understand and that often move him to see and record as a ghostly presence, separate from the lives around him. At one point, for example, he reports that Martin Pemberton first saw his father—himself a ghostly presence on the streets of New York after his supposed death—on a spring morning after a night of debauchery. McIlvaine says that Martin told another person who told him (that is, McIlvaine) that, on that morning, he (Martin) received oral sex from a young housemaid: "he held her head and felt the working muscles of her jaw and the rhythmic pulling of her cheeks" (56). McIlvaine's narration here takes on the quality of a reverie; the entire passage is marked with ellipses to indicate that he has fallen into a kind of mesmeric fantasy as he thinks about it.[17] He reports the scene of fellatio from Martin's point of view but also with an awareness of the woman's felt experience. Given McIlvaine's characterization of Martin in the narrative, along with nineteenth-century middle-class norms about sexuality, it seems unlikely that Martin told anyone this story. We can infer that McIlvaine is creepily imagining an intensely private scene he could not have witnessed, leaving us unsure whether he is fantasizing about being Pemberton or about being the woman. He is, in any case, a queer ghostly presence in that imagined bedroom.

The Waterworks is Doctorow's most recognizably gothic narrative.[18] The plot centers on old men who wish to live forever and who are glimpsed after their supposed deaths clinging, zombie-like, to life. In plot and characterization, it owes much to Hawthorne, Poe, Wilkie Collins, Arthur Conan Doyle, and George Lippard. The plot is occasioned by a "mad," sociopathic scientist determined to understand the mechanical processes of nature and convinced that human beings are accidents in the great scheme of natural history. Nature operates, Sartorius tells McIlvaine, "in total blindness, in the total disregard of a recognizable world that would give us comfort" (242). In Sartorius's vision, humans inhabit a gothic universe; they are pebbles tossed and flung by the waves, uncannily "alive" in their own minds but mere objects in the grand scheme of things. As an observer who sees largely through the eyes of others, McIlvaine is at different times metaphorically "taken" by others' gloomy, gothic perspectives. He sees through the eyes of the scientist Sartorius, who is ruthless in his pursuit of the truths of modern science; the painter Harry Wheelwright, who emphasizes the abject and the grotesque in his paintings of traumatized Civil War veterans; and the reporter Martin Pemberton, who eventually uncovers an even deeper conspiracy at the heart of his father's disappearance: that is, that the fortunes of wealthy men in the United States have been built on the slave trade, shoddy manufacturing practices, and graft. McIlvaine tells us that behind the headlines of "common, ordinary, everyday steamboat sinkings, prizefights, race results, train wrecks, and meeting of the moral reform societies [there is a] secret story" (64–5). My tale, he sighs, "is a story of invisible men, dead men or men indeterminately alive . . . of men hidden, barricaded, in their own created realm behind the thick walls of the brownstones of New York" (213–14), invoking at once ghosts, zombies, and all the specters of capitalism.

The tale is nominally written by McIlvaine but it is suffused with the ghostly voices and visions of other characters, presenting in its whole a bleak vision of modernity, the urban city, and the modern state. Writing many years after the events, McIlvaine reminds us again and again that the narrative is about the emergence of the "modern" world in the nineteenth century. Most of chapter 2 is about the machinations of Boss Tweed after the Civil War, which are "murderous in the very modern sense of the term" (10). McIlvaine repeatedly describes what he refers to as the experiences of "modern city life" (25), including alienation, dissociation, and heartlessness. Corporations and science have replaced religion; both are ruthless, both treat individuals as objects to be drained of vitality.

As in *Homer & Langley*, Doctorow edges toward allegory in *The Waterworks*. McIlvaine's narrative of events invests the search for Augustus Pemberton with allegorical significance. Augustus Pemberton stands in for the corporate profiteers of capitalism, Sartorius for a belief in the power of science to save us, the waterworks for the inhuman power of modern institutions, invented with good intentions but murderous in their consequences. But with McIlvaine's distorted first-person perceptions we are unable to discern whether the gothic allegory is simply a reflection of his mind, or whether it is in some way embedded in the reality of the emerging modern world. It is significant, I think, that Doctorow's first two published novels imagined evil or the uncanny as objective incursions from outside or above: in *Welcome to Hard Times* the Bad Man from Bodie appears from over the horizon to terrorize the town; in *Big as Life* the two naked giants appear magically and instantaneously in New York Harbor to unsettle the city's inhabitants. Doctorow charts the complex reactions of characters to these sublime incursions; in the first novel, the narrator (Blue) records events much in the way that Homer and McIlvaine do.

However, in *Homer & Langley* and *The Waterworks*, evil and the uncanny are imagined less as objective realities and more as products of consciousness itself. Both narrators are possessed by their stories, retreating further and further into the depths of their minds. Homer's "project" (201) is to record his family's descent: blind, typing on a Braille typewriter, increasingly "imprisoned" (205) by Langley's objects and booby traps, he is bound and bounded by his own doom. When Homer ends his narrative by comforting himself with the thought that his brother's hand is nearby, the reader knows that he is ignorant: Langley is already dead, and Homer is as alone in his darkness as all of us are in our consciousness. For his part, McIlvaine suggests that not only has his story over the years "grown into the physical dimensions of [his] brain," possessing him, but that he might have been dreaming an alternate reality all along:

> There are moments of our life that are like breaks or tears in moral consciousness . . . and the eye sees through the breach to a companion life, a life in all its aspects the same, running along parallel in time, but within a universe even more confounding than our own. It is this other disordered experience . . . that our ministers warn us against . . . that our dreams perceive. (220, ellipses in original)

It is impossible to tell if the gothic quality of his narrative is simply a projection of a mind that "long ago became content to live alone," and is now possessed by a story that has sprawled beyond his control; or whether the gothic darkness and secret mysteries that he writes about actually inhere in the world itself. McIlvaine notes at one point that "as I had brought in [to my narrative] the protagonist for my quest,

he brought with him, like a shadow, his opposite" (95). Here and elsewhere, McIlvaine expresses an uncanny passivity or lack of agency in
his narration. The conventions of this kind of story, he implies, demand
a certain outcome. Elsewhere, he says that the story really "belongs" to
Pemberton, whom McIlvaine repeatedly refers to as "my freelance. My
freelance" (251). He suggests a queer desire in that statement, but he also
implies that he is in fact owned or possessed by a story that is not his.
McIlvaine, as it turns out, is no more determinately alive than the "invisible" men he dreamed and dreams about; he lives through other men.
Significantly, Doctorow imagines McIlvaine as an editor, not a reporter.
McIlvaine does not write any stories, even his own. He does not even live
his own story. He desires to "own" the individual who can write stories,
and who has the energy to dig beneath the surfaces to uncover the "secret
story" (67) of the modern world, but he is himself alienated from the
position of author. It may be that we are all strangers, even to ourselves.

The Absurdity of Our Condition

The events in *The Waterworks* take place in 1871–2, although McIlvaine
writes about them long afterwards as an "old man" (235). Given that he
was present as a young man at the dedication of the Croton Reservoir
on Fifth Avenue in 1842, McIlvaine appears to be writing in the 1890s
or 1900s, perhaps even as late as the 1910s. Both *Homer & Langley*
and *Ragtime* begin around that very same period, suturing an entire
set of Doctorow's novels into a kind of history of the emergence of the
modern world.

City of God is sutured into this cluster of novels, as well. One of the
main characters, Thomas Pemberton (or "Pem"), seems to be descended
from the Pemberton family of *The Waterworks*. Given that Martin
Pemberton (in *The Waterworks*) was married in 1872, Pem would be
two or three generations younger, a grandson or great-grandson in
direct lineal descent. The narrator of *City of God* visits a hospice in
New York City in the 1990s expressly to interview "Old McIlvaine . . .
A newspaperman, a city reporter all his working life."[19] Logically, this
cannot be the McIlvaine of *The Waterworks*: he would be approxi-
mately 180 years old by this time. And yet in a kind of magical realist
way, Doctorow links the two novels.

City of God is narrated by Everett, a character who sounds and acts
suspiciously like the novelist himself. Both are born in New York City
in 1931, both have fathers who ran a small music shop, and both are
writers. Everett was created by an author whose first name was Edgar.

Everett shares other attributes that Doctorow knew most readers would recognize: he invents stories, and muses thoughtfully about religion, physics, literature, film, and the origins and ends of the universe. But Everett has other interests that may or may not have been Doctorow's; he is, for example, fascinated by birds.

Formally, *City of God* seems less obviously a written transcript of a single narrator, as are novels like *Homer & Langley*, *Welcome to Hard Times*, and *The Waterworks*. The novel's 103 unnumbered sections[20] are narrated by a variety of characters: Einstein, Wittgenstein, a confused Anglican priest named Thomas Pemberton, a Holocaust survivor, a reflective writer named Everett. Because the sections are unnumbered and because narrators shift fairly randomly, Doctorow forces readers to do a lot of work to grasp the logic of the narrative. The best way to understand it is as the written thoughts on a computer of one person, Everett, even though there are fewer references here (than in, say, *The Waterworks*) to the composition of a single manuscript.[21] Everett do the police in different voices. As his character Einstein says (alluding to the real-life Einstein's famous thought experiments), "This is my laboratory, here, in my skull" (36). Everett muses, begins several narratives, critiques standard pop songs, fantasizes, looks out his studio window. He writes. What goes on in his skull gets tapped into the computer.

His story contains few of the conventional trappings of the gothic. There are no claustrophobic mansions, dark conspiracies, mad scientists, or gloomy atmospheres. But it, too, is essentially a gothic tale. So, for example, after writing in his own voice about physics and astronomy in sections 1, 3, 8, 12, and 14, Everett first begins to voice the character of Einstein in section 21. In those very early sections Everett mentions his classmates at the Bronx High School of Science (Doctorow's own alma mater) who later became famous as physicists, as well as his own reading of the work of physicists like Steven Weinberg. In section 14, he notes that Einstein, more than some physicists, retained an idea of God as a creator, "the Old One," whose existence Einstein "tracked" in natural forces like gravity and light. Einstein's idea that the universe was created by the "Old One" is absurd, Everett writes, but not as absurd as the idea that it was "accidentally self-generated" (25). Both ideas trouble him because they provide no solid answers to "metaphysical" questions (12): either humankind is at the mercy of an inscrutable God or humankind is at the mercy of nuclear and cosmic forces beyond our final comprehension. Either way, as conscious entities, humans are at the mercy of nonhuman, frightening, alien forces. It is only after section 14 that Everett then begins to write in Einstein's voice (in sections 21, 25, and 29), as he tries to imagine how Einstein lived with such absurdity.

Thinking "as" Einstein—writing as if he were Einstein, in the "laboratory . . . in [Einstein's] skull"—Everett tries to locate some meaning in humankind's existence. Section 21 ends with "Einstein" recognizing the "theological visions and screams and terrors" that his theory of the constancy of the speed of light "produces in our brains" (39). In section 25, "Einstein" ponders the mind itself but shudders: "it is too vast, a space without dimension, filled with cosmic events that are silent and immaterial. For one's sanity it is preferable to track God in the external world" (44). In section 29, "Einstein" finds transcendent meaning in the bending of starlight but he does so as a way of staving off the realization that the Holocaust represented "the accelerating disaster of human history" (53). All three of these sections veer toward nightmare, toward a gothic sense that humankind is uncannily "alive" in a universe that has no sympathy, empathy, or even purpose.[22]

Everett is, in a sense, haunted by Einstein's voice, or perhaps more accurately by metaphysical questions prompted by Einstein's discoveries. Significantly, Everett discards Einstein's voice/thoughts after section 31, commenting that there may be other beings in the world (than just himself and Einstein) "suffering the same metaphysical crisis that deranges us" (62). That possibility is small consolation. Dropping Einstein, Everett then assumes the voice, thoughts, and method of Wittgenstein in sections 41, 53, 62, and 72. In the laboratory of Wittgenstein's mind, Everett ponders consciousness and language, and rejects the truths of physics as finally irrelevant to our "problem" as human beings (87). That "problem" is the uncanny philosophical dilemma of being an alien in our own home, of being conscious in a world oblivious to our consciousness: "The self . . . proposes the world is everything that is, but finds itself excluded from that proposition. . . . [It] can theoretically ascertain everything about the world except who and what it itself is" (125). Everett's Wittgenstein turns to movies as a kind of personal consolation: they are "pictograms flicker[ing] over you that are the opposite of language"; they are the opposite of linguistic, rational consciousness (155). They can console. But philosophically he ends at an impasse: "I am your guide to the infernal shambles of human reason, the shattered, unassembleable fractions of consciousness . . . the dreck of the real, our wrecked romance with God" (192, ellipsis in original).

In *City of God* Doctorow imagines a writer's mind as it obsesses over the absurdity of our condition. Everett sits at his desk and writes about the world, at times pondering metaphysical questions about our condition but at other times thinking about birds, about the philosophical underpinnings of popular songs, or about film as an art. In addition to speaking as Einstein and Wittgenstein (and, later, Frank Sinatra), he begins to write several narratives. One is a fantastic third-person narrative about a bored man who seduces a good wife only to then mistreat her and murder her husband; it is a "secular Enlightenment version of Amphitryon" invented in Everett's own "laboratory . . . in my skull" (52). The narrative begins as "a tale of subtle existential horror" in the vein of James M. Cain, only to morph into "a simple waxworks melodrama." Everett gives up on the narrative with the observation that "an author [must] honor the character of his idea and allow it to express itself in all its wretched insufficiency until it too reaches its miserable end" (85). Another is a gritty first-person narrative about a ten-year-old boy who survived the Holocaust; this narrative seems to end in a packed, suffocating train car headed to a concentration camp, but since the boy survived to father another character (in Everett's imagination) he logically could not have died at the concentration camp. Instead, Everett drops that narrative, and begins a new one about an ex-*New York Times* reporter determined to track down a former SS sergeant now living an unassuming life in Cincinnati. Everett imagines the reporter's desire to write a story that has a clear, unambiguous ending, as opposed to the stories one reads in newspapers in which "justice fails again and again to catch up in time to effect just endings" (187). This narrative devolves into absurdity as the reporter exacts vengeance by accidentally killing the former SS sergeant, and then in a follow-up effort accidentally kills a former Guatemalan death squad commander. Everett imagines the reporter achieving ethical narrative closure with, in essence, no agency of his own; his retributive murder of both men is uncanny and accidental.

Everett is tormented by his sense that he lacks agency. The universe seems indifferent and inscrutable. Stories come to him but they follow their own logic. He cannot control them. The longest and most successful narrative in Everett's imaginings focuses on Thomas Pemberton, an Anglican minister who abandons his training and Christian faith to convert to Judaism after falling in love with a younger, widowed rabbi. Pemberton actively confronts and shapes his doubts, and at the end is welcomed warmly into his partner's home, family, and religion. He finds a home but is still questing at the end of the narrative. Pemberton's story is one of enlightenment and love, not gothic terror. Everett, however, is unlike his character; he envies Pemberton his happiness, desires his wife (that is, Everett's own character), and is left yearning at the end for some kind of purpose in his artistic endeavors. At the very end, Everett's imaginings include a city beset by plagues, coups, violence, and martial law, but one that in the movie in his "laboratory" might be saved by Pemberton and his wife.

That is the way movies work, in Everett's mind. They obey their own logic of form. He sees film as "time-driven" and simplistic; it "never ruminates, it shows the outside of life, it shows behavior" (214). Movies are "illiterate events" (214), operating by a visual logic that appeals to the unreflective mind. In the movies, a city beset by plagues and violence can be saved (however implausibly) by a husband and a wife. Everett is attracted to film precisely because of this. He visits a film set at one point in the narrative and that leads him into a meditation on the ubiquity of film (105–10); he meets with a film director who wants him to write a screenplay for a complex metaphysical horror story (150–3); he attends an award ceremony for a renowned film director (236–8). Skeptical of film, Everett is surrounded by it. When he ends his narrative with a reference to his own imaginings as being similar to a movie—his characters as "the hero and heroine of the movie" (272)—he signals the way that his own mind (the mind of the modern writer) has become haunted by the impersonal logic of film.

Where film skates on the surface of things, however, "novels can do anything in the dark horrors of consciousness." Novels are truly gothic. They are not bound by time or space; in "the extensions of syntactical thought" they can achieve a "depth" of perception that is fundamentally different from what film can achieve (214). They probe the gothic dilemma that defines our human experience: being conscious in a world that is unconscious. Everett is like McIlvaine and Homer in his attempt to represent his perception of the world in a written narrative, though Everett has, in a sense, no other "narrative" than the emergence, repetition, and disappearance of his ideas and potential stories.[23] As with Homer, the sense that he is haunted belongs less to him than to the reader; he does not feel his musings as a form of haunting, but readers can see that "he" is a kind of ghost inside various machines: his skull, the entertainment industry, the created world, even stories themselves, which, as they fulfill generic conventions, simply follow their own logic, not an author's.

Much as we can see Homer's *unheimlich* situation in a refuse-strewn house more clearly than can he, we can see Everett's uncanny lack of agency in a refuse-strewn brain more clearly than can he. Everett's mind is filled with flotsam and jetsam: old songs, chance perceptions, a fascination with birds, books he has read, films he has seen, and on and on. His invented stories seem to belong to "him," but they turn out to obey laws of form and media that are not his. Several of his characters are happier and more engaged and active in the world than he is, sitting at his desk and recording the voices in his skull. While Everett's own brain is a gothic space, he nevertheless imagines a character who breaks free of at least some of the mental "confinement" that we inhabit. Pemberton leaves the Church, which he believes "lies upon the Present like a giant's dead body," and embraces a form of "evolutionary" Judaism. Everett is "fascinated by the power of this hodgepodge of chronicles, verses, songs, relationships, laws of the universe, sins, and days of reckoning . . . this scissors-and-paste" job called the Bible (115); it is a story and he is fascinated by how it has operated as a story. But Pemberton ends up rejecting it as insufficient for our needs in the modern world. Augustine's *City of God* marks for Pemberton an end to true questioning in the Western, Christian tradition. It, along with the Bible, has boxed us in. Pemberton comes to see Augustine's treatise, too, as a kind of novel, "doctrinal notions treated as if they exist, like characters in a Henry James novel" (222–3). What Judaism offers Pemberton is figured in the sections of Everett's narrative focused on the Midrash Jazz Quartet, as well as those sections when Sarah Blumenthal struggles to answer basic questions about faith: an open-ended, still-questioning faith about God and humankind.[24] Messianic longing, Pemberton comes to believe, is "a longing, a navigating principle, redemptive not on arrival but in never quite getting [there]" (248). However, one has to undo the gothic confinement to understand it: higher truths are "visible only to the unhoused derelict mind" (215), Pemberton says upon leaving the church.

While every page of Pemberton's copy of Augustine's *City of God* is "almost totally underlined" (222), Everett merely likes the *title* of Augustine's text. He perhaps has not read it. To Everett, the title conjures up not heaven but the modern city of traffic, coffee shops, and movie theaters. Everett is not as skeptical or questioning about the "city" as Pemberton is, or as Doctorow urges his readers to be. The city as Everett imagines it, like the Collyer mansion or the waterworks system in the earlier novels, edges toward allegory: it stands in for the proliferation, speed, and profound alienation of the modern world, and the way that that world insinuates itself into our brains in the form of stories, movies, images, sounds, a bombardment of information that urges us to perceive but not to think. Doctorow suggests that the modern city of God is finally in our brains, a gothic space of confinement where when we open a new door (or a new musing, or a new story thread in Everett's narration) we merely find ourselves again. The alternative, proposed ironically by a character invented by a character, is to "unhouse" the mind, to make it derelict. Only then would we release ourselves from the uncanny sense that behind every door in the world is only our own consciousness.

The trajectory I have traced in this essay leads unsurprisingly to Doctorow's final novel, *Andrew's Brain*, where the narrator is even more clearly trapped in the confining space of the skull. With his brain as a kind of jail cell, Andrew's consciousness is merely a record of "visions, dreams, and the actions of words and people [he does not really] know."[25] Even the brain, Andrew laments, is separate from consciousness: "We have to be wary of our brains. They make our decisions before we make them" (177). That novel, too, is a gothic story about the "dark horrors of consciousness." Like many of Doctorow's fictions, it demonstrates a tension between Doctorow's desire as a novelist to imagine and narrate from within the "trapped" consciousness of an individual and his desire as an allegorist to figure in the narrative a meaningful, objective, hidden meaning that is in the world itself: a waterworks that reveals secrets, a house that reveals our future. Though each of us is finally and uniquely separate from the world around us, we wish to locate and communicate truths about the world. We try to see through the doors and windows of the gothic house of consciousness, but there is only us. That tension is not only central to Doctorow's fiction, it is the *point* of his fiction. To me, it is neatly ironic that some film (and Broadway) producers have found so much inspiration in Doctorow's plots, because there is nothing more terrifying in his novels than the gothic lesson that we are finally all alone in our brains. That, in a way, is the allegory that Doctorow's gothic tales finally shadow forth. Consciousness is a lonely business. Repeat. Consciousness is a lonely business. Repeat.

Notes

1. I note that David Cronenberg's version of DeLillo's *Cosmopolis* was released in 2012, and Paul Thomas Anderson's version of Pynchon's *Inherent Vice* in 2014.
2. E. L. Doctorow, *City of God* (New York: Random House, 2014), 214. Subsequent parenthetical citations refer to this edition.
3. E. L. Doctorow, *The Waterworks* (New York: Random House, 2007), 219. Subsequent parenthetical citations refer to this edition.
4. E. L. Doctorow, *Homer & Langley* (New York: Random House, 2010), 7. Subsequent parenthetical citations refer to this edition.
5. Here and elsewhere in the essay I refer of course to Sigmund Freud's famous essay, *Das Unheimliche* (*The Uncanny*).
6. According to the fifth edition of the American Psychiatric Association's *Diagnostic and Statistical Manual of Mental Disorders* (DSM-V), there are six criteria for diagnosing hoarding disorder. (1) There is persistent difficulty discarding or parting with possessions, regardless of their actual value. (2) This difficulty is due to the perceived need to save the items and to the distress associated with discarding them. (3) The difficulty discarding possessions results in the accumulation

of possessions that congest and clutter active living areas and substantially compromise their intended use. If living areas are uncluttered, it is only because of the interventions of third parties (e.g. family members, cleaners, authorities). (4) The hoarding causes clinically significant distress or impairment in social, occupational, or other important areas of functioning (including maintaining a safe environment for self and others). (5) The hoarding is not attributable to another medical condition. (6) The hoarding is not better explained by the symptoms of another mental disorder. Herring critiques the way in which the concept of hoarding became pathologized in light of the Collyer story. On Doctorow's use of the Collyer brothers' story, see Patrick W. Moran, "The Collyer Brothers and the Fictional Lives of Hoarders," *MFS: Modern Fiction Studies* 62.2 (2016): 272–91.

7. In a 1991 interview, Doctorow noted how he had been influenced by Hawthorne, especially his idea of the "romance" and very specifically Hawthorne's allegorical "stories like 'The Minister's Black Veil,' 'The Birthmark,' [and] 'Wakefield'." E. L. Doctorow, "Fiction Is a System of Belief," interview with Christopher Morris, *Michigan Quarterly Review*, 30 (1991): 444.

8. Herring traces the way in which the actual brothers came to be seen as a figure for the encroaching "blackness" of Harlem as the neighborhood shifted from white-dominant to black. See Scott Herring, "Collyer Curiosa: A Brief History of Hoarding," *Criticism*, 53.2 (2011): 162–71.

9. Before Doctorow published *Homer & Langley*, Wutz argued presciently that the figure of "waste" or "garbage" was central to Doctorow's project: "The debris and residue he brings to the surface signify the dark mirror image of official culture pushed into the muck of invisibility, the return of the repressed seeking release through narrative exposure." See Michael Wutz, "Literary Narrative and Information Culture: Garbage, Waste, and Culture in the Work of E. L. Doctorow," *Contemporary Literature*, 44.3 (2003): 532.

10. Nathaniel Hawthorne, *The House of the Seven Gables*, ed. Robert S. Levine (New York: Norton, 2006 [1851]), 130.

11. Eric Savoy, "The Face of the Tenant: A Theory of American Gothic," in *American Gothic: New Interventions in a National Narrative*, ed. Robert K. Martin and Eric Savoy (Iowa City: University of Iowa Press, 1998), 6.

12. Wakefield (the character) appears briefly in Doctorow's short story "The Leather Man," in *Lives of the Poets* (New York: Random House, 2010 [1984], 71–2), and is then featured in the story "Wakefield," first published in the *New Yorker* in 2008 and republished in *All the Time in the World* (New York: Random House, 2011), 3–38. Robin Swicord's film version of the story was released in 2017. Hawthorne's short story "Wakefield" was first published in 1835 in the *New-England Magazine* and republished two years later in *Twice-Told Tales*.

13. My references here are to the "Preface" to *The House of the Seven Gables*, where Hawthorne says that the story is both a "Romance" and a "Legend." "The Reader," he teases, "may perhaps choose to assign an actual locality to the imaginary events of this narrative," but the author has chosen to avoid "anything of this nature" (3–4).

14. McIlvaine refers to it as an "inverted temple" a few pages later (60).

15. David L. Pike, *Subterranean Cities: The World Beneath Paris and London, 1800–1945* (Ithaca: Cornell University Press, 2005), 60. For a discussion and analysis of the development of the subterranean city in the nineteenth century, this book is invaluable.

16. Doctorow published an earlier version of chapter 24 as the short story "The Water Works" in *Lives of the Poets*.

17. At certain moments in the narrative, McIlvaine uses ellipses to indicate that his thoughts are becoming hesitant or unsure, or, as here, that they are departing from a strict reportorial style into fantasy.

18. Nearly all of the reviews of *The Waterworks* mention the gothic. Simon Schama, for example, noted that the novel owed much to "the 19th-century genre of the science-detection mystery . . . [though it is not] mere Gotham Gothic," *New York Times*, June 19, 1994. "The Water Works" was reprinted by Joyce Carol Oates in her influential collection *American Gothic Tales* (1996).

19. E. L. Doctorow, *City of God*, 245.

20. By "section," I refer to those places in the novel where the text has been marked with a divider of three short horizontal lines.

21. Doctorow in a 2012 interview makes a distinction between Everett, Pemberton, and Sarah, who are characters operating in New York City in the present time of the novel, and characters like Einstein, Wittgenstein, and the young boy in a Polish ghetto in the early 1940s, who are creations of Everett's. The novel "proposes itself as Everett's daybook as he becomes friends with Pemberton and, later, the rabbinical couple." See Wutz, "On the Craft of Fiction: E. L. Doctorow at 80," *The Contemporary West*, 29.1 (2012): 9. He goes on to say that "I had the freedom of writing as in a daybook where Everett would simply put down his thoughts as they occurred to him. It was, in a sense, accepting improvisation as a creative principle, giving in to the intuition of spontaneous connectives, and so that's how we find riffs in the voices of Einstein and Ludwig Wittgenstein" (ibid., 10). In my reading of the novel, that distinction essentially disappears: Everett in his "daybook" represents lived experience and imagined experience as equivalent, as in some sense indistinguishable. We cannot make an ontological distinction between Pemberton and Wittgenstein.

22. Doctorow surely knew Emily Dickinson's poem "The Brain—is wider than the Sky," where she asserts that the mind can "contain" the entire universe. See *The Poems of Emily Dickinson*, ed. R. W. Franklin (Cambridge, MA: Harvard University Press, 1999), 269. Dickinson, too, was deeply gothic in her sensibility.

23. In this way, *City of God* is a version of *Lives of the Poets*. The "lives" of writers are primarily lived in the "laboratory of the skull." In his 2003 book on the U.S. invasion of Iraq, Slavoj Žižek notes that Doctorow's 1984 collection of stories was a "hidden literary model" for his own meditations on the invasion. Doctorow's collection, Žižek says, comprises "six totally heterogeneous stories . . . accompanied by a novella which conveys the confused impressions of the day-to-day life of a writer in contemporary New York who, as we soon guess, is the author of the six stories." See Slavoj Žižek, *Iraq: The Borrowed Kettle* (London: Verso, 2005), 7.

24. It is important to note that Pemberton joins the Synagogue of Evolutionary Judaism, a small sect that refuses to let tradition (doctrine, law, language) impede a desire for "unmediated awe" (194). Doctorow implies that many forms of Judaism would be just as stultifying for Pemberton as the Christian Church. Osborne discusses how midrash as an open-ended commentary, and thus as a potential resistance to a fixed tradition, is a useful concept for several contemporary writers, including Doctorow: Monica Osborne, *The Midrashic Impulse and the Contemporary Literary Response to Trauma* (Lanham: Lexington Books, 2017).

25. E. L. Doctorow, *Andrew's Brain* (New York: Random House, 2014), 196.

Chapter 3

E. L. Doctorow as Short-Story Writer

Mark Azzopardi

Collected Stories may well have been E. L. Doctorow's final literary project.[1] "Selected, revised, and placed in order by the author himself shortly before he died," according to the dustjacket, *Collected Stories* contains fifteen short stories spanning almost the entirety of Doctorow's half-century writing career, from "The Songs of Billy Bathgate" (1968) to "Assimilation" (2010). Reading *Collected Stories* cover to cover demonstrates considerable thematic and generic continuity between Doctorow's short stories and novels, even as this collection falls short of the consummate instance of "late style" Doctorow that readers may have hoped for. Doctorow's revisions turn out to be minimal, amounting mostly to typographical and stylistic amendments of the originally published story. "The Songs of Billy Bathgate," Doctorow's first published short story, undergoes somewhat more extensive revision, with at least 1,000 words excised from the *Collected Stories* version. An entire song has been omitted, "She's too Good for Me," Billy's protest against the "disease of fame" and description of the elusive Lovegirl (now "Missy" in the *Collected Stories* version).[2] These revisions do not alter the meaning of the story as a self-reflexive parable of the pressures of artistry and commercial success, though one likely effect of *Collected Stories* is that the version of "The Songs of Billy Bathgate" most known to future readers will be the short story that first appeared in the 1968 *New American Review*, attributed to a Doctorow "just beginning to win recognition."[3]

In "Childhood of a Writer," Doctorow nominates "a short story entitled 'The Beetle'" as his first juvenile publication, a "teenage homage" to Kafka's "The Metamorphosis" published in the Bronx High School of Science literary magazine.[4] Beginning with "The Songs of Billy Bathgate" in the *New American Review*, the mature Doctorow published eighteen short stories between 1968 and 2010, a total increasing to as many as twenty-nine stories depending on whether published excerpts from his novels are included. The posthumous *Collected Stories* not-withstanding, Doctorow's short fiction is known primarily in the context of his book collections, *Lives of the Poets* (1984), *Sweet Land Stories* (2004), and *All the Time in the World* (2011), with publication of these collections creating a sporadic counterpoint to his twelve novels, three essay collections, and one play. Doctorow's theories of the novel, as a "system of knowledge" accommodating and rewriting various worldly discourses, and a "false document" imaginatively commingling history and fiction, have been well known to critics since *Ragtime* (1975); he has no corresponding theory of the short story.[5] His most sustained commentaries on the short story as a literary form are his introduction to *The Best American Short Stories* (2000), which he guest edited, his preface to *All the Time in the World*, and his occasional comments on his own stories and those of Kafka, Kleist, Poe, Joyce's *Dubliners*, and Sherwood Anderson.

Doctorow's introduction to *The Best American Short Stories* outlines one difference between the novel and short story:

> While there are exceptions—Isaac Babel or Grace Paley, for example, writers-for-life of brilliant, tightly sprung prose designedly inhospitable to the long forms—we may say that short stories are what young writers produce on their way to their first novels, or what older writers produce in between novels.[6]

On these terms, Doctorow falls into the latter category, though since his first novel, *Welcome to Hard Times* (1960), was not published until he was twenty-nine, this distinction is less applicable to his own story writing. Unlike Kurt Vonnegut, Doctorow did not finance his first novel by publishing short stories in the large-circulation general-audience weeklies *Collier's* and *Saturday Evening Post*, nor did he write "entry level" short fiction as a college student that he would later abandon for longer novels, as did Thomas Pynchon.[7] Prior to publication in the book collections, Doctorow's short stories appear at fairly regular intervals between his novels, in literary magazines containing fiction and criticism (*Paris Review, Virginia Quarterly, Kenyon Review*) and general-audience monthlies (*Esquire* and *The Atlantic*). Following *City of God* (2000), Doctorow's short fiction was published increasingly in the *New Yorker*, though readers may have a hard time accommodating his stories within the perhaps apocryphal tradition of the "*New Yorker* short story," given their diversity of subject matter and relative absence of comic writing.[8]

With these considerations in mind, the first conclusion to be drawn of Doctorow as a short-story writer is that his stories cannot be classified as apprentice work, or as fiction produced chiefly for the commercial magazine market, which in any case had all but dried up prior to 1968's "The Songs of Billy Bathgate." Yet even with his reasonably consistent publication of short fiction, Doctorow always considered himself principally a novelist. "I'm not a short story writer but a novelist," he said in a 1994 interview, a statement that can then serve as a second initial conclusion.[9]

Doctorow's comments on the primacy of the novel in his writing should be offset by the fact that critical attempts to differentiate the novel from the short story remain less than resolved. "Attempts to define short fictional forms and distinguish them from the novel are often in danger of tautology," cautions Graham Good, a view Doctorow endorses later in his *Best American Short Stories* introduction.[10] Here he takes issue with Frank O'Connor's influential argument in *The Lonely Voice: A Study of the Short Story* (1962) that the short story can be differentiated from the novel based on its predilection for "submerged population groups," or characters belonging to society's material and spiritual margins.[11] An abundance of novelistic counter-examples leads Doctorow to propose an alternative to O'Connor's essentially demographic hypothesis, offering that the short story's distinctiveness resides instead in its "scale":

> Smaller in its overall dimensions than the novel, it is a fiction in which society is surmised as the darkness around the narrative circle of light. In other words, the scale of the short story predisposes it to the isolation of the self.[12]

Scale is a name for the difference between what is represented in a story and what is only "surmised," implying that the short story's variously enabling contractions and selections create a range of possibilities when it comes to rendering time and character. While Doctorow's remarks here are too brief to sustain an entire theory of the short story in the manner of O'Connor, his emphasis on scale has the virtue of restoring to the short story a narrative orientation largely suppressed in *The Lonely Voice*. Wanting to avoid the tautology of defining the short story according to its length alone, O'Connor valorizes a strand of modern short-story writing running from Chekhov and Joyce through to Anderson and Salinger, his preference for stories organized around "the significant moment" or "something that springs from a single detail," meaning he has little substantial to say about short fiction based on what he calls "episodic interest" (*The Lonely Voice* has nothing to say about Hawthorne and precisely two sentences on Poe, for example).[13]

Doctorow's comments on scale gesture toward the short story's ir-reducibly narrative elements of plot and plotting, and can be profitably applied to his own short fiction, where "what shapes a story and gives it a certain direction or intent of meaning" is, more often than not, plot: storytelling that "develops its propositions only through temporal sequence and progression."[14] Belatedness and condensation organize narrative in the stories in *Lives of the Poets*, and *Sweet Land Stories* sees Doctorow part ways with the epiphanic short story most associated with Anderson's *Winesburg, Ohio* (1919). *All the Time in the World* offers an opportunity to revisit Doctorow's perennial intertextuality by way of his retelling of Hawthorne's 1835 tale "Wakefield." What follows will attempt not to exaggerate the achievement of a writer who, as Doctorow insists, will be remembered primarily as a novelist. We will proceed instead by acknowledging that Doctorow the short-story writer is an eminently different proposition than Doctorow the novelist, while remaining sensitive to the readerly pleasures and narrative complexities found in his less well-known career as a writer of short stories.

Lives of the Poets (1984): Possible Novels

We know *Lives of the Poets* by its subtitle, *A Novella and Six Stories*, the novella functioning to "strikingly fuse" the six "miscellaneous" nar-ratives preceding it by depicting the author of the stories as a character in his own right.[15] This interpretation of *Lives of the Poets* affixes a unifying structure on its six narratively unconnected short stories, the placement of the title novella at the end of the book investing each preceding story with retrospective continuity. On this reading, *Lives of the Poets* becomes an extended scene of writing created by Jonathan, letter-writing child in "The Writer in the Family" and middle-aged novelist in the novella.[16] Doctorow was referring to *Lives of the Poets* when he said "I'm not a short story writer," adding elsewhere that he considers the stories in *Lives of the Poets* "possible novels."[17]

Reading *Lives of the Poets* as a unified collection has a handful of dissenters,[18] and the problem with this interpretation is that something important is lost when its six short stories are subsumed into the auth-orial structure connecting "The Writer in the Family" at the beginning of the book with the title novella at its end. We can agree with Stephen Matterson that, in *Lives of the Poets*, "Doctorow's achievement . . . is an overall one," wherein "the stories are interdependent and contribute to a developing meaning," while insisting that the book's cumulative effect is one of disorientation, where differences between stories cannot be smoothed over entirely by installing Jonathan as the book's central intelligence.[19] An alternative reading of *Lives of the Poets* begins with the transition from Jonathan's last letter on behalf of his deceased father in "The Writer in the Family" to the spectacle of the anonymous child caught in underground machinery in "The Water Works." Whatever readerly pathos is summoned by the former story's ending all but vanishes when placed alongside the decidedly more macabre image of childhood that begins "The Water Works," with the latter story conspicuously shorn of the historical markers enclosing character and meaning in *The Waterworks* (1994). The ordering of the six stories in *Lives of the Poets* relies on spatial and temporal transitions that qualify and ultimately undo its continuity: the setting of "Willi" is a rural outpost of the Austro-Hungarian Empire, "Main Street" and "Mechanic Street" stand in for a decaying postindustrial community in "The Hunter," "The Foreign Legation" takes place in contemporary suburbia. The book's fluctuating continuity is embodied in its physical design, each story set off from the stories preceding and succeeding it by a title page and two additional blank pages.

Understanding *Lives of the Poets* as a short-story collection would involve approaching each story first with a view to its self-contained coherence, with "Willi" and "The Hunter" offering suggestive instances of Doctorow's management of time and plotting in the short form. For B. M. Eikenbaum, "the story must be constructed on the basis of some contradiction, incongruity, error, contrast," with "Willi" generated by the incongruity between childhood experience and its belated adult recollection.[20] This is the source of some of Doctorow's most lyrical writing in any form:

> I was resonant with the hum of the universe, I was made indistinguishable from the world in a great bonding of natural revelation. I saw the drowse of gnats weaving between the grasses and leaving infinitesimally fine threads of shimmering net, so highly textured that the breath of the soil below lifted it in gentle billows. Minute crawling life on the stalks of hay made colossal odyssey, journeys of a lifetime, before my eyes. (27)

A great deal could be said about this elaboration of self-consciousness, its emphasis on "revelation" in particular, since the story begins by pairing Willi's ecstatic pastoral vision with his discovery of his mother's lifeless body. Willi's discoveries are narrated in succession from the perspective of an adult looking back on childhood. Readers learn belatedly what they already know when the story begins, that Willi inadvertently brought about his mother's death and father's ruin by informing his father of his mother's secret romance with his tutor. The story's structure enacts its theme of unforeseen causality: the story begins with the adult Willi narrating the moment he finds his mother's body, moving backwards in time to describe his childhood relationship with his parents, and ending as he stands watching his father violently beat his mother. Offsetting Willi's exercise of childhood agency is the reader's gradual awareness that he survived the Holocaust as an adult, and what amounts to a repositioning of his life story within historical time also enacted in the story's concluding sentences: "This was in Galicia in the year 1910. All of it was to be destroyed anyway, even without me" (35).

The story's display of historical markers invites the reader to understand childhood as bounded by causal and historical circumstances narratable only decades after the fact. This is at odds with the initiation of mobile child protagonists into adult worlds in the roughly contemporaneous novels of education *Loon Lake* (1980), *World's Fair* (1985), and *Billy Bathgate* (1989), with "Willi" pointing toward an altogether more contingent experience of childhood agency that the climactic beginning of "The Water Works" makes clear. "Willi" is a "loss of innocence" story where the meaning of one's name can be read only backwards.[21]

"Willi" positions its title character within a wider set of historical determinations, whereas the next story in *Lives of the Poets*, "The Hunter," isolates a comparatively brief segment of time released from any explicit explanatory context. Narrative in "The Hunter" is condensed into a few days in the life of a female elementary school teacher, its use of limited third-person point of view giving the reader minimal access to the sequence of personal history bringing her into the story. Doctorow long ago nominated the "storyteller within the story" (Bruce Weber's words) as one of the defining conventions of his novels; the absence of any equivalent character in "The Hunter" is notable, especially considering that this story marks the first female protagonist in any of Doctorow's fiction.[22] Little about the nameless teacher's personal life is described to the reader other than that she is "young" (42), wears "opal teardrop earrings" given to her at her college graduation (42), was born in "the eastern part of the state" (45), and reads aloud at a retirement home on weekends (43). This effect is compounded by the narrator's piling up of declarative sentences starting with a pronoun, creating a catalog of actions lacking psychological cause. Of *Ragtime*, Fredric Jameson once said that the book's sentences conform to a "rigorous principle of selection" symptomatic of the postmodern novel's inability to self-assuredly render the past as did the historical novel à la Lukács; "The Hunter" employs a commensurately diminished language for somewhat more modest storytelling purposes, constructing a protagonist from whose psychological life the reader is largely excluded.[23]

The story's ambiguity makes its title episode all the more disturbing. After visiting the retirement home, the teacher runs to a ruined mansion overlooking the small town. She ascends to the second floor:

> She stands at the window and sees at the edge of the field a man in an orange jacket and red hat. She wonders if he can see her from this distance. He raises a rifle to his shoulder and a moment later she hears an odd smack as if someone has hit the siding of the house with an open palm. She does not move. The hunter lowers his rifle and steps back into the woods at the edge of the field. (44)

Running in Doctorow's short stories is typically an objective correlative for purposelessness. Morgan in "The Foreign Legation" takes up neighborhood running after his wife and children leave the family home, and in "All the Time in the World" the narrator's meandering cognition finds a physical analogue in his urban jogs. Here, the hunter's unexplained gunshot interrupts the teacher's movement across the small town, an apparently random intrusion lacking causal bearing on the story's beginning or ending. Critical comment that the female teacher is the real hunter identified by the title, owing to her pursuit of interpersonal attachments, is not untrue, but misses the story's more literal, terrifying quality.[24]

Lives of the Poets employs two types of ending. On the one hand, "The Writer in the Family" concludes with a moment of enhanced self-knowledge, as Jonathan realizes what his father's "dream for his life" had been prior to his early death (17). Withheld or denied knowledge is more characteristic of the book's other endings, where condensations of time yield cryptic final scenes observed by the protagonist: the dismembered leg within a maroon knee sock in "The Foreign Legation," the group of city workers standing together after their mysterious errand in "The Water Works." Even the paired revelations of "Willi" are narratable only belatedly. Critical literature on the epiphany is unanimous, that this signal feature of the modern short story possesses unique power in illuminating fictional character; the stories in *Lives of the Poets* point to a countervailing power in the absence of epiphany. "All my life I had been X until one day Y happened, and for the rest of my life I was Z," writes Mary Louise Pratt of epiphany narratives.[25] Denied this most satisfying temporal algebra, the ending of "The Hunter," as a photographer arrives at the elementary school to take a photograph of the teacher with her students, is as narratively inconclusive as its beginning and middle. Storytelling here cultivates an experience of time more or less impervious to sudden changes in a character's self-knowledge, introducing one of Doctorow's differences from the American writer most associated with the epiphanic short story, Sherwood Anderson.

Sweet Land Stories (2004): Plotting Against Sherwood Anderson

A "mournful chronicler" of "Midwestern provincialism" is how Doctorow describes Sherwood Anderson, with comparisons between Doctorow's *Sweet Land Stories* and Anderson's *Winesburg, Ohio* owing to both collections' interest in demographically ordinary, working-class characters inhabiting regional American geographical settings.[26] Yet Anderson's 1919 short-story collection has always amounted to "clearly a great deal more than a statement of disillusionment at country freshness gone stale or pastoral innocence tattered and vulgarized," and this is worth keeping in mind when assessing its possible connection with Doctorow.[27] Thematic resemblances between *Sweet Land Stories* and *Winesburg, Ohio* should not obscure the fact that Doctorow and Anderson remain fundamentally different narrative writers, especially when it comes to the epiphany and the genre of the integrated short-story cycle. Anderson's epiphanies arise from his stated objection to "plot[ting] short stories" (Frank O'Connor has high praise for Anderson in *The Lonely Voice*), with many of his short narratives organized around a single moment in time where meaning is temporarily, albeit dramatically, revealed simultaneously to character and reader.[28] While not an element of all the short stories in *Winesburg, Ohio*, the stories combining the character profile of the spiritually impoverished "grotesque" with the narrative device of the epiphany are among Anderson's most well known and anthologized: Ray Pearson's unspoken understanding with Hal Winters in "The Untold Lie," or Alice Hindman in "Adventure," at the moment she realizes her devotion to absent lover Ned Currie is not the cure for her loneliness but its cause.[29]

The five short stories in Doctorow's *Sweet Land Stories* proceed according to episodic progression rather than discrete moments of self-understanding. Indeed, Doctorow relishes the narrative and generic possibilities inherent in "plot[ing] short stories"; his introduction to *The Best American Short Stories* describes the authors selected by him for inclusion as "more disposed to the episodic than the epiphanic," and this describes well *Sweet Land Stories*' storytelling instincts.[30] Moreover, even with their similarly regional settings, the different *Sweet Land Stories* do not share fictional space, in that, unlike *Winesburg, Ohio*,

Sweet Land Stories do not interact with each other, and Doctorow's collection lacks any equivalent to the map sketched by the illustrator Harald Toksvig for Anderson's first edition that would affix knowable boundaries to his fictional geography.[31] Though he was referring to *All the Time in the World*, we can let Doctorow have the last word on his resemblance to Anderson: "There is no *Winesburg, Ohio*, here to be mined for its humanity."[32]

Plot in each of the *Sweet Land Stories* develops sequentially out of a proposition stated in the first sentence: "Mama said I was thenceforth to be her nephew, and to call her Aunt Dora" ("A House on the Plains"); "I had taken up with her knowing she was this crazy lovesick girl" ("Baby Wilson"); "She married Mickey Holler when she was fifteen" ("Jolene"); "When Betty told me she would go that night to see Walter John Harmon, I didn't think I reacted" ("Walter John Harmon"); "Special Agent B. W. Molloy, now retired, tells the following story" ("Child, Dead, in the Rose Garden"). Each first sentence summons two fictional characters into being who will be brought together or separated by the events of the story. The exception is "Child, Dead, in the Rose Garden," where Agent Molloy's disaffection from the characters around him, especially his younger FBI colleagues, will be partly what causes his retirement. Each initial speech act of naming, coupling, marrying, telling, and storytelling will be progressively and often ironically modified by the episodes that follow: a mother and son achieve financial security through fraud; a couple reform their wayward lives by stealing a newborn baby; a young woman finds comfort in isolation after a life of temporary attachment; a relationship ends following an extramarital liaison with a cult leader, the latter a West Kansas garage mechanic claiming to be God's earthly prophet. More mundane than mournful, Doctorow's stories are too worldly for the secular transcendence contained in the epiphany, his short narratives drawn instead to storytelling's more material complications.

"A House on the Plains" modifies its initial premise to point to narrative's potentially sinister motivations. Marshall Bruce Gentry is right to say that this story's self-described "happy ending" (12), wherein Earle and his mother burn down the title house after defrauding unsuspecting suitors, is "so macabre as to seem totally ironic," with the story's irony depending on the eighteen-year-old Earle's naïve perspective.[33] The "storyteller within the story" convention focusses the story through a character apparently unaware of the plot he is both narrating and participating in, giving the reader a very different version of events compared with the story Earle's calculating mother might have told. Time in "A House on the Plains" amounts to the few months it takes Earle and his mother to relocate to the countryside and establish a scheme to attract suitors, and, as in many of Doctorow's short stories, the forward movement of narrative is cultivated by temporal markers within the story: the change of seasons intensely felt by Earle after leaving his cherished Chicago, the steady arrival of suitors at the house, the accumulation of compound interest in his mother's recently opened savings account. Earle's narration is replete with cryptic references to his life with his mother before the story begins, creating density of character and motive by encasing his story within a series of unnarrated stories taking place before and after the events at the house. It is the burning of the house that transforms ambiguities in Earle's narration into a fully gothic mode, uncovering the hidden story of murder and serial deception behind his surface narrative. Of Poe, Doctorow says that his "contributions to the short story are the unmodulated voice—he starts high and ends high—and the embellished situation that serves for a plot."[34] Unlike Poe, the embellished plot of "A House on the Plains" requires modulation and, especially, elision, to allow Earle's narrative to arrive at its unexpectedly gothic conclusion.

Episodic plot structure is similarly mediated by genre conventions in "Jolene: A Life." The story selectively narrates the ten-year period in Jolene's life between the ages of fifteen and twenty-five, organizing her biography according to a picaresque pattern of incarceration and escape. Beginning Jolene's life story at age fifteen means she is an "orphan" when she first appears to the reader, as she is described by her future husband (69), and her father-in-law is sent to state prison for having sex with a minor. The reader's awareness of Jolene's repeated interpersonal entanglements is matched by her own sense of her life as a narrative. Jolene appears to be as curious as the reader about the formative effects of storytelling, and equally aware of its dangers: telling her "story" to the county psychiatrist places her in juvenile detention (63), and a lawyer refuses to hear her case against her abusive husband owing to her "past" (84). She ends her narrated life story as she started it, alone, moving into an apartment by herself after having to give up her baby. Thus does Jolene repeat her life's shaping design even as she attempts to evade it. She ends the story with thoughts of writing a graphic novel about herself, finding some consolation in the idea that her messy lived experience might achieve coherent form when communicated as narrative.

Sweet Land Stories' plot structures have an unexpected bearing on Doctorow's political writing. The collection's final story, "Child, Dead, in the Rose Garden," has been interpreted by Liliana M. Naydan as a timely reflection on personal and national trauma in the aftermath of the September 11 terrorist attacks, though this story was not viewed positively by all of the collection's original reviewers.[35] In this story, Agent Molloy investigates the discovery of a deceased child, Roberto Guzman, in the White House Rose Garden the morning after the National Arts and Humanities Awards, leading him to a plan by protestors to give "a kind of shock treatment" to Washington politicians covertly involved in the Texas energy industry (145). This short story "crosses the line from narrative into social criticism" according to David L. Ulin, and "here alone in the collection, Doctorow seems like a writer with an ax to grind."[36] However this story is interpreted, Ulin introduces an additional dimension to the "plot story" eschewed by Sherwood Anderson, in that a story believed to supply a political context absent from its beginning can be seen as violating its narrative premises. Certainly, the story's ending, Molloy's description of Guzman "rest[ing] in peace at the Arlington National Cemetery among others who had died for their country" (147), concludes the collection on a sentimental note uncharacteristic of the other *Sweet Land Stories*, differentiating "Child, Dead, in the Rose Garden" from the resolutely nondidactic "politics of indirection" Michelle M. Tokarczyk identifies in *E. L. Doctorow's Skeptical Commitment*.[37]

For that reason, "Child, Dead, in the Rose Garden" and its critical reception may perhaps be best understood in the context of Doctorow's contemporaneous political essays. If Doctorow is first and foremost a novelist, it could be said that, second, he is an essayist, rather than a short-story writer (his tenure as playwright for 1978's *Drinks Before Dinner* belongs at the bottom of the list). The original publication of the five *Sweet Land Stories* in *Virginia Quarterly* and the *New Yorker* between 2001 and 2004 partially overlaps with five political essays Doctorow wrote between 2003 and 2012, whose common theme is the "lingering miasma of otherworldly weirdness hanging over this country" in the years after September 11.[38] Other than "Child, Dead, in the Rose Garden," this view of American life features in only one of the other *Sweet Land Stories*, "Walter John Harmon," the story sharing with Doctorow's essay "Why We Are Infidels" the theme of religious literalism as a common denominator to both the United States and its ideological adversaries in the "war on terror." *Sweet Land Stories* was his first book after September 11, yet in reading these short stories alongside his political essays from roughly the same period it becomes apparent how little connection there often is between Doctorow's literary and political writings. This is where knowing something about the short stories enables a deeper insight into Doctorow's career. Almost to a story, Doctorow's short fiction avoids the topical subject matter and hortatory mode of address adopted by his political essays, and readers of *Ragtime* (1975) and *The Book of Daniel* (1971) will find little in any Doctorow story resembling those novels' celebrated metafictional reimaginings of American political history. In other words, Doctorow's stories demonstrate a side of his writing not immediately assimilable into the prevailing critical view of him as either "Citizen Doctorow" or "Prophet Edgar," which may go some of the way to explaining difficulties readers face in accounting for his stories, especially when it comes to one of Doctorow's least straightforward characteristics, his politics.[39] More specifically for *Sweet Land Stories*, it would not be irrelevant to note that Doctorow's first published work of fiction after 9/11, "Baby Wilson," makes no mention of "terrorist modalities" and "interagency cooperation" in the manner of "Child, Dead, in the Rose Garden" (124), focusing instead on the life of a small-time conman, who falls asleep "thinking what a great country this was" after his eccentric girlfriend kidnaps a baby (41).

All the Time in the World (2011): Retelling Hawthorne's Tale

A "tale told thrice," Birgit Spengler says of Doctorow's retelling of Hawthorne's "Wakefield," in *All the Time in the World*, though this marks the fourth iteration of the Wakefield story if we include its appearance in "The Leather Man" from *Lives of the Poets*. Here, a "Peeping Tom" is seen over a period of several months, "behind the residence of Mr. and Mrs. Morris Wakefield," who turns out to be none other than "the owner of the property" (71–2).[40] Doctorow's repeated use of a male character who disappears from his family home only to keep watch from nearby says a great deal about his narrative tendencies, making explicit the connection between storytelling and voyeurism latent in Hawthorne's 1835 tale. For both Hawthorne and Doctorow, the Wakefield story dramatizes a peculiarly male fantasy of escape from responsibility, a temporary stepping out of domestic and marital time, ending with the title character's belated return to the home. Hawthorne's Wakefield is largely a product of the narrator's imagination, a semi-remembered story from "some old magazine or newspaper" encountered years earlier.[41] The reader's knowledge of Hawthorne's Wakefield is mediated by the narrator's speculations, and Wakefield's departure from domestic life is treated as an undistinguished man's attempt at self-definition in crowded London. Doctorow's version of the story removes Hawthorne's transatlantic and conjectural narrative frame, allowing Wakefield to describe in his own words "a series of odd circumstances" that led to him taking up residence in his attic, with his wife and daughters living below (5). Doctorow's retelling also reduces Hawthorne's twenty-year timeframe to a period of several months, allowing the callously joke-like quality of Wakefield's unannounced return to domestic life to remain intact; the story ends as Wakefield's "good joke" at his family's expense arrives at its punchline (34).

Doctorow's use of a storyteller within the "Wakefield" story eroticizes the fantasy of leaving one's wife to observe her without her knowledge. We learn from Wakefield that "marital arguments" give him "that kind of blood stir you get in anticipation of sex" (5), and that he expected neighborhood husbands to arrive at the house to proposition his wife "the first chance they got" (16). Infidelity fantasies multiply within Wakefield's self-narrated psychology, from the time of his original attraction to his wife owing to her romantic involvement with his one-time best friend. Wakefield's departure unwittingly reactivates his marriage's foundational logic, causing his wife to reconcile with that former best friend. "The force of Mr. Hawthorne's tale lies in the analysis of the motives which must or might have impelled the husband to such folly," said Poe in his review of *Twice-Told Tales*.[42] Doctorow's ironic twist ending is more Krafft-Ebing than William Sydney Porter, rendering Wakefield's motives equal parts banal and psychosexual.

Wakefield shares outsider status with many of *All the Time in the World*'s characters; these short stories revolve around "people who, for one reason or another, are distinct from their surroundings—people in some sort of contest with the prevailing world," Doctorow writes in the collection's preface (ix). Plots in this collection negotiate the presence of an outsider within, in the form of a stranger's unannounced arrival in "Edgemont Drive," a citizenship scam in "Assimilation," and the theft of an eight-foot crucifix from a Lower East Side parish in "Heist." Doctorow's coolness toward Frank O'Connor in his introduction to *The Best American Short Stories* need not prevent *All the Time in the World*'s stories from being profitably interpreted as intrusions into the home, nation, and church by characters belonging to various "submerged population groups," even though none of the collection's stories quite matches "Wakefield" for insight into some of Doctorow's basic storytelling processes. The possibility of watching life continue in your absence is associated with hidden knowledge in "The Leather Man" as well as the *Lives of the Poets* novella, when the adult Jonathan, who lives alone after moving out of the family apartment, sees the lights of his apartment building while looking out of a window (137). This external view takes on additional meaning as a scenario that is, after all, an experience of living through one's own death. Living posthumously is what Wakefield experiences when he sees friends and family arrive at the house to console his wife, a scene already rehearsed in "A House on the Plains," when a disguised Earle returns to the burned farmhouse and the scene of his fabricated death (26). "Wakefield" is in this respect a continuation of existing Doctorow story situations almost as much as an intertextual adaptation of Hawthorne; perhaps this story's conflation of elegy and infidelity should be nominated as a generative principle at work in all Doctorow's storytelling, his short fiction at least.[43] To voluntarily live outside normal life creates a scene that is both funeral and sexual betrayal (with one's wife playing the role of adulteress and widow simultaneously), with Wakefield's inability to decide whether to delay or bring about this scene being what generates his self-told narrative.

A different type of outsider narrates "All the Time in the World," placed as the final story in both *All the Time in the World* and *Collected Stories*. "All the Time in the World" is loosely held together by the unidentified narrator's observations of everyday life, from the "naked girl dancing" in the apartment window across the street to the "cartoon logic" of people holding umbrellas in the rain (259). These observations appear as elements of the narrator's consciousness and are only minimally shaped by the causal and teleological conventions of plotted narrative; like his meandering city jogging, the narrator's language serves as a way to "pass the time," oriented toward "no destination" (262). For this reason, the story has more in common with the "still-life" or descriptive sketch of social manners identified by Brander Matthews's *The Philosophy of the Short-Story* (1901) than any story Doctorow has written previously.[44] "All the Time in the World" does make a valuable companion story to Doctorow's final published novel, *Andrew's Brain* (2014), in that both story and novel dramatize a consciousness's experience of being apart from the physical and social world. Story and novel also make unusually inventive uses of direct speech: "All the Time in the World" uses the narrator's repeated and mysterious telephone calls to interrupt his solitary experience as a mind thinking of itself thinking, while telling the entirety of *Andrew's Brain* through Andrew's therapy sessions and only minimal narratorial intervention is the chief cause of the novel's unstable epistemology.

"It's easy to see that the short form is not [Doctorow's] strongest," Jess Row writes in his review of *All the Time in the World*:

> A great short story has to function like a black hole, demanding our entire attention, drawing all available light into itself, but Doctorow's energies are too diffuse and variegated to achieve that effect often.[45]

The short stories vary in quality, it is true, and the sense that Doctorow never wrote the same novel twice cannot be said of his stories. Readers persuaded by John Updike's frowning censure of *Ragtime*'s "impudent, mocking shuffle of facts" may find Doctorow's short stories more congenial, the stories offering a basically more recognizable version of American history compared with the historiographically self-reflexive novels, on which his critical reputation largely rests (the short stories are also written by a more decorous Doctorow than the author who once described an unseasonably warm day as "the kind of day the crocuses get fucked").[46]

Yet it would be a mistake to read Doctorow's short stories solely on the terms set by his novels, and this is why the handful of stories that were incorporated into his novels, among them "The Water Works" into *The Waterworks*, "Heist" and "Untitled" into *City of God*, the *American Review* "Ragtime" into *Ragtime*, do not go much of the way to explaining what Doctorow is doing in the short form. Even Doctorow's suggestive phrase "possible novels" is at odds with the fact his short stories are not his novels. This may be another way of account-ing for Doctorow's minimal revisions to the stories assembled into the *Collected Stories*; *Collected Stories* is not an attempt by Doctorow the one-time Dial Press editor to create an artistically definitive edition of his short fiction by way of revising the originals, as is, say, Henry James's "New York Edition," regardless of what the dustjacket says of his editorial involvement in the retrospective collection. More suggest-ive are *Collected Stories*' omissions, chiefly "The Foreign Legation" and "The Leather Man" from *Lives of the Poets*, these stories appar-ently containing whatever it is Doctorow felt did not represent him as a writer.

To reconsider E. L. Doctorow in the sense this chapter has suggested would mean not to accept too quickly his remark that he is "not a short story writer but a novelist," his short stories revealing more of his inclinations as a writer of narrative fiction than his own more diffident self-evaluation. Doctorow's stories deserve a modest but not invisible place within his body of work, and are worth reading chiefly to see him writing in a format neither he nor readers accustomed to his novels are entirely comfortable with. Akin to the spirit of Walter Benjamin's "The Storyteller"—an essay Doctorow was fond of alluding to repeatedly—Doctorow's short stories demonstrate the side of a writer for whom there need be no embarrassment in telling a story or hearing a story told, in experiencing fiction take shape through narrative.[47]

Notes

1. E. L. Doctorow, *Collected Stories* (New York: Random House, 2016).
2. E. L. Doctorow, "The Songs of Billy Bathgate," *New American Review*, 2 (1968): 58. The omitted song features in Christopher D. Morris's book chapter on the story, one of the first extended critical discussions of Doctorow's short fiction. Christopher D. Morris, *Models of Misrepresentation: On the Fiction of E. L. Doctorow* (Jackson: University Press of Mississippi, 1991), 66–78.
3. Untitled editor's note, *New American Review*, 2 (1968): n.p.
4. E. L. Doctorow, "Childhood of a Writer," in *Reporting the Universe* (Cambridge, MA: Harvard University Press, 2003), 34.
5. "'Fiction Is a System of Knowledge': An Interview with E. L. Doctorow," *Michigan Quarterly Review*, 30.3 (summer 1991): 456; "False Documents," *American Review*, 26 (1977): 215–32.
6. E. L. Doctorow, "Introduction," in E. L. Doctorow, ed., *The Best American Short Stories 2000* (New York: Houghton Mifflin, 2000), xiii.
7. Kurt Vonnegut, "Introduction," in *Bagombo Snuff Box: Uncollected Short Fiction* (London: Vintage, 2000), 6–7; Thomas Pynchon, "Introduction," in *Slow Learner: Early Stories* (Boston: Little, Brown, 1984), 4.
8. Kasia Boddy, *The American Short Story Since 1950* (Edinburgh: Edinburgh University Press, 2010), 39.
9. "An Interview with E. L. Doctorow," in Christopher D. Morris, ed., *Conversations with E. L. Doctorow* (Jackson: University Press of Mississippi, 1999), 199.
10. Graham Good, "Notes on the Novella," in Charles E. May, ed., *The New Short Story Theories* (Athens: Ohio University Press, 1994), 147.
11. Doctorow, "Introduction," xiv.
12. Ibid.
13. Frank O'Connor, *The Lonely Voice: A Study of the Short Story* (Brooklyn: Melville House, 2004 [1962]), 23, 21, 50.
14. Peter Brooks, *Reading for the Plot: Design and Intention in Narrative* (Cambridge, MA: Harvard University Press, 1984), xi.
15. Benjamin DeMott, "Pilgrim Among the Culturati," *New York Times Book Review*, November 11, 1984: 1.
16. In-text citations refer to E. L. Doctorow, *Lives of the Poets: A Novella and Six Stories* (London: Michael Joseph, 1984).
17. "Fiction Is a System of Knowledge," 450.
18. Jonathan Yardley, "Ruminations and Regrets," *Washington Post*, November 11, 1984: BW3; Robert Towers, "Light and Lively," *New York Review of Books*, December 6, 1984; and Morris, *Models of Misrepresentation*, 133–8.
19. Stephen Matterson, "Why Not Say What Happened? E. L. Doctorow's *Lives of the Poets*," *Critique: Studies in Contemporary Fiction*, 34.2 (Winter 1993): 113–14.

20. B. M. Eikenbaum, "O. Henry and the Theory of the Short Story," in May, ed., *The New Short Story Theories*, 81.

21. Ann V. Miller, "Through a Glass Clearly: Vision as Structure in E. L. Doctorow's 'Willi'," *Studies in Short Fiction*, 30.3 (Summer 1993): 337.

22. Bruce Weber, "The Myth Maker," *New York Times*, October 20, 1985.

23. Fredric Jameson, *Postmodernism, or, the Cultural Logic of Late Capitalism* (Durham: Duke University Press, 1991), 24.

24. Morris, *Models of Misrepresentation*, 145.

25. Mary Louise Pratt, "The Short Story: The Long and the Short of It," in May, ed., *The New Short Story Theories*, 101.

26. E. L. Doctorow, "Sinclair Lewis's *Arrowsmith*," in *Creationists: Selected Essays, 1993–2006* (New York: Random House, 2006), 69. On the collection's similarities with Anderson, see Peter Wolfe, "Review of *Sweet Land Stories*," *Prairie Schooner*, 80.1 (Spring 2006): 206.

27. Ellen Kimbel, "The American Short Story: 1900–1920," in Philip Stevick, ed., *The American Short Story 1900–1945: A Critical History* (Boston: Twayne, 1984), 66.

28. Sherwood Anderson, "Form, Not Plot, in the Short Story," in Anne Charters, ed., *The Story and Its Writer: An Introduction to Short Fiction* (8th edition; Boston: Bedford/St. Martin's, 2011), 903.

29. Sherwood Anderson, *Winesburg, Ohio* (New York: Penguin, 1976 [1919]), 205, 117.

30. Doctorow, "Introduction," xv.

31. In-text citations refer to E. L. Doctorow, *Sweet Land Stories* (New York: Random House, 2005 [2004]).

32. E. L. Doctorow, "Preface," in *All the Time in the World: New and Selected Stories* (New York: Random House, 2011), ix.

33. Marshall Bruce Gentry, "Elusive Villainy: *The Waterworks* as Doctorow's Poesque Preface," *South Atlantic Review*, 67.1 (Winter 2002): 83.

34. E. L. Doctorow, "E. A. Poe," in *Creationists: Selected Essays, 1993–2006*, 13–14.

35. Liliana M. Naydan, "E. L. Doctorow and 9/11: Negotiating Personal and National Narratives in 'Child, Dead, in the Rose Garden' and *Andrew's Brain*," *Studies in American Fiction*, 44.2 (Fall 2017): 281–97.

36. David L. Ulin, "On Native Ground," *Nation*, June 28, 2004: 30.

37. Michelle M. Tokarczyk, *E. L. Doctorow's Skeptical Commitment* (New York: Peter Lang, 2000), 3.

38. E. L. Doctorow, "A Calamity of Heart," *Nation*, 291.9/10 (August 30, 2010): 27; "The White Whale," *Nation*, 287.2 (July 14, 2008): 28–32; "Why We Are Infidels," *Nation*, 276.20 (May 26, 2003): 11–12; "Narrative C," *Daedalus, Journal of the American Academy of Arts and Sciences*, 141.1 (Winter 2012): 118–25; "Unexceptionalism: A Primer," *New York Times*, April 29, 2012: SR6.

39. John Leonard, "The Prophet," *New York Review of Books*, June 10, 2004.

40. Birgit Spengler, "A Tale Told Thrice: Hawthorne, Doctorow, and the Intertextual Imagination," *Nathaniel Hawthorne Review*, 41.2 (Fall 2015): 48–82.

41. Nathaniel Hawthorne, "Wakefield," in *Twice-Told Tales* (Columbus: Ohio State University Press, 1974 [1835]), 130.

42. Edgar Allan Poe, "Nathaniel Hawthorne," in *Essays and Reviews* (New York: Library of America, 1984 [1847]), 574.

43. In contrast to Geoffrey Galt Harpham, "E. L. Doctorow and the Technology of Narrative," *PMLA*, 100.1 (1985): 81–95.

44. Brander Matthews, "*The Philosophy of the Short-Story*" [1901], in May, ed., *The New Short Story Theories*, 77.

45. Jess Row, "From His Own Playbook," *New York Times Book Review*, April 3, 2011: A18.

46. John Updike, *Due Considerations: Essays and Criticism* (New York: Ballantine, 2008), 294; E. L. Doctorow, *The Book of Daniel* (New York: Random House, 1971), 300.

47. Walter Benjamin, "The Storyteller: Observations on the Works of Nikolai Leskov," in *Walter Benjamin, Selected Writings, Vol. 3: 1935–1938*, trans. Edmund Jephcott, Howard Eiland, and others, ed. Howard Eiland and Michael W. Jennings (Cambridge, MA: Belknap Press of Harvard University Press, 2002), 143–66.

Part II

Politics, Allegory, Difference

Chapter 4

Submerged Politics and the Artist

Nicholas Murgatroyd

E. L. Doctorow's status as one of the last great American political novelists is a recurrent theme in the obituaries that appeared after his death in 2015, but such discussions make surprisingly scant reference to Doctorow's genre fiction. *Welcome to Hard Times* (1960) is mentioned as the first step in his writing career, but is treated more as a challenge to the genre model of the Western than the nihilistic examination of the American dream it can be argued to be, while there is little or no reference to Doctorow's return to genre fiction in the late 1980s with *Billy Bathgate* (1989) and 1990s with *The Waterworks* (1994). Yet this is a grave critical oversight. For while the two later genre novels are difficult to categorize, with *Billy Bathgate* simultaneously *Bildungsroman*, a gangster fiction and a love story, and *The Waterworks* both a gothic novel and a work of detective fiction, as well as an investigation into religion, science, and the nature of narrative, a close reading of either novel suggests that they are in fact as political as any of Doctorow's more overtly political works, such as *The Book of Daniel* (1971) or *Andrew's Brain* (2014).

However, despite Doctorow's claim that *The Waterworks* was "the most profoundly political thing" he had ever done,[1] it is perhaps little surprise that critics have failed to detect the political content of these texts, for, as this chapter will argue, Doctorow's assumption of the genre tropes of crime and detective fiction is a reaction by Doctorow to a period when he felt that political novelists in the United States were anathema to a culture in which dissent was discouraged in American fiction. In this reading, both *Billy Bathgate* and *The Waterworks* can be viewed as what John Whalen-Bridge has termed "submerged political novels,"[2] which, like the mirrors in the bar where the Schultz gang are killed in the former novel, "have the peculiar power . . . to show you what is otherwise not there" and thereby smuggle political narratives into the mainstream.[3] Yet although he used this tactic successfully in both novels, my focus here is particularly on *The Waterworks*, a narrative which, at the same time as it questions the political culture of the time, also questions the artist's role within that culture and the challenge of how to create without being implicated in the society he or she seeks to critique.

Doctorow's nonfiction from the 1980s and early 1990s provides the critic with ample evidence of his dissatisfaction with the political and cultural climate of what might be termed the "long Reagan era," stretching from Ronald Reagan's investiture in 1980 to the defeat of George Bush Senior in 1992. For example, as early as 1984's "The Beliefs of Writers," he claimed that "examination of society within a story" in the United States "places a work in aesthetic jeopardy," and he bemoaned the difference in the reception of U.S. political novelists and their contemporaries in the Eastern bloc.[4]

This frustration may, on first impression, explain his work's apparent drift from the overtly political nature of *Loon Lake* (1980), the contemporaneous short fiction of *Lives of the Poets* (1984), the coded memoir of *World's Fair* (1985), and the genre fiction of *Billy Bathgate* (1989) and *The Waterworks* (1994). As early as *Lives of the Poets*, Jonathan, the narrator of the titular novella and seeming authorial foil for Doctorow, finds himself blocked by the conundrum of how to write in Reagan's America without the output being what Raymond Williams identifies as "a form of contribution to the effective dominant culture."[5] The writing at the novella's end which "cures" his writer's block is not by Jonathan but by the youngest child of the immigrant family he has taken into his apartment:

> Little kid here wants to type. OK, I hold his finger, we're typing now, I lightly press his tiny index finger, the key, striking, delights him, each letter suddenly struck vvv he likes the v, hey who's writing this? every good boy needs a toy boat, maybe we'll go to the bottom of the page get my daily quota done come on, kid, you can do three more lousy lines.[6]

The political act of taking in the immigrant family leaves Jonathan robbed of control at his desk ("hey who's writing this?"); the lines he produces are meaningless, fated to receive no audience, the repeated "vvv" a symbol not of artistic release but of repetitive, irresolvable conflict.

Yet however much Doctorow's nonfiction suggests he shared of Jonathan's frustration, he did not abandon the idea of writing political fiction altogether. For both *Billy Bathgate* and *The Waterworks* can be read beyond the conventions of the genres they borrow. Although there is not space here to list the full range of political allusions in *Billy Bathgate*, various facets of the Schultz gang—from their patho-logical hatred of income tax to their blind faith in the freedom of the market, their smashing of unions to their self-interested courting of the Roman Catholic Churchfind parallels with the Reagan administration's "gangsterdom of spirit," while it seems an unlikely coincidence that both Schultz and Reagan enjoyed the same nickname of "Dutch."[7] *The Waterworks* may, by contrast, function as more of a critique of Bush Senior's era and its gung-ho capitalism, but it is equally political.

In writing these novels of submerged politics, Doctorow performs a genre version of the "ventriloquial drone" the young Edgar practices at the close of *World's Fair*.[8] Indeed, one reading of the ending of *World's Fair*, where the child Edgar goes back to the time capsule he has buried in order to rescue the ventriloquist's manual before walking away into an adverse wind, is as a hidden manifesto for Doctorow's switch to genre. While the high sales of both *Billy Bathgate* and *The Waterworks* exemplify success in terms of placing them before the reading public, the ventriloquial strategy of these political novels imitates Melville's strategy of "hoodwinking the world."[9] As Whalen-Bridge identifies in his description of *Moby-Dick*, in such novels "political content dives beneath an ocean of literariness."[10] They simultaneously represent an act of rebellion in their smuggling of critique into the mainstream and an acknowledgment of the precarious nature of the writer's position in such a society, a tacit admission that such critique offered overtly would most likely have a negative impact on the writer's career.

Alongside other writers of the American Renaissance, particularly Hawthorne and Whitman, Melville had clearly been on Doctorow's mind after the mid-1980s: his preparatory notes for *Billy Bathgate* include several references to *Moby-Dick* and the possible writing of a nineteenth-century narrative,[11] while the title character's initials of BB and his status as youngest member of Schultz's crew may be a covert reference to *Billy Budd*. Similarly, his notes for *The Waterworks* twice include a plan for the novel to unfold in what Doctorow terms "the one-day span" of *The Confidence-Man*,[12] and the opening of his original draft begins with McIlvaine reflecting, among other things, on a national "literature just proposing itself."[13]

Yet there is also evidence in the archive to suggest that Doctorow, whose career exemplifies a readiness to change narratorial strategy from novel to novel, had little intention for *The Waterworks* to be another submerged political novel in the spirit of *Billy Bathgate*, or, indeed, for it to be anything like the novel he eventually published. Every other Doctorow novel in the archive (which runs from *Welcome to Hard*

Times to *The March*, published in 2005) has a clear genesis from its first draft to the published version, with elements of the published novel identifiable from an early stage. By contrast, *The Waterworks* began life as a very different novel, called *The Soul*, the workings for which are so developed that Doctorow completed and revised a full draft before he reimagined it as what would eventually become *The Waterworks*.[14]

The Soul exists as a shadow counterpart to *The Waterworks* in much the same way as the New York of the latter corresponds to the New York of the 1990s: it is simultaneously recognizable as *The Waterworks* and distinct therefrom. The basic narrative is there of the disappearance of Martin Pemberton (originally called Bram, perhaps as a tribute to Bram Stoker, author of *Dracula*) and Sartorius (originally called Rufus) keeping aging businessmen alive via blood transfusions from kidnapped orphans. However, rather than a detective novel, it is largely a gothic fantasy, with sensational paraphernalia more akin to Poe than any other nineteenth-century American writer, culminating in Emily and Bram making love in the sanatorium shortly before the sight of the supposedly dead Augustus Pemberton drives Emily insane.[15]

The draft's main difference to the eventual novel, however, lies in its structure and its thematic concerns. Rather than the first-person narrative he had used in *Billy Bathgate* and would repeat in *The Waterworks*, Doctorow's original strategy was to utilize an encyclopedic narrative similar to *City of God*, with a bricolage of competing narratorial voices, including Grimshaw, Emily Tisdale, Martin Pemberton, and Sarah Pemberton, and found texts that range from faxes sent by a present-day author to a catalogue of Harry Wheelwright's paintings.[16] In evidence of what Michael Wutz identifies as Doctorow's recycling of narrative elements, several of these passages, or slightly modified versions, appear in *City of God* (2000), including a shorter prose version of the narrator's brother's adventures in World War II.[17] Yet surprisingly little of this draft is narrated by McIlvaine: his is one voice among many, often used as a voice opining the changing nature of the city, a foil to the other voices who—as suggested by the original title—are often less concerned by the city's politics than by the theological questions that Doctorow would explore more deeply in *City of God*.

Doctorow's practice of leaving drafts undated offers few clues as to exactly when works were composed, but there is a clear indication that the reorientation of *The Soul* into *The Waterworks* occurred in 1991, and coincided with the drafting of his essay "The Character of Presidents," inspired by the 1991 U.S. presidential election. The urge to engage with political questions appears to have come to predominate, and, ultimately, to have shifted the book's main focus away from its original theological preoccupation. This is seen in a typewritten sheet dated "6/5/91," which bears both part of a draft of the essay and of *The Waterworks*, now narrated solely by McIlvaine. The draft of the essay declares that:

> This President is a terrible liar. He lied about his opponents in the primaries, he lied about his opponent in the election. He lies about his involvement in shadowy para government operations of the past, and he lies about why he is doing what he is doing in the present.[18]

This is almost identical to the eventual published version:

> Mr. Bush is a man who lies. [. . .] Vice President Bush lied about his opponents in the primaries, and he lied about Mr. Dukakis in the election. President Bush lies today about the bills he vetoes, as he lies about his involvement in the arms-for-hostages trade with Iran [. . .] He lies about what he did in the past and about why he is doing what he is doing in the present.[19]

Where the two versions of this critique of George Bush Senior differ is in the draft's analysis that: "No one can out shout him because no one has as many microphones, TV screens, headlines at his disposal as a president." This dilemma of Bush's domination of the press, if not culture as a whole, directly mirrors Boss Tweed's corruption of the press in *The Waterworks*, just as McIlvaine represents the kind of "brave journalist" Doctorow hopes "may expose [President Bush's] lies a year from now."[20] Thus it seems evident that part of Doctorow's decision to switch to McIlvaine as a single narrator was linked to the desire to once more engage with the practices of the Reagan–Bush era through another submerged political novel, one that would attack what Doctorow termed "the oligarchical presumption that no one but an executive citizenry of CEOs, money managers, and the rich and well-born really matters."[21]

However, while *Billy Bathgate* with its ingénue narrator simultaneously repelled and attracted by the energy of a monomaniacal leader may suggest *Moby-Dick* as its Melvillean model for a submerged political novel, *The Waterworks* bears closer relation to a different Melville work, "Bartleby, the Scrivener" (1853). For example, both *The Waterworks* and "Bartleby" share similarities in their predominantly lower Manhattan geography, including visits to the Tombs prison, and in their narrators' shared fascination with a lowly employee. However, their most overt similarity may lie in their evocation of how the dominant form of capitalism co-opts the existence of its workers. When, for example, McIlvaine laments "O my Manhattan!,"[22] this echo of the final words of "Bartleby, the Scrivener"– "Ah Bartleby! Ah humanity!"[23]—so early in the novel serves as a veiled invitation to the reader to view the characters as being equally as enmeshed in the political hegemony of the Gilded Age as those in "Bartleby" are of antebellum New York. In doing so, it raises the same question of how resistance to the dominant might be achieved as Melville's work engaged with over a century before. Yet, through clear parallels with the dominant economics of the 1980s and early 1990s, *The Waterworks* also invites the reader to reflect on possible avenues of resistance in their own time.

That Doctorow intends the reader to view the novel both as something more than a simple work of formula fiction and as a metaphor of the present is apparent from the outset. McIlvaine's introduction of Martin Pemberton in the first paragraph as someone whose words people "wouldn't take [. . .] as literal truth," though he was "a critic of his life and times" (3), suggests a disjunction between representation and reality, but paradoxically implies that accurate social criticism may come from this failure to tell the literal truth. This veiled invitation to see another truth within what follows is reinforced by the ending of the first chapter, when McIlvaine admits that he "interpreted what [Martin] had said as a metaphor, a poetic way of characterizing the wretched city that neither of us loved, but neither of us could leave" (8).

This signposting of a secondary meaning becomes a recurrent narrative strategy and is partly achieved by both oblique and direct reference to the reader's present. For example, McIlvaine confesses to not being "exactly complacent about our modern industrial civilization" (4), and this adjective "modern," which sits uneasily between McIlvaine's past and our contemporary moment, is then repeated a further ten times in the novel. A similar effect is achieved through McIlvaine's tendency to speculate in the present tense, thus highlighting the link between the depicted past and the present moment of reading, as well as through the use of other temporally ambiguous terms such as "now" in: "It was a hard world, but are we less hard now?" (66) and "our," particularly in the final chapter's opening line: "Finally, after all, I have been talking about our city" (246).

Yet nowhere is the correlation between the past and the present made more explicit than when McIlvaine describes his city as standing "to your New York City today as some panoramic negative print, inverted in its lights and shadows . . . its seasons turned around . . . a companion city of the other side" (59).[24] Like several others in the novel, this passage bears an almost word-for-word resemblance to Doctorow's essay "The Nineteenth New York," in which he is explicit about the relations between the past and the present, declaring that "the century is still with us, the ghostly nineteenth [. . .] a companion city of the other side, some moral hologram generated from an unknown but intense radiation of historical energy and randomly come to imprint on our dreaming brains."[25] Published the year following "The Character of Presidents," and also appearing in draft form in the archival workings for *The Waterworks*,[26] the essay appears in retrospect to be a declaration of metaphorical intent for the novel that he would publish two years later.

In addition to such invitations to read the novel in relation to the present day, frequent allusions to the financial practices of the Gilded Age also encourage a reading of the novel as a metaphor of the economic experience of New York during the long Reagan era. It would, of course, be difficult to write a novel set in the Gilded Age without referring to the economic climate of the time, when capitalism was so dominant that Charles King, the president of Columbia University, declared in 1858 that "This city is the creation of Commerce."[27] However, references throughout *The Waterworks* to "Wall Street thieves" (4), "the inane social doings of the class of new wealth" (21), the destruction of homes for commercial buildings (33), "the defiance that you get from much money when it combines with little taste" (81), and the volatility of the markets (172) appear pointedly designed to conflate in the reader's mind the Gilded Age and what David Harvey terms the "casino economy" of the Yuppie era,[28] "with its accoutrements of gentrification, close attention to symbolic capital, fashion, design, and quality of urban life" (332).

However, I would argue that a key element in Doctorow's critique of the neoliberal dominant in *The Waterworks* is what probably constitutes his most inventive adaptation of a genre fiction formula. For although *The Waterworks* is a detective novel replete with missing persons and, in Donne, a masterful police detective who combines Auguste Dupin and Sherlock Holmes, its plot derives ultimately from a fictional element more closely associated with horror: the undead. This element manifests itself in Martin's father, Augustus Pemberton, who—with other aged financiers—is kept alive by Doctor Sartorius via rudimentary blood transfusions from young orphans. It is, of course, possible to read this genre element simply as a playful ploy on Doctorow's part, a subversion of the customary practice of having a detective investigate a death by instead having a detective investigating why some characters remain alive, albeit in an almost catatonic state. Yet both the novel and other material suggest Doctorow had a far more serious design for these super-rich undead than a simple desire to subvert the generic formula.

That these financiers are supposed to represent the elite of Doctorow's own time is hinted at in the introduction to *Jack London*,

Hemingway, and the Constitution, published in 1993, a year before *The Waterworks* was published. Doctorow discusses the state of the nation in the immediate aftermath of the Cold War, and notes:

> In this final decade or so, with the mandate of a populace compliant with ruling circumstances, the last administrations of the cold war conflated its ideology with the capitalist principles of the nineteenth century. Deregulating industry, dismantling social legislation of benefit to anyone but their core constituencies, abjuring law enforcement where the law was not to their liking, and politicizing the courts, they distributed the enormous costs of the cold war democratically among all the classes of society except the wealthiest. The effect on our national standard of living was as a vampire's arterial suck.[29]

In *The Waterworks*, this "vampire's arterial suck," symbolized by the blood transfusions, is for the immortal benefit of both the financiers and Boss Tweed, thereby implicating big business and government in this illegal practice and in the citywide corruption, whose "effect on the city," McIlvaine claims, "had been like a vampire's arterial suck" (151). This implied collusion between business and government is further supported by archive material, in which one note shows Doctorow's aim to make it clear:

> that whole society [is] implicated in Rufus' continuance of the animation of the capitalist dead, a selective conspiracy of wealth and science.[30]

The "animation of the capitalist dead" may initially seem a dramatic flight of fancy, but if we follow McIlvaine's invitation to see societal critique behind the literal truth of words, then the underlying purpose of Doctorow's invention becomes clear. For when the financiers bankroll Sartorius's experiments in search of immortality, they mimic the actions of the corporations that came into being in the Gilded Age and changed the American capitalist landscape forever, and still dominate it today. As Alan Trachtenberg argues:

> The corporation embodied a legally sanctioned fiction, that an association of people constituted a single entity which might hold property, sue and be sued, enter contracts, and continue in existence beyond the lifetime or membership of any of its participants.[31]

This desire to effectively escape death and make the fruits of capital eternal, albeit for a select few, is gradually revealed as the central motivation for the crime in *The Waterworks*. When McIlvaine interviews Sarah Pemberton about her "monstrous thieving husband," she recalls how Augustus assured his doctor "he had no intention of dying at any foreseeable time in the future" (76–8). Augustus's belief in his possible immortality is based on a process at the root of which lies capital. This is signaled by the repetition of the verb "buy" when Doctorow reveals the disappearance of the children whose blood makes the animation possible:

> "[. . .] I aver an' detest there is a man going about these nights offerin' to buy up loose children."
> "Buy them?"
> "Exactly so."
> (91–2)

This capitalist belief that money makes anything possible, including immortality, is further emphasized when Martin Pemberton's long speech detailing his father's plot ends with their hope that Sartorius would recompose "their lives piece by piece [. . .] reconstituting them metempsychotically as endless beings" (200).

Though this deregulated corporation of financiers may not bear strict correlation to any specific present-day corporation, their business practices recall the corporations of the final years of the Cold War, ranging from their collusion with government to their hiding place at the waterworks, the steel and glass construction of which prefigures the "legion of steel and glass corporate headquarters" that Marshall Berman argues sprang up in the United States in the twentieth century in imitation of London's Crystal Palace.[32] These misguided financiers represent "the persistence of evil" (4) practicing irresponsible forms of capitalism that place profits above all else and ignoring "the plague of homelessness, disempowerment, and impoverishment" that blighted both the Gilded Age and the Yuppie era.[33]

Nevertheless, this does not mean that *The Waterworks* is an outright attack on capitalism per se, as some of Doctorow's detractors might argue. *The Waterworks* may be a politically submerged novel, but it constitutes less a complete rejection of capitalism than a signaling of its dangers. While *Billy Bathgate* may at times appear in thrall to the gangster capitalism of Schultz's gang and the eternal possibility of numbers/ money to reinvent themselves, through setting *The Waterworks* in the Gilded Age, Doctorow highlights the moment in which corporate interests began to "preempt the idea of the larger community, the national ideal, the United States as the ultimate communal reality" and provides a riposte to the triumphalist narrative of capitalism that followed in the wake of the end of the Cold War, asking what the price of that victory had been.[34]

Doctorow's answer to that question may lie in his decision to begin *The Waterworks* and end "The Nineteenth New York" with Abraham Lincoln's funeral, an event which, as Doctorow makes clear in the essay, formed "a commencement procession for our century."[35] If, as Wyn Kelley argues, nineteenth-century New York represented a labyrinthine city in which rising rents and increasing social stratification challenged "the ideology of liberty and justice for all" central to "American democratic individualism,"[36] for Doctorow Lincoln's death appears to represent the moment when such ideology was replaced by a new dominant, the "soulless, social resolve" that favored business above all else.[37] By representing that moment, Doctorow returns to the pre-history of our era, the beginnings of a system that would reach its apotheosis in the last years of the Cold War, in which he felt "the Right's chastisement of the ungrateful known as Morning in America" manifested "a social and cultural pathology" that "constituted an act of national self-mutilation all the more astonishing for the greatness of the country that performed it."[38] Thus, the black dye that stains the buildings for weeks after Lincoln's funeral is a symbol of grief for a political idealism that will never be recovered, a lament for what is already lost that evokes the Whitman of both "Crossing Brooklyn Ferry" and "When Lilacs Last in the Dooryard Bloom'd."

Thus, although Michelle Tokarczyk reads *The Waterworks* as an endorsement of the possibility of small-scale community action against corrupt officials, I would argue that Doctorow's novel engages with American politics on a much wider, national scale.[39] For although, in the interests of plot, McIlvaine, Donne et al. triumph over the financiers and love manifests itself in the twin marriages that end the book, the "heroic" characters in *The Waterworks* represent more than victors at a local scale. In their clinging to an ideology of justice and truth, they are little more than representatives of what, to borrow Raymond Williams's term,[40] we may call the "residual" of the ideals of American democracy, where personal interests supersede those of the corporation, however powerful the latter may be.

Doctorow's critique of the apparent lawlessness and self-interest of sections of corporate America at the end of the twentieth century, and of the government's role in assisting them, is an attack on a dominant that has ensconced itself as the American status quo. Yet however much the novel may manifest Doctorow's moral outrage at the state of America, its nostalgic recall of a more democratically idealist spirit is unlikely to disturb the hegemony of the financial and political elite. Its anger is tinged with resignation, its weight of despair negated by the commercial need to produce a happy ending.

For a submerged political novel to be effective, it needs to be both read and interpreted. We need only consider the fate of *Moby-Dick* in Melville's time to see how a lack of readers can effectively suppress even the most skillful of submerged political writing, while in its sanitized version of the past, the 1991 film adaptation of *Billy Bathgate* offers an example of a "reading" of Doctorow that ignores the novel's submerged politics. As I have argued above, through such passages as the invitation to see New York as a "negative print" of the present day, Doctorow invites the reader to enact a reading of *The Waterworks* that transcends the literal and grasps its submerged politics, but such passages are prompted by what we might term an "anxiety of interpretation" that is perhaps unavoidable for the writer of any submerged political novel. In effect, without resorting to didacticism, it is impossible for the novelist to ensure that the novel's submerged critique will not be lost in the reader's engagement with the plot.

Yet in *The Waterworks* this anxiety of interpretation appears to form part of a wider reflection on the position of the socially responsible artist in society. *The Waterworks* achieves this reflection through Doctorow's skillful deployment of the novel's several creator figures: McIlvaine, Martin Pemberton, and the painter Harry Wheelwright. In doing so, as I will outline below, Doctorow underlines the compromises the artist must face in his attempt to speak out against the dominant culture.

McIlvaine first visits Wheelwright as part of the investigation into Martin's disappearance. Here, his initial impression of Wheelwright as a society painter who lives by flattering the rich is challenged by what he sees in the studio. Donne and McIlvaine disturb the painting of a live model, but rather than a society heiress it is a Civil War veteran who "had one arm cut off above the elbow, the reddened skin of the stump sewn together like the end of a sausage" (96). The studio walls, in an echo of Baby's collage in *The Book of Daniel*, display a mix of other "maimed and disfigured veterans painted in unflinching detail [and] the more academic portraits or fashionable New York scenes designed for the market," a mélange in which McIlvaine recognizes a "conflicted mind [. . .] the critique, and the necessity of earning a living, side by side" (97). What starts as the description of an artist's studio ends in a summary of the conflict that faces any socially responsible artist in a capitalist society, between the demands of the market and the need to be true to one's own vision.

This episode in Wheelwright's studio serves as a prelude to McIlvaine's own experience of a similar conflict. For McIlvaine's narration of *The Waterworks*, his moment of becoming a writer, happens long after the events, mostly because he has been silenced by political interests. He remembers that, accompanying Donne to interview Wheelwright, "I felt as if I was giving up . . . my diction . . . for his" (95). On this occasion, McIlvaine's surrendering of his voice to the interests of the state is in the public interest: he keeps the secret Wheelwright reveals in order to help Donne solve the case. Yet shortly after, he finds himself silenced for more insidious reasons when presented with details of the full scale of Boss Tweed's corruption. McIlvaine feels "this story was so monumental . . . the truth so overwhelming in its demands" that it must be published; instead, the fact that "Tweed committed advertising to our pages—unnecessary, and very profitable, city advertising" (150) ensures his publisher refuses to run the story and the corruption remains hidden from the public.

This second silencing of the artist figure, along with the compromised position of Wheelwright, is, I would argue, symbolic of Doctorow's own frustrations as a writer. If *The Waterworks* represents an investigation into the role of the artist vis-à-vis the dominant, then the lesson here is that, as Berman argues in his analysis of Marx:

> Modern culture [is] part of modern industry. Art, physical science, social theory . . . all are modes of production; the bourgeoisie controls the means of production in culture, as in everything else, and anyone who wants to create must work in the orbit of its power.[41]

McIlvaine's vain attempt to speak out against the Tweed Ring therefore constitutes a metaphor of the situation in which the socially committed artist finds himself in America, where all forms of media are subsumed "into one smooth reality-laundering revenue stream that is in fact a ready-made highly suggestive simulacrum of state-controlled media."[42] As a result, however much artists wish to criticize or act for social justice, they can only do so within the "orbit" of the regime's power; are allowed only to raise their voice to the volume the structures of power are prepared to tolerate. If the conglomerated publishers etc. represent a "simulacrum of state-controlled media," it is impossible to criticize the state fully and openly through its own mouthpiece without being marginalized. Though artists may be capable of producing submerged political novels, as workers in the capitalist system they must ensure that the politics remain submerged or risk losing their livelihood.

This reading is further supported by Doctorow's recycling of the short story "The Water Works" toward the end of the novel. Originally appearing as the second story in *Lives of the Poets*, the story's unnamed narrator recounts a visit to the New York reservoir in which he tracks an anonymous figure into the machinery of the water works, watches him load the corpse of a drowned urchin into his carriage, and then returns to see the workers "dividing some treasure among themselves" and drinking whisky.[43] At only four pages in length, it is perhaps the collection's most enigmatic story and, placed as the second story, effectively represents the first mature work after Jonathan's initial story of his grasping of the power of the writer's independence. Yet archival evidence shows that Doctorow originally planned this story either to open or to end the collection, thus suggesting that it plays a significant role in *Lives of the Poets* despite Doctorow's eventual decision to begin with "The Writer in the Family."[44]

Perhaps the significance of the story's role only really becomes clear in *The Waterworks*, when it is recycled as McIlvaine's dream of Sartorius, but with two subtle additions (217–20). In both versions of the episode, the narrator feels that the Sartorius figure "acts on the presumption of partnership, as if he were on watch for our mutual benefit" (217), but only in the later version does the Sartorius figure look back at the narrator after collecting the dead body: "He glances back at me over his shoulder as the carriage races off, the bright black wheel's spokes brought to a blur. He smiles at me as at a complicitor" (219).

After narrating this look, which draws him into complicity in the act, McIlvaine states: "Finally you suffer the story you tell. After all these years in my head, my story occupies me, it has grown into the physical dimensions of my brain" (219). The simple act of witnessing makes the artist figure complicit in the regime he wishes to critique objectively, unable to refuse the "presumption of partnership." This point is underlined by the final change Doctorow makes to this scene. In both versions of the episode, the water workers who have retrieved the dead child from the water divide "some treasure among themselves" after the exit of the Sartorius figure.[45] Yet where in the first version the narrator ends the story by noting the water workers' love of ritual, here, in McIlvaine's dream, rather than ignoring him, they "call out to me to come join them. I do . . ." (219). This dream enactment of Althusser's interpellation, the notion that everyone is helplessly enmeshed in society the moment they respond to its call, suggests a resignation on Doctorow's part to the dilemma of writing a submerged political novel. For however critical socially responsible authors may be of the state, they can be so only through a state-controlled media, and thereby inadvertently supports the regime through a process of normalization even as they seek to subvert it. The submerged political novel can smuggle political fiction into the genre-dominated mainstream, but it forever runs the risk of making the critique it contains appear safe, its subversive intent one more thing to consume uncritically and unthinkingly.

Thus, at the close of *The Waterworks* we see Doctorow, through McIlvaine, re-acknowledge the conflicted position of the artist in contemporary America that he had explored in both "The Beliefs of Writers" and *Lives of the Poets*. As political fiction is as much a commodity as any other kind of literature, it seems impossible for the writer not to be implicated in the very processes he seeks to criticize. It seems therefore little coincidence that in this book, whose narrator is "sensitive to architecture" (57), the dream of complicity takes place at the reservoir that once stood on the site of the New York Public Library. For if the Gilded Age established that the "power to say what was real, what was America, seemed now safely in the hands of property, wealth, and the word 'Culture',"[46] Doctorow's novel suggests that this remains the case in contemporary America.

Culture, symbolized by the library, and capital, symbolized by the reservoir beneath whose walls the undead financiers appear to Martin Pemberton, are inextricably linked, the one built on the other. It is the socially conscious writer's task to negotiate between the two poles in his attempt to reveal the truth, yet he can never fully escape the web of complicity the ties between the two create. Even as he attempts to subvert the expectations of the state-controlled media, whether through encyclopedic or submerged political fiction disguised as genre, he remains a part of that system.

This does not mean, of course, that Doctorow abandoned the idea of the political novel after *The Waterworks*. Political concerns remain apparent in some of the storylines of *City of God* (2000) and return to the fore with *The March* (2005), which manages to be both a historical depiction of the Civil War and a response to the contemporaneous Gulf War, just as they are there in *Homer & Langley*'s (2009) historical sweep of the twentieth century and most overtly in *Andrew's Brain* (2014), excoriating George Bush Junior. Yet while each of these novels is political in its own way, none of them re-employs the assumption of genre tropes that Doctorow employed in *Billy Bathgate* and *The Waterworks*. The fate of the political novelist in America may not necessarily have improved in the final decades of Doctorow's writing career, but he appears to have abandoned the strategy of the submerged political novel and replaced the ventriloquial strategy with one in which the dissenting voice is more clearly his, however faintly it may have been heard in the dominant culture around it.

Notes

This chapter is based on part of a Ph.D. thesis at the University of Manchester, which was fully funded by the U.K. Arts and Humanities Research Council, which also part-funded the author's trip to the E. L. Doctorow archive at the Fales Library, New York University.

1. Christopher D. Morris, ed., *Conversations with E. L. Doctorow* (Jackson: University Press of Mississippi, 1999), 211.
2. J. Whalen-Bridge, *Political Fiction and the American Self* (Chicago: University of Illinois Press, 1998), 46.
3. E. L. Doctorow, *Billy Bathgate* (New York: Random House, 1989), 300.
4. E. L. Doctorow, *Jack London, Hemingway, and the Constitution: Selected Essays, 1977–1992* (New York: Random House, 1993), 112.
5. Raymond Williams, "Base and Superstructure in Marxist Cultural Theory," in *Culture and Materialism* (London: Verso, 1980), 31–49.
6. E. L. Doctorow, *Lives of the Poets* (New York: Random House, 1984), 145.
7. Doctorow, *Jack London*, 86.
8. E. L. Doctorow, *World's Fair* (New York: Random House, 1985), 288.
9. Herman Melville, "Hawthorne and His Mosses," *The Literary World*, August 17 and 24, 1850: 125–7 and 145–7; reprinted in R. Weaver, ed., *Billy Budd and Other Prose Pieces*, (London: Constable, 1924), 123–43.
10. Whalen-Bridge, *Political Fiction and the American Self*, 46.
11. Archive, 35.012. All archive quotes are taken from "The E. L. Doctorow Papers," MSS #56; Series 2A (Novels), Fales Library, New York University Archives. The numbers refer to the box and the folder numbers; for example, 39.005 is box 39, folder 5. The full catalogue is available at <http://dlib.nyu.edu/findingaids/html/fales/doctorow/dscref2173.html> (last accessed May 2019>.
12. Archive, 39.005.
13. Archive, 38.003.
14. Archive, 38.003–10.
15. Archive, 38.004: 263–77.
16. Archive, 38.003.
17. Archive, 39.004. See also E. L. Doctorow, *City of God* (New York: Random House, 2000), 189–206.
18. Archive, 39.004, unnumbered page.
19. Doctorow, *Jack London*, 98–9.
20. Archive, 39.004.
21. Doctorow, *Jack London*, 96.
22. E. L. Doctorow, *The Waterworks* (New York: Random House, 1994), 6. Subsequent parenthetical citations refer to this edition.
23. Herman Melville, "Bartleby, the Scrivener: A Story of Wall Street" (1853), in R. Midler, ed., *Billy Budd, Sailor and Selected Tales* (Oxford: Oxford University Press, 1997), 43.

24. Ellipses in quotes from *The Waterworks* are Doctorow's own unless enclosed by square brackets.

25. Doctorow, *Jack London*, 145.

26. Archive, 38.019.

27. Quoted in Sven Beckert, *The Monied Metropolis: New York City and the Consolidation of the American Bourgeoisie, 1850–1896* (New York: Cambridge University Press, 2003), 69.

28. David Harvey, *The Condition of Postmodernity* (Oxford: Blackwell, 1990), 332.

29. Doctorow, *Jack London*, xii.

30. Archive, 38.017.

31. Alan Trachtenberg, *The Incorporation of America* (New York: Hill & Wang, 1982), 83.

32. Marshall Berman, *All That Is Solid Melts into Air: The Experience of Modernity* (2nd edition; London: Verso, 2010), 248.

33. Harvey, *Condition of Postmodernity*, 332.

34. E. L. Doctorow, *Reporting the Universe* (Cambridge, MA: Harvard University Press, 2003), 104.

35. Doctorow, *Jack London*, 145.

36. Wyn Kelley, *Melville's City: Literary and Urban Form in Nineteenth-Century New York* (New York: Cambridge University Press, 1996), 96.

37. Doctorow, *Jack London*, 147.

38. Doctorow, *Jack London*, xii. This introduction, written in March 1993, is the final piece Doctorow published before *The Waterworks* and offers further evidence that the end of the Cold War was paramount in his thinking while composing the novel.

39. M. M. Tokarczyk, *E. L. Doctorow's Skeptical Commitment* (New York: Lang, 2000).

40. Williams, "Base and Superstructure in Marxist Cultural Theory," 40.

41. Berman, *All That Is Solid*, 117.

42. Doctorow, *Reporting the Universe*, 105.

43. Doctorow, *Lives of the Poets*, 24.

44. Archive, 43.005.

45. Doctorow, *Lives of the Poets*, 24; *The Waterworks*, 219.

46. Trachtenberg, *The Incorporation of America*, 232.

Chapter 5

Redeeming the National Ideal: Revisiting E. L. Doctorow's *The Book of Daniel* and Its Political Implications

Jieun Kwon

I

As many critics have pointed out, Louis Althusser's theory of ideology shifts focus from a validating framework (i.e. truth versus falsity) to a discursive one through which the individual incorporates himself or herself into the symbolic social order.[1] For him, ideology is "a system (with its own logic and rigor) of representations (images, myths, ideas of concepts, depending on the case) endowed with a historical existence and role within a given society."[2] What Althusser denotes is that one adopts society's dominant knowledge and values—such as "images, myths, ideas of concepts"—to represent social reality and define one's position within the social order. With this process, ideology turns a pre-social individual into a socialized subject by "'recruit[ing]' subjects among the individuals (it recruits them all), or 'transform[ing]' the individual into subjects (it transforms them all)."[3] Given that, Althusser's theory connotes both representative and incorporative dimensions of ideology—representative in that it re-articulates the cultural vocabularies commonly used within society, and incorporative in that it sutures individuals to society's dominative mode of thought.

Ideology as a discursive means of social suturing is a key element in Sacvan Bercovitch's critique of American literature and its political implications. According to him, ideology functions to provide "the ground and texture of consensus . . . the system of ideas inwoven into the cultural symbology through which 'America' continues to provide the terms of identity and cohesion in the United States."[4] Through the consensus process of incorporating social values and rhetoric, "America" becomes a symbolic terrain whereby the nation's dominative logic is re-iterated and thus its ideological cohesion is reassured. Bercovitch defines this consenting impulse as a distinctive pattern in American literature, continuing from Puritan writings to the American Renaissance works. He particularly directs attention to the antagonistic relation between self and society, which is offered in these works as a form of social criticism. In his view, this kind of social subversion is already part of the main lexicons in American political discourses, in which individual dissent has been acknowledged as a socially consented form of harness-ing a better national future. Therefore, the surface value of rupturing from the social ironically serves to buttress the unified significances of "America":

> The immemorial response of ideology . . . has been to redefine protest in terms of the system, as a complaint about shortcomings from its ideals, or deviations from its myths of self and community. Thus the very act of identifying malfunction becomes an appeal for cohesion. (366)

For Bercovitch, this mechanism of absorbing radical impulse into the national identity is the very basis of how ideology functions within American literature. The political criticism offered in it serves to testify to the cultural hegemony of liberal democratic ideals, and in this process, the authors construct politically subversive narratives in such a way that the latter become culturally identified with the nation's fundamental logics: in Bercovitch's own words, "the classic American authors . . . were imaginatively nourished by the culture, even when they were politically opposed to it" (16).

Bercovitch's argument provides a theoretical framework crucial in appreciating E. L. Doctorow's *The Book of Daniel*. To discuss this matter, we need to turn first to the general receptions of the novel. While widely disagreeing about the value of its political intention, most critics agree on its radicality in critically reconfiguring national identity. The text's description of the Rosenberg trial as well as its unrelenting attack on Cold War politics led Joseph Epstein to label it a typical representative of "the adversary culture." For him, Doctorow's antagon-istic stance against the mainstream American society is "an intense distrust of [this] country that borders on hatred."[5] On the other hand, those who highly valorize Doctorow's political criticism retain the same opinion about the radicality embodied in the text. David S. Gross, for instance, argues that Doctorow is "the radical writer or intellectual or political activist," whose vision of the nation's identity is fundamentally "a terrible and negative one."[6] Similarly, Paul Levine situates Doctorow within the subversive tradition of Melville's "the power of blackness" by asserting that the author is one of the "American writers who have treated America in various eras as a gigantic mistake."[7]

Despite opposite political stances in these two camps, the general criticism of *The Book of Daniel* shares a common premise that Doctorow's critical distance from American society automatically signals his radical denial of that society altogether. This premise is reinforced by the symbolic solution that the novel offers: Daniel Isaacson, the protagonist, completes his political subversion by refusing any tie with society and thus radically deserting the latter. What these criticisms fail to perceive, however, is that under the dissenting gesture of the text lies the desire and even the necessity to redeem the legitimacy of American liberal democratic principles. Doctorow mentions that the ultimate aim of his political works is to reconfirm the spirits of the U.S. Constitution: "[I]n this county the reference has to be the Constitution; and the political analysis, Marxist or otherwise, will have to develop from just such elemental biblical perception, from what we are in our mythic being, not from what Europe is."[8] Embodying absolute worth and authority, which are tantamount to "mythic" and "biblical perception," the Constitution signals for him the nation's exceptionality that distinguishes it from Europe (or any other nation, for that matter). Seen in this light, the narrative construction of *The Book of Daniel* betrays the same ideological logic that Bercovitch detects in American literature: its political critique of reality serves to reinvigorate the value of ideals sustaining the nation's coherence, and thus it politically dissents from society by way of culturally consenting to its fundamental logics. Therefore, one might conclude that the text's radicality can be defined rather as a vigorous reform within the system than as a complete denial of society that those criticisms commonly assume.

Bimbisar Irom re-evaluates the political implications of individual dissent in *The Book of Daniel*. Detecting impulses of engaged politics in its otherwise Rortian ironist retreat, he argues that the text provides "a moment of intervention to rethink the entrenched positions that read the post-1960s aesthetic as either enervated retreat or engaged praxis."[9] This essay shares the same assumption that the text conveys a fundamentally political gesture in its seemingly private retreat. One step further, this essay aims to show that Doctorow's individual subversion is an effective means to connect the private and the public, in terms that it serves to reinvigorate the socially consented discourses of liberal democracy. Section II of this essay examines how Doctorow utilizes conspiracy theory as a way to construct his political criticism of the Cold War U.S. The main argument of this part is twofold. On one level, it traces the genealogy of conspiracy theory as a form of political criticism. As we shall see in detail later, conspiracy theory enables one to imagine politics in a way that the mechanism of consensus democracy cannot or will not permit. On another level, conspiracy theory tends to offer individual dissent as the ultimate outcome of its political criticism. In demonstrating how "evil" conspiracies truncate the ideal state of the nation, conspiracy narratives heavily invest in the autonomous and marginalized individual as the main agency to convey social criticism. I will argue that Doctorow faithfully continues the genre's tradition by beginning with the conspiratorial suspicion of consensus democracy and ending with the sanction of Daniel's personal subversion.

Whereas section II shows how the conspiratorial framework in *The Book of Daniel* articulates the text's dissenting impulse against American society, section III explores its consenting aspect, by tracing the transformation process of a dissentive individual into an Althusserian national subject. This transformation largely arises from the inner logic of conspiracy theory itself. American conspiracy theory as a genre reveals a distinctive pattern: that is, the necessity to guard and reaffirm national ideals by way of identifying "enemies" of the nation. In the case of *The Book of Daniel*, the national ideal is mainly materialized in the form of liberal individualism—or, more precisely, the age-old conflict between self and society. Taking these elements into account, I hope to show that the conspiratorial political criticism in *The Book of Daniel* is a perfect example of the Bercovitchian model of political dissensus/cultural consensus. By conforming to the traditional role that conspiracy genre has played throughout American history, *The Book of Daniel* reveals under its surface of radial rupture from society the desire to reconfirm that very society's ideological cohesion.

II

Before getting into *The Book of Daniel*, I will briefly recapitulate the theoretical background of conspiracy theory as a form of political criticism. Quite contrary to the traditional view of conspiracy theory as a pathological delusion disrupting the normal perception of self in relation to the world,[10] recent critics find in its unorthodox status the very potential of political criticism. Mark Fenster argues that the unofficiality of conspiracy theory serves "as a strategy of delegitimation in political discourse."[11] In a similar vein, Daniel Hellinger valorizes it for offering "the underprivileged" an opportunity to "challenge elites to explain why they have contradicted republican ideals."[12] Conspiracy theory as a populist attempt to engage with the nation's political discourse is further elaborated by Fredric Jameson. According to him, conspiracy theory is a form of what he terms "cognitive mapping," through which one tries to restore a cohesive social order in the complex networks of late capitalist society:

> [Conspiracy theory] is an unconscious, collective effort at trying to figure out where we are and what landscapes and forces confront us in a late twentieth century whose abominations are heightened by their concealment and their bureaucratic impersonality . . . [T]his is what used to be called self-consciousness about the social totality.[13]

Conspiracy theory as an act of cognitive mapping provides a kernel to a larger collective discourse: it connects an individual narration of conspiracy with the historical significances of the event, and it thus enables us to recognize the working order of society, which Jameson calls "the social totality." Given that, conspiracy theory seems to be a perfect example of his earlier argument about the collective utopian desire in popular culture. For him, all forms of mass culture convey a utopian desire through which such forms imagine beyond social contradictions and anxieties: "[E]ven the most degraded type of mass culture . . . remains implicitly, and no matter how faintly, negative and critical of the social order."[14] Therefore, however "degraded" in representing social realities and histories, conspiracy theory ultimately leads to the impulse to criticize the status quo and to imagine a better collective destiny.

Considering that the value of conspiracy theory lies in its unofficial— or, "degraded" and "delegitimat[e]"—status, conspiracy theory can be understood as part of the "subjugated knowledges" theorized by Michel Foucault:

> I believe that by subjugated knowledges one should understand something else, something which in a sense is altogether different, namely, a whole set of knowledges that have been disqualified as inadequate to their task or insufficiently elaborated: naïve knowledges, located low down on the hierarchy, beneath the required level of cognition or scientificity. I also believe that it is . . . a popular knowledge though it is far from being a general commonsense knowledge, but is on the contrary a particular, local, regional knowledge, a differential knowledge.[15]

As popular and local knowledge, conspiracy theory perfectly embodies Foucault's notion of subjugated knowledge. On the one hand, its unofficiality puts it in a marginalized position in relation to official history, and this hierarchy of knowledge is maintained under the name of consensus democracy and its entailed notion of transparency in decision-making processes. The marginalized position, on the other hand, enables conspiracy theory to problematize the implicit connection between power and knowledge. Conspiratorial imagination sees historical knowledge as ultimately an institutionalized kind, whose construction and distribution are believed to be dictated by institutional authorities. Under this rubric, one might argue that the value of conspiracy theory lies on drawing attention to the very process in which certain knowledge turns into an official discourse through collusion with power.

The idea that conspiracy theory, as subjugated knowledge, functions to reveal the complicity between power and official knowledge is resonant in *The Book of Daniel*. Doctorow claims in numerous interviews that the main aim of his conspiratorial representation of history is to bring to light the problem of authority monopolized by factual history. Echoing Foucault's knowledge hierarchy, he points out the rigid classification of historical narratives based on scientific instrumentality. According to him, modern Western societies have given the primary authority to factual and documentary narratives, which he calls "the power of the regime," while literary or nonscientific languages, which he dubs "the power of freedom," have been devalued.[16] As a means to break away from this hierarchy, the author attempts to evaluate historical representation not by validation but by signification. That is to say, historical narrativization is for him a process of endowing meanings to the past rather than a mimetic replica, and therefore "there is no fiction or nonfiction as we commonly understand the distinction: there is only narrative."[17]

As the focus shifts from historical validation to its signification, so does the Rosenberg trial presented in *The Book of Daniel*. According to Doctorow, depicting the trial as a governmental conspiracy is "true, whether it happened or not. Perhaps truer because it didn't happen."[18] The conspiratorial imagination can be "truer"—i.e. "more significant"—than factual history, for it opens up a discursive space where the working mechanism of power/government comes to the fore. In this regard, Doctorow's view of conspiratorial history shares the same premise as Jameson's cognitive mapping, in that conspiratorial thinking tries to configure the social working order hermeneutically sealed and thus inaccessible to the ordinary mind. Doctorow's criticism of the Cold War period is epitomized in his attempt to refute the commonly consented notion of American innocence—that is, the belief that reality faithfully lives up to the nation's founding principles. For him, recent governmental activities testify to the incongruity between national ideals and reality: "[A] message of the twentieth century [is] that people have a great deal to fear from their own governments . . . It is the nature of the governing mind to treat as adversary the people being governed."[19] Daniel, a son of Paul and Rochelle Isaacson, who are fictional surrogates of Julius and Ethel Rosenberg, rephrases the author's argument:

> The final existential condition is citizenship. Every man is the enemy of his own country. EVERY MAN IS THE ENEMY OF HIS OWN COUNTRY. Every country is the enemy of its own citizens . . . In war the soldier's destruction is accomplished by his own Commanders. It is his government which places a rifle in his hands, puts him up on the front, and tells him his mission is to survive. All societies are armed societies. All citizens are soldiers. All Governments stand ready to commit their citizens to death in the interest of their government.[20]

The military metaphor evokes two different yet reciprocal levels of relation between individuals and the government. At a more explicit level, individuals take an antagonistic position against the government, in which citizenship is not a means of identification with the latter but a symbol of the battlefield to secure their "existential" rights. At a different level, the paragraph indicates that individuals are at a war not only *against* their government, but also *for* it. They are required to die defending the nation's cause, and the government's role as a "Commander" is to "plac[e] a rifle in his hands" and ask citizens to die "in the interest of" it. Citizenship as an "existential condition" takes on a new meaning in this light: as a symbol of bounded responsibility with the country, it dictates one's existence by asking citizens to sacrifice their lives for a great cause.

The idea that individuals are not merely the enemy of the system but also a pawn of it is the main thread of Doctorow's criticism of Cold War America. For the author, the Isaacsons were sacrificed so as to maintain the cohesion of national Cold War ideology. Questioning the government's convicting the Rosenbergs on a communist espionage opens the door to the suspicion about Cold War logics, and this in turn leads to admitting that the whole society sustained by these logics is at great peril. Therefore, as Robert Lewin succinctly puts it in the novel, "the only alternative to admitting our bankruptcy of leadership and national vision was to find [communist] conspiracies. It was one or the other" (222). Lewin's observation reveals that Cold War American society was also responsible, if only partly, for the deaths of the Isaacsons. By embracing the official verdict and thus avoiding the uncomfortable question on national identity, American society readily conformed to the dominant political order of the time. The governmental Cold War policy supported by social conformity seals the Isaacsons' fate. As Jacob Asher tells Daniel, "[this] is not a period that our historians will be proud of us. We are in the mood that someone should pay for what we find intolerable" (118). The overriding image of individual sacrifice for collective fate is reinforced by the name "Isaacson." As Susan Brienza points out, it alludes to Isaac in the Old Testament.[21] Much as Isaac's near sacrifice is for his family to reconfirm its religious tie with God, the Isaacsons are sacrificed for the sake of their "national family" to reassure its ideological unity and to reclaim national innocence.

Given the deeply compromised status of Cold War American society, it is hardly surprising to see that Daniel's resistance takes a form of complete alienation from it. He defines himself as "a psychic alien" (34), who voluntarily marginalizes himself by refusing any tie with the social. As I briefly mentioned in section I of this essay, the formation of the autonomous individual is less an isolated case in *The Book of Daniel* than highly symptomatic of many conspiracy narratives. Timothy Melley asserts that conspiracy theory "promote[s] forms of hyperindividualism—extraordinary desires to keep free of social controls by seeing the self as only its truest self when standing in stark opposition to a hostile social order."[22] Melley's argument is elaborated by both Robert Alan Goldberg and Fenster, whose main focus is on the hermeneutical function of conspiratorial individualism. According to Goldberg, the dissenting individual in conspiracy narratives is manifested not through actual action but, rather, through one's ability to interpret society: "Whether men or women act on the information [gained by conspiracy theory] is less important than their sense of revitalization in discovering the truth."[23] Similarly, Fenster argues that "the relationship of character to history is largely cognitive and based on the collection, sorting and interpreting of information," and thus the politics of the conspiratorial individual can be summarized as "the cognitive act of interpretation."[24]

Daniel's attempt to construct his own autonomy by distancing himself from society exactly overlaps with this individualist model. The enlightened status of Daniel, which enables him to correctly interpret social totality, provides a platform to successfully resist conspiracy-ridden society. Daniel as an enlightened individual is clearly shown in his ability to "make connections"—the hermeneutic ability to grasp the ideological logic behind his parents' death. This practice of interpretation is, for Daniel, a token of his radicalness: "The idea is the dynamics of radical thinking . . . The radical discovers connections between available data and the root responsibility. Finally he connects everything" (140). More to the point, making connection is also a mark of difference between him and other family members. The family's physical and symbolic deaths—his parents are executed, his sister Susan goes insane, and his foster parents, the Lewins, are mentally destroyed by their vain effort to win the trial—result from their inability to realize that it is impossible to get justice within the system. For Daniel, Robert Lewin's absolute belief in the American judicial system is a naïve idea at best and unwitting complicity with the unjust system at worst: "We are dealing here with a failure to make connections. The failure to make connection is complicity. Reform is complicity. . . Innocence is complicity" (226–7). Paul Isaacson is also innocent enough not to understand the gap between social justice as an ideal and reality: "[Y]ou couldn't help feeling that the final connection was impossible for him to make between what he believed and how the world reacted. He couldn't quite make that violent connection" (32). The final and only connection Paul makes is his own electrocution. With the help of electricity that flows into his body and connects it to death, he "finally connects everything" (140). If he could not make connections due to his trust in the system, he can now, with his own death that completes the betrayal of his trust. The idea of innocence as the main cause of one's demise continues in Susan. As her attempt to "get inside and create help" (80) and its subsequent failure lead to insanity and suicide, Daniel once again identifies innocence with the absence of interpretative ability: Susan "died of a failure of analysis," for "nothing [she] did ever lacked innocence" (301, 275).

Daniel's attempt to disclaim family innocence and break away from society is manifested in his refusal to participate in collective movements of the time, notably the New Left. During the Pentagon march, Daniel feels that there is an impenetrable wall between him and other participants. He is "unable to share the bruised cheery fellowship of his companions" (256), and his feeling of isolation "has robbed the day of genius" (255). Daniel's dissatisfaction with the New Left is, on one level, based upon his observation that it has become a sort of spectacle through media. Artie Sternlicht, a fictional prime figure of the movement, regards the march ultimately as a television show: "Do something and be a celebrity . . . Be there! We'll be on television. We're gonna overthrow the United States with images!" (140). Disappointed with the New Left movement, Daniel concludes that "[t]here was nothing to it. It is a lot easier to be a revolutionary nowadays than it used to be" (257). On another level, Daniel's dissociation from the movement arises from the fact that he is none other than a son of the Isaacsons:

> I live in constant and degrading relationship to the society that has destroyed my mother and father. I will never be drafted . . . I could burn my draft card on the steps of the Pentagon and nothing would happen.

Nothing I do will result in anything but an additional entry in my file. My file. I am deprived of the chance of resisting my government . . . I am totally deprived of the right to be dangerous. (72)

As offspring of traitors who committed "the only crime defined in the Constitution" (167), Daniel is already stigmatized as the nation's biggest enemy. Under the circumstance, any act of political protest existing within society, such as burning the draft card or participating in the march, loses all of its significance: it will be nothing but "an additional entry in my file"—an additional proof of the already proven. Daniel's desire to be part of a collective struggle, therefore, ironically ends up making him realize its futility.

The government entrapped by Cold War ideologies, the conformed society, and the ineffectiveness of collective resistance—all of these compel Daniel to find a way to revolt on his own terms. At the risk of repetition, what is significant in Daniel's personal dissent is that it is equivalent to and often exchangeable with his interpreting ability. Daniel as a "criminal of perception" (31) underlines the immediate connection between interpretation and social transgression: the illicit act of transgression implied in the "criminal" metaphor is enacted foremost by his "perception," upon which his interpretative skills rely. As "the ability to know" surpasses all other aspects of political revolt, Daniel's dissent turns into a psychological kind whereby its subversive power lies in knowing the truth rather than taking action with the knowledge. As he mulls over:

In the late afternoon the sun burned on the windows of downtown Boston as if someone was flashing signals with a mirror. This was my window. I pretended the signals were for me . . . What gave me immense satisfaction was the thought that anyone who tried to intercept the signals, and decipher them, would fail. No matter who, the FBI or the Nazis, nobody not standing right here in this window could read the signals exactly as they were sent or understand them as they were meant to be understood . . . [The feeling] pulses out of him like a radio wave, out of all parts of him at once, and it needs . . . But if he could accommodate any part of his body the feeling wouldn't leave, it would still be there in all parts of him at once, each cell of his body radiating its passionate need. (218)

History flashes signals to him, and he is the only one who can manage to grasp their full meaning. The sole claim on proper interpretation is, for Daniel, a badge of difference from the society: it endows him with a sense of autonomy, by distinguishing him from the rest of society. Social alienation as a form of empowerment is further elaborated in

Daniel's description of increasing self-integrity. As the last part of the paragraph implies, the integrity of his knowledge is transferred into that of his body. By endowing the power emanating from interpretation onto his body and thus internalizing it, his *self* as well as his interpretation become impervious to institutional interventions and social co-option. The significance of knowledge—and of the ability to know, by extension—in Daniel's protest seems clear enough. Not only is it a means of creating a symbolic distance between him and society, but it is also a determining factor in materializing his subjectivity as an autonomous individual. Under this rubric, Daniel's individuality takes a form of "knowing subject," whose enlightened status is both the starting point and the final goal of his self-alienation.

Given these circumstances, one might conclude that Daniel's political dissent serves to harness the completion of his subjectivity rather than actual political praxis. If it begins with an attempt to reconfigure social totality against consensus democracy, it ends with positing an autonomous individual as the ultimate outcome of its social critique. In addressing subjectivity formation, the novel presents individual marginalization in two contrasting ways. As we saw in Daniel's observation on his family's victimhood, individuals are involuntarily marginalized from the mechanism of power at both a cognitive and a practical level: they are unable to grasp its full meanings, let alone to participate in decision-making. On the other hand, marginality can be also empowering in Daniel's case, in the sense that it is a token of his autonomy accelerated by his voluntary alienation from the conformed society. Given that, one might argue that Daniel's personal dissent is both a symptom of and a symbolic solution to the problems of Cold War America. As a symptom, it reflects the anxiety that one's full individuality cannot be accomplished within the social boundary; and as a symbolic solution, it fantasizes a way of reclaiming the unencumbered individual, whose distance from society is regarded as an effective means of ameliorating social defects.

III

Patrick O'Donnell sees conspiracy theory as a suturing process whereby the individual integrates with stories of the collective, notably those of the nation:

> [Conspiracy theory] is intimately linked to the formation of individual subjects within a specific national regime precisely to the extent that

they view themselves as citizens of a nation, defined as an assemblage of behaviors, laws, boundaries, and invested historical narratives . . . The paranoid subject [is] . . . interpellated into collective narratives of nation, identity, and destiny.[25]

At one level, O'Donnell's argument refers to the thematic aspect of conspiracy theory, in which the individual engages with the nation's collective fate by investing on historico-political events shaping national identity. At a higher level, his argument brings attention to the process of subject construction through conspiracy theory. As is evident in his terminologies, O'Donnell's argument signals a process similar to that of Althusserian interpellation. By investigating socio-political events and thus propelling himself or herself into the collective identity of the nation, the individual turns into a historically unified subject. In this process, conspiracy theory functions to take the role of ideology—ideology in the Althusserian sense—in which the individual is integrated into the symbolic social order as "an assemblage of behaviors, laws, boundaries." O'Donnell concludes that conspiracy theory is a kind of identification process between the individual and the nation: through the interpellation of the theory, "crucial differences between agency and national or other identificatory fantasies are collapsed," and "self and nation become one."[26]

The Book of Daniel also undergoes the process of constructing a national subject. As we saw in the previous section, Daniel embodies the liberal individualist model of subjectivity based upon autonomy and self-control. Considering that liberal individualism is "the deepest identity" of the U.S.,[27] Daniel neatly fits into the description of an Althusserian subject interpellated into national principles and values. Daniel as a national subject renders a somewhat paradoxical situation—paradoxical at least to the non-American mind. His identification with the national ideology is manifested through his alienation from national community. Phrased another way, the unity between him and American society is actualized precisely through his rupture from that society's boundary. This situation leads to two questions crucial to understanding Daniel's individual dissent. First, what is the theoretical connection linking Daniel's self-alienation with his embodiment of a national subject? If these two statuses are, in their own natures, not in an automatically causal relation with each other, then it seems worth discussing the logic that binds the two. The second and more important question is about the need to redress the novel's radicality. If Daniels' radical break from society is completed with his compliance to its most fundamental logic, then how should one evaluate the nature of its radicality?

Before investigating the matter of radicality, we will first turn to the logical basis of Daniel's individual dissent. One possible answer to the marriage of alienation and interpellation can be found within the internal structure of conspiracy theory. As Melley's book title *Empire of Conspiracy* aptly summarizes, there are numerous examples in American history that interpret socio-political events through the lens of conspiracy. From the American Revolution, the Illuminati, the nineteenth-century Populist movement, McCarthyism, to more recent incidents such as the JFK assassination and 9/11, the historical events that deeply inform and shape national identity have engendered a possibility of evil conspiracy at work.[28] In spite of various subjects and often conflicting ideological intentions, these narratives have a common denominator—the quest for Americanness. They all lament how far the conspiracy-ridden reality strays from the principles of American liberal democracy, and underline the urgency to redeem the latter.[29] David Brion Davis argues that the heavy investment of the genre in Americanness reflects "the desire to recover an imperiled heritage through self-purification."[30] Given that, conspiracy theory might be seen as another manifestation of the American Jeremiad tradition, at least in terms of social purpose and function. Like the American Jeremiad tradition exhorting the fallen condition of reality in comparison with the spirit of the newly found nation, conspiracy theory functions to reconfirm Americanness by way of discovering the "enemies" threatening it. This logic provides a teleological link between social critique and social identification. In a situation where the shortcomings of reality stress the legitimacy of ideals, the critical distance from social reality becomes a means to ensure one's unity with the nation's principal values.

Doctorow continues the tradition of American conspiracy theory by faithfully following its dualistic logic of assent/dissent. He invariably underlines in a number of interviews the absolute worth of the Constitution. According to the author, "[t]hat we don't manage to live up to it [the Constitution] is the source of all our self-analysis."[31] In the same vein, he also asserts that "[w]e would build on what we already have, we would go out in the barn (which is the Constitution) and tinker. And it's the failure to recognize *that* which has always brought programmatic radicals up short in this country."[32] The significance of the Constitution is resonant in *The Book of Daniel*. Daniel identifies himself with a number of "traitors" in American history, who cast a critical eye on the compromised status of their own societies. Among the list of names, which includes Benedict Arnold and his wife, Peggy, General Robert E. Lee, and Aaron Burr, Daniel singles out Edgar Allan Poe as the most representative model of his personal revolt:

[H]istorians of early America fail to mention the archetype traitor, the master subversive Poe, who wore a hole into the parchment and let the darkness pour through . . . First he spilled a few drops of whiskey just below the Preamble . . . A small powerful odor arose from the Constitution; there was a wisp of smoke which exploded and quickly turned mustard yellow in color. When Poe blew this away through the resulting aperture in the parchment the darkness of the depths rose, and rises still from that small hole all these years incessantly pouring its dark hellish gases like soot, like smog, like the poisonous effulgence of combustion engines over Thrift and Virtue and Reason and Natural Law and the Rights of Man. It's Poe, not those other guys. He and he alone. It's Poe who ruined us, that scream from the smiling face of America. (177)

This paragraph appears at first glance to describe Poe damaging the Constitution to reveal its dark side, and thus it seems to contradict Doctorow's belief in the Constitution. However, closer inspection betrays a quite different effect. That the smoke rises from below the hole in the parchment indicates that the Constitution is a kind of surface concealing the darkness below it. The act of making a hole is therefore to reveal the ugly reality lurking behind the screen of the Constitution—in Doctorow's own words, it is to reveal "that scream from the smiling face of America."[33] Moreover, Poe's act to put a hole "just below the Preamble" further attests that he leaves the letters of the Constitution intact. Thus understood, the role of Poe as "the archetype traitor" is not to problematize the Constitution itself but to ensure its value as the symbol of national covenant. Individual subversion as a chief vehicle to reclaim national ideals continues in Daniel. As a true inheritor of Poe, Daniel criticizes Cold War America and its claim to national innocence: "My country! Why aren't you what you claim to be?" (40). By envisioning the discrepancy between the ideal and the actual, Daniel equates political amelioration to the renewal of national spirit.

Considering the significance of national ideals in Doctorow's political criticism, the nature of its radicality comes into view more clearly. Doctorow's criticism of Cold War America is undoubtedly radical, precisely to the extent that it calls for a vigorous change in the contemporary social order. However, this kind of radicality is not identical to the systemic refusal that Daniel's self-marginalization rhetorically claims: rather, it serves to reinforce the ideological cohesion of the nation by appealing to its most fundamental logic. In order more effectively to illuminate this matter, Bercovitch demarcates political dissent from cultural consent: according to him, as quoted above, "the classic American authors . . . were imaginatively nourished by the culture, even when they were politically opposed to it."[34] There is no denying that the distinction between political dissent and cultural consent has a direct bearing upon *The Book of Daniel*. It is politically oppositional, yet this radical impulse is redirected into the service of the nation's cohesive identity. Seen in this interpretative framework, Trenner's aforementioned acclamation of the novel as a continuation of "the power of blackness" bears more implications than he probably intended. *The Book of Daniel* shares with these works not only the critical edge of political criticism, but also the refusal to abandon national ideals.

The significance of cultural consent is further increased by Daniel's individuality. Individual autonomy and self-control are, on one level, part of the national principles that Daniel tries to reclaim. Yet as we saw earlier, it also functions as a *means* to materialize the impulse of returning to the ideal. That is to say, liberal individualism in *The Book of Daniel* is posited as a legitimate political statement, through which Daniel articulates his dissent and harnesses national ideals. As has been argued by numerous theorists, individualism has taken a peculiar turn in the American imagination, in such a way that individual self-autonomy is regarded as an effective vehicle to promote communal good.[35] Since it is not my aim to exhaust the course of theoretical development regarding the subject, I will limit my discussion to its characteristic that is, I believe, crucial in understanding Daniel's subversion. Cyrus Patell distinguishes positive liberty from negative liberty in conceiving individual freedom. Negative liberty is "freedom from" social constraints and authorities, while positive liberty is "freedom to" participate in communal activities and commitments.[36] According to Patell, American liberal individualism has been conceived in such a way that negative liberty and positive liberty are conflated with each other, and thus that individual freedom not only signifies individuality but also comes to benefit the whole of society:

> [W]e cannot understand the continuing persuasiveness of individualism as an ideology in the United States without comprehending the way in which its official narrative sets negative liberty and positive liberty into a teleological relation . . . The official narrative inherits Locke's negative conception of freedom as freedom from restraint but claims that negative liberty inevitably transforms itself into a form of positive liberty that nurtures communal institutions.[37]

The "teleological relation" between negative and positive liberties provides a theoretical framework that propels individual autonomy into legitimate political discourse. As negative liberty subsumes the role of positive liberty, individuality comes to signify not selfishness but a token of one's indivisible membership to society. This membership is, to be sure, a negative kind: it is the independent status from society that guarantees communal interests. This negative membership constitutes, as Patell points out, the "official narrative" of American individualism. As a culturally consented form, individual autonomy provides an official vocabulary in conceiving the role of the individual within the political terrain.

Given these circumstances, one might conclude that Daniel's individual subversion is a doubly assenting move. On one level, it appeals to the most fundamental basis of national identity under the name of the Constitution, in which the "radical" project of breaking from the present is profoundly shaped and informed by the past. On another, liberal individualism as a means of articulating this self-purifying impulse is part and parcel of official lexicons sustaining the cohesive identity of the nation. In this regard, the political radicality of *The Book of Daniel* should be reassessed, if partly. At the risk of repetition, it certainly expresses a form of radical transgression against Cold War American society. Yet, at the same time, its radical subversion aims to renew the absolute belief in the nation's fundamental tenets. Therefore, quite contrary to Epstein's criticism of the novel as the representative of "the adversary culture," *The Book of Daniel* rather reveals the desire and even necessity to return to the very ideals that Epstein wants to uphold.

Notes

This essay was first published in *Studies in the Novel*. It appears here with slight authorial correction. Kwon, Jieun. "Redeeming the National Ideal: Revisiting E. L. Doctorow's *The Book of Daniel* and Its Political Implications." *Studies in the Novel*, 46.1 (2014), 83–99. © 2014 Johns Hopkins University Press and the University of North Texas. Reprinted with permission of Johns Hopkins University Press.

1. Fredric Jameson argues that the Althusserian ideology is "a representational structure which allows the individual subject to conceive or imagine his or her lived relationship to transpersonal realities such as the social structure or the collective logic of History." Fredric Jameson, *The Political Unconscious: Narrative as a Socially Symbolic Act* (Ithaca: Cornell University Press, 1981), 30. Terry Eagleton evaluates the Althusserian ideology in a similar manner: "Ideology is not primarily a matter of 'ideas': it is a structure which imposes itself upon us without necessarily having to pass through consciousness at all. Viewed psychologically, it is less a system of articulated doctrines than a set of images, symbols and occasionally concepts which we 'live' at an unconscious

level." Terry Eagleton, *Ideology: An Introduction* (London: Verso, 1991), 148–9. Based upon these arguments, one can argue that the Althusserian ideology refers to a process of social integration through which individuals recognize, negotiate with, and sometimes internalize the dominant ideas of society. I will use the term "ideology" strictly in the Althusserian sense, particularly in positing liberal individualism as one of the dominant ideologies of the U.S.

2. Louis Althusser, *For Marx*, trans. Ben Brewster (New York: Random House, 1969), 231.
3. Louis Althusser, *Lenin and Philosophy and Other Essays* (New York: Monthly Review Press, 2001), 118.
4. Sacvan Bercovitch, *The Rites of Assent: Transformations in the Symbolic Construction of America* (New York: Routledge, 1993), 355. Subsequent quotations are cited parenthetically within the text.
5. Joseph Epstein, "A Conspiracy of Silence," *Harper's* (November 1977): 80; 77–92.
6. David S. Gross, "Tales of Obscene Power: Money and Culture, Modernism and History in the Fiction of E. L. Doctorow," in Richard Trenner, ed., *E. L. Doctorow: Essays and Conversations* (Princeton: Ontario Review Press, 1983), 138,128.
7. "Interview with Paul Levine," in Trenner, ed., *E. L. Doctorow*, 57.
8. "Interview with Richard Trenner," in Trenner, ed., *E. L. Doctorow*, 52.
9. Bimbisar Irom, "Between 'Retreat' and 'Engagement': Incomplete Revolts and the Operations of Irony in E. L. Doctorow's *The Book of Daniel*," *Studies in American Fiction*, 39.1 (Spring 2012): 81.
10. Given that conspiracy theory is often based upon the paranoid view that a hidden world order is secretly controlling individuals, the notion of paranoia has been the central issue in discussing the mechanisms of conspiracy theory. According to Sigmund Freud, paranoia can be defined as a hyper-hermeneutic act. See Sigmund Freud, *The Standard Edition of the Complete Psychological Works of Sigmund Freud*, ed. James Strachey (23 vols., London: Hogarth Press, 1953), vol. 7. Freud's comment on Schreber indicates that paranoid subjects withdraw themselves from "the catastrophic" world that they interpret as threatening the self, and in doing so, the normal relation between them and the world goes awry: "[T]he end of the world is the projection of this internal catastrophe; for his subjective world has come to an end since he has withdrawn his love from it" (70). Another important theorist to note in this matter is Richard Hofstadter. See Richard Hofstadter, *The Paranoid Style in American Politics and Other Essays* (Cambridge, MA: Harvard University Press, 1996). Although his criticism on conspiratorial paranoia strictly focuses on the conservative atmosphere of 1960s America (in particular, Barry Goldwater's presidential nomination in the Republican Party) and thus it has lost its critical momentum in historical terms, it might be still worth mentioning his

theory because it is one of the earliest to add the political dimension of conspiracy theory to psychological paranoia. For Hofstadter, the biggest problem that conspiracy theory engenders is that its political view seriously cripples the principles of consensus democracy: "The paranoid tendency is aroused by a confrontation of opposed interests which are totally irreconcilable, and thus by nature not susceptible to the normal political process of bargain and compromise" (39). In both cases, conspiracy theory/paranoia is viewed as a pathologized state in which one fails to perceive the "proper" working order of the world (which is normalized psychological adaptation to the world and the democratic decision-making processes, respectively) through the distorted lens of conspiratorial fear.

11. Mark Fenster, *Conspiracy Theories: Secrecy and Power in American Culture* (Minneapolis: University of Minnesota Press, 1999), xii.
12. Daniel Hellinger, "Paranoia, Conspiracy, and Hegemony in American Politics," in Harry G. West and Todd Sanders, eds., *Transparency and Conspiracy: Ethnographies of Suspicion in the New World Order* (Durham: Duke University Press, 2003), 206.
13. Fredric Jameson, *The Geopolitical Aesthetic: Cinema and Space in the World System* (Bloomington: Indiana University Press, 1992), 2–3.
14. Fredric Jameson, "Reification and Utopia in Mass Culture," *Social Text*, 1 (Winter 1979): 144.
15. Michel Foucault, *Power/Knowledge: Selected Interviews and Other Writings 1972–1977*, trans. Colin Gordon, Leo Marshall, John Mepham, and Kate Soper (New York: Pantheon Books, 1980), 82.
16. E. L. Doctorow, "False Documents," in Trenner, ed., *E. L. Doctorow*, 17.
17. Ibid., 26.
18. "Interview with Paul Levine," 69.
19. "A Spirit of Transgression," Interview with Larry McCaffery, in Trenner, ed., *E. L. Doctorow*, 46.
20. E. L. Doctorow, *The Book of Daniel* (New York: Plume, 1996), 72–3. Subsequent parenthetical citations refer to this edition.
21. Susan Brienza, "Writing as Witnessing: The Many Voices of E. L. Doctorow," Ben Siegel, ed., *Critical Essays on E. L. Doctorow* (New York: G. K. Hall & Co., 2000), 193–215
22. Timothy Melley, *Empire of Conspiracy: The Culture of Paranoia in Postwar America* (Ithaca: Cornell University Press, 2000), 25.
23. Robert Alan Goldberg, *Enemies Within: The Culture of Conspiracy in Modern America* (New Haven: Yale University Press, 2001), 240.
24. Fenster, *Conspiracy Theories*, 112–13.
25. Patrick O'Donnell, *Latent Destinies: Cultural Paranoia and Contemporary U.S. Narrative* (Durham: Duke University Press, 2000), 17, 19.
26. Ibid., 13.
27. Robert N. Bellah, Richard Madsen, William M. Sullivan, Ann Swindler,

and Steven M. Tipton, *Habits of the Heart: Individualism and Commitment in American Life* (Berkeley: University of California Press, 1996), 142.

28. For the historical narratives of conspiracy theory, see David Brion Davis, ed., *The Fear of Conspiracy: Images of Un-American Subversion from the Revolution to the Present* (Ithaca: Cornell University Press, 1979), which is an excellent collection of documents written by contemporaries of various conspiracies from 1773 to 1968.

29. With the common interest in liberal democracy, Americanness in the genre turns into something similar to an "empty signifier." Ernesto Laclau employs the term to explain the role of liberal democracy within political movements. See Ernesto Laclau, "Constructing Universality," in Judith Butler, Ernesto Laclau, and Slavoj Žižek, eds., *Contingency, Hegemony, Universality: Contemporary Dialogues on the Left* (London: Verso, 2000), 281–307. For him, liberal democracy as the ultimate and common goal for all political movements constitutes "the empty signifier" or "the floating signifier" (305), in the sense that its universality is maintained without being reduced to concrete and local aims (such as women's liberation, class struggles, racial equality, or national independence). This idea is part of Laclau's well known concept of hegemonic struggle: the empty universality of liberal democracy is a site where each particular group comes together and forms a hegemonic bloc. At some level, liberal democracy in conspiracy theory functions like Laclau's concept, to which people with different goals commonly subscribe. In the case of conspiracy theory, however, the matter of universality brings about a more complicated situation. As liberal democracy becomes an empty signifier, the two groups with competing interests and opposite national visions claim that it is they who truly represent Americanness and therefore the other is the nation's enemy. There are indeed numerous examples in American history on this matter. To take one example, conspiracy narratives from the anti- and the pro-slavery camp were constructed in a strikingly similar way: by commonly appealing to American values. William Goodell and James Paulding, an anti- and a pro-slavery activist respectively, appropriated the same principles, such as "civil liberty" and "rights of the people," for their own political agendas. See William Goodell, "Slavery at War with Our Liberties," in Davis, ed., *The Fear of Conspiracy*, 109–11; James Kirke Paulding, "Abolitionism Is the Product of a Foreign Plot," in Davis, ed., *The Fear of Conspiracy*, 135–8. When the former argues that "the continuation of the slave system must of necessity involve the loss of liberty to the free" (110), the latter replies that "abolitionists are marked by an utter disregard, a ferocious hostility to those laws and institutions . . . to the existence of civil government and the principles of liberty" (137). Thus understood, one might argue that liberal democracy as an empty signifier has also

a rhetorical function in conspiracy theory, through which one posits oneself as a true heir of Americanism while condemning the opponent as a conspirator.

30. Davis, ed., *The Fear of Conspiracy*, xxiii.
31. "Interview with Paul Levine," 57.
32. "Interview with Trenner," 55; emphasis in original.
33. The idea of social injustice concealed beneath the nation's presumed innocence is a continuing theme in Doctorow's works. Williams, an African-American garbage collector, lives in the cellar of the Isaacson house. Although his story is purely anecdotal and thus has nothing to do with the plot of *The Book of Daniel*, it enriches Doctorow's notion of the concealed injustice of American society. Daniel is curious yet fearful about Williams because he always detects "the smell of his [Williams's] constant anger" (90). The fact that Williams lives in a cellar further symbolizes the invisible yet nonetheless existing understructure of American society. Anticipating the Black Power Movement as well as the Civil Rights Movement of the next decade, Doctorow describes Williams's unseen presence as an unsettling element capable of shaking the very foundations of the house. Listening to the rattling sound of Williams sorting garbage cans in the cellar, Daniel imagines it to be "like a storm under the earth, like a storm that would raise the foundation of the house" (91). A similar idea is presented in *Ragtime*. The novel begins with the remark that "[t]here was no Negroes. There were no immigrants" in turn-of-the-century America (3–4). This remark is, however, soon negated by Coalhouse Walker, an African-American, whose Model T Ford is vandalized by Irish workers. After a series of futile attempts to amend the problem within the boundary of law, he becomes an anarchist and declares a one-man war against the society that does not allow him to get justice within the system. As is the case with Williams, Doctorow dramatizes Coalhouse's experience by contrasting it to the innocent surface of American society, "the smiling face of America".
34. Bercovitch, *The Rites of Assent*, 16.
35. In order to discuss the peculiar dimension of American liberal individualism, it might be helpful to turn first to the origin of the term "individualism." Raymond Williams makes a distinction between individuality and individualism in the European usage. "Individuality," which signals the break from the European medieval order, conveys primarily two meanings—the uniqueness of each individual, and the indivisible unity with a certain group/society. "Individualism" was coined much later, by a French theocrat, Joseph de Maistre, who saw French society dominated by "deep and frightening division of minds, the infinite fragmentation of all doctrines . . . carried to the most absolute individualism." Cited in Richard O. Curry and Lawrence B. Goodheart, eds., *American Chameleon: Individualism in Trans-national Context*

(Kent: Kent State University Press, 1991), 13. According to Williams, what makes individualism different from individuality is its lack of indivisible character: its primary concern is not communal good but individual interests and freedom. Under this circumstance, the reception of individualism was harsh in Europe, mainly due to its failure to embrace individuality. Alexis de Tocqueville argues that individualism tends toward social dissolution, for it "disposes each citizen to isolate himself from the mass of his fellows . . . [H]e gladly leaves the greater society to look after itself." See Alexis de Tocqueville, *Democracy in America*, trans. Henry Reeve (New York: Schocken, 1961 [two vols., 1835, 1840]), 506. In stark contrast, individualism was well received in the U.S., to the extent that it had become a national identity. Forty years after de Tocqueville, James Bryce observed that "individualism, the love of enterprise, and the pride in personal freedom, have been deemed by Americans not only their choices, but their peculiar and exclusive possessions." Cited in Yehoshua Arieli, "Individualism and National Identity," in Curry and Goodheart, eds., *American Chameleon*, 167. Also, and perhaps more interestingly, American individualism has developed into a mixture of individualism and individuality. As we will see soon in Patell's argument, American liberal individualism combines negative liberty (individualism) and positive liberty (individuality as the indivisible unity with society).

36. Cyrus R. K. Patell, *Negative Liberties: Morrison, Pynchon, and the Problem of Liberal Ideology* (Durham: Duke University Press, 2001), 14.
37. Ibid., 19.

Chapter 6

"A Rearrangement of Molecules": On Doctorow's Perpetual Motion Machines

Julian Murphet

Freaks

"Freak" is a term of endearment, or not quite, in *The Book of Daniel*, a generational badge of honor, and in the mouth of Artie Sternlicht, it is almost a program.

> "You've got PLP down here, and a W. E. B. Du Bois, and the neighborhood reformers, and Diggers like me, and some black destruct groups, and every freak thing you can think of. Eventually we'll put it together, we'll get our shit together. All the freaks will get it together. Then we won't be freaks anymore. Then we'll be a clear and present danger."[1]

To be a freak in the end days of the 1960s is ontologically to be pre- or proto-revolutionary, a Rancièresque "part of no part" unhinged from the national myth but not yet fused into any more meaningful totality—jetsam and flotsam of the left, adrift in the fallow period of economic contraction and mounting crisis. It is for Sternlicht a potent political waiting game, a coalescence-to-come: "When the Federales wake up and see I'm not just some crazy acid-head, when they see that all the freaks are together and putting it together we will be set up for the big hit or the big bust or both," as he puts it (156–7). But that isn't what the novel itself thinks, since it isn't what Daniel thinks, who treads delicately around the freaks of the New Left in his excruciating progress back to the Old Left, represented by his martyred parents. And it isn't what history was to have thought either. The freaks, after all, remained trapped in their dissociation, by the FBI as much as by their own lack of cohesion.

In fact, the most striking freak of this novel is Daniel's sister, Susan, quondam comrade of Sternlicht, but whose hospitalized apotheosis as a *starfish* is perhaps the novel's most powerful single image: "Today

Susan is a starfish. Today she practices the silence of the starfish. There are few silences deeper than the silence of the starfish. There are not many degrees of life lower before there is no life" (213). This degree of physical and mental aberration, her proximity to the remoter territories of the animal kingdom, associates Susan with the carney folk with whom Joe works in *Loon Lake*—the "Living Oyster," the "Wolf Woman," and of course "Fanny the Fat Lady," who meets her terrible end as a moonlighting employee of the Hearn Bros. carnival's travelling freak show. Their distance from the human, however, turns out not to be the most remarkable thing about them. "There was about all of them," remarks Joe, "freaks and family, such competence that you almost wondered how normal people got along. There was a harmony of malformation and life that could only scare the shit out of you if you thought about it."[2] In the right, outcast conditions, freaks attain a dangerous, even terrifying "harmony" with one another, a solidarity that imperils the consistency of the surrounding social formation. It doesn't make them particularly likable. "The Fingerlings were mean little bastards, they were not really a family but who could tell? They all had these little pug faces. They used to get into fights all the time and only the dwarf could do anything with them" (21). These are midgets, and there will be more to say about them; the striking thing here is their air of violent menace, rendered in starkest relief by their degree of disconnection from society at large.

The freaks' "harmony of malformation" extends to the world of *Ragtime*, too, where it manifests at the soirée of Mrs. Stuyvesant Fish amid the "[c]reatures with scaled iridescent skins and hands attached to their shoulders, midgets with the voices of telephones, Siamese twin sisters who leaned in opposite directions, a man who lifted weights from iron rings permanently attached to his breasts," in fact, "the entire sideshow of the Barnum and Bailey circus."[3] Their presence triggers an ethic of solidarity in the evening's star performer, Harry Houdini (former circus employee), who, charmed backstage by Lavinia Thumb, "the widow of General Tom Thumb, the most famous midget of all" (32), extemporizes a routine for the circus folk instead of the assembled ruling class. Later, the little girl and the Little Boy visit the freak show at Atlantic City, walking "quietly among the exhibition stalls of the Bearded Lady, the Siamese Twins, the Wild Man from Borneo, the Cardiff Giant, the Alligator Man, the Six-Hundred-Pound Woman" (195), and realizing a thrilling affinity with these creatures of a parallel world.

At the world's fair of *World's Fair*, Edgar Altschuler takes his girl Meg to the Odditorium, "where the freaks were shown, terrible-looking poor beasts . . .: a half-bearded man/lady . . .; something that had fur all over its body; male Siamese twins joined at the hip; a man with enormous webbed feet; a man who claimed to be made of rubber and who proved it by suspending heavy weights from rings in his chest . . .; a woman in a basket who had no arms or legs, just little flippers at the shoulders and hips, which were covered with woolen pink gloves and pink booties; and so on."[4] And then, more wonderful still, Little Miracle Town, "the community of midgets":

> The midgets were grown-ups, they acted with all the assurance and confidence of grown-ups—they really ran things all by themselves—except that they were tiny, with tiny voices as if they talked through telephones. They had little pug faces, like Mickey Rooney. They looked up in your face and patronized you. (264)

The extensive repetitions and overlaps are all to the point here. We get the sense of an *idée fixe*, an authorial obsession that Doctorow is obliged to revisit, in almost identical terms, from text to text, like Beckett's silhouettes of father and son, or Faulkner's spotted horses. Even Homer, the blind narrator of *Homer & Langley*, identifies with "Quasimodo, the hunchback of Notre Dame—this poor defective."[5] In Doctorow's work, being a freak means being branded, herded, exhibited, and above all *exploited* by the eye of normality; set apart from the world, having it put at a distance, so that its gaze might be felt in all its ambivalently sentimental malevolence.

All of which comes full circle in *Andrew's Brain*. When Andrew absconds with Briony, the "girl of [his] dreams," and she takes him to visit her parents in "a little seaside town about an hour south of Los Angeles," he little expects the company awaiting him.[6] Too "politically correct" to refer to them as midgets, Andrew opts for "Diminutives" as his term of reference. These Diminutives, Bill and Betty, are especially eloquent in the space of the Doctorow canon, serving as belated mouthpieces for the accumulating political unconscious of his career-long litany of freaks. Displaying remarkable literary perspicacity for an uneducated entertainer, Bill heaps scorn on Mark Twain's fudged ending of *Huckleberry Finn* and proceeds to offer a penetrating analysis of L. Frank Baum's *The Wizard of Oz* as an allegory:

> "See, what the moral is, is don't rely on me, don't trust me, my rule is a scam, you've got the stuff to run things yoursels. You and your comrades. All you got to do to take over is get up your courage, use your brain, everones your equal, 'cept for some at the top, of course, and the world's your oyster. That's communist allegory, according to some." (73)

This pugnacious left hermeneut also knows precisely where the cardinal points of his allegorical exegesis are grounded, in his own experience:

> "The yellow brick road, well, that's the way to the gold. The Wicked Witch, well, she's the West, you see, meaning us, and with all those flying monkeys being her military forces, if you don't do something she will be even worse than the phony Wizard. And I know who the Munchkins stand for. Believe me, I'm the authority on that." (73)

In the company of these Diminutives and their like-sized comrades, who end up doing various vaudeville numbers, Andrew finds himself subject to that most unexpected of American emotions, "almost too much to bear—happiness. I felt it as something expressed from my heart and squeezing out of my eyes" (75). Seeking the truth of this experience, one of the most joyous in all Doctorow, Andrew learns that Bill and Betty met as part of a touring ensemble in Europe, Leo Singer's Lilliputians. The show was "essentially vaudeville . . . Circus acts like jugglers, and wire walkers, people who could play the fiddle behind their back, everything you could think of. The attraction was their size and how many things they could do anyway that people would come to see and marvel at" (77). It is just as Joe thinks of the freaks in *Loon Lake*, and as Edgar and Meg do in *World's Fair*: they can do everything we can do and more, and they're only two feet tall! Disadvantage is dialectically transformed into advantage—*better than*, not lesser than. But like Joe, who comes to focus on Sim Hearn as the able-bodied impresario of the operation—"His real genius was in freak dealing. Where did he get them? Could they be ordered?" (22)—so too Andrew turns his thoughts to Leo Singer himself, "Clearly an operator who infantilized these people, made a spectacle of them, and made himself a fortune in the process" (78) by dealing Munchkins to Hollywood. Under that aegis, joy gives way to its opposite, searing thoughts of "serfdom, indentured oppression . . . Baiting bears, that's what I mean, the European culture of bearbaiting. Freak taunting. Jew killing" (79).

It turns on a dime, this affective ambiguity of the freaks in Doctorow. On the one hand, a swelling and nameless pleasure: the delight taken in sheer cooperative capability and aesthetic harmony as performed by agents not fully human, and therefore somehow more than human. On the other, the long shadow of atrocious exploitation, a market in bodies, the invidious ethics of the spectacle, and what such perfected harmony in the spotlight reflects back at its violent and predatory social environment. The "communist allegory" that Bill spins out of Baum's classic befits his station as the single most articulate spokesperson for the community of freaks dispersed among the novels of E. L. Doctorow. "I know who the Munchkins stand for. Believe me, I'm the authority on that." Who would doubt it? But do we? Have we been in any position to make sense of the eternal return of these figures in book after book of the Doctorow oeuvre, who must, after all, and precisely because they insist on reappearing, stand for something more than themselves in an allegory we have yet properly to disambiguate?

Some orientation might come from one of the stories assembled in *Lives of the Poets*, which Douglas Fowler described as "a study in the official American police attitude."[7] This is "The Leather Man," and is unusual for Doctorow in taking, exclusively, the police or FBI as its vocal home base. One of the authorities, a theorist of surveillance and control, is speculating about a rise in the temperature of the left, not in its official parties and institutions, but, far more menacingly, in a sort of collective unconscious, slowly knitting itself together among the disassembled and disenfranchised, the drifting lumpens and isolates of the Imperium: "what is new is the connection they're making with each other, some kind of spontaneous communication has flashed them into awareness of each other, and hell, they may as well have applied to the national endowment as a living art form."[8] Again we find the same link that Joe makes between the cooperation of misfits, the aesthetic dimension, and a nebulous political danger to the status quo; and the network of aesthetic-political affects that Bill, the Diminutive, distils from Baum and the variety theatre. Its reiteration in the mouth of the police, however, has the singular advantage of forcing a nomination, obliging the spectral menace to take explicit conceptual form in order to be surveilled and infiltrated. Articulating a lay theory of *ostranenie*, the speaker tries to capture what it is to live as a freak or "Leather Man" on the fringes of the social order: "What is the essential act of the Leather Man? He makes the world foreign. He distances it. He is estranged. Our perceptions are sharpest when we're estranged. We can see the shape of things" (74). The types who belong to this class of spontaneous political formalists are as follows:

> 0001. MEMBERS OF THE CLASS: feral children, hermits, street people, gamblers, prisoners, missing persons, forest-fire wardens, freaks, permanent invalids, recluses, autistics, road tramps, the sensory deprived. (See also astronauts) (70)

And there is our keyword buried in a list of what looks like a partial *dramatis personae* of the Doctorow universe; it is, if you like, that universe with all the celebrities and impresarios turned down. And now, thanks to the necessity of forcing a name in the police order of things, we begin to see what our suspected allegory might be about. The "freak" is the emblematic representative of a much larger class in Doctorow's fiction, a distributed underclass of misfits and the unfit, non-belongers who never put down roots because it is their function to tramp, tour, disappear, and reappear in the fluorescent panopticon of the large metropolis only as a smear or blur in one's peripheral vision. Once it is named, too, there is no stopping the viral contaminations of its logic, which can apply even to the brutalizers themselves:

> Your feelings are broken down by plurality, you don't stop, you keep moving, it becomes your true life to keep moving, to keep moving emotionally, you find finally the emotion in the movement. You are the Leather Man, totally estranged from your society, the prettiest women are rocks in the stream, flowers along the road, you have subverted your own life and live alone in the world, your only companion your thoughts. (74)

The principle at stake is finally named here, "to keep moving," and we shall see now that it offers the most important key to the oeuvre as a whole, and endows the freaks with their ultra-representational function as the self-subverted community most subject to *the imperatives of collective movement*. The freak show must be propelled forward, from town to town, to promote its novelty and scandal afresh in each location; and with it evolves a backstage ethical life that has nothing to do with exploitation or profit, a communal "harmony of malformation" that irradiates everything it genuinely touches, and fuels the engines of a "communist allegory" that nobody who is gripped by its spectacle can fully disavow. It is, of course, with the young that it leaves the deepest political impressions.

Movement vs. Stasis

All this allows us to aver that there is a fundamental dialectic in Doctorow's spatial imagination, that I can characterize no better than to describe it in terms of an alternation between inveterate patterns of belonging and errant trajectories of passage. There are certain novels devised to articulate and occupy a given space: *Welcome to Hard Times*, *World's Fair*, much of *Billy Bathgate*, *The Waterworks*, the present-tense of *City of God*, and *Homer & Langley*. These last five, indeed, mark Doctorow out fair as one of the greatest novelists of the greater New York metropolitan area, and their prodigious reconstructions of vanished urban worlds demonstrate the virtuous fixity of his spatial understanding of the United States. He distils a national essence out of a square mile, or, in the case of *Homer & Langley*, a single townhouse. Perhaps this last novel can stand as a type of the very principle here: a novel so enclosed upon itself spatially that it is forced to express an entire, prolonged episode of national history, in a bravura demonstration of the novelist's powers to pull imaginary rabbits out of real hats.

But then there are the novels which pull in the opposite direction, away from spatial fixes, and toward a logic of sheer mobility and flux whose aesthetic exhilarations are unlike those of any other American writer in my experience, above all *Ragtime* and *The March*, but also very much including the geographical restlessness of *The Book of Daniel* and the drifting center of gravity formed by Joe in *Loon Lake*, as well as the delightful spatial eccentricities of *Andrew's Brain*. From the perspective created by this remarkable motility of the narrative engine, the previous emphasis on spatial rootedness appears deathly and entropic, condensed into that terrible figure of the starfish in *The Book of Daniel* already mentioned:

> Slowly her legs spread, her feet slide over the mattress and her toes hook into the crevice between the mattress and the spring. Her arms move outward; her hands curl over the edge of the mattress and find the same ledge. She holds her bed in her hands and by her ankles. (213)

Susan's stillness might associate her figuratively with the freaks in the street, but medically it amounts to a kind of death in life, an asymptotic approach to the horizon of the inorganic, a lowering of becoming into mere being. Against this rictus of fixity, we have Daniel's insatiable desire for movement at all costs, his traversal of the continent itself, in a quest for liberty, understood as the negation of his parents' arrest, imprisonment, and electrocution.

This tension between spatial arrest and agitated movement can be felt as a molar dialectic across Doctorow's body of work; but it is implicit as well in the architecture of individual novels, as best seen in what I take to be the singular formal masterpiece of his career, namely *Loon Lake*, whose unique aesthetic success consists (on this reading) in its internalization of the dialectic at issue. For *Loon Lake* dramatizes the contradiction between stasis and movement, and goes a long way toward establishing that contradiction as perhaps the definitive alternating current of Doctorow's fiction. Joe himself is precisely a drifter, an itinerant autodidact in the great *Bildungs* tradition of Doctorow's voracious young narrators—his Billys, Edgars, and Daniels. Joe's restless itinerary and association with the freaks of the traveling show, his tendency to skate across the surface of things, meet their structurally opposing principle in the sprawling compound of Loon Lake itself, landed property as a signature of capitalist success and the promise of its dynastic succession. Property translates the American drive to accumulate into security and privilege, and insofar as it arrests the free-floating trajectory of Joe's quest for experience, it infects his own drive with the dangerous fantasy of its metamorphosis into *fame*—surely one of the most enduring thematic preoccupations across Doctorow's novels. *Loon Lake* turns upon this structural antagonism between landedness and homelessness, wealth and freedom, property and drift, an opposition undone by the fact that wherever he goes in corporate America, Joe invariably comes face to face again with F. W. Bennett, Loon Lake's ubiquitous landlord, whose property (in an allegory of capitalism itself) extends in every direction and makes a mockery of free movement. The breathtaking final page stages the fateful conversion of drift into duration, affiliative wandering into filiative persistence in place, that is so characteristic of Doctorow's cynicism as a political writer. So many of his "capable boys" (and even Tateh himself) turn into ruthless businessmen, captured by a principle of stillness that internalizes "restlessness" as a different kind of endless dynamic: the profit motive.

It is worth pointing out in passing that Doctorow's signature women characters, Clara Lukacs, Drew Prescott, and Evelyn Nesbit, are perfectly amoral creatures of transcendental homelessness (Clara is a Lukacs for a reason).[9] Like Poe's quintessential figure of the Man in the Crowd, these women move hungrily from place to place to soak up the intensities of this or that cluster of people, this or that lover, before moving on once more. They personify the novels' exceptional interest in what does not stay still, in what moves without a thought for duration or, indeed, character as such. And in that, they represent, in part, precisely money itself, that restless circulating medium of exchange that stays still at its own peril; as indeed Emma Goldman explicitly tells Evelyn Nesbit in a crushing character analysis.[10] But this means that they represent movement and circulation in a very different way from the young men, who are ambivalent figures of a metamorphic *Bildung*, their early impulsive transience finally transmogrifying into the terrible stasis and stature befitting a leader of men in the corporate state.

But now is a good time to insist that this dialectic between mobility and stasis is everywhere being disrupted, not only by the representational principle of money and accumulation, but by a higher-order opposition, between property and rent. The painstakingly recreated streetscapes of the Bronx in *The Book of Daniel*, *World's Fair*, and *Billy Bathgate* carry within them a virus of instability and incipient eviction occasioned by the fact that neither the Isaacsons, the Altschulers, nor the so-called "Bathgates" own property in the first place. As renters of modest lower-middle or working-class domiciles, these families are exposed to an imperative of displacement and impermanence that affects the descriptive economy of the prose, always spring-loaded with a surcharge of nostalgia predicated on loss. Indeed, the Isaacsons are removed to prison and their children scattered, the Altschulers (of *World's Fair*) are forced by economic circumstances to relocate to a new apartment building in a less salubrious part of town, and the "Bathgates" await either the ruin or the redemption of Billy's unsentimental education.

The main tradition of American literature has, by and large, preferred not to think about rent; its obsession with property, ownership, small towns, and suburbs has tended to blind it to the motley instabilities and anxieties associated with the modern urban rental economy. In an economy of domestic ownership and inheritance, something like Bachelard's "poetics of space" is able to flourish for literature, and the passional networks that make literary forms endure through acts of commemoration and naming. In Doctorow, too, the upscale home in New Rochelle where *Ragtime*'s Family lives,[11] the Collyer mansion on upper Fifth Avenue where the action of *Homer & Langley* takes place, the august Romanesque mansion—"very substantial, lending substance to those who lived there"[12]—where the mysteries of *The Waterworks* are resolved, not to mention the estate of Loon Lake itself: these properties are, if you like, "owner-occupied," and are not subject to the fluctuating rates of return that speculators in property seek to stabilize through a machinery of absolute exploitation. "Land and property rent in central locations," writes David Harvey, "does not arise out of the land's marginal productivity but out of the processes which permit absolute and, even more importantly, monopoly rents to be charged."[13] To be a renter in the modern American city is to be subject to a logic of exploitation that unseats the denizen from the very concept of place; it is to be ceaselessly offered up to a precarity and a structural violence that issues from the conjoined threats of eviction and cyclical rent increases. It is a logic that the renter-protagonist of Pynchon's *Inherent Vice* finds crystallized in the perfect scorn of his class enemy, Crocker Fenway: "People like you lose all claim to respect the first time they pay anybody rent."[14] But it is felt, on the whole, as an existential alienation from the very place where one dwells, and from the communities of which one is a part.

In Doctorow's novels, it turns out that the best way to inhabit such a rental economy is by way of a phenomenological internalization of the

principle of drift itself: not to sink roots into the concrete jungle, but to
flit through it like the homeless shadow you are always about to become,
and look back at it with an element of wonder. This discovery of the
unheimlich within the *heimlich* receives no better treatment than in the
extraordinary episode of the *Hindenburg* zeppelin as it floats grandly
above Edgar Altschuler's world on Mt. Eden Avenue:

> My mouth dropped open. She sailed incredibly over the housetops, and
> came right toward me, just a few hundred feet in the air, and kept
> coming and kept coming and still no sight of the tail of her. She was
> tilted toward me as if she were an enormous animal leaping from the
> sky in monumental slow motion . . . She did not make the harsh raspy
> snarl of an airplane, but seemed to whisper. She was indeed a ship, a real
> ship in the sky. She moved like an airship. The enormity of her was out
> of scale with everything, out of scale with the houses and the cars on
> the street and the people now shouting and pointing and looking up; she
> was like a scoop of sky come down to earth, or a floating building, or a
> populated cloud. (156–7)

This, until the trip to the fair itself, is the signal event of the text of
World's Fair, a narrative book without a plot, and it raises the issue decisively: what if the novels of settled location, the books of Manhattan
and the Bronx and New Rochelle, are secretly orchestrated by a hovering
weightless logic of motion, peopled by a floating population of renters
able, as here, to project their condition onto the skies as a vision of
sublimity, a state of limitless exception? To be adrift above the streets, to
hover in motion as beneath you the buildings begin to look like so many
anchors and chains, is this not the very aspect of freedom implicit in the
anxiety of a rental economy?

It is a utopian suggestion, to be sure, but one that seems in deep
accord with the way these novels wage representational war against
the nightmare vampirism of property, as in *The Waterworks* or J. P.
Morgan's library in *Ragtime*, or indeed Loon Lake itself. Even the world
of Dutch Schultz, in *Billy Bathgate*, for all it is ringed round by vast
amounts of money and includes somewhere (though only speculatively)
actual property and real estate, is presented in this way: for the gang is
permanently "on the lam" with Dutch, moving from warehouse to hotel
to brothel in an effort to escape detection. It is a movable feast of vulgar
appetites and rash behavior, a lurid fantasy of working-class liberty that
will not settle into place, will not become a property. The gang is itself
a kind of doomed zeppelin, a spectacle of levitating rootless drift that
the rubes and street kids gawp at with the same mixture of awe and
dread. It is only Billy himself who, repeating the lesson of *Loon Lake*,

finally transforms this principle of chaotic dislocation into the settled propriety of a respectable bourgeois.

What, then, of the novels that openly embrace and model their own formal apparatus upon the economy of movement? We think here of two novels in particular: *Ragtime* and *The March*, surely Doctorow's most ambitious books and united in more ways than one at the formal level. They are fraternal volumes, twins even, in their giddy, kaleidoscopic applications of a narrative perpetual motion machine. Of *Ragtime* I want to mention only a couple of things, above all the sense throughout, evident in its breezy tone and paratactic delivery, of a novel built out of newspaper ephemerality, as though it were a scrapbook of illuminated vignettes arranged in loosely chronological sequence but with the sense that each page is a kind of center in its own right. This democratic equivalence of the materials, at least until the Coalhouse Walker plot assumes dominance, is also a refusal to establish any base of operations, even the very house itself: it is a resistance to the law of groundedness and a declaration of independence from propriety. Which is why this purported "historical novel" is really a species of fantasia, whose fundamental formal principle is the Ovidian one that the Little Boy learns from his classicist grandfather, a protean logic of metamorphosis and metaphor—"that the world composed and recomposed itself constantly in an endless process of dissatisfaction" (92)—whereby a bluebottle fly in your screen door can become a Model T car bearing the famous escape artist you've just been day-dreaming about to your very door. The formal principle that orchestrates the wildly improbable meetings and transitions between the locations and characters of this text is essentially the Freudian one of oneiric wish fulfillment: every conjunction that can be imagined is duly effected by the book's fantastical dream-work. *Ragtime*'s method is that of magical realism, its giddy phantasmagoria of the historical déjà vu a prodigious evasion of the reality principle. And that makes it the literary equivalent of crack cocaine, an utterly addictive satisfaction of the narrative erogenous zones.

If *Ragtime* achieves its miraculous narrative momentum on the basis of an economy of the dream-work, how does *The March*, its closest relative in the canon, manage its own formidable onward drive? The answer to that is, for once, squarely located in the material itself, since this is Doctorow's "war novel" and we are plunged helplessly into General William Tecumseh Sherman's famous military campaign to end the Civil War by sweeping through Georgia and up into the Carolinas. This means that the book is at liberty fully to indulge Doctorow's formal attraction to ceaseless narrative movement without either the resort to wish fulfillment or the corrective impulse of a restraint in property and real estate. For in the context of the great march, property has been annulled: there is only strategy, the military genius of flanking, feinting, amassing, possessing, consuming, discarding, and moving forward. Ancestral mansions and warehouses alike are treated as temporary billets, churches become field hospitals, bridges are burned, and the emancipated slaves are drawn into the vortex created by the army's rapid progress, like a river of landless humanity. Although from the outside it looks like one of the great anomalies of Doctorow's career, situated so far from the familiar haunts of the Five Boroughs, in fact *The March* serves as something like a *summa* of everything that animates this oeuvre with dynamism and drive. And as if in confirmation of this unique status, the book offers us the clearest signs of something like an all-embracing Balzacian or Faulknerian textual universe in Doctorow's fiction: for here is the father of Coalhouse Walker, falling in love on the march and founding the family that will bring the stalwart hero of *Ragtime* into the world; and here is Wrede Sartorius, immigrant medical genius and central character of *The Waterworks*, beginning his American career as a member of the great collective cast of this book. *The March* is a kind of origin myth for the entire Doctorow canon, sprung from the Civil War as the fault line in national space whence the whole effort emerges to map the American experiment as a tension between the freedom to roam and the proprietary subsumption of "primitive accumulation" in the legalisms of capital. But it also the only novel from which capital itself has been summarily banished. There is no money in this book; exchange value has been reverse engineered into barter and the economy of the gift. Property is reimagined as what you have to give to the ex-slaves in order to get them off your back: forty acres and a mule. And free at last from having to factor in what capital does to human relations, the narrative can openly declare its author's abiding passion, which is to say, movement and transformation as such.

Savannah, we read, "was alive with the movement of men and animals, so that it seemed as if the streets themselves were moving, that the city in its dimensions had come apart from the land and was fluttering loose in the blow."[15] In such a space, there is no further distinction between the city and the zeppelin that sails above it: the city has been raised to the status of what floats. Land is movement. In the early dialogue between Dr. Sartorius and Emily Thornton, things are clarified further:

> I confess I no longer find it strange to have no habitation, to wake up each morning in a different place, he said. To march and camp and march again. To meet resistance at a river or a hamlet and engage in combat. And then to bury our dead and resume the march.

You carry your world with you, Emily said.

Yes, we have everything that defines a civilization, Wrede said. We have engineers, quartermasters, commissary, cooks, musicians, doctors, carpenters, servants, and guns. You are impressed?

I don't know what to think. I've lost everything to this war. And I see steadfastness not in the rooted mansions of a city but in what has no roots, what is itinerant. A floating world.

It dominates, Wrede said.

Yes.

And in its midst you are secure.

Yes, Emily whispered, feeling at this moment that she had revealed something terribly intimate about herself. (61)

And something terribly intimate, we might feel, about the author himself, who here reveals his hand most completely. For what has his life's work been but a protracted effort to discover such "floating world[s]" within the cracks left by those "rooted mansions" that anchor a civilization down in chains of property? There is security, we learn, in the experience of being uprooted, set adrift in space, which now shines with meaning, the significance of the encounter; "transcendental home-lessness" becomes a new kind of home; when "you carry your world with you," you discover the steadfastness of a community (exactly like the freaks') completely transparent to itself, even as it constantly loses old cells and acquires new ones. But when it all begins to wind down, the campaign over because successful, the old world begins to stabilize once more, and the transient utopia of a world of Huck Finns, a floating world of trekking Jack Londons, dissipates, in the key of melancholy. Here is Sherman himself musing on what must now come to an end, which is to say, radiant spatial meaning as such:

> Though this march is done, and well accomplished, I think of it now, God help me, with longing—not for its blood and death but for the bestowal of meaning to the very ground trod upon, how it made every field and swamp and river and road into something of moral conse-quence, whereas now, as the march dissolves so does the meaning, the army strewing itself into the isolated intentions of diffuse private life, and the terrain thereby left blank and also diffuse, and ineffable, a thing once again, and victoriously, without reason, and, whether diurnally lit and darkened, or sere and fruitful, or raging or calm, completely in-sensible and without any purpose of its own. (359)

There are few moments as powerful as this in Doctorow's work. It is the novelist posing as the great military strategist, mourning that we are not constantly at war, which is to say, writing novels, making glorious meanings out of the insensible territories of a "diffuse private life." Against that dull re-establishment of the reality principle, he proposes the art of forgetting what is proper to you, and lighting out for the territory. Here at the novel's end is Stephen Walsh comforting little Pearl, whom Doctorow has reimagined from *The Scarlet Letter* as an emancipated child slave possessed of an innate nobility:

> He touched her face and brushed the tears. Nothing stays the same, he said. Not David, not Sartorius, not the army on the march, not the land it trod, not the living, and not even the dead. It's always now, Stephen said with a sad smile for poor Albion Simms [the man with the spike in his head who loses all short- and long-term memory]. (356)

In the Ovidian space where everything becomes something else, there is no history; it is always now. The spatial becomings that define the art of E. L. Doctorow precipitate the utopian amnesia of all radical transformations. On the march, provisional alliances are made and broken, love blooms and withers, care and responsibility are passed from one to the next, people assume new guises and forms, nothing is stable or permanent. So it is at last with all Doctorow's fiction, which promises (however distantly) the jubilee of a collective metamorphosis that cancels all debts and renews all relations.

"A rearrangement of molecules"

Ovid has his counterpart in modern physics, of course. Albert Einstein, one of the writer-narrator Everett's insistent ventriloquists in *City of God*, informs that book's radical ontology. Moving from the premise that "There is nothing in the universe that can be proven to move absolutely without reference to something else in the universe, or for that matter without reference to the universe in its entirety,"[16] Einstein is led to think about the planets, "about their formation—how, from amorphous furious swirls of cosmic dust and gas, everything spins out and cools and organizes itself into a gravitationally operating solar system . . . And that this has apparently happened elsewhere, that there are billions of galaxies and stars beyond number" (62), so that the novel itself can openly proclaim its protean, sacred-secular vision of our world as one tremendous Heraclitian fire and flux:

> The [tectonic] plates collide, ride over one another, crack, and great upheavals of the sea floor rise gasping into mountain ranges, enormous

volcanoes in the seafloor create islands that bob up in the oceans, the earth's crust quakes, shivers us into different shapes, we buckle and cleave, storms assail our heavens, our mountains shake thunderous avalanches of snow down upon our valleys, our Arctic and Antarctic ice floes crack like the bones of God, our wind-worn dunes of desert pile up to bury us, maniac tornadoes fling us about and thump us against the ground like rag dolls, great floods of viscous burning lava bury our villages, and in all this fury of planetary self-fulfillment, we spin about an axis and roll around the sun, and our oceans are pulled and pushed by lunar tides, our oceans roll in waves which exist apart from the water they pass through, our atmospheres are shot through with electromagnetic frequencies, and we stand abroad our terrains totally magnetized by the iron core at our center, with our skies at night tumbling with asteroids and flashing with the inflamed boreal particles of solar winds that flare like the luminous eyes of saber-toothed tigers circling the darkness beyond our fire. (82–3)

The rhetoric is equal to the thought: that all is in incessant movement and transformation, and can best be portrayed through the transformative figures of metaphor and simile. And there is nothing more threatening, more disabling, to the very idea of a police order of things, than that the world is woven of flux and impermanence, motion and dissolution. As Doctorow once said in an interview:

Einstein, for instance, infuriated the Nazis. Einstein was coming up with a universe in which nothing stayed the same very long. Things kept transforming and there was no space without time, and energy became mass and mass became energy. They saw all this relativism as a great threat to their psychic security.[17]

And so we return again to our police seminarian, grappling with a terrible foreboding about the new connections springing up, unconsciously, between the atomized members of a dispersed majority, trying to articulate "not a theory of a subversive class, but an infrastructure of layered subversion, perhaps not conspiracy at all. That something has happened like a rearrangement of molecules."[18]

Doctorow's art, I want to end by saying, was committed entirely and across its long arc to those subtle, sometimes imperceptible "rearrangements of molecule[s]" that can happen without a moment's notice on the basis of a cosmic constancy of movement at the level of the infrastructure, and which, now and then, with or without intention, break new figures out of the common ground. Where those figures might travel, how they will fare, and what degree of salience they are given to attain, are all entirely unpredictable. The forces of reification and "the isolated intentions of diffuse private life" work tirelessly to recapture and constrain the disorderly passages of these gleaming meteors of becoming: property and fame, the police order of things, death itself, all cloaking the great adventure in a logic of meaningless similitude, "the terrain thereby left blank and also diffuse, and ineffable, a thing once again." But the books exist, magnificently, to declare against all odds that *these freaks have lived* and drifted, striven and flared, against the blank terrain, and etched their passages in the stars that fall like glitter from these pages.

Notes

1. E. L. Doctorow, *The Book of Daniel* (London: Picador, 1982), 139. Subsequent quotations are cited parenthetically within the text for this title and after initial citations for the Doctorow volumes that follow.
2. E. L. Doctorow, *Loon Lake* (New York: Random House, 2007), 21.
3. E. L. Doctorow, *Ragtime* (London: Picador, 1985), 32.
4. E. L. Doctorow, *World's Fair* (New York: Random House, 2007), 263.
5. E. L. Doctorow, *Homer & Langley* (London: Little, Brown, 2009), 136.
6. E. L. Doctorow, *Andrew's Brain* (London: Little, Brown, 2014), 64.
7. Douglas Fowler, *Understanding E. L. Doctorow* (Columbia: University of South Carolina Press, 1992), 115.
8. E. L. Doctorow, *Lives of the Poets* (New York: Random House, 1984), 68.
9. Georg Lukács treats the subject of "transcendental homelessness" in his epochal study *Theory of the Novel*, trans. Anna Bostock (London: Merlin Press, 1971), 70–83.
10. "Somehow every dollar paid over to you has resulted in [Thaw's] profit. And you will be left with a finite amount of money that you will spend and waste until you are as poor as when you started." Doctorow, *Ragtime*, 71.
11. A reproduction of Doctorow's own home.
12. E. L. Doctorow, *The Waterworks* (New York: Random House, 2007), 156.
13. David Harvey, *Social Justice and the City* (revised edition; Athens: University of Georgia Press, 2009), 188.
14. Thomas Pynchon, *Inherent Vice* (London: Jonathan Cape, 2009), 346.
15. E. L. Doctorow, *The March* (New York: Random House, 2005), 123.
16. E. L. Doctorow, *City of God* (London: Little, Brown, 2000), 36.
17. Christopher D. Morris, ed., *Conversations with E. L. Doctorow* (Jackson: University Press of Mississippi, 1999), 70.
18. Doctorow, *Lives of the Poets*, 74.

Chapter 7

Cocks, Corsets, Clocks: E. L. Doctorow and the Tunnel of Love

Alexander Howard

Cocks

I want to open with an old-fashioned instance of resolutely down and dirty mudslinging. Here is Bo Weinberg's surprisingly creative and impressively detailed take on the presumed sexual proclivities of his business associate and soon-to-be executioner, the mobster Dutch Schultz:

> I didn't beg you, I told you to let the girl go. I spoke to you as if you were still human. But all you are is a cocksucker. And when you can't find a cock to suck you pick up scumbags off the floor and suck them. That's what I think of you, Dutch.[1]

What to make of these wonderfully evocative epithets? To begin, we should recall that Bo spits out these rich verbal formulations while bound and physically immobile, "sitting hunched over a chair there with his feet entubbed in the deckhouse of a boat running without lights past Coenties Slip across New York Harbor and into the Atlantic" (10). One could be excused—given the character's immediate predicament—for thinking this a remarkably poor choice of words. Indeed, one could also be forgiven for thinking that Bo could have picked a slightly better time to pick a fight with the man who—up until recently at least—has been paying his wages. All the more when one recalls that the employer in question has been known from time to time to rub the eyes of his enemies with rags smeared with the discharge from gonorrheal infections. In equal measure, however, this heroically suicidal act of last-ditch defiance makes a great deal of sense. Bo Weinberg is, after all, a well-liked man of great "spirit" (12). Yet there is more to the man's appeal than merely this. It turns out that this singular specimen is also something of a looker. Bo, we are told,

was a handsome man, with smooth shiny black hair combed back
without a part from a widow's peak, and a swarthy Indian sort of face
with high cheekbones, and a full well-shaped mouth and a strong chin,
all set on the kind of long neck that a tie and collar dresses very nicely.
Even hunched over in the shame of his helplessness, with his black tie
askew on his wing collar and his satiny black tuxedo jacket bunched
up above his shoulders, so that his posture was subservient and his
gaze necessarily furtive, he suggested to me the glamour and class of a
big-time racketeer. (12)

The "me" in these lines is the eponymous narrator of E. L. Doctorow's
mid-career masterpiece, *Billy Bathgate* (1989). There are a number
of things we might say about the wealth of information contained in
the passage just quoted. Certainly, there is much to be said as regards
the overtly homoerotic aspect of Billy's reflections. If so inclined, one
could feasibly make much of the close and loving attention that Billy
pays to Bo's face while describing him for the benefit of the reader.
Notice, in particular, the emphasis placed on the avowedly chiseled
quality of Bo's facial features during this dramatic moment. One might
also consider the manner in which Billy's eroticized description of Bo's
visage almost immediately starts to pitch into something approaching
the troubling condition of racialized objectification. And what are we
to make, finally, of the altogether abject nature of the disquieting and
sexualized scene being brought to life before the reader's very eyes?
Do not the references to shameful helplessness and necessarily furtive
subservience serve to complicate our understanding of Bo's traumatic
final moments? If nothing else, I think it entirely reasonable to argue
that something slightly strange seems to be going on at this specific
juncture in Doctorow's novel. But why choose to linger on this isolated
moment? The answer to that question is relatively straightforward and
speaks to the concerns of the present disputation. Put in the simplest
terms possible: this chapter strives to interrogate the hitherto overlooked
relationship in Doctorow's novels between conceptions of sexuality,
intimations and representations of erotic yearning, conceptions and accurately historicized performances and approximations of masculinity,
and occasionally geographically specific forms of political radicalism.
Moreover, I want in particular to bear down critically on moments such
as the one just mentioned because these passages hint at the presence
of what we can describe as a queer—and at times a queerly radical—
current that pulses almost undetected through many of Doctorow's
celebrated works. But before we turn our attention to certain of those
curious moments, scattered as they are throughout Doctorow's fictional
oeuvre, I propose first to say a little something about fashion and the

importance of personal style. I want to do so here as we shall have cause to revisit the topic of self-presentation on more than one occasion in this discussion.

As the expansively descriptive passage surveyed above suggests, the titular narrator of *Billy Bathgate* has a keen observational eye when it comes to the issue of sartorial flair, or lack thereof. Consider Billy's description of his notorious employer, the aforementioned Dutch. Put simply, the rather embarrassing fact of the matter is that

> even in his finest clothes Mr. Schultz seemed badly dressed, he suffered a sartorial inadequacy, as some people had weak eyes or rickets, and he must have known this because whatever else he was up to he would also be hiking up his trousers with his forearms, or lifting his chin while he pulled at his collar, or brushing cigar ashes from his vest, or taking off his hat and blocking the crown with the side of his hand. (12)

Dutch, clearly, is absolutely hopeless when it comes to the interrelated fields of personal grooming and individual dress-sense. "Without even thinking about it he tried constantly to correct his relationship to his clothes, as if he had some sort of palsy of dissatisfaction," Billy notes, "to the point where you thought everything would settle on him neatly enough if he would stop picking at it" (12). We can productively contrast these observations with Billy's subsequent reflections regarding the rather enigmatic figure of Harvey Drew, the first husband of the woman that our inquisitive narrator more often than not refers to as "Miss Lola Miss Drew" (46). Billy goes to great lengths when reminding us that we are dealing with an impressively large man,

> very well groomed in a tweed suit with a vest into the pocket of which he inserted his hand as if he had some sort of pain under the cloth, except that as he came toward me he didn't appear to be in pain, and in fact looked quite healthy and like a man who took care of himself. Not only that but he commanded respect, because without thinking I stepped out of his way. (42)

This passage serves to confirm what we already know: Billy likes to gaze at "very well groomed" men—particularly spruced up male subjects who take good care of their bodies. But why—to pose yet another question—focus on this well heeled minor character? The answer has less to do in this instance with attire, and more to do with what—or rather, *whom*—Harvey has been doing lately. Lest the reader of this postmodern *Bildungsroman* forget, Dutch has just asked Billy to keep an eye on Miss Lola Miss Drew. This Billy does with much alacrity and gusto, accompanying Lola all the way back to her suite at the Savoy-Plaza

Hotel in New York. This is where he meets the bowtie-wearing Harvey. Here is the passage in which Billy describes their initial encounter:

> I was left standing in this doorway looking into a room that was a private library with glass-enclosed bookcases and a tall leaning ladder that rolled on rails and an immense globe in its own polished wood framework, and light that came from two brass table lamps with green shades at either end of a soft sofa, on which were sitting two men side by side, one somewhat older than the other. What I found remarkable, the older was holding the younger's erect cock in his hand. (42)

Professing the view that it makes "things so much easier, living on an ex-planationless planet" (43), Billy casts his inquisitive gaze in the direction of Harvey's anonymous squeeze:

> With thumb and forefinger the fellow on the couch removed an anti-macassar from the sofa and dropped it over himself. He looked up and laughed in a way that suggested that we were complicitors, and I realized he was working-class, like me. I had not at first glance understood this. He appeared to be wearing mascara on his eyes, they were certainly bold and black eyes, and his black hair was slicked down without a part, and his bony wide shoulders were draped with the tied sleeves of a collegiate sweater with an argyle pattern of light maroon and gray. (43)

This deceptively rich and ambiguous piece of prose seems in a very real sense to be haunted by the dashing and alluring specter of Bo Weinberg. To start, notice how certain aspects of the description of Harvey's unnamed paramour chime with the earlier one proffered as regards Bo. I am thinking specifically in this instance of the line about the younger man's black hair being "slicked down" without any sort of parting. All we would need to complete the picture here is a widow's peak. Notice, too, the emphasis that Doctorow's narrator places in this passage on the "bold and black eyes" of the mascara-wearing young man currently sitting with his cock out. What are we to make of these arresting eyes of the very darkest hue? In a way, the presence of such light-absorbing organs of sight serve to yoke this passage with the aforementioned one about poor old Bo. That passage, as we have seen already, is full of references to the most brilliant of non-colors. Bo's "satiny" tuxedo and accompanying tie are most definitely black, as is his lustrous and "shiny" hair. But what of his eyes? Are these black too? Billy does not say. Perhaps he simply cannot see clearly enough. That was certainly the sense we got when reading that earlier passage. Recall also that Bo's posture in his final minutes, at least up to the moment when he lets rip in the general direction of Dutch Schultz, "was subservient and his gaze necessarily furtive." Bo was trying desperately, in other words, to keep his head down. Conversely, the black-eyed and laughing "fellow" positioned on Harvey's sofa is not looking down but rather up. How best to interpret the upturned facial gesture of this wide-shouldered proletarian complicitor? It strikes me as anything but furtive. In that case, then, perhaps we might describe it in terms of defiance or maybe even insouciance? Ultimately, it is difficult to say with certainty. What we *can* say with a degree of certainty, however, is that this gaze belongs to a young man who moves in social and sexual circles unfamiliar to Billy and far removed from those in which characters such as Bo Weinberg tend to mix.

We have here, in short, a fictional character who seems almost to have stepped directly out of the pages of George Chauncey's historical account of gay urban social and cultural life in New York City during the nineteenth and twentieth centuries. "In the half-century between 1890 and the beginning of the Second World War," Chauncey writes, "a highly visible, remarkably complex, and continually changing gay male world took shape in New York City."[2] This world, in Chauncey's reckoning, "included several gay neighborhood enclaves, widely publicized dances and other social events, and a host of commercial establishments where gay men gathered, ranging from saloons, speakeasies, and bars to cheap cafeterias and elegant restaurants" (1). But what, we might ask, of the queer subjects making their way through these urban milieus? "The men who participated in that world forged a distinctive culture with its own language and customs," Chauncey submits,

> its own traditions and folk histories, its own heroes and heroines. They organized male beauty contests at Coney Island and drag balls in Harlem; they performed at gay clubs in the Village and at tourist traps in Times Square. Gay writers and performers produced a flurry of gay literature and theater in the 1920s and early 1930s; gay impresarios organized cultural events that sustained and enhanced gay men's communal ties and group identity. Some gay men were involved in long-term monogamous relationships they called marriages; other participated in an extensive sexual underground that by the beginning of the century included well-known cruising areas in the city's parks and streets, gay bathhouses, and saloons with back rooms where men met for sex. (1)

Some men would have continued to meet in private. That much is assuredly obvious. Yet it also rather misses the point that Chauncey strives time and time again to make in these extracts and indeed throughout his crucial work of queer historical revisionism. "The gay world that flourished before World War II has been almost entirely forgotten in popular memory and overlooked by professional historians; it is not supposed to have existed. This book seeks to restore that world to history," Chauncey adds, "to chart its geography, and to recapture its culture and politics" (1). Two things stand out here. The first of these has to do with the interwoven issues of memorialization and historical effacement, and also—as we will see shortly—resonates when read in relation to certain of Doctorow's longstanding thematic preoccupations. The second point of interest here relates to the first and is site-specific. Eric Garber reminds us that in New York during

> the so-called Harlem Renaissance period, roughly 1920 to 1935, black lesbians and gay men were meeting each other on street corners, socializing in cabarets and rent parties, and worshipping in church on Sundays, creating a language, a social structure, and a complex network of institutions.[3]

Privileging as it did conceptions of inclusivity, the queer community that flourished in Harlem during this historical era attracted, in Garber's formulation, "white homosexuals as well as black, creating friendships between people of disparate ethnic and economic backgrounds and building alliances for progressive social change" (318–19). Inclusivity and progressive social change thus seem to have been the orders of the day in the equally queer enclave of Greenwich Village. Cristanne Miller foregrounds as much when reminding us of the fact that "Greenwich Village in the 1910s was home to New York's first visible middle-class gay subculture."[4] But it would be wrong to describe the queerly oriented Village as uniformly middle class. We need also to bear in mind at all times that Greenwich Village was, in the opening decades of the twentieth century, a veritable hotbed of class-based analysis and political radicalism. Step forward Emma Goldman.

This world-famous anarchist thinker and agitator was a prominent fixture and highly visible public figure in the Village. While living in lower Manhattan in the early twentieth century, Goldman edited the important feminist periodical *Mother Earth*. This monthly magazine—which ran between 1906 and 1917—sought to perform a number of functions. It strove, for instance, to concentrate public attention on questions pertaining to radical educational reform. "If education should really mean anything at all," Goldman asserts,

> it must insist on the free growth and development of the innate forces and tendencies of the child. In this way alone can we hope for the free

individual and eventually also for a free community, which shall make interference and coercion of human growth impossible.[5]

Pay close attention to the emancipatory language Goldman chooses to use here. I mention this as Goldman uses similar language when writing about the feminist struggle. "History tells us that every oppressed class gained liberation from its masters through its own efforts. It is necessary that woman learn from that lesson," Goldman declares, "that she realize that her freedom will reach as far as her power to achieve her freedom reaches" (167). There is, to be sure, a socio-sexual element to Goldman's analysis of the feminist movement in the United States. "Through these masterly psychological sketches one cannot help but see that the higher the mental development of woman," Goldman reasons,

> the less possible it is for her to meet a congenial mate who will see in her, not only sex, but also the human being, the friend, the comrade and strong individuality, who cannot and ought not lose a single trait of her character. (163–4)

This passage, which hints at a link between the birds and bees and possibilities of personal liberation, is typical of Goldman. Red Emma's understanding of sexuality comes more clearly to the fore in the following extract. "It is essential that we realize once and for all that man is much more of a sex creature than a moral creature. The former is inherent," Goldman posits in an unpublished piece on the question of modern schooling, "the other is grafted on. Whenever the dull moral demand conflicts with the sexual urge, the latter invariably conquers. But how? In secrecy, in lying and cheating, in fear and nerve-racking anxiety" (148). Goldman has no truck with hypocritical moralizing of this sort. "Verily, not in the sexual tendency lies filth," she continues, "but in the minds and hearts of the Pharisees: they pollute even the innocent, delicate manifestations in the life of the child" (148). The point that Goldman is making here is that bourgeois moralizing as regards sexuality always has negative psychological and physical consequences. This much becomes evident when Goldman turns her attention to the familiar yet elusive term that the philosopher Alain Badiou has attempted to wrest from the clutches of "the comfort zone limited by regulated pleasures," especially the clutches we tend to associate with life spent laboring under the sign of late capitalism.[6] "Love, which should be the impetus for the harmonious blending of two beings," Goldman opines in a turn of phrase that would not seem out of place in Badiou's twenty-first-century treatise on precisely the same topic, "today drives the two apart as a result of the young into an overwrought, starved, unhealthy sexual embrace" (149). How might we begin to rectify this starkly and depressingly unsatisfactory state of interrelated societal and sexual affairs? The solution that Goldman proffers is both far-reaching and refreshingly simple: rip it up and start again.

Still, I recognize that all this talk of education and emancipation in the essays of Emma Goldman might strike some as digressive. We seem, for a start, to be drifting away here from our earlier mentions of queerness as latent and manifest in the work of Doctorow. Equally, it is important to remember that initial appearances are more often than not fairly deceptive. Mark Steven, for one, suggests, in a formulation referring back to the earlier critical work of Raymond Williams, that a central thematic trope underpinning a significant amount of Doctorow's mature prose is that of "the knowable community."[7] Knowing this, it is easy to grasp why a historical personage like Goldman—who consistently emphasized the importance of community in her various writings and public addresses—would appeal to Doctorow. But I think we can go even further than this. I want now to suggest that the version of Goldman we have come to associate with Greenwich Village in fact has much to tell us about the way in which queerness is figured in Doctorow's long fictions. Come to think of it, that formulation doesn't quite get to the heart of the matter. Specifically, and this is a point that we will return to in the next section of our disquisition, it is the fictionalized version of Emma Goldman that makes a number of decisive appearances in the seminal novel *Ragtime* (1975) who has much to tell us about the way in which—as mentioned earlier—queerness and radicalism can be said to mingle in unusual and climactic ways at certain site-specific locales and moments in Doctorow's prose. What, though, of the novel with which we began? What does *Billy Bathgate* tell us about non-normativity in Doctorow's work? I want now to round out this section by drawing attention to the fact that—aside from some dimly recollected instances of "homo wrestling" and a fleeting reference concerning "an attempted sodomizing" buried deep in the pages of *The Book of Daniel*[8]—*Billy Bathgate* contains the sole example of explicit and directly reported male-on-male, non-heteronormative sexual behavior featured anywhere in Doctorow's long-form fiction. And just to be clear, I don't just mean in *Billy Bathgate*, but rather in *any* of his novels. Given the sheer volume of fictional characters and imagined historical personages populating the pages and various historical ages of Doctorow's socio-cultural and economically sensitive novels, this disparity strikes me as just a little bit peculiar. But then again, perhaps not. After all, we are dealing here with a novelist often thought to be, as John G. Parks once put it, "critical of the fiction of the private life."[9] Besides, there is absolutely nothing wrong with sticking with what you feel most comfortable writing about. Yet that begs the question: what does Doctorow feel most comfortable writing about? Doctorow is, to my mind, comfortable when writing about at least three things. Following the critical lead established long ago by Fredric Jameson, Doctorow is interested in and perhaps most comfortable when writing about historical effacement—especially when it becomes time to treat "the disappearance of the American radical past, of the suppression of older traditions and moments of the American radical tradition."[10] And it goes almost without saying that Doctorow is on sure and comfortable footing when writing about New York City. Lastly, I want now to advance the slightly unconventional claim that Doctorow is clearly comfortable writing, in his own words, "about intimacies" and about "personal relationships,"[11] as well as writing about the various trials and tribulations pertaining to and facing the American family over the course of the long twentieth century.

Corsets

I propose in this section, which doubles up as a survey of Doctorow's fictional oeuvre, to investigate the interplay between the three areas of interest outlined above. Where better a place to begin than with the American family? More precisely: where better to begin than with the *straight* American family. But why the straight American family specifically? Simply because, however weird and upsetting things might get—and I am thinking primarily here of the self-destructive and at times physically abusive Isaacson family dynamic on display in *The Book of Daniel*—Doctorow's collected works consistently display a clear interest in, an engagement with, and perhaps a desire to shed light on the intimate workings, seemingly endless permutations of, and constraints associated with what we might choose to term the nuclear heteronormative familial. Witness the behavior of certain of the afore-mentioned Isaacsons:

> He ran his right hand over her buttocks. The small of her back was dewy with sweat. She shivered and the flesh of her backside trembled under his hand. He tracked the cleft downward. Triangulated by her position it yielded a slightly sour smell of excrement. He teased the small hairs of her tiny anus. Then, with the back of his hand, he rubbed her labia lying plump in their nest between the upturned soles of her feet. (74)

The derriere being fondled in these lines is that of Phyllis Isaacson; the right paw is that of her troubled husband, Daniel. The sexual situation described here—brief foray into the realm of anal play and all—is self-evidently straight. But it is also worth keeping in mind that Phyllis and Daniel have decided to have it off on the front seat of their ever so slightly knackered old jalopy, while their blissfully unaware baby quite literally sits in the back seat. In this sense, then, irrespective of what you might think of Daniel and Phyllis's shared parental decision-making, it is possible to speak of this sexually explicit and intimate sequence in terms of the heteronormative familial: man, woman, child. When we choose to do so, though, we need also to acknowledge that everything about this moment is cramped, claustrophobic, and most manifestly the opposite of anything remotely erotic. This much is confirmed when Daniel orders his long-suffering wife

> to kneel on the seat facing her side of the car, and to bend over as far as she could, kneeled and curled up like a penitent, a worshiper, an abject devotionalist. Weeping, she complained that the car was too small and she too big to get comfortable that way. (74)

And things only get worse for the forlorn Phyllis, whose backside Daniel proceeds to brand with the car's cigarette lighter, "three concentric circles of heating element glowing orange in a black night of rain upon the tender white girlflesh of [his] wife's ass" (74).

Violence—sexualized and otherwise—is also present in Doctorow's first published novel. "Colt gave every man a gun," we read near the start of *Welcome to Hard Times* (1960), "but you have to squeeze the trigger yourself."[12] A plethora of different releases are most definitely sprung in this revisionist orgy of unbridled and ejaculatory brutality. Meditate, if you will, on the following passage, which is taken from the novel's utterly despondent final chapter:

> In front of his bar lies the Russian, scalped expertly. The bullet he got was in his stomach—a red stain over his apron—he must still have been alive when John Bear reached him. As much as it was the sight of Zar, who once struck the Indian from behind, which got me to take my books out here and sit down and try to write what happened. I can forgive everyone but I cannot forgive myself. I told Molly we'd be ready for the Bad Man but we can never be ready. (211)

As the reference to the skillfully performed scalping contained in this extract suggests, we are dealing here with a relative outlier in Doctorow's novelistic canon. *Welcome to Hard Times* is, above all else, best understood as Doctorow's fictional repurposing of the Old American West. It features, to be sure, a variety of tropes associated with the Western novel. Doctorow's debut contains, for example, a demonic intruder of the sort instantly familiar to readers of this long-established genre: the aforementioned "Bad Man" from Bodie. But it is also worth recalling that this savage tale, for all its slightly hackneyed ruminations about the nature of good and evil, revolves around a hastily assembled family unit. This elementary heteronormative grouping comprises the town mayor and record-keeper Blue, the brutalized former prostitute Molly, and the orphan Jimmy. Suffice it to say, things do not pan out all that well for this particular familial unit, positioned as it is against a harsh and unforgiving landscape in which the coyotes roam, smoke fumes rise, and embers glow "on the ground like peepholes to Hell" (31). Cacodemonic peepholes or not, though, the fact of the matter remains the same: what we have here is a novel that is in a concrete fashion preoccupied with the formation of familial units.

Familial issues also come to the fore in Doctorow's decidedly less demonic *City of God* (2000). This is a novel, lest we forget, which terminates not long after the marriage of Tom Pemberton and Sarah Blumenthal in New York, a service attended by their respective children. This act of union serves as temporary ballast of sorts. "We have only our love for each other for our footing, our marriages, the children we hold in our arms," the reader notes, and "it is only this wavery sensation, flowing and ebbing, that justifies our consciousness and keeps us from plunging out of the universe."[13] While this familial ballast is evidently of an imperfect and temporary variety, the very presence of such a symbolic stabilizing weight in the narrative ensures that Doctorow's novel ends on what might be described as an optimistic note. On a relatedly hopeful front, consider the manner in which the narrative framework of the earlier *World's Fair* (1985) serves to evoke the shared dreams, aspirations, and desires of Rose, David, Edgar, and Donald Altschuler. "Yet our dreams and desires were great shadows on the sun," recalls the novel's primary narrator at one point, "the enormous looming fearful attacks of unnamed chaos of the heart."[14] Consider, too, the ways in which other prominent characters in this text spend significant portions of time reflecting on their past experiences in certain sections of New York itself. It is here that the three themes mentioned earlier begin to interweave:

When we went out we went down to the Village, Greenwich Village. It was very much the thing then. Your father had a gift for making friends, meeting people, and he naturally gravitated to people of intelligence, people with fine minds and radical ideas. Well, in the Village that's the way things were, lots of young people thinking new thoughts and living differently from everyone around them. We knew Maxwell Bodenheim, who was then a very well-known Village poet, we even met Edna Millay, who was already well known outside the Village. (29)

These memories belong to the narrator's mother, Rose. What we have here is an instance of the road not taken. It is only in retrospect that Edgar's mother comes to appreciate that she and her husband once upon a time "had wonderful friends. Only now do I see that ours [our lives] could have gone in an entirely different direction" (29). What are we to make of this sepia-infused recollection? I find the references to the incorrigible nonconformist Bodenheim and the openly bisexual Edna St. Vincent Millay telling. In terms of the latter, heed in particular Millay's most renowned quatrain:

My candle burns at both ends;
It will not last the night;
But ah, my foes, and oh, my friends –
It gives a lovely light![15]

Evidently biographical when considered in relation to what is commonly known about Millay, the incandescent "First Fig" was published as part of *A Few Figs from Thistle* (1923). The indelible image of the burning candle can be read in at least two ways. The first of these pertains to Millay's well documented bohemianism. The second speaks loudly and clearly to notions of the writer's bisexuality. As the delightful and oft-cited anecdote included in Max Eastman's *Great Companions* (1959) attests, the first female poet to win the Pulitzer Prize famously had little interest in sexual binaries. Eastman describes how he once parleyed with Millay

about the highly colored notions that prudishly conventional people have about those who take sex, so to speak, in their stride. The narrowing down, in American usage, of the words moral and immoral to apply only to the minute question whether one obeys a formula or his own selective good taste in sexual relations seemed lamentable to us both. But what would the psychoanalysts do if people were direct and simple about things?[16]

Eastman then relates how Millay, who believed all analysts to be in some way psychologically inhibited, told him that on one occasion "at a party she was sitting alone nursing a bad headache when a young doctor approached and said that he had been watching her and thought he might be able to help her if she would allow it" (91). The stripling analyst, in Eastman's wry recounting,

> got up and closed the door, then came back and requested her permission to ask a few questions. After a long and roundabout approach, he finally brought out, with much hesitation and several false starts, a momentous:
>
> "I wonder if it has ever occurred to you that you might perhaps, although you are hardly conscious of it, have an occasional erotic impulse toward a person of your own sex?"
>
> "Oh, you mean I'm homosexual!" she exclaimed. "Of course I am, and heterosexual too, but what's that got to do with my headache?" (90–1)

We will return to the issue of psychoanalysis—and certain of the famous practitioners associated with the so-called "talking cure"— when it comes time to discuss *Ragtime* in greater depth. First, though, a sentence more on Millay and her understanding of life's rich pageant. Far from prudish, this notable bon vivant had no reservations when it came to embracing everything that life and sex had to offer. Not so Doctorow's Rose. She trades a possible life spent in the bohemian Village for a more or less unexceptional family, a stolidly modest apartment in the Bronx, and a relatively healthy pinch of regret. In a similarly melancholic, regretful, and familial vein, we might also think a while on Doctorow's very last novel. Recall, in particular, a hallucinatory passage contained in *Andrew's Brain* (2014)—a passage in which the titular character imagines his deceased wife, Briony, "doing cartwheels and handstands and somersaults on the kitchen table."[17] Reflect, too, on those lines near the end where the babbling narrator talks of how he would like nothing more than to read to his daughters, as Mark Twain once "did to his little girls, making up stories to help them get to sleep" (197). As the reader knows, though, that's not likely going to happen anytime soon. Andrew's first daughter dies long before the narrative even gets going. And matters are surely compounded by the fact that Doctorow's principal character has been locked up in some sort of institution for the best part of a decade when the book ends.

But perhaps things aren't quite as simple as we've just made them out to be. Take the formally ambitious *Loon Lake* (1980). The notion of the nuclear heteronormative familial features prominently in this experimental novel, which is otherwise mainly concerned with the machinations of industrial labor relations during the Great Depression. In equal measure, however, matters are a bit more ambiguous than they are in the majority of the narrative fictions mentioned above. For while the novel's protagonist—Joe of Paterson—certainly yearns for a family he might one day call his own, he appears profoundly conflicted about such affairs. Joe admits as much to his girlfriend, Clara, not long after they share a dinner together at the Jacksontown Inn:

> I sat on the side of the bed next to her, whispering in her ear, "You don't realize what you've done to me. Me, the carney kid! You're making an honest man of him, it's horrible. I have all these godawful longings to work to support you, to make a life with you, I want us to live together in one place, I don't care where, I don't care if it's the North Pole. I'll do any fucking thing to keep you in bonbons and French novels, Clara, and it's all your fault."[18]

Joe doesn't know what he really wants. Clara, on the other hand, seems quite sure of herself. In her own words: "That's the crying shame of it" (157). But what is it that Clara wants? Clara doesn't seem all that interested in bonbons. Rather, it seems fairly self-evident that she wants Red James's wife. Doctorow makes this perfectly clear in a passage written from Joe's perspective:

> Clara didn't think much of Red James but she never said no to one of their invitations, she had fixed on young Sandy, in that way she attached to people who interested her, locking on her with all her senses. I sometimes became jealous, actual jealous, I felt ashamed, stupid it was the diversion I had hoped for, it was just what I had counted on, I jammed myself when I saw the way Clara looked at Sandy, watched every move she made. (174)

To put it as politely as possible, Joe isn't the sharpest tool in the shed. He is almost willfully oblivious to—or perhaps even "jammed" by—the exceedingly obvious when it comes to the question of Clara's behavior:

> Worrying about survival was something new to her and she was engaged by it, as by the little baby, the smell of milk and throwup, a bath in a galvanized-tin tub with water made hot on a coal stove, and all the ordinary outcomes of domestic life which presented themselves to her as adventure—how could I feel anything except gratitude! I thought every minute with Sandy James put Clara's old life further behind us, I felt each day working for my benefit I was a banker compounding his interest. (174–5)

Preoccupied as he is here with idle fantasies of accumulated wealth, Joe fails to spot what is obviously transpiring between Clara and Sandy. But the clued-up reader most surely does understand what is in fact going on. And it is perhaps here that the sensitively attuned reader begins to discern the presence of that previously mentioned non-normative undercurrent pulsing through Doctorow's body of writing.

Building on this assertion, I want now to propose that what can be said of *Loon Lake* might just as easily be said of a novel such as *The March* (2005). Admittedly, the thematic concerns underpinning this piece of historical prose seem at first glance to have little to do with the overarching narrative preoccupations of *Loon Lake*, let alone with the line of non-normative inquiry that we have been cleaving to in this chapter. Yet a closer inspection of the contents of *The March* complicates things significantly. I want first to argue that this novel speaks to the sorts of performative activities we have come to associate with Butlerian understandings of queerness—especially those pertaining to self-presentation and personal finery. In turn, I want to propose to that this late novel speaks to notions of the familial. In particular, I want to suggest that Doctorow's novel—in a gesture that wouldn't be out of place in select works of twenty-first-century queer theory—proffers something approaching the condition of a critique of the nuclear hetero-normative familial model we have been discussing. It certainly isn't all that much of a stretch to suggest that this piece of long-form fiction is preoccupied with conceptions of intimate kinship. "When the war began," Doctorow writes,

> Emily had not understood what the war meant. It meant the death of everyone in her family. It meant the death of the Thompsons. She felt hollowed out, as if there was nothing left of her to mourn them. The power of war and what it had done seemed to wipe away her past until this moment.[19]

Emily's aged father agrees with this analysis. With tears of self-pity welling up in his watery eyes, Old Thompson reflects on the way in which the onset of

> war had destroyed not only their country but all their presumptions of human self-regard. What a scant, foolish pretense was a family, a culture, a place in history, when it was all so easily defamed. And God was behind this. It was God who did this, with the Union as his instrument. (54)

What are we to make of the reference to the familial contained in this passage? The tone is evidently bitter. But that comes as no surprise. After all, we are dealing in this instance with a character whose entire way of life has been exposed for what it really is: a historical abomination. The better question to ask here is perhaps this: are things quite as bleak as the desiccated elder Thompson suggests when it comes, among other things, to the familial? The answer isn't necessarily all that clear cut.

Certain of the characters we encounter in *The March* have different takes on the Union forces sweeping through the South. Witness the following scene, for instance, which is anything but despondent. "But everyone was merry," the revealingly paternalistic Lieutenant Clarke notes of the inebriated Union soldiers in his charge,

> chattering and laughing. Sergeant Malone wore the Massah's top hat and cutaways over his uniform. They had found some old colonial militia hats for the slave children. Private Toller had donned a flouncy dress, and each and every man, including the two old Negroes, was smoking a cigar. (14)

Reading this, one is struck immediately by the quasi-Rabelaisian quality of the scene, which seems in a sense to be approaching the condition of the carnivalesque (and which also contains a fleeting reference to cross-dressing). Think, too, on the way in which the festive and intimate episode being described here might be said to resonate when considered in relation to expanded conceptions of the familial. "The sociality of Doctorow's novels is consistently that of extrafamilial intimacy," the aforementioned Mark Steven confirms, "and its dominant affect might be described as propinquity, closeness, or attachment."[20] Notions of propinquity and on occasion highly problematic forms of attachment come to the fore in *The March*. "The whips cracked," Doctorow states,

> the wheels rolled, the horses were urged to a trot. Clarke, riding on, saw from the corner of his eye the white nigger girl. She had stood apart, not having joined the others aboard the train, and there she was now, in her bare feet with her grand red-and-gold shawl tied around her, watching them go. Later, Clarke would wonder why he didn't think it ridiculous that she required a special invitation. He swung his mount around, cantered back, leaned over, and grabbed her hand. You'll ride with me, missy, he said, and in a moment she was behind him in the saddle, with her arms wound tightly around his waist. (14)

Siobhan B. Somerville tells us that the notion of "race" always "refers to a historical, ideological process rather than to fixed transhistorical or biological characteristics: one's racial identity is contingent on one's cultural and historical location."[21] We need to keep this in mind when considering the bare-footed figure who captures Clarke's attention in the passage previously quoted. By far the most sympathetically drawn character in *The March*, Pearl is the illegitimate daughter of a female slave and a former plantation owner, John Jameson. The girl "with skin as white as a carnation" (356) assumes a number of important roles in Doctorow's narrative. Characters are drawn to Pearl. That is to say, they quickly become attached to her. Some want to care for her. For others Pearl is an object to be gazed upon. Some even dream idly of starting a family with her. On that last note, Pearl's prominent presence in the novel also serves to remind the reader of the hypocrisy of the specifically heteronormative dynamic characteristic of the aristocratic Southern families featured in *The March*—predicated as such an asymmetrical dynamic is on notions of accumulated and inherited capital and systematic forms of sexual exploitation. This becomes clear when Pearl's path crosses with that of her gravely injured father on an improvised hospital ward in the oldest city in the state of Georgia. Pearl calls on him to

> open your eyes and look on the daughter of your flesh and blood. Your eyes is closed, but I know you listenin. I know you hear me. And if you worryin about me I can promise no man will ever treat me like you did my mama, nosir. So you needn't worry 'bout your Pearl. She here in Savannah now an thas just to begin. She going far, your Pearl. She will take your name to glory. Scrub it up of the shame and shit you put it. Make it nice and clean again for peoples to remember. (113)

Pearl's attire at this precise juncture in the narrative also warrants attention. Doctorow describes the moment when John Jameson's wife turns and finds

> herself looking up at the child who had haunted her life. Pearl wore the sky-blue Union trousers under her skirt and a uniform sash around her waist, and held a stack of white towels in her arms. Her hair had grown longer and she wore it pulled back and tied in a bun. Mattie had not shed a tear, sitting beside her unconscious husband. Now the tears filled her eyes. (111–12)

As to whether the tears that begin to cloud Mattie's vision prevent her from appreciating the extent of Pearl's rather unconventional hospital costume – that remains unclear. What is clear, however, is the fact that this is not the first time in the novel when Doctorow lingers upon on the topic of Pearl's personal wardrobe:

> Pearl bathed herself with soap and a basin of cold water every evening in Clarke's tent while he stood guard outside. Then she went to sleep in a fly tent he'd put up next to his own. He wanted the men to know that she

was under his protection but that his behavior was honorable. After the first few days of snickering and talking among themselves, they seemed to understand and accept the situation at face value. They, too, became protective. It was Sergeant Malone who came up with a drummer-boy uniform for her. At first she was pleased. They were camped in a pine grove at the time, and she came out of her tent, having wriggled into the tunic and trousers, and stood for all of them to admire her, though everything was just a mite too big. There was a hat too, and silver buttons that she rubbed to a shine. But then she grew thoughtful. (43)

We mentioned before that pretty much all the characters who meet Pearl develop strong attachments to her. This is what we find in the extract above. The Union soldiers under Clarke's command have taken a liking to Pearl. That is why they are trying to find ways to care for her and to protect her identity. (Note, too, the characteristic emphasis on extrafamilial sorts of attachment present in the passage.) The best solution they can come up with is to dress her in the sort of regimental outfit usually reserved for adolescent boys. This leads to yet another in-stance of wartime cross-dressing. And it goes almost without saying this instance of gendered mimicry comes attached to a host of figurative and literal associations. Having donned the clothing, Pearl is now expected to play the instrument associated with this historically gender-specific military position. Pearl expresses significant reservations about taking on such a role:

> I ain't never played no drum, she said.
>   Nothing to it, Malone said. We'll show you how.
>   Sompun wrong bein a white drum boy, she said to Clarke.
>   What?
>   I too pretty fer a drum boy. I not white, neither, if white be.
>   Clarke said, By and by, Pearl, the black folks will have to go back.
>   Those are the standing orders of General Sherman. You don't want to go back, do you? (43–4)

This exchange is revealing: it serves to anticipate the way in which the logics of race and sexuality come to underpin this particular instance of performativity. While it is most surely problematic when read in terms of contemporary theory, a fictional moment such as this is still important; it certainly makes sense for Doctorow to include it in *The March*. Among other things, it functions as a broadly accurate creative nod in the direction of the actual instances of performativity that were documented during the historical period in question.

It is common knowledge that many women donned male military clothing during the Civil War. Many of these women did so in order to fight. This they did despite being forbidden from enlisting. "Men were not the only ones to march off to war. Women bore arms and charged into battle, too. Women lived in germ-ridden camps, languished in appalling prisons, and died miserably, but honourably," DeAnne Blanton and Lauren M. Cook declare, "for their country and their cause just as men did."[22] Yet the fact remains that the very idea of a woman enlisting was a cause for much in the way of moralistic and gendered handwringing. "The rise of Victorian social and cultural ideals in antebellum America reinforced the existence of separate spheres of influence for men and women. Men's sphere was in worldly pursuits and providing for home and family," Blanton and Cook note,

> while women were confined to bearing and raising children and overseeing the private world of the home. The cult of true womanhood dictated that women always appear as demure, submissive, pious, and concerned only with home and family. Women who gave any appearance of stepping outside of highly restrictive female roles risked being labelled "not respectable." (3)

This explains why women chose to disguise themselves as men during the Civil War. They had to do so not only in order to enlist, but to avoid being characterized as disruptive and socially improper. No wonder, then, that the behavior of a figure like Mary Edwards Walker caused such widespread consternation among the chattering classes in the mid-1860s. The sole female recipient of the Medal of Honor, Walker was, in the estimation of Elizabeth D. Leonard,

> a deeply controversial and, in some cases, even a deeply reviled figure, despite her passionate and unwavering commitment to the soldiers' medical care, because she flatly and explicitly (and often quite testily) rejected the unspoken expectation that she should balance her practical challenges to Victorian ideals about gender with at least the appearance of fundamental conformity.[23]

So as to be clear here: the noncombatant Walker did not at any stage deign (à la Doctorow's Pearl) to masquerade as a male Union soldier in the Civil War. A qualified physician, Walker rose to prominence during the conflict working—as will surely be of interest to readers of Doctorow's post-Civil War era novel *The Waterworks* (1994)—in a formal capacity as a surgeon. Walker also served as a Union spy. Her undercover activities eventually led to her capture by Confederate soldiers on April 10, 1864. Doctor Walker caused something of a stir during her time as a prisoner of war. The problem had everything to do with the issue of personal attire. She flat out refused to wear the prison garb thrust in her direction. By all accounts, Walker considered the outfit unbecomingly feminine. This refusal was wholly characteristic. Walker was, as is well known, a passionate believer in gender equality and dress reform. Eschewing societal convention, Walker preferred to wear clothing traditionally thought of as masculine. The visual historical record also reveals that Walker was partial to a top-hat or two. Unfortunately, this did not go down all that well with the majority of Walker's social peers. Leonard goes as far as to declare

> that "properly" dressed (and behaved) women nurses and aid activists, or women traveling with the army as cooks, laundresses, and morale boosters, or women who transformed their purported talent for gossip into the standard tool of an effective spy—indeed, even women masquerading as men in order to enlist—simply failed to provoke the sorts of wartime and postwar gender anxieties that Mary Walker's story did. (108)

These remarks help us to better understand precisely what it was that people found so troubling about Walker. It seems that the reason for such social consternation had less to do with purportedly unconventional behavior than it did with perceived acts of sartorial impropriety.

Walker, it bears repeating, was consistent and insistent when it came to the topic of self-presentation. Walker cared not a jot what other people thought about her penchant for male attire, believing as she did in egalitarianism and gender equity. Walker was in this sense ahead of her time. Yet these admirable social and political commitments served to land her in hot water on a number of occasions. Those same commitments in fact landed her in jail repeatedly, on the charge of male impersonation. "Ambiguous gender, when and where it does appear," Jack Halberstam reminds us, "is inevitably transformed into deviance, thirdness, or a blurred version of either male or female."[24] Sadly, this seems to have proven all too true in Walker's case. "All of this leads one to wonder whether things might not have gone just a bit more smoothly for Walker if she had made the decision early in her public life to assume a thoroughgoing male identity," Leonard speculates,

> as women who chose to enlist as soldiers did by necessity, at least for a period of time. Then, at least, she might have won the sympathy of those who thought they "understood" her, who thought that what she really wanted was to *be* a man, not just to enjoy the same rights and opportunities as one, though this was not, in fact, true in her case. As it

turns out, Walker's very refusal to adopt such a tactic when she believed she should not have to earned her the enduring sympathy of very few. (109)

Though I have profound reservations about the way in which Leonard appears to lay the blame squarely at Walker's feet here, the broader point she is making in this passage is useful nonetheless. It reminds us of the simple historical fact that unruly women—especially unruly women engaged in socially subversive and highly visible acts of gender performativity—tend to rub more conservatively minded people the wrong way.

All of which brings us somehow to Doctorow's most famous novel. The justly acclaimed *Ragtime* also contains depictions of socially unruly women—certain of whom take great pleasure in rubbing people in ways that the more conservatively minded might erroneously consider wrong. *Ragtime* opens with these words:

> In 1902 Father built a house at the crest of the Broadview Avenue hill in New Rochelle, New York. It was a three-story brown shingle with dormers, bay windows and a screened porch. Striped awnings shaded the windows. The family took possession of this stout manse on a sunny day in June and it seemed for some years thereafter that all their days would be warm and fair.[25]

We all know that the agreeable conditions mentioned here eventually take an altogether inclement turn. Various energies encountered in the novel threaten to pull Doctorow's characteristically heteronormative family apart. I want to suggest that these charged energies, which speak to notions of emancipation and impact characters such as Mother's Younger Brother, are in equal measure politically radical and radically non-normative. But first, a word or two about the Austrian who strove in 1909 to trouble and transform public understandings of sexuality in the United States. Doctorow notes that

> Freud's immediate reception in America was not auspicious. A few professional alienists understood his importance, but to most of the public he appeared as some kind of German sexologist, an exponent of free love who used big words to talk about dirty things. At least a decade would have to pass before Freud would have his revenge and see his ideas begin to destroy sex in America forever. (30)

How are we to read this tonally curious passage, which is at once weirdly flat and strangely hyperbolic? It seems as if Doctorow's tongue is planted firmly in his cheek. The image conjured in this extract is exquisite: the great Sigmund Freud reduced to the state of a jilted and resentful avenging angel bent on nothing more than the wholescale destruction of the social bonds and psychic relations undergirding everyday existence in the United States. Nor is it the only such delicious image to feature in the pages of *Ragtime*. "Their ultimate destination was Coney Island," Doctorow writes elsewhere in the novel,

> a long way out of the city. They arrived in the late afternoon and immediately embarked on a tour of the three great amusement parks, beginning with Steeplechase and going on to Dreamland and finally late at night to the towers and domes, outlined in electric bulbs, of Luna Park. The dignified visitors rode the shoot-the-chutes and Freud and Jung took a boat together through the Tunnel of Love. The day came to a close only when Freud tired and had one of the fainting fits that had lately plagued him when in Jung's presence. (32–3)

This passage is arguably even funnier than the last. Freud comes across as a hopeless neurotic here. He is evidently hung up on Carl Jung in some emotional and possibly even physical capacity. How else are we properly to understand the psychological roots of the involuntary "fainting fit" that Freud falls prey to at the end of his day—or, if you prefer, his *date*—with Jung? There is clearly no doubt about it: try to deny it as he probably might, this fictionalized version of Freud is clearly and chronically lovesick. (One also wonders whether Doctorow's Freud might have caught a glimpse of one of those gay male beauty contests mentioned by Chauncey.) Be that as it may, though, it would be wrong to suggest that Doctorow pokes fun at Freud in order to discredit him or his myriad achievements in the field of psychiatry. There is, for one thing, real tenderness to be found in Doctorow's fictional rendering of Freud. And we also know that Doctorow always had a soft spot for the sorts of opinions held by Freud and his fellow psychoanalytic travelers.

He certainly had a lot of time for the ideas espoused by Wilhelm Reich. The noted author of *Character Analysis* (1933) was, in Doctorow's estimation,

> second only to Freud in the early days of psychoanalysis. He was spectacular but always troublesome, always difficult. He kept going, always being Reich, until he ends up with the orgone box, and, in the last days of his life, shoots down UFOS with tin cans. He was the same man, always.[26]

Doctorow also thought very highly of the way in which Reich, who was a passionate believer in the transformative power of free love, sought to side-step stifling societal conventions. Doctorow makes this clear in a passage from *Ragtime*:

> The common wisdom is that there has been a retreat from a certain kind of political development or communal education. I'm not sure that's true. If you think of the early Wilhelm Reich, for instance, as a man who tried somehow to accommodate or bridge Freudian insight into Marxist sociology, then this is a very clear part of the process. Reich came to believe that there is no hope for political progress until people can be freed from their neurotic character structures. (47–8)

There is a simple reason why all this talk of communal education and freedom from neurotic strictures should strike us as familiar. These were the same views espoused by another prominent figure associated with the free love movement, the anarchist thinker Emma Goldman. Tellingly, we see evidence of such emancipatory thinking in *Ragtime*. One sequence in the novel stands out in this regard. The one I am thinking of is set in a brownstone located somewhere on the Lower East Side. Goldman plays an important role in this geographically specific set-piece, as do Mother's Younger Brother and Evelyn Nesbit. Having schooled Nesbit on the importance of personal integrity, sisterhood, and "love and freedom" (49), Goldman instructs the young model to get into bed and to remove her corset. Neither character appreciates that she is being watched by Mother's Younger Brother, hidden as he is in a wardrobe. The situation escalates quickly and before long everything comes to a shuddering climax. Here is the glorious, multi-orgasmic moment in question:

> Her feet pointed like a dancer's and her toes curled. Her pelvis rose from the bed as if seeking something in the air. Goldman was now at the bureau, capping her bottled emollient, her back to Evelyn as the younger woman began to ripple on the bed like a wave on the sea. At this moment a hoarse unearthly cry issued from the walls, the closet door flew open and Mother's Younger Brother fell into the room, his face twisted in a paroxysm of saintly mortification. He was clutching in his hands, as if trying to choke it, a rampant penis which, scornful of his intentions, whipped him about the floor, launching to his cries of ecstasy or despair, great filamented spurts of jism that traced the air like bullets and then settled slowly over Evelyn in her bed like falling ticker tape. (54)

This scene practically reads itself. Responding to Red Emma's queer caresses of Evelyn Nesbit, Mother's Younger Brother both figuratively and actually falls—or, if you will, *comes*—out of the closet. This is, I want to argue, the originary moment and primal scene of Mother's

Younger Brother's political radicalization. Turned on by Nesbit and inspired by Goldman's emancipatory anarchist rhetoric, Mother's Younger Brother trades the nuclear heteronormative familial for a radical life spent on the communal revolutionary fringe, taking up as he subsequently does with imaginary and historical figures of the ilk of Coalhouse Walker and Pancho Villa. In this sense, then, I think it at the very least possible to say that for a brief, beautiful, and wholly beatific moment, Doctorow's masterwork tantalizingly suggests—to adapt an old avant-garde axiom of which the *Un Chien Andalou* (1929) referencing author of *The Book of Daniel* would have surely been aware—that radicalism will be non-normative, or it will not be at all.

Clocks

In lieu of a definitive and fittingly pithy conclusion, the question I want finally to pose in this opened-ended coda runs as follows: how might we begin to position these non-normative moments in relation to Doctorow's fictional oeuvre in its totality? Truth be told, I'm not entirely sure. But I do find it striking that one of the more memorable moments in Doctorow's late work centers on two immobilized elderly bachelors sitting side by side, trussed up in a manner reminiscent of poor Bo Weinberg, listening to the gentle ticking of a grandfather clock. The scene in question features in the underrated *Homer & Langley* (2009). As with so many of Doctorow's novels, this compassionate and evocative piece is set in New York. Much critical ink has already been spilt on the two siblings who came to fascinate Doctorow late in his career. The reclusive Collyer brothers were the stuff of local urban and journalistic legend in mid-twentieth-century New York. This had partly to do with where and how Homer and Langley Collyer chose to live. The inheritors of a four-story brownstone in Harlem, the brothers rarely left the house and refused to pay their taxes. Despite being offered eye-wateringly large amounts of money by real estate agents, they also refused to countenance the idea of selling their home. As a result, an aura of mystique began to build up around Homer and Langley. This helps to explain why they hit the international headlines in the spring of 1947. It all started with an anonymous phone tip. The caller claimed that there was a dead body in the Collyer residence. Patrick W. Moran tells of the way in which the patrol officer dispatched in response to the mysterious call

> entered the brownstone to discover that Homer, who was blind, rheumatic, and paralytically dependent on his younger brother, had died from

starvation. Unable to find Langley, authorities called for an eleven-state manhunt, while the New York police began to search the dangerously cluttered building. The rooms were so crammed with objects that the only passage to be found was through an elaborate labyrinth of booby-trapped tunnels. After a two-week search, during which time the police excavated nearly 150 tons of trash, Langley's body was uncovered ten feet from where Homer had died. Ensnared by one of his own booby traps, he had been crushed under an avalanche of baled newspapers and bundled detritus.[27]

It isn't all that difficult to understand why this tragic and dramatic tale would appeal to Doctorow. Most obviously, it gave him yet another opportunity to write about his beloved New York. Further to that, the story of the real-life Homer and Langley seemed to trigger something in Doctorow. His decision to fictionally extend the lifespan of the Collyer brothers by a whole ten years speaks volumes in this regard. Born in the Gilded Age, Homer and Langley walk the earth for the best part of a century in Doctorow's novel: they live through and in effect bear witness to both World Wars, the Spanish flu pandemic, the Wall Street Crash and the subsequent Great Depression, the onset of the Cold War, the lasting political shame of Watergate, and the social and cultural fallout associated with the disastrous Vietnam War. In short: the strange case of the Collyer brothers affords the novelist a late-career opportunity once more to pass comment on the wider arc of American history. Finally, and somewhat unexpectedly, the flesh-and-blood Collyers also permit Doctorow the opportunity to revisit certain topics broached in earlier works, such as *Loon Lake*. Specifically, they allow for an extended fictional meditation on idiosyncratic forms of accumulation.

Moran describes how "the Collyers have become mainstays in con-versations about hoarding. Many popular and diagnostic accounts of the phenomenon, in fact, begin with a short narrative of their deaths and discovery much like the one above" (273). Scott Herring concurs with this assertion. He also suggests that the "Collyers were unwit-tingly pivotal in constructing a paradigm shift in hoarding as a curious abnormality—a shift that helped make chronic the gradual psycho-pathology of gross disorganization."[28] The key word here is the last one: disorganization. "In the wrong place at the right time," Herring argues, "the Collyer brothers helped catapult chronic disorganization to a national—and swiftly international—prominence that would assume infamous proportions thanks to newspapers, magazines, popular novels, and other forms of media" (183). This notoriety had partly to do with the sort of stuff they sought to hoard. Unlike, say, Doctorow's Joe of Paterson, the Collyers had no pronounced interest in the accumulation of material wealth. They were drawn instead to trinkets and objects that most would characterize as materially worthless. The contemporary press made much of the Collyers' fondness for curious objects. "As police extracted items," Herring writes, "a new definition of hoarding as the aberrant accumulation of a person's disorganized things coalesced, and a new definition of the hoarder as a material and mental deviant rather than a mere eccentric came into view" (178). Acts of purportedly aberrant accumulation were now more often than not defined specifically in terms of queerness. The treatment of Homer and Langley confirms this. Their reclusiveness was often held up as proof of their queerness. So, too, the fact that they both chose to remain single and childless. This is something that comes to the fore in Moran's account of the innuendo-driven public scrutiny that the real Homer and Langley had to endure. "Whatever may have been their sexual orientations," Moran posits,

> the two brothers failed to comply with the heteronormative mandates of midcentury American culture. Their urge to accumulate objects was perceived as a type of selfish provisioning rather than as an amassing of wealth to be passed along to a child. Here and elsewhere, the Collyers were easy to cast in the role of the childless queer miser. (279)

That being so, what are we then to make of Doctorow's fictionalized depictions of Homer and Langley? Moran suggests that Doctorow goes to great lengths in the novel "to 'straighten out' the Collyers' desires and ambiguous object choices" (218). There is, I think, something in that. This is, after all, a novel that goes into significant—and significantly overwrought—detail when discussing heteronormative notions of romantic desire and attendant acts of "lovemaking," as Moran notes (151). Yet it also seems significant that nothing familial or even remotely fruitful comes of such lovemaking. Miserly or not, the simple fact remains that all the brothers have, in the end, is each other. Homosocial affection thus comes to trump heteronormative futurity in *Homer & Langley*. As to whether that was Doctorow's intention, who could say? But I'm pretty confident that both of the Emma Goldmans we've encountered in these pages would have been on board. And that surely counts for something.

Notes

1. E. L. Doctorow, *Billy Bathgate* (London: Plume, 1998), 11–12. Subsequent parenthetical citations refer to this edition.

2. George Chauncey, *Gay New York: Gender, Urban Culture, and the Making of the Gay Male World, 1890–1940* (New York: Basic Books, 1994), 1. Subsequent quotations are cited parenthetically within the text.

3. Eric Garber, "A Spectacle in Color: The Lesbian and Gay Subculture of Jazz Age Harlem," in Martin Duberman, Martha Vicinus, and George Chauncey, Jr., eds., *Hidden from History: Reclaiming the Gay and Lesbian Past* (New York: Penguin Books, 1991), 318. Subsequent quotations are cited parenthetically within the text.

4. Cristanne Miller, *Cultures of Modernism: Marianne Moore, Mina Loy, and Else Lasker-Schüler* (Ann Arbor: Michigan University Press, 2007), 97.

5. Emma Goldman, *Red Emma Speaks*, ed. Alix Kales Shulman (New York: Humanity Books, 1998), 139. Subsequent quotations are cited parenthetically within the text.

6. Alain Badiou, *In Praise of Love*, trans. Peter Bush (London: Serpent's Tail, 2012), 10.

7. Mark Steven, "Community and Apostrophe in the Novels of E. L. Doctorow," *Studies in American Fiction*, 45.1 (spring 2018): 122.

8. E. L. Doctorow, *The Book of Daniel* (London: Penguin Modern Classics, 2006 [1971]), 201. Subsequent quotations cited parenthetically within the text are from this edition, and after initial quotations from the editions of the Doctorow volumes that follow.

9. John G. Parks, "The Politics of Polyphony: The Fiction of E. L. Doctorow," *Twentieth Century Literature*, 37.4 (winter 1991): 454.

10. Fredric Jameson, *Postmodernism, or, the Cultural Logic of Late Capitalism* (London: Verso Books, 1991), 24.

11. Paul Levine, "The Writer as Independent Witness," in Christopher D. Morris, ed., *Conversations with E. L. Doctorow* (Jackson: Mississippi University Press, 1999), 43.

12. E. L. Doctorow, *Welcome to Hard Times* (New York: Plume, 1996), 32.

13. E. L. Doctorow, *City of God* (New York: Random House, 2000), 304.

14. E. L. Doctorow, *World's Fair* (New York: Random House, 1985), 61.

15. Edna St. Vincent Millay, *Collected Poems* (New York: Harper Collins, 2011), 127.

16. Max Eastman, *Great Companions: Critical Memoir of Some Famous Friends* (New York: Farrar, Straus & Cudahy, 1959), 90. Subsequent quotations are cited parenthetically within the text.

17. E. L. Doctorow, *Andrew's Brain* (London: Abacus, 2014), 93.

18. E. L. Doctorow, *Loon Lake* (London: Macmillan, 1980), 156–7.

19. E. L. Doctorow, *The March* (New York: Random House, 2005), 33–4.

20. Steven, "Community and Apostrophe in the Novels of E. L. Doctorow," 123.

21. Siobhan B. Somerville, *Queering the Color Line: Race and the Invention of Homosexuality in American Culture* (Durham: Duke University Press, 2000), 7.

22. DeAnne Blanton and Lauren M. Cook, *They Fought Like Demons: Women Soldiers in the American Civil War* (Baton Rouge: Louisiana State University Press, 2004), 1. Subsequent quotations are cited parenthetically within the text.

23. Elizabeth D. Leonard, "Mary Walker, Mary Surratt, and Some Thoughts on Gender in the Civil War," in Catherine Clinton and Nina Silber, eds., *Battle Scars: Gender and Sexuality in the American Civil War* (Oxford: Oxford University Press, 2006), 106. Subsequent quotations are cited parenthetically within the text.

24. Jack Halberstam, *Female Masculinity* (Durham: Duke University Press, 1998), 20.

25. E. L. Doctorow, *Ragtime* (London: Macmillan, 1975), 3.

26. Harvey Blume, "Fuse Arts Interview: The Late E. L. Doctorow—Reduced to Art," *The Arts Fuse*, July 24, 2015 <http://artsfuse.org/131611/fuse-arts-intervie8w-the-late-e-l-doctorow-reduced-to-art> (accessed October 14, 2018), n.p.

27. Patrick W. Moran, "The Collyer Brothers and the Fictional Lives of Hoarders," *MSF: Modern Fiction Studies*, 62.2 (summer 2016): 272–3. Subsequent quotations are cited parenthetically within the text.

28. Scott Herring, "Collyer Curiosa: A Brief History of Hoarding," *Criticism*, 53.2 (spring 2011): 162. Subsequent quotations are cited parenthetically within the text.

Part III

Narrative, Media, and Cognition: The Case of *City of God*

Chapter 8

Literary Neutrinos and the Hot Dark Matters of Doctorow's *City of God*

Nathan D. Frank

But where is the novel?
A. O. Scott, "A Thinking Man's Miracle"

Try this trick and spin it, yeah . . .
The Pixies, "Where Is My Mind?"

The use of *neutrino* as a trope to indicate the capability of transgressing and reconfiguring boundaries aptly fits any object of inquiry that, following Karen Barad in *Meeting the Universe Halfway: Quantum Physics and the Entanglement of Matter and Meaning* (2007), achieves as its ultimate status a "great democratizer," or a "realization of a mobility and reach that knows no bounds" (246). Barad observes, for instance, that "information technologies are often touted as the neutrino of the geopolitical-economic-social-cultural landscape, passing through matter as if it were transparent, innocently traversing all borders . . . with undiscriminating ease and disregard for obstacles" (245).[1] Whether information technologies, digital media, or the narrative technologies of print media, the quality of a neutrino obtains when media or technologies "democratize" their "landscapes" by rendering ontological differences between incompatible objects irrelevant, or even nonexistent. That, from the perspective of a neutrino, there would be no difference between black holes and white holes suggests that a democratized landscape is so neutral that nothing registers positively or negatively in *any* terms, physical or otherwise. Neutrinos, true to their etymology, see/enact/perform/seek/enjoy/uphold/enforce only diminutive neutralities. Great democratizers are also great minimizers of difference.[2] They are their own existence, for their own sake, to the blissfully noncontradictory degree to which things like minds can only aspire. No quantum theory has yet posited "a neutrino in consideration of itself."

This just in . . . the elusive invisible heretofore only deduced neutrino has a detectable mass. How is this verified? There's this cult of neutrino physicists, and all over the world they're building great huge tanks to hold heavy water deep inside mountains, under the Aegean Sea, on the bottom of Lake Baikal in Siberia, in tunnels under the Alps, below the Antarctic ice cap . . . so they can watch the flying neutrinos that slip so easily, effortlessly through the diameter of the earth, like bats at night flooping behind your ear and lifting your strands of hair with their wing wind—and detect with powerful light sensors the miniscule voltage emitted by the neutrinos plunging through the dark giant tanks of pure heavy water. . .[3]

My colleague here is so into his own mind
No wonder he's in the dark
No wonder he doesn't see anything.
Lighting up the twists and turns of his brain
With all the voltage of a neutrino
He's dancing with his shadow
Dancing in the darkness of his mind.
(157)

So, *bitte*, what is our problem? Not the nature of the universe, therefore, but . . . what? The mind in consideration of itself? The self that proposes the world is everything that is, but finds itself excluded from that proposition? The I or self that can theoretically ascertain everything about the world except who and what itself is—as the subject of its own thinking? (125)

E. L. Doctorow's *City of God* (2000) syncopates a number of refrains across its traversals of evolutionary biology, quantum theory, ordinary-language philosophy, and theology. The recurrent phrase describing languages as "intonative systems of clicks and grunts and glottal stops and trills," for instance, interlocks with the Wittgenstein-attributed reflection that "even if all possible scientific questions be answered, the problems of life have still not been touched at all." Interspersed among these is a running rumination on what several of the different narratorial voices refer to as "a mind in consideration of itself." Each phrase articulates a methodologically distinct approach to mediations of reality or apprehensions of the world, without which we cannot process, understand, or appreciate the "unmediated awe" (194) that comes with existence.

The connection that I want to make between neutrinos and minds takes Doctorow's cues from *City of God* in seeking to articulate these approaches, and—in attempting to negotiate between them—to center a mediatic meditation on the concept of *mind* in order to think of novels *qua* minds, and to think of minds *qua* objects. In short, I capitalize on Doctorow's neutrino–mind discourse in order to broaden my concept of "transmentality" in contemporary metafiction.[4] I do not mean "to center" *mind* in the normative sense, nor do I mean to leave the concepts of *mind* and *object* overly general or unqualified. Rather than privileging the reading in which "a mind in consideration of itself" emerges as the most illuminating of *City of God*'s refrains, I embed this phrase as the literal center of a thought process that, like Doctorow's Wittgenstein, glides across a spectrum of propositions, beginning with the most conventional and commonplace premises, and advancing toward the most ambitious and nuanced possibilities: it thus becomes the fulcrum upon which to leverage "minds in consideration of neutrinos" and "neutrinos in consideration of minds." I do not go so far as to suggest "neutrinos in consideration of neutrinos," for the simple reason that "neutrinos in consideration of minds" is already so far reaching and defamiliarizing in terms of flipping subject–object relations as to provoke the next move.

Minds in Consideration of Neutrinos

The Reverend Dr. Thomas Pemberton (Pem, Father) is the Yale-bred, heterodox priest, rector of St. Timothy's, Episcopal, in the Bronx, in process of converting to Judaism while his marriage crumbles and his bishop gently strips him of authority over his parish; his consideration of things like neutrinos is filtered through his father-in-law, Everett, a conservative politician-come-writer aspiring to capture Pem's spiritual biography (among other things) in fictionalized form. But long before *City of God* arrives at anything like an interrogation of the "unmediated awe" that Pem-through-Everett confronts, as Pem's participation in a reform synagogue steadily increases, it is wonder at the "obligated awe" of "the average astronomer doing his daily work" that opens the novel (4). In this opening, Everett appears to ventriloquize the beginnings of Pem's doubt by sketching the implications of a Christian God audacious enough to be "involved" in the creation of the universe according to the most contemporary scientific theories, such as the Big Bang that purportedly got matter moving, or the anticipated Big Crunch that will end it all by having the universe "fly back into itself" (12).[5]

As with most intellectual and progressive theologians, Pem's hang-up is not with any perceived *in*compatibilities between the secular and the sacred—"reason and faith, rather than being incompatible, are complementary"[6] (162)—but rather with the metaphysical horrors that would attend the very compatibilities themselves, and which Pem (according to Everett) intuits acutely:

> Does the average astronomer doing his daily work understand that beyond the celestial phenomena given to his study, the calculations of his radiometry, to say nothing of the obligated awe of his professional life, lies a truth so monumentally horrifying—this ultimate context of our striving, this conclusion of our historical intellects so hideous to contemplate—that even one's turn to God cannot alleviate the misery of such profound, disastrous, hopeless infinitude? (4)

The question is rhetorical but sincere, as is clear from the way that Pem dwells on it. Shortly after positing it, he returns—in the wake of expressing his incredulity at the theoretical terms and acronyms devised by his "average astronomers," terms like Big Bang and Big Crunch, acronyms like WIMPs for weakly interacting massive particles and MACHOs for massive compact halo objects—with another question, now more pointed, his stance now more explicit:

> Are these clever fellows mocking themselves? Is it a kind of American trade humor they practice out of modesty, as the English practice self-denigration in their small talk? Or is it bravery under fire, that studied carelessness in the trenches while the metaphysical rounds come in?
>   I think they simply are lacking in holy apprehension. I think the mad illiterate priest of a prehistoric religion tearing the heart out of a living sacrifice and holding it still pulsing in his two bloodied hands . . . might have had more discernment. (12)

At issue here, following Barad once again, this time in her rehearsal of representationalism, is an unsettling insight concerning "knowledge (i.e., representations)," and, by extension, representations as mediations between "the known (i.e., that which is purportedly represented)," and "the existence of a knower (i.e., someone who does the representing)."[7] Pem, like Barad, questions representationalism's adequacy: how can "WIMP" or "MACHO" be said to "represent" what is at stake in the very terms themselves, that is, as sufficient stand-ins for "that which is purportedly represented," and thus as effective connectors between the "knowers" and the "known"? Though "the word *explosion* is inadequate" for capturing "some original particulate event or happenstance" (3; emphasis in original), Pem's distrust of the astronomers' lexicon in the service of metaphysical trench warfare anticipates Adam Levin's precocious Gurion ben-Judah Maccabee in *The Instructions*, who, after holding forth on the merits and limitations of radiometric dating to determine the age of the earth and in interpreting *Genesis* in front of Rabbi Unger at the Solomon Schecter Torah Study, answers the very question that calls representationalism onto the carpet. Having explained to his rabbi and his peers that carbon dating is based "on rates and con-stants and constant rates of decomposition that no one can really know," and, further, that "it also doesn't matter . . . because all that matters is do you know what radio-isotopes are?," Gurion drives his point home by flaunting that he, Gurion, has "no idea what radio-isotopes are . . . but neither does Rabbi Unger, so he's scared of what they could be."[8] Gurion makes clear in this passage that, as knowledge fails—potentially as a function of fear, but definitely as a function of the representationalist shortfall[9]—so does any possibility of a linguistic representation mediat-ing between "knower" and "known," as the word *radio-isotope* fails in this instance to bridge the gap between subject and object. Doctorow and Levin, then, together suggest that WIMPs and MACHOs are terms born of insecurities about "what they *could* be."[10]

If we were to imagine Father Pem in some hypothetical and inter-textual encounter with Gurion, surely we would imagine him approving; he would confirm (along with most readers) that Gurion exhibits "dis-cernment" in "holy apprehension." Pem would be drawn to this Jewish boy from Chicago in the same way that he is drawn to Joshua and Sarah Gruen, the rabbinic couple who lead the small-but-growing reform movement in the Synagogue of Evolutionary Judaism on West Ninety-Eighth Street. It is among the Gruens and in their rethinking of Judaism that Pem discovers a nexus in which immediacy and democracy, attributes of the neutrino, complement each other, a nexus in which Pem accepts and embraces the limits and failures of linguistic representa-tionalism just as he discovers with Sarah that "the glory of Judaism is its intellectual democracy" (249). In other words, Pem detects two intersecting ways of bypassing the representationalism of words, which combine for him as a form of mediation that allows greater access to reality, the world of objects: God and His infinitely expanding universe sit more comfortably together without their human-given names impli-cating and delimiting each other. If Pem's problem is that "even one's turn to God cannot alleviate the misery of such profound, disastrous, hopeless infinitude," then perhaps the words *God* and *infinitude*, as bridges between Pem and that which he struggles to apprehend, need to be rearticulated. Or, as Pem puts it to God directly while delivering his own marriage toast at his wedding with Sarah Gruen, ". . . I think we must remake You" (268).[11]

At this point, *City of God* echoes and updates the rest of Doctorow's corpus insofar as Pem sits comfortably alongside a cast of protagonists for whom representationalist failures facilitate social critique. Consider John Williams's reading of Arthur Saltzman,[12] who notices that "on the one hand, the artist-figures who populate each [Doctorow-authored] book try unsuccessfully to represent reality; on the other they manage to critique American social institutions with powerful irony."[13] As Saltzman and Williams are both writing well before the publication of *City of God*, their readings presciently concatenate *City of God* with such works as *The Book of Daniel* and *Loon Lake*. Pem's decision to "remake" God is in lock-step with the protagonists of these earlier novels, Daniel Isaacson and Joseph Korzeniowski, in their respective calls for a new model, a new representation of what they (the knowers) have learned (the known), without an adequate language to express what they have learned (knowledge). For Pem, this isochronal dilemma means that the first of his two alternatives (immediacy) provides a basis and a template for the second (Judaism), since he finds in Judaism's intellectual democracy an affirmation of his unmediated experience with God.

But what is this immediacy? The immediacy that I have in mind is lodged in *City of God*'s synoptic premise, the event that (aside from the Big Bang) occasions its existence and determines its action: a stolen cross from Pem's sanctuary mysteriously makes its way to the rooftop of the Gruens' synagogue, where Joshua discovers it after his wife, Sarah, reads about the theft in what Everett records as "the *Times*."[14] In a later conversation, one of the many in which Pem and Everett drink together, Everett is suspicious of Pem's claim that he, Pem, has been given a sign by God in the form of the cross on the roof of the synagogue. Pem's use of the word "sign" and the fact that his sign is itself composed of symbols (a cross, a synagogue) prompts me to offset some loaded connotations by stressing a reading in which it is clear *to him* that *his* use of "sign" does indicate immediacy: he is "still, happily, thankfully vulnerable to one aspect of the ancient apprehension" (91), and this apprehension "is a thunderous silent thing" (92). Galvanizing his point to Everett that meaning might be more *immediately* conveyed through this sign than through linguistic representation, Pem says: "Listen, I'll just say this one thing. You place a big brass cross down on a synagogue roof, what could you be doing? Well, you could be doing with one brilliant stroke everything I've been translating into language for you" (92). What I am reading as "immediate" in this passage refers very specifically to the lack of mediation between knower (Pem) and known (i.e., whatever *im-mediate* meaning inheres in this nontranslated situation); it does not refer here to its more colloquial meaning as "instantaneous," as is clear from Pem's explanation that

[a] sign is a sign. And when you know it's a sign, that's enough. That's how you know it's a sign. It is not something whose meaning is instantaneous. It doesn't light up on Broadway. And it's not something you go looking for, it has to come to you. That's what signs do, they come to you. There is moment to this thing, where you know something . . . has finally happened. (92)

Reinforcing how "one brilliant stroke" and the translation of that brilliant stroke "into language" differ in terms of conveying meaning—that is, in terms of immediacy versus mediation—are the very critiques and analyses that extend the novel's attempt to translate a wordless gesture into linguistically represented meaning. In Harold Bloom's introduction to *Modern Critical Views: E. L. Doctorow*, for instance, Bloom reads the "transfer of the cross from church to synagogue" as "a transfer that [Pem] himself will follow, when he becomes a Jew, a rabbi, and the husband of the widowed Sarah."[15] In this tidy reading, we see Bloom converting the wordless gesture of a stolen holy symbol into words, and then the words into meaning, just as Pem and Everett continually attempt to do throughout *City of God*'s narration. We also see Bloom reading "transfer" according to metaphor in that the utility of metaphor is precisely its ability to "transfer" or "carry over" meaning (*meta*: over, across; *pherein*: to carry, bear). Metaphor is language's version of mediation *par excellence*, and though Bloom does not explicate it as such, the fact that he connects a transfer of an object to a transfer of subjectivity is itself a critical transfer that highlights the immediacy of a cross on the roof of a synagogue.

Novel and critique are thus both bound by representationalist attempts to translate, to mediate; it is the impulse of knowers to use language so confidently. But what happens when these confident makers of knowledge begin to examine their own representations (or critiques), not as mediations between knower and known but as objects to be known in their own right? Or when their representations examine themselves? What happens when consciousness slips into self-consciousness? What happens when minds shift from consideration of things like neutrinos and radio-isotopes to consideration of things like themselves?

Minds in Consideration of Themselves

Prima facie, the novels of E. L. Doctorow and those of Joshua Ferris have little in common, even among critical audiences sensitive to their respective brands of formalistic experimentation and thematic preoccupations, yet they overlap so remarkably that I begin "minds in consideration of themselves" by way of a thumbnail sketch of my theoretical approach to Joshua Ferris's *Then We Came to the End* (2006).[16] Were it not for the fact that Ferris and Doctorow both engage the impacts of proliferating digital media on their characters' spiritual lives at the millennium through their print narratives, and that they both do so via novels that (I argue) achieve textual minds, such a comparison might appear obtuse or smack of an attempt to forward a contrarian agenda.[17] Once articulated, however, this fact of remarkable overlap between the two novelists and their work becomes so stubbornly conspicuous as to recall Doctorow's own defense of how he portrays Milledgeville's geography in *The March* (2005), wherein he explains to Marshall Bruce Gentry of the *Flannery O'Connor Review* that "[t]hese are facts. You can't ask for my research and then, as it turns out to be accurate, claim that I'm trying to persuade you of something."[18] Indeed, Doctorow's relationship to facts and his penchant for fictionalizing history are major axes whose coordinates illuminate *City of God*'s grandiose grid, just as they illuminate *The March* along with most of his other novels; it is a relationship that complicates his interrogation of "unmediated awe" in *City of God* by going to the heart of the representationalist's dilemma.

Meanwhile, Joshua Ferris differs significantly from Doctorow in his treatment of factuality and historicity; their shared points of contact, which feed into those commonalities listed above, have more to do with their abilities to dramatize the limits of their chosen genres such that something new originates from within the old, from within established generic structures that they choose to inhabit and exploit. This might sound parasitic, but for Bruce Kawin, who develops the concept in *The Mind of the Novel: Reflexive Fiction and the Ineffable* (1982), what appears as formalistic appropriation is really more of a symbiotic exchange that takes place within the interactive environments that categories of genre subtend.[19] Kawin's notion of a "mind of the text" prefigures Christopher D. Morris's "fiction [as] a system of knowledge,"[20] and it occasions what I call "an experience [on the reader's part] of unexpected, contrapuntal interaction with an intentionally subversive system [the mind of the text] pushing against its own limits, rather than some indivisible backdrop of experience against which the text operates,"[21] by which I mean that when reader and text encounter each other on the terrain of the new media ecology, *they dynamically shape and sustain each other*. The environment in which the text finds itself is that of fluid readerly consciousness. By denying the possibility of the text's interaction with "some indivisible backdrop of experience against which the text operates," I also suggest that *mind* be conceived as "a divisible and interactive interface" between otherwise "incompatible" entities (242), a definition inspired by Louis Armand's proposition "that *mind* is constituted solely in the separation or interface of the representable and the unrepresentable, on the cusp of verifiability, analogy, metaphor or mimesis, or as the division between that which thinks and that which makes thinking possible."[22]

In addition to his notion of *divisibility*, then, I take Armand's utilization of *interface* and support it with Alexander Galloway's theory in *The Interface Effect* (2012), in which he claims that interfaces are designed, in my paraphrase, to mediate between that which "separates the logics of history and its representational forms."[23] In his own words, Galloway claims that interfaces are ultimately concerned with "the impossibility of thinking the global in the here and now, of reading the present as historical. Thus the truth of social life as a whole is increasingly incompatible with its own expression."[24] Galloway thus joins Doctorow, Barad, and others in doubting representationalism's accuracy and efficacy.

For Kawin as for Galloway (and as for Joseph Tabbi, toward whom we head), literary attempts to write the "impossible"—whether the impossibility of articulating the "ineffable" (Kawin) or of "thinking the global in the here and now" (Galloway)—necessarily involve ascending levels of metafictional self-consciousness, or reflexivity.[25] Kawin cites authors ranging from Shakespeare to Beckett to Ron Sukenick, whose symbioses *precede* these reader–text interchanges, and indeed give rise to the interactive environments of generic categories, first by performing transactions between reality and imagination/life and art, demonstrating in these transactions "that reality and imagination are mutually enriching and mutually sustaining categories; in some of [Sukenick's] stories, art and life are symbiotic, while in some, they create each other. In the Kabbalist terms borrowed by Edmond Jabès, the 'black fire' of the Torah is written on the 'white fire' of the silent parchment; the unsaid allows and underlies the saying."[26]

Kawin is hardly the first literary theorist to have proposed an art–life or a reality–imagination symbiosis (Oscar Wilde's Platonic dialectic of the Aristotelian model of mimesis in *The Decay of Lying* comes most readily to mind), but to my knowledge he is the first to have strapped the language of symbiosis together with the Kabbalah and the Torah in so succinct a passage; to have the language of evolutionary biology working in tandem with the language of mystic Judaic theology; and to have launched them as a single narratological rocket fueled by Wittgenstein-flavored language analogies. Kawin's work crystallizes here as indispensable to a reading of how *City of God* answers what Geoffrey Galt Harpham calls "the abiding question of the relation between thematics and technique."[27] Perhaps less obviously, it also comports presciently with the work of Joshua Ferris and to the steadily growing cohort of contemporary novelists who cannot avoid writing in the gaps[28] between information-based futures and faith-based traditions, between mimetic representation and generative creation, between fact and fiction, history and the present, the truth of social life and its own expressions, language and mind, matter and materiality, object and subject. There is no doubt that Ferris and his contemporaries, ranging from Dave Eggers to Richard Powers, write in these gaps to caution against a ubiquitous digital connectivity permeating and pervading the lives and relationships of humanity in the twenty-first century.[29] The creative genius of these authors manifests in their attempts to cope with hyperconnectivity, attempts that vary not only between the authors but within their oeuvres. *Then We Came to the End*, for instance, enacts a formal subversion of what Uri Margolin calls the *"we" narrative*, and in this way inserts a mindful presence into an aperture between what the text is calling an unnamed "you" and "me."[30] Alternatively, Ferris fills gaps differently with his third novel, *To Rise Again at a Decent Hour* (2014), which thematically challenges the culture of social media and the prevalence of smart phones and iPads, contemptuously referred to throughout the novel as "me-machines," thereby occupying a space between social expectations and individual resistances to these expectations, which essentially amounts to another way of filling the you–me, or the we–they, or the self–world, or the subject–object divide.

Gap, then, clearly emerges as a keyword, coming hot on the heels of a discussion concerning the limitations of representationalism; it also rounds out my theoretical approach to *Then We Came to the End* insofar as I deploy Jenny Sundén's articulation of "affect between the analog and the digital."[31] This *between* in her subtitle clarifies the gap that she fills, but it also positions *affect* as the interface between the two incompatible entities. In addition, the way that Sundén fills this gap gives us our mileage toward a reading of *City of God*, since she explores the gap between the digital and the analog by brilliantly identifying cyberpunk as a genre that houses both facets—the digital and the analog—just as *City of God* furnishes its own mind–neutrino gap. Moreover, the visibility of one emerges in this genre precisely as the absence of the other.[32] This updates the old trick of knowing something according to what it's not, by knowing something according to its own competing characteristics (a slight adjustment to dialectic), and Sundén interpellates this trick as *transing*:

To . . . trans the digital . . . is to transcend, transgress, or otherwise bend the boundaries of media (and bodies) . . . The "punk" in steampunk works as a critical tool in that it provides ways of bending, or hacking, or reimagining the past . . . When steam . . . transes the digital, this is a process that highlights the materiality of the digital, as well as its connectedness with other temporal orders and technological forms. Steampunk . . . is a reconsideration, or transing, of the (digital) present.

> . . . Trans also draws attention to material specificity. Transgressions accentuate the transgressed medium, or body. A transgression of a category, a body, a form, makes visible the category itself, its material specificity. (146–7)

The transcendence and transgression of boundaries here suggests an affinity between anything with the ability to *trans* something, and a neutrino; remarkably, my Sundén-inspired transing of mind in *transmentality* also, therefore, suggests an affinity between minds and neutrinos. It is true that this affinity is based on analogy, just as, for Kawin, textual and novelistic minds are imitations and analogies: representations. Kawin's reliance on analogy invites a two-pronged attack on any notion of an *actual* mind of the novel: first, the charge that analogy-based methodologies are weak (Barad, for one, is anti-analogy *tout court*); and second, that regardless of strengths or weaknesses, analogies are not real and thus never escape representationalism.

Our way out of this is to bracket analogy momentarily and to recognize that gaps are phenomenologically real, even as they go by different names (margins, footnotes, thresholds, liminality, fault lines, betweenness, incompatibility). Treatments of gaps are real, too, and they also go by different names (inquiry, representation, critique, media/mediation, interface, dialectic, transing, Timothy Morton's "gapsploitation"). I built transmentality by drawing on Morton's mesh en route to Sundén's transing. Morton replaces all of "nature" (where gaps occur) with "mesh," turning it toward interconnectedness and interdependence precisely by transing it: "Mesh can mean the holes in a network and threading between them. It suggests both hardness and delicacy."[33] Morton's mesh could be said to describe, trans, or treat gaps. In any case, I give Morton credit for providing the impetus for gap treatment and for squaring things off with his signature "gapsploitation" in *Hyperobjects*, in which "irony is the aesthetic exploitation of a gap between 1 + *n* levels of signification. Irony means that more than one thing is in the vicinity. Irony is the echo of a mysterious presence. For there to be irony, something must already be there," something like a *phor* under its *meta-* "levels of signification."[34]

Yet a gap separating Kawin's *The Mind of the Novel* from Morton's *Hyperobjects* remains. What falls between an understanding of a textual mind according to analogy and the understanding of a mind, textual or otherwise, according to object-oriented ontology (OOO)? I believe that a concern for the fate of the print novel in a new media ecology leads the likes of John Johnston, Joseph Tabbi, and Michael Wutz to fill this gap with a combination of media theory and a re-evaluation of what literary narrative, in the wake of Pynchon and DeLillo, is most suited to accomplish. Building upon each other's research and collaborating, these scholars manage to harness a sense of urgency in order to turn the representationalist corner such that print narrative could be taken seriously precisely as that "divisible and interactive interface" that mediates between otherwise "incompatible" entities, that is, *as the thing-in-itself* and not just a model of it.

Taking print narrative as the thing-in-itself first requires a recognition of the gaps that it fills, that is, recognizing its mediacy but also its immediacy. Michael Wutz, in *Enduring Words: Literary Narrative in a Changing Media Ecology*, recognizes Doctorow, along with authors ranging from Frank Norris and Malcolm Lowry to Richard Powers, as one writing in the same gaps, or "the fault lines of media-technological shifts,"[35] as do Joshua Ferris and other novelists previously discussed. He then observes that Doctorow "inserts" *City of God* into the very gap that Sundén puts all of cyberpunk into, that of "the alphanumeric gap left by the binary code, extending from film and television to other discourses such as journalism, history, and science, literally by spelling out what has been left out of these knowledge domains" (17–18). But Wutz also recognizes a two-way gap–mind dynamic when he remarks on the "gappy and multiply spatial nature of cognition" (176), a remark indicating that minds themselves *contain* gaps (divisibility) just as they *occupy* gaps (interface).

Of course, it takes an ecological awareness for such recognition to happen, and it probably does not hurt that the environmental language of the so-called "new media ecology" dovetails historically with the evolutionary language of a species logic, that the print novel has recently been anthropomorphizable to an unprecedented degree since people worry about its extinction along with their own. In note 17 to this chapter, I cite Tom LeClair's language about "books that *know* [emphasis added] and show what we as a people and a species need to understand in order to have a future," and then I suggest that this "know" can be literalized. Here a metaphor's necessity to "transfer" or to "carry over" meaning is effaced, as the need to translate between "one brilliant stroke" and whatever sits across a gap from that stroke goes away. Another way of putting it would be to say that the novel no longer transfers meaning from author to reader but *from itself to itself*: no gap. Literalized knowing in a text, as articulated by Nancy Armstrong in *How Novels Think* to be historically and "quite literally" "one and the same" as the "individualism" of the "modern subject,"[36] and to be in command of a "polygenetic imagination" that allows "novels [to] understand individualism as the one thing that keeps Europeans from going over to the dark side and losing their humanity" (108), for example, is thus a move toward overcoming representationalism.[37] The metaphoric anthropomorphisms are de-mediated, rendered *im*mediate, stripping language of its meta-aspects and letting it exist alongside Barad's known entities as meta-stripped *phors*.

Beyond LeClair and Armstrong's knowing books, it is worth briefly sampling a smattering of the anthropomorphic language used to describe Doctorow's metafiction as a way of suggesting just how thoroughly ingrained is the critical intuition that these *phors* tucked away in metaphor are immediate to themselves. In a riveting media analysis of "the image," Harpham references *The Book of Daniel's* "anxious insight into the image's powers."[38] Kathryn Ludwig argues that "the characters and the text" of *City of God* "perform the struggle of reading prophetically."[39] In the previously mentioned interview between Doctorow and Gentry, Doctorow himself describes *Ragtime* as having "its own irreducible identity."[40] Granted, this is widely accepted as conventional shorthand, not meant to be taken literally in all cases. If pressed, Harpham may claim that it is Doctorow's "anxious insight" represented in the book, and not the book's own emotions; Ludwig could say that Doctorow is doing the "performing" by way of his representations; Doctorow's attribution of "identity" to *Ragtime* may not be adequate for either an anthropomorphic or even a conscious identity. I also acknowledge that things like having an identity or performing a reading are not exclusively human functions: nonhumans identify and perform, too, and they do so both literally and metaphorically. Yet I remain unconvinced that such qualifications categorically attend such a pervasive critical convention. I find it more productive to allow for a certain slippage from the qualified idiom of convention to an unintended literalization (except, of course, in Armstrong's case, where literalization is explicitly the point) of the idiom precisely because such slippage provides an opportunity for insight. I may not have full confidence in the intentionality behind *all* of these critical constructions, but neither do I doubt the intellect of *any* who articulate them. Rather, I believe they are *onto something*, as they sometimes verge excitingly toward an explicit avowal that the convention, as metaphor in its own right, speaks to the *phors* lurking within. Consider, for instance, how close Tabbi comes to stripping the convention of its meta-trappings when he reads Johnston:

> Although Johnston does not say it in so many words, this narrative continuity, which the novelist must *construct* among "partially connected media systems," functions very much like the conscious mind, which responds to gaps in modular awareness and incommensurable representations by creatively linking them into a workable mental image or patchwork representation.[41]

While Tabbi still reads the novelist's construction as analogous to "the conscious mind" and sticks to representationalist guns, the fact that he wants to explicate what Johnston "does not say" "in so many words" means that he is scraping away at Johnston's metaphor; Tabbi is not so much attempting to *transfer* Johnston's meaning as to *touch* it.[42] Wutz, noting Tabbi's claim that "print media . . . might recognize itself, at the moment it is forced to consider its own technological obsolescence, as a figuration of mind with the new media ecology" (xi), scrapes away in a similar vein, wanting to touch Tabbi's meaning in the same way that Tabbi wants to touch Johnston's, except that Wutz becomes the first in this trio to scrape past a "figuration of mind" to excavate, at long last, a *phor* buried beneath layers of meta-.[43] And it just so happens that the *phor* is mental.

Following Tabbi, Wutz begins with the anthropomorphic statement that "novels . . . share an acute media-ecological awareness,"[44] and while he languishes a bit in the representationalist quicksand by continuing to think of novels as cognitive "models" with "thematic and formal parallels" to minds (18), he pulls out of it decisively when he asserts that "literary narrative may *see itself* as the repository of specific notions of information and knowledge in the digital moment of the present, when these very terms are subject to negotiation" (24, emphasis added). *City of God* in particular is "a novel trying to engage the imponderables of twentieth-century thought" (182). Finally, Wutz's description of *The Waterworks* as "*a novel that understands itself* " (156, emphasis added) does away with a need for those representationalist "models" and "parallels," that is, of any "cognitive distance necessary to translate history into knowledge" (18) precisely because there is no longer any "distance" between history and knowledge once knowledge becomes coterminous with the knower and the known, as must surely happen if we take *literally* that "a novel understands itself," which is tantamount to saying that knowledge knows just as it can be known.[45]

Neutrinos in Consideration of Minds

> Is this a stretch? But think of the contingent human mind . . . The per-
> meable mind, contingently disposed for invasion, can be totally overrun
> and occupied by all the characteristics of the world, by everything that
> is the case, and by the thoughts and propositions of all other minds
> considering everything that is the case . . . as instantly and involuntarily
> as the eye fills with the objects that pass into its line of vision.
>
> So we, too, are subjected to a kind of quantum weirdness, defined in
> our determinacy by how we are measured . . .[46]

If the knowledge of a representation knows just as it can be known,
then *City of God* joins *The Waterworks* not only as a novel that is
aware of itself, but as a novel whose awareness is predicated precisely
on its divisibility and interactivity. More specifically, *City of God* joins
The Waterworks insofar as Wutz recognizes in the latter that "the narrator's highly responsive role" is that of "a decentered and perpetually
self-correcting node processing parallel narrative fractals."[47] By adjust-
ing the singular narrator in this statement to account for *City of God*'s
multiple narrators, we get an apt description of the novel as one in
which the many narrators are highly responsive to each other and to
their environments, self-correcting in relation to the emergence of new
voices but also to new information informing these voices. Though
Robert Alter is unaccountably grumpy[48] about *City of God* as a literary
achievement, he nonetheless gives an excellent rehearsal of what we
might call the novel's narratorial ecology, for which it is well worth
quoting him at length:

> There are ten or more different narrators, all sounding like each other,
> though they have different aims and preoccupations. One of the most
> prominent of these is Everett the novelist, a fictional stand-in for
> Doctorow, who exhibits roughly the same biographical data as Edgar,
> the protagonist of Doctorow's autobiographical novel *World's Fair*. In
> the course of interacting socially with Pem the priest and Sarah the rabbi,
> Everett provides the reader with narratives of his father's experience in
> World War I and of his older brother's experience in World War II,
> the evident connection with the novel as a whole being the horrors of
> twentieth-century history. In the same loose connection, another sub-
> sidiary narrative follows the story of an unemployed journalist who
> dedicates himself, ineptly but aided by spectacular coincidence, to ex-
> acting private vengeance from war criminals who have taken refuge in
> the United States. And more difficult to connect with anything else is
> the bizarre story (the narrator himself calls it "a simple waxworks melo-
> drama") of a man involved in an adulterous affair who assumes total

domination of his mistress, and then takes on the physical appearance and the public identity of her rich husband, reducing him to penury. Another lurid instance of man's inhumanity to man, perhaps.

Through all these narrative strands, Doctorow labors to weave a large philosophical tapestry that will bring together Judaism and Christianity, two world wars, the death camps, the emotional upheavals of private life, and the ephemeral existence of a terraqueous globe supporting conscious life, under the aspect of eternity. To this end, he begins his novel with a two-page meditation on space, time, and the Big Bang, moving rapidly from physics to theology. Here he makes the tactical error of including among his narrators both Einstein and Wittgenstein.[49]

I am in no position to offer a better sketch of divisibility or interactivity from a *representationalist* standpoint, but I am equipped to comment upon the putative "looseness" of the novel's connections as well as the merits of including both Einstein and Wittgenstein from the *transmental* vista. For it is precisely in the looseness of its connections that *City of God* coheres into what Bloom describes as an "astonishing fusion" of narratorial voices,[50] and that the avatars of Einstein and Wittgenstein so effectively *trans* each other that what at first appears to be their competing worldviews turns out to be just as astonishing a fusion of words, images, and propositions (and just as coherent) as the "first-rate polyphony" of the narration.[51] Einstein considers minds and God by way of neutrinos and dark matter; Wittgenstein considers neutrinos and dark matter by way of minds and God. In their own ways, they consider (in)finitude. These thinkers are *Weltanschauung* transers—*but only if/when taken together*, as in Sundén's reading of cyberpunk, as in a transmental reading of *City of God*.

If, as I stated earlier, taking print narrative as a mind first requires a recognition of the gaps that it fills, tantamount to a recognition of its immediate mediacy, then the next requirement is a recognition that this mind's field of vision tries to include itself, tantamount to a recognition of its democracy. But just as we cannot see our own eyeballs without mirrors or photographs or other representationalist mediations, neither can a novel see the *phor* of itself without building out metaphorical layers (hence, metafiction). Tabbi summarizes this limitation in his reading of Richard Powers's epigraph to *Galatea 2.2*, the poem by Emily Dickinson in which "The brain is wider than the sky,/For, put them side by side,/The one the other will contain/With ease, and you beside." Tabbi comments that "'[y]ou' differ from your 'brain' only in that one is seen *observing* the other . . . . This self-variation in language is what throws off the symmetry between subjects and objects, the inside and the outside of theory; it creates a wobbling or doubling-back on itself, in which 'brain' can both contain and be contained by what it perceives."[52]

This is why *City of God* holds Pem's direct experience with his nonverbal "sign" at a series of gradual removes, revealed as the text backs up to watch itself "wobbling," and wobbling all the more for doing so. Pem's interiority, for instance, is revealed as only his interiority as imagined and fictionalized by Everett (the changing of the actual newspaper to *The Times*, for example), and then even that is revealed as Everett's archive of research—notes, emails, audio recordings of their drinking conversations, and so on. In their "brilliant stroke" conversation, for instance, there is this line by Everett: "Well, I can't [inaudible]. . ." (92), implying that this particular novelistic conversation, aimed at elucidating Pem's interiority, is to be taken as an attempt to transcribe, an attempt which is itself nested within an attempt to reimagine, another attempt which is in turn nested within an attempt to represent, nested within an attempt to transfer original meaning. Each of these attempts is Morton's "$1 + n$ levels of signification" and creates a new gap (or nest) inside the original gap between Pem and the world.

Everett is acutely aware that as he tries to write in the gap, he only creates more gaps. This is why, after welcoming readers into his "laboratory, here, in [his] skull" (which of course he cannot see), he laments that "[t]here is nothing in the universe that can be proven to move absolutely without reference to something else in the universe, or for that matter without reference to the universe in its entirety" (36). Or later, when he imagines this reflection as one that Einstein must have tried to put between himself and the world: "The entire problem of mind is of enormous interest, and yet it demands a superhuman courage to dwell on. The mind considering itself—I shudder; it is too vast, a space without dimension, filled with cosmic events that are silent and immaterial. For one's sanity it is preferable to track God in the external world" (44).

Detection of mind, then, cannot rely on mind itself, it cannot be purely meta-, and it cannot be purely subjective. For N. Katherine Hayles,

> [t]he situation is akin to a relativistic scenario of a spaceship traveling at near light speed: the clocks on board by which one might measure time dilation are themselves *subject* to the very phenomenon in question, so accurate measurement of dilation effects by this means is impossible. Needed are approaches broad enough to capture the scope of the changes underway, flexible enough to adapt to changes in criteria implied by technogenetic transformations, and subtle enough to distinguish between positive and negative outcomes when the very means by which judgments are made may themselves be in question.[53]

My singling-out of the "subject" in this passage is in order to trans it into an object, which is an altogether different course of action from what Hayles urges by characterizing the "approaches" that are "[n]eeded." Hayles means to turn the clocks from subjects to objects, but in a different way: she finds their "outside" and aims something "broad," "flexible," and "subtle" toward them, like an outer Everett toward an inner Pem. The problem that I have with her method is that "dilation effects" are her true object, not the measuring devices. Hayles is correct about having relativized measurement techniques but wrong about having stepped outside of time itself. Intriguingly, the approaches that Hayles calls for really become extensions of the thing that they seek to relativize. She is describing interface, and, depending on the complexity of these approaches (which sound considerable), they are probably also highly divisible and interactive.

City of God is one step ahead in this regard. Knowing that it cannot step outside of itself, it finds another way to relativize and objectify itself—the novel as a mind transes its own putative immateriality with the neutrino, which is effective because a neutrino is the closest thing to a mind's outside that *City of God* ever finds. The novel is right there with Hayles in imagining light-speed spaceships and performing various other "thought experiments," but none of them gestures toward any kind of meaningful outside. Even wondering what "things look like just at the instant's action at the edge of the universe" (4) yields no truly helpful outside. But if a neutrino is detectable based on its mass, which is in turn detectable based on its ability to pass unimpeded through other things with mass, like giant underground water tanks, and if the existence of the human mind is so far beyond dispute as to be held at a specialized remove from the world of objects (including the metafictions that supposedly model them), then *my* question, which *City of God* put into *my* mind, is whether a neutrino can pass through a mind.

If so, does that mean that a mind has a detectable mass? And if not, does that mean that minds do not exist? Or does it mean, as Grzegorz Maziarczyk and Joanna Teske suggest, that minds are "immaterial,"[54] or, following Wioletta Chabko (in the same volume as Maziarczyk and Teske), as she reads the metafiction of Jonathan Safran Foer, that "what is abstract and immaterial is conceptualized in terms of what is physical and available to our perceptual and sensory faculties"?[55] When Wutz describes the project of *Enduring Words* as work that "circumscribes the novel's awareness of its location within (and endurance in) a modern media ecology,"[56] he highlights in succinct fashion the overarching themes of this celebratory essay: namely, a novel's self-awareness (taken to a literal level), and the ecology within which this awareness operates.

But if a mind is immaterial, how can it locate itself? How can "Doctorow suggest[] that the serious novel . . . acquire important cultural legitimacy by *locating itself* in the interstices of contemporary knowledge and information production" (133, emphasis added)? Is not *City of God* aware of itself, not necessarily as an instance of the "aesthetics" of the endless "proliferation" that Marie-Laure Ryan identifies as the dominant mode that "contemporary culture practices,"[57] but rather as a proliferation of endless gaps, of endless endlessness, even as it inserts itself into the alphanumeric gap of cyberpunk? Is it not therefore assuming with Wutz that it has actual and not just metaphoric *location*, singing along with The Pixies, asking over and over, "*where* is my mind?" And is it not in keeping with the a priori thought experiments of *City of God* itself that, on blasting a neutrino through a mind, the neutrino would trans the mind's immaterial subjectivity into a material and therefore locatable object, helping us to answer A. O. Scott and The Pixies at once by locating the mind of the novel as the embodied filler of a localized gap?

Notes

1. Barad's mention of information technologies in this instance is actually in order to correct the misperception that they *are* neutrino-like when, in fact, they "do *not* produce a flat spacetime manifold, a level playing field; on the contrary, in some cases they exacerbate the unevenness of the distribution of material goods . . ." See Karen Barad, *Meeting the Universe Halfway: Quantum Physics and the Entanglement of Matter and Meaning* (Durham: Duke University Press 2007), 246; emphasis added. My use of her quotation here serves to illustrate not only the neutrino's characteristics *but also* the desirability of these characteristics for those invested in fostering such things as democratization, inclusiveness, and (for lack of a better word) cholarchy.

2. Jeffrey Bilbro makes a similar statement regarding "difference," or the putative lack thereof, in the post- and nonhuman philosophies that espouse what Levi Bryant famously calls *The Democracy of Objects* (Ann Arbor: University of Michigan Press, 2011) by responding to Timothy Morton's *The Ecological Thought* (Cambridge, MA: Harvard University Press, 2010) with the critique that Morton's "rejection of ontology trivializes identity and *precludes real difference*, and thus real love" (emphasis added). See Jeffrey Bilbro, "Review: *The Ecological Thought*," *Christianity and Literature*, 61.4 (2012): 695. While I disagree with Bilbro's assertion that Morton's work rejects ontology— Morton is, after all, a leading proponent of object-oriented ontology

(OOO)—and therefore that identity and difference are precluded on these grounds, I do contend that OOO is inherently an anti-essentialist campaign and that Morton's dedication to "strange strangers" provocatively minimizes ontological difference while maximizing scalar difference, as becomes clear in *Hyperobjects: Philosophy and Ecology After the End of the World* (Minneapolis: University of Minnesota Press, 2013). A Donna Haraway-inspired Barad treats difference quite explicitly in her promotion of a diffractive (as opposed to reflective) mode of reading, since such a method "attends to the relational nature of difference; it does not figure difference as either a matter of essence or as inconsequential: [here quoting Haraway] 'a diffraction pattern does not map where differences appear, but rather maps where the effects of differences appear'" (Barad, *Meeting the Universe Halfway*, 72). Reading minds and neutrinos "through each other," diffractively, thus registers the *effects* of their differences while avoiding the pitfalls of reproducing sameness that comes with reflective reading.

3. E. L. Doctorow, *City of God* (New York: Random House, 2000), 20. Subsequent parenthetical citations refer to this edition.

4. Nathan Frank, "The Mind of *Then We Came to the End*: A Transmental Approach to Contemporary Metafiction," in Grzegorz Maziarczyk and Joanna Teske, eds., *Explorations of Consciousness in Contemporary Fiction* (Amsterdam: Brill Rodopi, 2017).

5. Barad refers to what I have called "the most contemporary scientific theories" as "our best theories" (*sic passim*) on the grounds that "it is a mistake to think that normative concerns entail a normative foundationalism or progressive conceptions of knowledge and history." Barad, *Meeting the Universe Halfway*, 407, fn. 19.

6. *Complementary* here is a tricky word, since, according to quantum theory, it resonates with Bohr's principle of complementarity. According to Barad, Bohr explains complementarity "by considering two mutually exclusive ways [of interacting]". Barad, *Meeting the Universe Halfway*, 154. Later, Barad describes two other ways of interacting (imaging and manipulating) as "complementary, that is, mutually exclusive modes of operation" (358).

7. Barad, *Meeting the Universe Halfway*, 46–7.

8. Adam Levin, *The Instructions* (San Francisco: McSweeney's, 2010), 44.

9. I take no issue with representation as a mode in and of itself, a mode that I take to be, by turns, a necessary, inevitable, and/or desirable literary function, as should be clear from my panegyric of Levin's novel, which I cite specifically as an instance in which the fantasy of "a perfectly accurate representation" is representation's high ceiling, a fantasy "in which the novel acts so perfectly as an interface that it erases any incompatibility between communicators of different worlds." See Frank, "The Mind of *Then We Came to the End*," 240. My issue is with an ideology that cannot fathom anything beyond

representation, a mode that, in reaching its heights, seems to foreclose critical considerations of "a condition in which literary texts refer to the conditions they create instead of referring to the conditions that create them." Nathan Frank, "Remapping the Present: Dave Eggers's Spatial Virtuality and the Condition of Literature," *Reconstruction: Studies in Contemporary Culture*, 14.4 (2014): 1.

10. A similar argument is made in Don DeLillo's *White Noise* when Heinrich, son of Professor J. A. K. Gladney, asks, ". . . what is a nucleotide? You don't know, do you? Yet these are the building blocks of life. What good is knowledge if it just floats in the air?" Don DeLillo, *White Noise* (New York: Penguin, 1984), 148. Following Barad's schematization allows us to piggyback on Heinrich's rhetoric to wonder: "What good is *representation* if it just floats in the air?"

11. I am indebted to Michael Wutz for pointing out that "Sarah grounds her evolutionary notion of God on the assumption that 'human history does show a pattern at least of progressively sophisticated metaphors,' thus (much like Einstein) as much demystifying as elevating the divine to a concept in synch with progressive 'metaphysical and scientific sophistication'." Private correspondence; see Doctorow, *City of God*, 256. It is the "at least" in Sarah's observation, however, that tempers even a "sophisticated" metaphor's ability to "remake" God, minimizing metaphor's ability to mediate the truly and irrevocably immediate.

12. Arthur Saltzman, "The Stylistic Energy of E. L. Doctorow," in Richard Trenner, ed., *E. L. Doctorow: Essays and Conversations* (Princeton: Ontario Review Press, 1983), 73–108.

13. John Williams, *Fiction as False Document: The Reception of E. L. Doctorow in the Postmodern Age* (Columbia: Camden House, 1991), 77. See Paul Levine, *E. L. Doctorow* (New York: Methuen, 1985), 75.

14. But which Pem, in conversation with his biographer Everett, disputes, and which adds a telling wrinkle to Everett's representationalist enterprise. See Doctorow, *City of God*, 48.

15. Harold Bloom, "Introduction," in Harold Bloom, ed., *Modern Critical Views: E. L. Doctorow* (Langhorne: Chelsea House Publishers, 2002), 4.

16. Frank, "The Mind of *Then We Came to the End*".

17. Here I echo Tom LeClair's preface to *The Art of Excess: Mastery in Contemporary American Fiction* (Chicago: University of Illinois Press, 1989), in which he states that he would "like to think that [his] criteria for evaluation are reasonable and eclectic, serving no eccentric or masked ideology," and that he is "ultimately concerned with survival value—not necessarily books that will last the ages, but books that know and show what we as a people and a species need to understand in order to have a future" (viii). Thus his (and my) clear-eyed plea to have a marginalized vocabulary reconsidered in light of burgeoning theoretical advances is driven by an *overt* and *urgent* sense that books

can "know" in a way that is vital to the future of humanity; this essay extends the spirit of LeClair's preface by attempting to *literalize* the anthropomorphic "know" in what amounts to his disclaimer, and finds itself sandwiched between Kawin and Armstrong. A notable recent addition to this line of scholarship comes by way of Antje Kley and Kai Merten, eds., *What Literature Knows: Forays into Literary Knowledge Production* (Berlin: Peter Lang, 2018), especially the contribution by Ann Spangenberg, who reads (what I call) the mind of David Mitchell's *Cloud Atlas* in an article entitled "'We are only what we know': Knowledge in David Mitchell's *Cloud Atlas* (2004)."

18. Marshall Bruce Gentry, "E. L. Doctorow in Milledgeville: An Interview," *Flannery O'Connor Review*, 11 (2013): 32; 31–7.

19. Bruce Kawin, *The Mind of the Novel: Reflexive Fiction and the Ineffable* (Princeton: Princeton University Press, 1982). This is not to say that parasitic modes of consciousness are not to be taken seriously. In a reading of Peter Watt's *Blindsight* (2006), for instance, Justyna Gallant explains that "[w]ith consciousness defined in the novel as a parasite and a mistake in the evolutionary process, we are encouraged to separate cognition from consciousness and concentrate on the processes presented in the text rather than on character construction." Justyna Gallant, "Creations of the Posthuman Mind: Consciousness in Peter Watt's *Blindsight*," in Maziarczyk and Teske, eds., *Explorations of Consciousness*, 27.

20. Christopher D. Morris, "Fiction is a System of Knowledge: An Interview with E. L. Doctorow," *Michigan Quarterly Review*, 30 (1991): 439–56.

21. Frank, "The Mind of *Then We Came to the End*," 238.

22. Louis Armand, "Introduction," in Louis Armand, ed., *Mind Factory* (Prague: Litteraria Pragensia, 2005), 7–8, 1–9.

23. Frank, "The Mind of *Then We Came to the End*," 230.

24. Quoted ibid.

25. While Kawin and I clearly agree on reflexivity's heuristic value, I join Barad in noticing its limits as well, evidenced by the fact that this essay progresses beyond "minds in consideration of themselves" and moves toward diffractive over reflexive reading. See note 2 above. Moreover, even critics wanting to highlight the reflexive qualities of Doctorow's novels, or the reflexive effect that they have on readers, are quick to temper their observations in this direction in light of countervailing tendencies throughout Doctorow's novels that seem to push against overtly reflexive (and therefore postmodern) techniques. Williams paraphrases Paul Levine's refusal "to call Doctorow a postmodern writer as the term is often used—he is postmodern perhaps in his refusal of master narratives, but humanist in his insistence on the relevance of literature to life. He especially avoids grouping him with the 'self-reflexive school,' although it is hard to read *The Book of Daniel* or

Loon Lake without seeing that quality." John Williams, *Fiction as False Document: The Reception of E. L. Doctorow in the Postmodern Age* (Columbia: Camden House, 1991), 77. See Levine, *E. L. Doctorow*, 19. This statement expands easily to include *City of God* as at once postmodern in its reflexivity while resolutely humanist in its relevance to life.

26. Kawin, *The Mind of the Novel*, 212.

27. Geoffrey Galt Harpham, "E. L. Doctorow and the Technology of Narrative," *PMLA*, 100.1 (1985), 81, 81–95.

28. Barad, in an attempt to update Ian Hacking's version of entity realism, supplements his motto of "Don't just peer, interfere" with her own "Not simply intervene, enact the between." Barad, *Meeting the Universe Halfway*, 359.

29. Or at least "permeating and pervading the lives and relationships *in Western and developed countries on a large scale* in the twenty-first century." While I want to be sensitive to inequalities in terms of access to hyperconnectivity, I want to be equally sensitive to the zero-sum dynamic in which a lack of access in certain parts of the world is not only a direct result of access elsewhere, but in which this asymmetry directly contributes to a very different but nevertheless real experience of that very access that occurs elsewhere, such as people on the receiving end of drone strikes, or of the invasive activities of multinational corporations.

30. Uri Margolin, "Telling Our Story: On 'We' Literary Narratives," *Language and Literature*, 5.2 (1996): 115–33.

31. Jenny Sundén, "Technologies of Feeling: Affect Between the Analog and the Digital," in Ken Hillis, Susanna Paasonen, and Michael Petit, eds., *Networked Affect* (Cambridge, MA: MIT Press, 2015).

32. In "The Mind of *Then We Came to the End*," I demonstrate that Sundén's rendering visible of the one thing against the perceived absence of the other is analogous to N. Katherine Hayles's work in *How We Think: Digital Media and Contemporary Technogenesis* (Chicago: University of Chicago Press, 2012) in rendering the properties of narrative visible in database and vice versa. Both cases rely on an extrapolation of Steven Pinker's definition of virtuality in *Words and Rules* (1999) as the latent presence of irregular (verb) forms lurking within "the category of regular forms"—"forms that *would* be created" based on a particular logic, but which remain uncreated mental abstractions until irregularity replaces them by instantiating unexpected conjugations. See Steven Pinker, *Words and Rules: The Ingredients of Language* (New York: Harper Perennial, 2011 [1999]), 280; original emphasis.

33. Morton, *The Ecological Thought*, 28.

34. Morton, *Hyperobjects*, 173.

35. Michael Wutz, *Enduring Words: Literary Narrative in a Changing Media Ecology* (Tuscaloosa: University of Alabama Press, 2009), 10.

36. Nancy Armstrong, *How Novels Think: The Limits of Individualism from 1719–1900* (New York: Columbia University Press, 2005), 3.

37. Though it must be noted that individualism teams up with representationalism as part and complicit parcel of the flawed ideology of neoliberalism. I draw on and synthesize Barad and Rachel Greenwald Smith to make this point in my reading of Karen Tei Yamashita's *Tropic of Orange* (1997). In this respect, the individualism of a novel with a mind might therefore serve a neoliberalist agenda even as it undercuts its representationalist tenet.

38. Harpham, "E. L. Doctorow and the Technology of Narrative," 32.

39. Kathryn Ludwig, "Finding the Prophetic in Failure: A Postsecular Reading of E. L. Doctorow's *City of God*," *Religion and the Arts* 19 (2015), 230; 230–58.

40. Gentry, "E. L. Doctorow in Milledgeville: An Interview," 33.

41. Joseph Tabbi, *Cognitive Fictions* (Minneapolis: University of Minnesota Press, 2002), 51; original emphasis.

42. Barad paraphrases fundamental aspects of Bohr's complementarity principle by concluding that "even the notion of proximity takes separation too literally." Barad, *Meeting the Universe Halfway*, 359.

43. Bruce Kawin provides another articulation of "layers of meta-" in the fourth chapter of *The Mind of the Novel* by describing metanarratives that have "one foot planted squarely in the limits of language and another in the complete range of experience" as being contained within "frames under pressure," frames which, when scaffolded, support "the energy of [a novel's] rhetoric." Kawin, *The Mind of the Novel*, 141, 142.

44. Wutz, *Enduring Words*, 8–9.

45. See note 42 for Barad's Bohr-driven claim that "proximity takes separation too literally." This is her conclusion; the premise beginning this sequence has to do with "the relation between knower and known," which she (through Bohr) claims "is much more intimate than either the notion of intervention or even the shift from sight to touch suggests." Barad, *Meeting the Universe Halfway*, 359. From another perspective, my claim that "knowledge knows just as it can be known" is at once of a contemporaneous piece with the Kawin–LeClair–Armstrong–Kley/Merten–Spangenberg line of scholarship (see note 17 above) *but also an anachronism* according to the historical view that "[o]ne of the most deeply entrenched narratives about the Scientific Revolution and its impact describes how knower and knowledge came to be pried apart" and that "[a]s long as knowledge posits a knower, and the knower is seen as a potential help or hindrance to the acquisition of knowledge, the self of the knower will be at epistemological issue." Lorraine Daston and Peter Galison, *Objectivity* (New York: Zone Books, 2007), 39, 40.

46. Doctorow, *City of God*, 243–4.

47. Wutz, *Enduring Words*, 18.
48. Or perhaps Alter's grumpiness *can* be accounted for. In an interview conducted by Wutz (2012), Doctorow speculates that it could be the perceived biblical aspects of *City of God* that has "Alter so upset": "Now I didn't see the book as having a biblical model behind it until about the time I had Everett say that. In short, without any conscious planning on my part, the book managed to affect the scissors-and-paste, sewn-together form of the bible. The first person to pick that up was Mary Bahr, at the time the managing editor at Random House. She said, you've constructed a bible. Then it occurred to me, maybe that's what got this fellow Alter so upset: he is a biblical scholar, who has translated the bible. Presumably he is religiously observant. (He is also the Alter who once said that *The Book of Daniel* and Joe Heller's *Catch-22* were anti-American novels. He's from the love-it-or-leave-it school of literary criticism [Laughter].)" Michael Wutz, "On the Craft of Fiction—E. L. Doctorow at 80," *Weber—The Contemporary West*, 29.1 (2012): 10; 2–17.
49. Robert Alter, "*City of God*," *New Republic*, March 6, 2000.
50. Bloom, "Introduction," 3.
51. Wutz, *Enduring Words*, 139.
52. Tabbi, *Cognitive Fictions*, 22.
53. Hayles, *How We Think*, 81–2; emphasis added.
54. Grzegorz Maziarcyk and Joanna Teske, "Introduction," in Grzegorz Maziarczyk and Joanna Teske, eds., *Novelistic Inquiries in the Mind* (Cambridge, MA: Cambridge Scholars Publishing, 2016), 1.
55. Wioletta Chabko, "Multimodal Experience: 21st Century Meaning-Making Strategies as Captured in Jonathan Safran Foer's *Extremely Loud and Incredibly Close*," in Maziarczyk and Teske, eds., *Novelistic Inquiries in the Mind*, 120.
56. Wutz, *Enduring Words*, 4.
57. Marie-Laure Ryan, "Texts, Worlds, Stories: Narrative Worlds as Cognitive and Ontological Concept," in Mari Hatavara, Matti Hyvärinen, Maria Mäkelä, and Frans Mäyrä, eds., *Narrative Theory, Literature, and New Media* (New York: Routledge, 2016), 12.

Chapter 9

City of God / City of Bits: Signs, Signals, Noise

Michael Wutz

The word "message" to me is a dirty word. A message is something that can be delivered briefly and concisely in a few words, and if I thought anything in my book could be reduced to that, then I wouldn't have written the book.
E. L. Doctorow[1]

During one of his ruminations in *The Waterworks*, narrator and newspaper editor McIlvaine—a kind of Machiavellian mastermind pulling the narrative strings—reflects on the conditions of urban existence: "In modern city life you can conceivably experience revelation and in the next moment go on to something else. Christ could come to New York and I would still have a paper to get out."[2] A meditation on the obliviousness of high-speed metropolitan culture, it is also meditation on the, seemingly imperceptible, coexistence of the sacred and the profane, and as such looks forward to one of the central preoccupations in Doctorow's next novel, *City of God*: the putative presence of the divine, now relocated from postbellum America to the turn of the millennium. Similarly, McIlvaine reports verbatim the eyewitness (or, better, ear-witness) account of the final words of one of the novel's major criminals, Boss Tweed, who stumbles through Cuba in a delirious state: "tweet, tweet, he says, over and over, I am tweet, which has no meaning . . . He is impoverished of language but with grand ideas. . . Oh, yes, he says, my city is the city of God."[3] An even more direct preview of Doctorow's next novel, with its canonical nod to St. Augustine, it also broadens the modern search for the divine to include language and the process of meaning-making, and—if only in retrospect—could be seen to playfully anticipate today's tweets of a different sort.[4]

Communication and information flow, encrypting and deciphering, and—as Tweed's tweets make (un)clear—translating noise into meaning, whether secular or spiritual, are indeed one of the hallmarks of Doctorow's oeuvre, and they are in particularly close proximity in the two novels written in the 1990s. What *The Waterworks* and *City of God* also share, arguably more so than Doctorow's earlier narratives— which often center on the myths of American history—are reflections on the novel's location within the ecology of media, be it the ecology of the late nineteenth century, with its telegraphs, telephones, and newspapers, or the ecology of the late twentieth century, including digital film and electronic communications technologies. In *The Waterworks*, McIlvaine surrenders his "newspaperman's metaphysics" (166) by acknowledging that not all stories are "reportorially possible," and eventually crafts a literary narrative of the events he has heard and witnessed, as if to juxtapose the breezy efficiency of journalistic factuality to the reflexive discursivity of the novel (207–8). In *City of God*, I argue, Doctorow goes to the very heart of the matter and probes the very nature of a sign and signification. In the following section of this essay, "Signs Taken for Wonders," I map the various signs and signals—material and spiritual, linguistic and electric, biologic and electronic—circulating within the narrative field, and how their signification is dependent on specific discourse communities. Information theory, in particular, here serves as a useful heuristic to distinguish sense from nonsense, signal from noise. In the subsequent section, "Communicative Ground Zero," I locate Doctorow's metafictional reflections on meaning-making within the human sign system language itself, chiefly by juxtaposing the positions of two of the novel's most memorable personae—Ludwig Wittgenstein and Albert Einstein—on communication, and above all, on listening and decoding. If the one ends in the despair of communicative silence because of insurmountable linguistic blockage—the infinitely regressive metaphoricity of human speech—the other embraces the sonorous noise of various sign systems to reconcile modern physics with metaphysics. The last section, "Negotiating the Terrain," invokes Michel Serres's notion of the Northwest Passage (a tutelary spirit for much of the essay) to pursue the novel's focus on sound and noise into the domain of media culture. I suggest that Doctorow understands humanity as noise makers, whose sophisticated media technologies have not only not facilitated global understanding, but instead helped produce the carnage of modernity. I suggest as well that Doctorow understands the novel as a productive noise-making machine embedded within the sound cloud of the present, a medial subset capable of translating the din produced within the larger culture into its own, however tenuous and tentative, system of order, a minor noise echoing within, and against, the echo chamber of the larger media ecology. If *City of God* thus dissolves the aesthetic constraints of the (traditional) novel, it does so to foreground the contemporary proliferation of codes unprocessable in any single medium, instead favoring an appropriately inchoate textual whole forever resisting closure and coherence.

Signs Taken for Wonders

Doctorow is a writer, not a philosopher, linguist, or information theorist, and he has repeatedly insisted that "novelists are rarely original thinkers, but somehow instinctively pick up on things that are articulated as ideas more articulately by other people."[5] Hence, holding a narrative body of work up to the conceptual rigors of semiotics, semiology, or mathematics would not only do violence to the spirit of his writing, but also to its imaginative capaciousness. Still, the predominant models of modern sign and information theory no doubt variously circulate in his novels. Trained in philosophy—both Continental and American—during his student days at Kenyon, but also alive to the intellectual currents of his day, Doctorow certainly had a working knowledge of Ferdinand de Saussure's understanding of a sign as a "two-sided psychological entity" linking a signifier (the sign itself) randomly to a signified (its meaning) as they are coupled within a synchronic linguistic system.[6] For a novelist in the making, such an emphasis on the arbitrariness, or instability, of meaning, and its radical dependence on context, became a rich quarry for reflections on slippage and signification.

At the same time, Doctorow became also likely familiar with the groundbreaking semiotics of Charles Sanders Peirce, the American pragmatist who offered, not a dyadic conception of the sign (as did de Saussure), but a triangulation between sign, object, and an interpretant.

> I define a sign as anything which is so determined by something else, called its Object, and so determines an effect upon a person, which effect I call its interpretant, that the latter is thereby mediately determined by the former.[7]

Adding, in essence, a (human) reader to the formula of meaning making, and taking it out of linguistics into all possible domains, Peirce offers a generalized theory of meaning making that, on one level, is operative in Doctorow's numerous first-person narrators construing their own world from the proliferating tangle of signs within which they find themselves enmeshed. What Peirce says of himself about decoding the world, in fact, is true of Doctorow as well, especially a novel with as much of an encyclopedic impulse as *City of God*:

it has never been in my power to study anything,—mathematics, ethics, metaphysics, gravitation, thermodynamics, optics, chemistry, comparative anatomy, astronomy, psychology, phonetics, economics, the history of science, whist, men and women, wine, metrology, except as a study of semiotic.[8]

Complementing these more narrowly linguistic and broadly semiotic models, notions of information theory—even more wide-ranging than Peirce's sweeping system—also course through Doctorow's work. Typically associated with Claude E. Shannon, an engineer at Bell Laboratories working in the wake of World War II, and his landmark paper, "A Mathematical Theory of Communication," information theory centers on the transmission and reception of information via various processing channels. If perfect communication takes place by allowing a receiver (Peirce's interpretant) to decode a message in its entirety, without loss, that constitutes friction-free flow, which in reality is only a theoretical, albeit desirable, possibility. In practical terms, virtually all channels of communication—from the alphabet to pheromones, and smoke signals to the ethernet—are fraught with interference or, more commonly, noise. Thus, if information theory seeks to maximize information flow, it is the noise in the channel that determines the degree of successful communication, or, to put it differently, the degree of uncertainty in the amount of information traveling to the receiver. Not unlike the slippage of signs within de Saussure's synchronic linguistics, Shannon's model reflects on (and, in his case, solves mathematically) the probability of information loss, or decrease in error, when channels, as they always do, produce static. For a novelist as much concerned with signs and their semantic instability as Doctorow—all hearkening back to "the venerable ancestry of hermeneutics," as he put it in *City of God* (115)—Shannon's abstract model of signaling couldn't help but be translated into narrative terms.[9]

Consider what amounts to a veritable typology of signs and signals, and their attendant channels, embedded throughout the novel. Told in the form of extended and probably computer-generated notebook entries—and occasional taped conversations—by Everett, the novel's organizing consciousness, *City of God* registers, above all, signs of God in the modern metropolis. Thomas Pemberton, the doubting Thomas and soon-to-be-defrocked Episcopalian priest, recognizes in the cross stolen from his church, and its miraculous reappearance on the rooftop of a synagogue, a form of numinous signaling, and he insists to Everett that "A sign is a sign. And when you know it's a sign, that's enough" (91–2). Preparing for his eventual conversion to Evolutionary Judaism, the incident ushers in his spiritual rebirth free from the shackles of traditional theology, and one that recognizes God's ministry not in the desert—the biblical site of revelation—but "in this bloody, noisy, rat-ridden, sewered, and tunneled stone and glass religioplex. Isn't that what the sign says? But therefore visible only to the unhoused derelict mind" (214). Similarly, when the eminent scientist Murray Seligman—whose very name suggests soulful holiness—advocates for an evolutionary notion of God and belief, a baffled Pem understands his testimony as a "signal" of the "Ways of God" suggesting "a religious agency in our lives" (254).[10] Crucially, in both instances, Pem insists that talking about such revelation "is ruinous, it turns it to shit" (92), and he takes Everett to task for having "erroneously, gloriously assumed you could write a book about it!" (254), thus not only questioning the very foundations of Everett's (and Doctorow's) craft and reflecting on the limits of linguistic representation, but also illustrating the—in this case, insurmountable—noise produced by language. To verbalize orally or in written form what is, in essence, ineffable is to negate the experience altogether. What is needed, Pem observes, is, not a novelist, but a "Divinity Detective," operating more intuitively and receptively, to spot the fingerprints of an absent presence existing outside the realm of language (17).[11]

More properly electronic signals are shot through with noise but can suggest divine illumination as well. Trying to survive in the Kovno ghetto, young Yehoshua Mendelsohn sees in the shortwaves coming from their "glowing" Grundig a clear sign of divine messaging. Staring into the "illuminated cosmos of radio frequencies," and tuning out the static enveloping these pockets of signaling, he nurtures the idea that "numbers were the imperishably true handiwork of God," and would eventually allow prisoners to "perceive the Messiah when he came" (97). Similarly, closer to the historical present, Pem receives an anonymous email telling of the mysterious whereabouts of the cross (26), and, while at one point entreating God once more to "[s]end me an Email" (42), sees the divine encoded in "the blinking cursor" on his screen (8). Pulsing electrons here function, not as digital noise preventing illumination, but as a *deus ex machina* up to date, a cybergod coursing through computerized networks.[12]

At the same time, *City of God* also features signs and signals (de)coded in secular terms. If objects and electr(on)ic media communicate the divine to recipients (or interpretants) so inclined, others receive those messages differently, if not as white noise altogether. To Everett's brother Ronald, for example, a "radio man" during World War II, "the reliable glow of the radio tubes" beams a faint stability in a world of daily chaos, not the religious radiance with which Yehoshua imbues it (168–9). What is more, when German Messerschmitts demolish their B-17, the already considerable static in his radio switches to complete silence, that is, to the complete improbability of successful messaging—Mayday or otherwise: "The cabinetry of his gauges and lights and glowing tubes / . . . seemed all at once to fall in upon itself / like a sandcastle / The lights went out / The intercom went dead" (175). Communication, the novel insists, is not only always contingent on the discourse community within which a particular transmission takes place, on the shared language or sign system, verbal or otherwise, that provides the interpretive framework for meaning-making, but also on a functioning infrastructure and the suppression of enough channel noise to make such transmission reasonably possible.

Thus, ghetto historian Mr. Barbanel chronicles the activities of the Nazis in "a neat Yiddish, like stitches sewn into a page, the characters very small," not only because that may come easiest to him, but also to protect his archive from immediate legibility (94). Yiddish, in that sense, becomes a kind of code, with little noise beyond the idiosyncrasies of Barbanel's clean hand. Similarly, in an instance of extraordinary ingenuity, Everett's father remembers the last remnants of his Yiddish—"a Germanic dialect to hush and soften and make melodic that language of expectorated shrapnel"—and passes himself off as a Prussian to his enemies. His verbal stunt, too, serves as a code, a linguistic camouflage predicated on a shared (and hybridized) sign system, just as the very distortion of German as a, literally noisy, sandwiching of two languages—further enhanced by shouting "from cupped hands"—ensures his survival, and thus the novel itself (138). In yet other instances, paralleling Ronald's malfunctioning radio, when the communications network of Pershing's troops is blown to smithereens, what would otherwise have been decipherable messaging instantly reduces to an "impenetrable war code" (131), much like the "indecipherable messages" Ronald sees stenciled in the sky by German contrails and tracer flares (176).

City of God extends such (in)decipherable systems into the world of animals as well. Avian gobbledygook lies outside human language, but as a specimen of the human species, Everett observes the sophistication of birds. Always in the evolutionary vanguard, birds have developed sign systems, as when crows, in search of food on the docks, suggest an "[a]dvance party, a patrol. If they like what they find, the flocks will follow squawking and croaking in the waterside trees," eventually crow(d)ing out other birds because they "are smarter and bigger and noisier and they commune" (52). Canada geese secure their survival by flying south in the fall, except when interference undoes their collective piloting. If there is "a honking false prophet among them"—the singular noise in their presumably communal harmony—they might return to the ground and, if fed by well-meaning humans, "stay beyond their time and freeze to death" (153). Swallows similarly gather for their annual passage but—in a sustained play on communication—"have a weakness for telephone wires, they can't resist their linear communal perch." Abandoning their cloud formation for serial alignment, "a few suggest to the rest a break in their migration until they clear out of the sky" and settle "shoulder to shoulder on the cursive telephone cable, pole to pole," there to array themselves "for some celestial concert only they can hear" (153).[13]

In the insect world, Everett observes the signaling of an ant colony in Central Park. Controlled by ganglia rather than brains, they communicate "chemical messages [that] were synapsed back and forth" and rely on "genetically programmed little nervous sympathies" to bring about decisions. A dispersed knowledge cluster, they function "almost like parallel processors, or in fact our own cortical structure of neurons," each comprising "one cell of a group brain, . . . an invisible organ of thought that is beyond the capacity of any one of them to understand" (241–2).[14] Interested in cognition, as Everett's analogous thinking already makes clear, he speculates that "the ants' invisible organ of aggregate thought" might parallel the signal exchange within a human crowd, each possessed of "the integrity of the individual will" yet reacting in both sequential and parallel unison if necessary. Reminiscent of the autopoiesis of a gargantuan cell, he suggests that objects alien to a crowd, such as a "purse snatcher," are "isolated, surrounded, ejected, carried off as waste," and that humans, while "individually and privately dyssynchronous," participate in "the pulsing communicating cells of an urban over-brain" (243).[15] And such an over-brain, in turn, relays messages not (only) through a sophisticated linguistics but a (conceivably even more sophisticated) high-speed, spatio-temporal exchange of signals—perhaps undular like a frequency surge—with little or no static or redundancy.

Thus, not only has life on earth evolved innumerable biologic, linguistic, and electr(on)ic forms of communication, each with its own chain of signification and protocols of decoding, but *City of God* also seems to say that such sign systems have been surprisingly effective in ensuring species-based safety, propagation, and, in the final analysis, survival, even in the face of communicative breakdowns, error messages, or noise in their various channels (which are naturally inaudible to and rarely observable by human ears and brains). If not all sign systems are as complex and efficient as verbal language—a point that could be easily argued—they yet suggest that *Homo sapiens* is part of an evolutionary continuum partaking as much in nonverbal and instinctive as much as in verbal and rational methods of communication. Extending from basic electric impulses and body language to complex forms of verbal interaction, humans inhabit what Reverend Pemberton describes as a "primatial over-soul" (11), thus not only weaving the novel's central tensions into one of his neologisms, but also intimating that the species, for all its communicative sophistry, may not be all the distant from, yet out of touch with, the languages of its evolutionary progenitors.[16]

Communicative Ground Zero

The foundational human sign system underlying these reflections on sign systems is of course language—printed English, more properly— the noisy channel within which *City of God* unfolds its narrative(s), even as the very proliferation of signs it seeks to absorb strain against linguistic representation and the formal constraints of the (traditional) novel. Reverend Pemberton notably describes it as "one of Your inventions, one of Your intonative systems of clicks and grunts, glottal stops and trills" (and in the same breath describes God as "the Lord our Narrator, who made a text/ from nothing" [42]). That phrase works its way through *City God* like a leitmotif and becomes a platform for linguistic philosophizing and, as its very description as an apparatus of crude voicing suggests, communicative noise. Ludwig Wittgenstein, the preeminent modernist thinker about all things semantic, and one of the most notable inventions in Everett's cabinet of characters, observes that "the language of Western philosophical thought [is] choked with pretentious baroque tchotchkes," suggesting in a poetry as only a philosopher can, that such systemic overload does not facilitate, but prevent, communication (87). Like his intellectual counterpart in the realm of science, Everett's version of Albert Einstein, Wittgenstein refuses to speak until the age of four and concludes, in a major reservation about the limits of linguistic containability and communicability, that "[e]ver since, in all philosophy I have done, I have distinguished the truths that can be spoken from the truths that exist only in silence" (86). While Wittgenstein, marked by the unspeakable carnage of the Great War, does not go there, it is precisely within this extra-linguistic vacuum that Pem's god resides.

Einstein, for his part, in his own language, so to speak, complements Wittgenstein's reflections on sound and silence. Listening in on the hum of the electric motors in his father's shop, he hears "a soft sound, with tone to it, a language of total elision, with inseparable words, the meaning instantaneous and at the same time incomplete" (43), suggesting a sign system distinct and coherent, yet discrete and chaotic at the same time; it is almost as if he were reflecting directly on Shannon's ratios of sound and meaning, channels and noise, yet to be formulated, and on a system paradoxically inaudible to human forms of meaning-making. Indeed, if such an elusive tonality sounds vaguely analogous to the wave/particle duality he contemplates elsewhere in the text, Einstein's rhapsody on "the system of music" carries overtones of the Newtonian universe, whose mechanical elegance his own work radically relativized. Beginning to grasp that "notes were intervals, relationships of number, and that sound was a property of these relationships," he understands such constellations as "the proposal of a self-contained and logical construction." Much like the radio frequencies were for little Yehoshua, music for the young violinist becomes "a totally reliable cosmos," a quasi-religious experience, with "the character of the inevitable, as in great mathematics, which always seem to be made of pre-existent truths" (45).[17] In either case, such systems of signs communicate, with various degrees of (im)precision and channel noise—both literal and figurative—and are based on networks of interdependent propositions to bring about meaning.

It is Einstein, too, who generalizes about the most fundamental relationship between most systems of signs: communication or, more precisely, the transfer of meaning not just from one system participant to the other, but within various systems themselves. Tongue-tied until age nine, "as if dealing with a foreign tongue, which, as it turned out, I was" (the German of his youth), he reflects, "What does it matter—all language is a translation from something else and I have lived in that something else for seventy-three years" (43). As if reprising his own translation of Newtonian physics into the world of quantum mechanics (in the language of mathematics, and English, his second foreign tongue), Einstein not only observes that one system of scientific order grows out of another; he also suggests that even as radical a rupture as the paradigm shift from the mechanics of the Enlightenment to a theory of, both Specific and General, Relativity (during a particularly unenlightened period of human history) is fundamentally a matter of code-switching, during which one system of signs is replaced with another. Translation, in such a model, requires a reconceptualization of the universe away from planetary balances and interdependencies to subatomic waves and particles, with their crucial shifts from predictabilities to probabilities.

For that very reason, Einstein is able to translate, without contradiction, the language of science into the language of religion, or, to put it differently: to establish communication between the realms of physics and metaphysics. Following the gravitational acceleration of the Holocaust as an expression of centuries of religious discrimination, Einstein concludes that "the traditional religious concept of God cannot any longer be seriously maintained." Instead, he understands "certain irreducible laws of the universe as a transcendent behavior. In these laws, God, the Old One, must be manifest" (53). Similarly, Everett's classmate, the Nobel physicist Murray Seligman, in a riff on Einstein, describes a god that is co-extensive with knowledge of dark matter and string theory—an agent/agency that can "make solid reality, or what we perceive as reality, out of indeterminate, unpredictable wave/particle functions . . . out of what finally may be the vibration of cosmic-string frequencies" (252). Given the right transmission key—here once more inflected with the noise of particle amplitudes—even two systems as seemingly incompatible as modern science and religion can be brought to communicate with one another, or be understood within one another.

The crucial transmission key—not to say, its universal translator—underlying human language and its discourse communities is metaphor, the figure of speech establishing relationships between ideas and objects, or carving a path between signs to make meaning possible. In his discussion of the arche-messenger, Hermes, Michel Serres has famously noted:

> Metaphor, in fact, means "transport." That's Hermes's very method: he exports and imports. He invents and can be mistaken—because of analogies . . . —but we know of no other route of invention . . . [T]ransport is the best and worst thing, the clearest and the most obscure, the craziest and the most certain.[18]

In City of God, indeed, as it must in any utterance, such metaphorical transport is de rigueur and, while often free of friction, often fraught with static and semantic tension. For Everett, flocks of crows on the docks, rather than in suburban woods, their natural habitat, become "a mixed metaphor" (52). And when he explicates "Stardust," one of the standards played by the Midrash Jazz Quartet, he reflects how peculiar it is for the singer "to invoke in the name of lost love/ the cinderous products of a nuclear conflagration." Massively jarring and contradictory in itself, such a comparison, Everett observes, bespeaks "metaphorical desperation" (72)—a comparison ironically compounded by the metaphorical nature of his explication itself. Most prominently perhaps, as an instance of effecting easier communicative transport over time, Sarah grounds her evolutionary notion of God on the assumption that "human history does show a pattern at least of progressively sophisticated metaphors," thus (much like Einstein) as much demystifying as elevating the divine to a concept in synch with progressive "metaphysical and scientific sophistication" (256). Metaphorical equivalencies, however clear and obscure, silent and noisy, underlie the operations of language; they open corridors of connection, tubes of transport, and provide conduits of meaning-making.

Significantly, all the major players in the novel recall primal and primary moments of connectivity that suggest transport and transmission. Wittgenstein states, in a series of propositions: "My first memory is of the grand staircase in my home in the Alleegasse, Vienna," adorned with sidewalls of Carrara marble that "provided reflections, to infinity, of a person ascending to the great foyer" (86). Etched into Einstein's memory—and encoded in his very name, Ein-stein, the One-Stone— are the paving stones of his hometown, all individually chiseled such that they represent "an infinity of decisions under one plan, an intent to make a passable street." Impressed by their patterning and the "revelation that he walks on the thoughts of dead men," he observes, "the paving stones of Ulm, my medieval birthplace, became my first memory—not my mother's breast, not my bed, not my desperately loved toy, but a street—a way of passage from here to there" (43). And a nostalgic Everett laments the fracturedness of modern life, and similarly contemplates the city as the traces of the dead, while looking at silver prints of old New York:

> I am looking at times when people had a story to enact and the streets they walked upon were narrative passages. What kind of word is *infrastructure*? It is a word that proves we have lost our city. Our streets are for transit. Our stories are disassembled. (46)

All are focused, if not fixated, on routes and pathways that allow for exchange, or translation.

For Wittgenstein, of course, the spiral passage—with its suitably Platonic overtones—does not become a stairway to heaven, but an impasse of communication, even as he switches from vertical/helical to horizontal/linear transport by buying "a notebook with ruled lines" (87).[19] Still, "the pretentious baroque tchotchkes" of the language of Western philosophy—its (always inflated) metaphoricity—prevents clean communication and reduces all language, by its very nature, to noise. What remains for him is to weep on the shores of a Norwegian fjord to deafen the sound of silence and, eventually, to observe: "that even if all the possible scientific questions are answered, *our problem is still not touched at all*" (87). Einstein, by contrast, does not run into such an epistemological dead end. His lateral passage, while not necessarily friction free, allows for translation between systems of thinking and believing—from new physics to old religion, each with its miraculous leaps of faith—without abandoning his belief in communication at all. He warns against the widely held claim that "the man in the street cannot be made to realize what I'm talking about," and that the myth of the disheveled genius, built up by "the press and the radio people," has "relieved you of thinking about what I have to say" (38). And Everett, shuttling back and forth between these two thinkers, in a kind of transport dialectic, translates these divergent voices into his own, synthetic narrative *City of God* that is not as much horizontal or vertical as much as spatial and dimensional, and in the process re(con)figures narrative form as a, forever incoherent, semiotic totality awash in a sea of codes.[20]

Negotiating the Terrain

City of God, Everett's own narrative (rite of) passage and translation, is grounded in Serres's own widely known metaphor of transport: the Northwest Passage. Serres has repeatedly observed that "the passage between the Atlantic Ocean and the Pacific, to the north of Canada, . . . is very difficult and complicated to negotiate," and as such is a suggestive "image for the passage between the humanities and the exact sciences."[21] Elsewhere, Serres has observed that, much as the Northwest Passage is sprinkled with "shores, islands, and fractal ice floes," so "[b]etween the hard sciences and the so-called human sciences the passage resembles a jagged shore, sprinkled with ice, and variable . . . It's more fractal than truly simple."[22] Everett's assembly of notebook entries is of course such an attempt to negotiate the terrain—already much traversed—between the humanities and the sciences, including not only physics, linguistics, and religion, but other domains of knowledge as well. Like Serres, he negotiates the obstacle course of disciplinary exchange by navigating (through) the flotsam and jetsam of blockages that have, traditionally, prevented conceptual flow and rapport. Einstein and Pemberton, especially, his two most fleshed-out characters, seem not so much to tiptoe, but rather plunge, into debris-filled waters to establish connections and cohesion.

I want to build upon this model of passage by returning from geographic to auditory space: that is, by pursuing the novel's focus on sound and noise into the domain media culture, the whole machinery of sound-making (and image-making) within which literary fiction is embedded. While *City of God* opens numerous channels between the humanities and sciences—much in keeping with Doctorow's polemic that fiction is "an ancient way of knowing, the first science"[23]—it also opens such passages between its own sign system(s) and the sound-based media that constitute the twentieth-century media ecology.[24] In the first instance, I suggest, Doctorow adjudicates on the disproportion between increasingly sophisticated media technologies and their effect of estrangement. Their development has not only not led to a corresponding increase in global understanding, but in fact facilitated the carnage of modernity (and thus carries Doctorow's general skepticism about human progress to the level of media technology). In the second instance, I submit, Doctorow crafts a textual assembly that exceeds the aesthetic constraints of the (traditional) novel—an unorthodox assembly functioning both as noise maker and, at the same time, in an information-theoretical way, as a noise processor, translating the larger cultural disorder into its own system of order. Embedded within the broader ecology of media, which it maps within its textual space, this assembly can, as a lower-level sorting operator, identify the noise of culture and release that noise productively into the system it seeks to complicate and critique.[25]

City of God maps the spectrum of modern and contemporary media technologies. Email messages and conversations on the phone and recorded on tape punctuate the narrative as much as does the occasional, blinking cursor, not to mention discussions of analog and digital film. At the same time, Everett chronicles much of the communications system that has given rise to the modern mediascape within his own family, and often in the context of war. In prose-poetic passages, he declares that his father, Ben, became a Navy "signal officer" for ground communications during World War I, and that "communication was his speciality/ as it has been the speciality of all men in my family," beginning with his immigrant grandfather who "took up the printer's trade" (130). Aware that "light shutters and semaphoring/ depended on the open sea"—his original training being for service on a ship—he also knows that land-based "telegraphy and telephony" became useless once German barrages destroyed "the cables and wires" and left their general "as ignorant of the truth of his battle/ as some wretched infantryman crouching alone inside his uniform" (131). Switching to "carrier pigeons," which would quickly be shot, he transforms himself and his troops into a "company of runners" (paralleling Yehoshua in Kovno) to relay news from the front, always belated, to headquarters (132).

During World War II, it is Everett's older brother Ron who serves as a "radioman," on a B-17 of the Army Air Corps, with Everett reiterating that his family—his grandfather no less than his father, brother, and he himself, the novelist—are "disposed to communication" (168). He spotlights his brother's delight at "the numbered dials" and "the needle gauges" of his equipment (169), and notes that, during an amorous outing in England, the "heavy portable radio" brought along by his love interest switched itself on—presumably from interfering static—only to play a "shortwave speech of Hitler's/ Sounding like the spillage from an upended toolbox of / nails and nuts and bolts" (171). Back in the air, German attacks, as in the case of his father, demolish his communications apparatus, but not before the bomber's payload "delivered its stern message to the Germans" (177). Everett surmises that Ron saw nations so blinded by their history as to be susceptible—or, better, receptive—to radio-controlled demagoguery. As he puts it: "to be instantly enlistable to the causes/of murderous storytelling/From the mouths of its most monstrous twentieth-century impresarios,/the loudspeaking sociopaths who always know/ whom to blame" (179). And following his crash-landing in France, he "put[s] together some working radios/for the local Resistance" to counterbalance this acoustic threat (183).

Through these biographical snippets, *City of God* thus foregrounds the history of modern media technologies in times of global war—from its telegraphic beginnings to the dominance of acoustic communications technologies. As progressively more authentic signaling systems, from dots and dashes to the wireless broadcast of vocal flows, such systems could conduct warfare and defense maneuvers as much as mobilize the masses through fine-tuned message-bullets. What the, largely cabled and cryptic, signaling systems of the Great War could not yet accomplish, the *Volksempfänger* (a.k.a. "Goebbels' Snout") and Radio Rome could: transmit the radiogenic idiolects of Hitler and Mussolini into waiting ears. If their speeches sound like the noise of "spillage from an upended toolbox" to some, to others they may be the balm on a mind deformed by hate and prejudice. As soon or as long as hardware and software are on the same wavelength, so to speak, the messages will get through. It is once more, as it always is, a question of media infrastructure or communications network, code community, and of the ratio between signal and noise, highlighted by radio as the very medium that gave rise to the very notions of interference and static in the first place.

More importantly, *City of God* suggests as well that the level of humanity's media-technological sophistication does not correlate with its theoretical promise (and premise) of global communication, understood as building toward planetary peace rather than the mobilization of troops and ordnance—or malleable minds, as the case may be.[26] Everett punctuates his assessment of the media of war with allusions to many of the century's most egregious butchers—from King Leopold

II of Belgium and Hitler to Stalin and Pol Pot (268 and 186)—to insist that increased facility of communication has done little not to make the twentieth century the bloodiest on record. The evidence of history makes him as skeptical of media technologies as his mother is of the "phone answering machine," the "last technology that she didn't understand and trust" (130).

Significantly, upon his return into civilian life, Everett's father fails to establish himself in the "record player business,/ as a distributor of soundboxes," as if to suggest that "the tinny voices of Rudy Vallee and Russ Columbo" are, finally, no match for mesmeric speeches traveling on shortwave frequencies (167–8). War, the novel states, is the ultimate primal sound, the humanely created Ur-noise against which, in a humanistic spin on things, constructive messages have to bring themselves into relief. Everett's father is so focused on his job—to deliver messages to headquarters—that he can, ironically, drown out the surround sound of war itself. But when the muddied treads of a German tank are spinning above him, he imagines its toil as "the primordial conversation," a "terrible din, mechanical yet voiced as human,/ a thunderous chest-beating boast of colossal,/ spittingly cruel, brutish, and vindictive fury" (134).[27] And when, in his final act, he storms into the moonscape of a littered no-man's land, a "maniac animal scream [is] issuing from him"—half-intentional and half-instinctive—as if (echoing Wittgenstein) to assure himself of his own presence, and that message and noise, sense and nonsense, are always closely aligned.

Enter the novel. A medium of print that assumes the reader's silent capacity for projection, it too, like war, sits on the keyboard of the human sound console. *City of God* is full of meditations on medial limits, as when Wittgenstein, desperate about the liminality of language, extolls the nonverbal virtues of film. Pictograms, he observes, "do not have to create analogs of the world in grammatical propositions, as language does, . . . do not have to map the world with sentences, but are already there, simply and without effort, in it and of it" (155).[28] Countering such im-mediate claims about film, Everett celebrates the cognitive and emotional interiority offered by the "literary experience," which "extends impression into discourse. It flowers to thought with nouns, verbs, objects. It thinks. Film implodes discourse, it de-literates thought, it shrinks it to the compacted meaning of the preverbal impression or intuition or understanding" (214). And while Pem insists that "no writer can reproduce the actual texture of living life" (47), Everett yet understands the novel as a wafer of micro-pathways channeling readerly empathy, or, to put it differently, as a medium allowing for information exchange: "A story on the page is like a printed circuit/ for our lives to flow through./A story told invokes our dim capacity/to be alive in bodies not our own" (181).[29] What is more, he continues, is that he understands such emotional and cognitive flow, ideal(istical)ly, as an acoustic event: "You would want the whole planet in voice/and the totality of intimate human narrations/composing a hymn to enlightenment" (181). It is by giving voice or sounding out the sum total of all narratives that full human true communication could be achieved.

Like his narrating stand-in, of course, Doctorow knows that such an orchestration of all possible humane stories is pure utopia, a humanist's cry of despair at the inhuman behavior of humanity. Similarly, he has acknowledged time and again that serious fiction has long been condemned to the status of a cottage industry, a senescent medium swallowed up by the global avalanche of schlock and taken seriously by only a few. And far from pitching print culture over and against the obliterating dominance of the screen, he has observed that literary form itself has been inflected by visual media: "the rhythms of perception in me, as in most people who read today, has been transformed immensely by films and televisions."[30] The narrative fractals that constitute *City of God*, in fact, show pronounced elective affinities to filmic montage and even model as a template for our discontinuous minds suffering cognitive dispersion.

At the same time, he invests his medium with particular significance by contemplating its relationship with and within the media apparatus of contemporary culture through the tropes of acoustics and information signaling. Embedded as a subset within the sound cloud of the present, the novel produces its own noise, however faint, which rubs against the noises of its surrounding media ecology. While, of necessity, not being as loud as the, sometimes, bruitist barrage of bits and bytes—that was the preserve of the realist and modernist novel—it is yet capable of staging that din and translating it into a kind of (tenuous) order resistant to the messages of mass-mediated dominance. William Paulson has noted that "[i]f literary texts appear as paradoxical objects in a world of information, it is because of the ways in which they both complicate information with noise and bring meaning and order out of disorder and play."[31] *City of God*, with its sustained emphasis on sound and meaning, encryption and decryption, does precisely that, and it can do so because Doctorow surrenders the novel's formal integrity—its signifying harmony, so to speak—in favor of a semiotic space that features a cacophony of signs no longer containable within one medium or a predominant scale of meaning. When Everett, on a different metaphorical register, speaks of the Bible as "a hodgepodge of chronicles, verses, songs, relationships, laws of the universe," and as a "scissors-and-paste job" that, in its original form, was "inconsistent, defiant of common sense, and cryptically inattentive to the ordinary demands of narrative," he no doubt also alludes to the formal—that is, semiotic—chaos that is *City of God*.[32]

As a form of dissonant in-tonation, *City of God* thus locates itself within the larger system of noise-making, including the noise of war, and acts as a frequency switch between orders of order and disorder and sense and nonsense. It acknowledges the open-endedness of any system of signification, including its own system of signs, operating as they all do within competing rhizomes of codes in the media ecology of the present. If *City of God* makes possible the fluid deciphering of signals alternately codable as secular and theological, scientific and mystical, material and immaterial, etc., it also acknowledges the incompleteness of such deciphering and the necessity for rethinking the—especially ambitious—novel's generic constraints. Only then, as Doctorow memorably put it, can "the larger consciousness, if there is such a thing, [be] advanced a quarter of a tenth of a thousandth of a millimeter."[33]

Notes

1. Christopher D. Morris, ed., *Conversations with E. L. Doctorow* (Jackson: University Press of Mississippi, 1999), 108. Later parenthetical in-text references are to this edition.
2. E. L. Doctorow, *The Waterworks* (New York: Random House, 1994), 25. Subsequent parenthetical citations refer to this edition.
3. E. L. Doctorow, *City of God* (New York: Random House, 2000), 244. Subsequent parenthetical citations refer to this edition.
4. As Doctorow put it in 2012: "The traditional trouble is between truth as people find it in empirical investigation and truth that the fiction writer finds. But now we are in a new kind of trouble. It comes of the screening of every possible experience, with whole populations carrying around pocket screens, and reducing communication to 140 characters. If Henry James were alive today, he would take himself out." Michael Wutz, "On the Craft of Fiction—E. L. Doctorow at 80," *Weber*, 29.1 (2012): 14.
5. Morris, ed., *Conversations*, 197.
6. Ferdinand de Saussure, *Course in General Linguistics*, eds. Charles Bally and Albert Sechehaye, in collaboration with Albert Riedlinger, trans. and intro. Wade Baskin (New York: McGraw-Hill, 1966), 66.
7. Charles Sanders Peirce, *The Essential Peirce*, (Bloomington: Indiana University Press, Peirce Edition Project, 1998), vol. 2, 478.
8. Charles Sanders Peirce, *Semiotics and Significs*, ed. Charles Hardwick (Bloomington: Indiana University Press, 1977), 85–6.

9. "A Mathematical Theory of Communication" was first published in 1948 in the *Bell System Technical Journal*, before being re-released as a slim book, with Warren Weaver, under the title *The Mathematical Theory of Communication* the following year.

10. For a critique of *City of God* on religious grounds (which turn out to be largely political), driven by Doctorow's presumed misunderstanding of Anglicanism, see Bruce Bawer, "The Faith of E. L. Doctorow," *Hudson Review*, 53.3 (2000): 391–402. I don't share Bawer's claim that Doctorow is "engaged in a malignant and programmatic distortion of the truth" (400), but suggest instead a semiotic and information-theoretical analysis that reframes such distortions as noises of communication.

11. Significantly, it is not only Pem, but Rabbi Joshua Gruen as well who devours detective fiction (30), thus suggesting not only that both "learn the trade" (8)—their divine sleuthing—from a (however disreputable) literary genre, but also adding yet another layer to the complicated question of rendering the divine in language.

12. Building on Paul Ricoeur and Jerome Bruner, among others, Hannah Bingel has identified a number of "fictions of spirituality" in contemporary American literature, including *City of God*. See Hannah Bingel, "Fictional Narratives and Their Ways of Spiritual Worldmaking: (De-)Constructing the Realm of Transcendence in *City of God* by Way of Metafiction and Multiperspectivity," in Vera Nünning, Ansgar Nünning and Birgit Neuman, et al., eds, *Cultural Ways of Worldmaking: Media and Narratives* (Berlin: DeGruyter, 2010), 287–306. Such fictions, she observes, "explore religious subject matters on a meta-level drawing attention to how religious faith is constructed and unfolds in mutual exchange with a culture's stories of God and the sacred"; such fictions "range from the religious novel at one end of the spectrum, to the novel that finally denies any transcendentally oriented world construction at the other" (296–7).

13. In Doctorow's last novel, *Andrew's Brain* (New York: Random House, 2014), animal communication and survival receive substantial attention as well (e.g. 120–3).

14. Such parceled information-sharing is a biological case study of distributed cognition that echoes Gregory Bateson's notion, in *Steps to an Ecology of Mind* (Chicago: University of Chicago Press, 1972), that organic forms ineluctably participate in "pathways and messages outside the body," which then accumulate into a kind of expanded consciousness, but "of which the individual mind is only a subsystem" (467).

15. For autopoietic systems (from cells to complex organisms), the extraction of waste—of unwanted or no longer useful matter—too, is a form of noise that has to be eliminated in order for the system to restore itself to order at a higher level. See, for example, the ground-breaking work of French biologist Henri Atlan now available in English, *Selected*

Writings: On Self-organization, Philosophy, Bioethics, and Judaism, ed. Stefanos Geroulanos and Todd Meyers (New York: Fordham University Press, 2011).

16. As E. O. Wilson observes: "If all verbal communication were stripped away, we would still be left with a rich paralanguage that communicates most of our basic needs: body odors, blushing, and other telltale reflexes, facial expressions, postures, gesticulations, and nonverbal vocalizations, all of which, in various combinations and often without conscious intent, compose a veritable dictionary of mood and intention." Edward O. Wilson, *Consilience: The Unity of Knowledge* (New York: Alfred A. Knopf, 2003), 158.

17. To put it out of the way: it would be fruitless to reconstruct the historical accuracy of the observations made by Wittgenstein and Einstein. While Doctorow mentions Wittgenstein (Morris, *Conversations*, 165) and cites Einstein in *Reporting the Universe* (Cambridge, MA: Harvard University Press, 2003), 114, his, or rather, Everett's, figures are products of the imagination serving the vision of his fiction. Notwithstanding his despair, for example, Wittgenstein was a profoundly god-fearing, albeit conflicted, thinker, and Einstein's musings on music, while not implausible, might more credibly have come from the mind of Wittgenstein, who, like several of his brothers, was musically gifted. That is also true of the biographical accuracy of Everett's brother Ronald and their father, who share a lot with Doctorow's own family— such as the father's onetime ownership of "a record and radio and musical instrument store." Morris, *Conversations*, 69.

18. Michel Serres and Bruno Latour, *Conversations on Science, Culture, and Time*, trans. Roxanne Lapidus (Ann Arbor: University of Michigan Press, 1995), 66. The modern *locus classicus* for the universality of metaphor is George Lakoff and Mark Johnson, *Metaphors We Live By* (Chicago: University of Chicago Press, 1980). Observing that "the essence of metaphor is understanding and experiencing one kind of thing in terms of another" (5), they devote a section of their book to "orientational metaphors" that are grounded in embodied being and suggest the spatial mobility underlying linguistic concepts (14).

19. See Wittgenstein's concluding observation in *Tractatus Logico-Philosophicus* on language: once the reader has "climbed out" through his propositions, "(He must so to speak throw away the ladder, after he has climbed up on it)". *Tractatus Logico-Philosophicus*, intro. Bertrand Russell, trans. C. K. Ogden (London: Kegan Paul, Trench, Trubner & Co., 1922), 90.

20. The, even for Doctorow unorthodox, form of *City of God* has drawn attention repeatedly. Observes A. O. Scott: "To call this a novel of ideas would be half accurate. The ideas are certainly there . . . But where is the novel?" *New York Times Book Review*, March 5 2000, 7.

21. Chapter 3, Michel Serres, in Raoul Mortley, *French Philosophers in Conversation* (London: Routledge, 1991), 58.
22. Serres and Latour, *Conversations on Science, Culture, and Time*, 70.
23. Morris, *Conversations*, 181.
24. *City of God* of course also offers numerous reflections on film. The novel's sustained emphasis on sound, acoustics, and noise, however, requires separate treatment, as does the tension between visual culture and print in itself.
25. Writing during World War I, George Lukács, in *The Theory of the Novel*, theorized that modern narrative form is an expression of "transcendental homelessness," a thesis that is much at the heart of *City of God*. George Lukács, *The Theory of the Novel: A Historico-Philosophical Essay on the Forms of Great Epic Literature*, trans. Anna Bostock (Cambridge, MA: MIT Press, 1971), 41. Unlike Lukács, however, Doctorow is, nearly a century later, much less affirmative about the ability of the novel to bring about cultural healing.
26. As historian J. H. Robertson put it, in *The Story of the Telephone*, "All the world's telecommunications facilities . . . which should have been turned to peaceful uses, were set to the frantic uses of war." Quoted in Stephen Kern, *The Culture of Time and Space 1880–1918* (Cambridge, MA: Harvard University Press, 1983), 275.
27. In an analogous experience at the very end of the war a generation later, Everett's brother Ron is "Unable at times to know/ . . . If the screaming he heard was the engine's/ or his own" (183).
28. Wittgenstein's point anticipates Friedrich Kittler's description of the media ecology of the late nineteenth century, when print culture (a symbolic system of mediation) was increasingly being replaced by sound and film recordings, understood as the physical effects of the real—that is, sound and light waves. See Friedrich A. Kittler, *Gramophone, Film, Typewriter*, intro. and trans. Geoffrey Winthrop-Young and Michael Wutz (Stanford: Stanford University Press, 1999), 1–19.
29. That phrase first appears in Doctorow's landmark essay "False Documents." Doctorow, *Jack London, Hemingway, and the Constitution: Selected Essays 1977–1992* (New York: Harper, 1994), 151.
30. Morris, *Conversations*, 80.
31. William R. Paulson, *The Noise of Culture* (Ithaca: Cornell University Press, 1988), 50.
32. *City of God* is, indeed, Doctorow's encyclopedia akin to Joyce's *Ulysses* and *Finnegans Wake*. Joyce famously observed that "I am quite content to go down to posterity as a scissors and paste man for that seems to me a harsh but not unjust description." *The Letters of James Joyce*, 2 vols., ed. Stuart Gilbert and Richard Ellmann (New York: Viking, 1966), vol. 1, p. 297; letter to Georges Antheil, January 3, 1931. Doctorow seems to echo that phrase.
33. Morris, *Conversations*, 181.

Part IV

Tributes

Chapter 10

E. L. Doctorow: Inhabiting History

Jennifer Egan

I've been thinking a lot about E. L. Doctorow's work during the past few years, as I've wrestled to write a novel set before my lifetime.

There are more layers to the challenge of writing "historical fiction" than I had realized.

The first, obviously, is just to do enough research to really move around in a period. That means not just knowing what people wore and what kinds of cigarettes they smoked, but knowing what the past would have felt like to people alive in *that* present. What were people remembering? What were they nostalgic for? What were they reacting against?

All of that is the bare minimum.

The next challenge is to digest that knowledge until it disappears, and the reader can follow a story without being aware of how much work it took for the writer to have the confidence to tell it.

There is a third level of achievement in the realm of historical fiction that I wouldn't be aware of if I hadn't read Doctorow—he defined it, and it's where his work lives. In that realm, a writer has such knowledge and authority about the period he's taken on, AND its historical context, that he can revel in his research and have it STILL feel essential.

Who else could get away with a detailed six-page description of traveling from the Lower East Side to Boston for $2.40 using the interurban street railway lines, as Doctorow does in RAGTIME?

Doctorow's novels do more than occupy an historical moment; they own it, manipulate it, frolic with it, and become intertwined with it in our memories.

Chapter 11

The Polyphonic Past

Don DeLillo

From the Lower East Side and Hell's Kitchen they went up to the Bronx. A little less crowded but not for long. The pushcarts, the knife grinders, the ice men hauling tonged blocks up the tenement stairs. The Bronx was blunt stuff, but beautiful too—the strength of plain lives and roomfuls of noisy relatives.

Years later the sons and daughters, many of them, came back to Manhattan. Became teachers, doctors, tax accountants, artists. What did they bring with them? A conflict, possibly, between the old voices, the accents, the dialects, the intonations, the street life, the slatted shadows of the Third Avenue El, the alleyways and fire escapes—a conflict between this and the great crazy sun-dazed spectacle of the larger culture, the larger geography, the longed-for goal of their grandparents, the place with the shining name, mystical and futuristic—America.

E. L. Doctorow resolves this conflict in the truest and deepest way, through the language he devises, the sentences he works, beats, bends and stretches.

In Doctorow, fiction redeems history through the tonal prose and through the voices the writer sets in fitful rhythms of harmony and opposition.

In *Loon Lake*, *Ragtime* and elsewhere in this fiction, there is a community of voices, a family in fact, all those adenoidal relatives from Tremont Avenue—and those voices are placed in conflict with the monolith, the monotone of history, the single uninflected voice of the state, the corporate entity, the enormous talking product that floats in the sky.

In Doctorow's work, language is a kind of democratic experiment. We see the writer's intuition shaping itself into a narrative strategy, a little like a coloring agent plunked in a pail of water. The exuberant prose of *Billy Bathgate*, the driving winding page-long sentences do not seem designed, at first, to do anything but be exuberant. But in fact they work against the falsehearted promise of great gangsterish power and wealth. There is an endless tension between the living sentences, the innocent hurtling eager prose, and the tight bleak voice that whispers in opposition—the monotone chant of money and brutal privilege.

Those of us who are New York-born know that a thing and its ironic modulation are basically inseparable. They exist in the same subatomic flutter. In *Ragtime*, history and mock history tool along together. The deceptively easy sentences gradually reveal an epic energy of vision. And the sunny warmish syncopated tone yields repeatedly to moments of cruelty and injustice. The voices here—middle-class, poor, lonely, black, real, fictional, magical, third-person, first-person—these voices inflect the distance between the narrator and his subject. The fake objectivity of the history writer is humored, toyed with, played against and finally dismissed.

Ragtime, ragamuffins, rag people, rags—the discarded *shmatte* of the machine-driven culture. And from *The Book of Daniel*, another novel of interweaving materials—dialogues, documents, essays, multiple endings—this sentence: "It is History, that pig, biting into the heart's secrets."

Does the writer want to write himself out of the old streets, to find social mobility as an artist? And he's not just a writer but a novelist, which means his obsessions last for years and so do the blessings of possibility. He wants to be free of strictures and limitations but he doesn't want to betray his history, his crowded and polyphonic past. In Doctorow's case the work is often set in the past and so the requirements of loyalty are doubly intense. But so are the pleasures of invention, and this is where he finds his strength—in the sentences, the long and short of it, the push and shove, the faithful and mindful lilt, the swing of a phrase that's informed by lost time.

In Doctorow we find prose that has a kind of architectural integrity. It belongs to this book, not another. It is alive to every possibility in the material. It is bright, living and often lyrically grand.

That great and shaky institution, the social novel, still wants to live. And this is precisely where Doctorow's work is situated, in the grain of American possibility, in the clash of voices and forces, and in the way in which plain lives can take on the cadences of history.

The novelist knows this eerie feeling. He writes his book in isolation to the sound of a thousand voices.

Chapter 12

A Half Century of Friendship and Literary Greatness

Victor S. Navasky

I got to know E. L. Doctorow in 1964 when he became the Editor-in-Chief of the Dial Press, and I was putting out a small magazine of political satire called *Monocle*, which we dubbed "a leisurely quarterly." That meant it came out twice a year. Later we ended up calling it a "radical sporadical" which appeared with the regularity of the UN police force—whenever there was an emergency and whenever we could solve the financial crisis. Edgar got a kick out of it. And since *Monocle* had gone into the book packaging business we ended up doing a number of projects together, and when I moved to Washington to work on a book of my own, Edgar hired me as Dial Press's Washington scout. But the way I really got to know him was when, in 1966, the *New York Times* featured a short, unsigned news item about how the stock market had tumbled because of what the headline called a "Peace Scare."

Which naturally got *Monocle*'s small band of peacenik satirists thinking. Suppose the government had appointed a task force to plan the transition from a wartime economy, and the task force concluded that we couldn't afford it because our entire economy was premised on the threat of war and without this threat it would collapse? The report therefore was suppressed, and *Report from Iron Mountain: On the Possibility and Desirability of Peace* was born.

Although all of its footnotes (except for two trick ones) were to real sources, the report itself was, of course, a hoax. But we needed a publisher who would list it as nonfiction and not let their sales division know otherwise. In Edgar Doctorow, along with Dial Press publisher Richard Baron, we found the perfect co-conspirators. When a reporter from the *New York Times* called to ask whether it was a real, government-commissioned study, Doctorow advised him: if you don't believe it, check out the footnotes. And when the reporter called the Johnson White House, the officials—not knowing whether or not the Kennedy administration had commissioned such a report—simply responded, "No comment." *The Times* ran a front-page story saying this possible hoax was possibly a real secret government document, and the book ended up on *The Times* bestseller list.

I knew that Doctorow had already written a novel that had been made into a movie with Henry Fonda called *Welcome to Hard Times* (which Edgar used to joke was "the second worst movie ever made"), but little did I suspect that *Iron Mountain*—navigating the complicated line between fact and fiction—was to prefigure Doctorow's remarkable career, as he went on to write a series of novels—not least among them *The Book of Daniel* (inspired by the case of Julius and Ethel Rosenberg), *Ragtime*, and *The March*—which in addition to everything else they did, used real (and fake) history to raise critical historical, political, moral, and cultural questions.

Conflict-of-interest alert: I owe Edgar Doctorow. When in the late 1970s *The Nation* came up for sale and my erstwhile colleague Hamilton Fish told me he would raise the money to buy it if I agreed to be the editor, it was Doctorow who wrote a check to Hamilton for $10,000 of what he called "walking around money," while Hamilton sought to raise the $1 million we would need to buy the magazine and grow it to the point where in theory it might become self-sustaining. (Little did we know.) When *The Nation*'s owner, James J. Storrow, Jr., balked at signing an agreement that would give our group (which at the time was cash-short) a legally binding option to purchase the magazine, if we raised the required capital by the end of the year, it was Doctorow (along with a small group of supporters, including Ralph Nader, W.H. "Ping" Ferry, and others) who attended a small meeting to persuade the reluctant Storrow that the Navasky–Fish team should be chosen over the other twenty would-be buyers.

After we went into business, over the years Edgar proceeded to contribute twenty-two articles, meditations, speeches, and editorials to our pages. They ranged from his thoughts on "The Rise of Ronald Reagan" (1980) and why it was wrong for PEN's president (and former Doctorow author) Norman Mailer to invite Secretary of State George Shultz to address its annual gathering (Ed sat on PEN's board, as did I). He also contributed his always original meditations on such subjects as "The State of Mind of the Union" (1986) and "A Citizen Reads the Constitution" (1987), not to mention his subversive reflections on "Why We Are Infidels" (2003).[1]

Not only that, but Edgar, who had been at Kenyon College with Paul Newman (Edgar liked to say that it wasn't until Newman graduated that he started to get the good parts in campus plays), set up a dinner date for himself, me, Paul, and his wife, Joanne Woodward. It took three months to arrange, but the result: Newman became the magazine's largest outside financial supporter, never once trying to intervene in editorial policy.

By this time, Edgar and I had (slowly) become fast friends, consulting each other on drafts of speeches and articles in advance of publication (although Edgar had the good sense never to ask my opinion of any of his fiction in advance). Along with our spouses, Helen (whom Edgar called "Captain Tidy") and my wife, Annie, we were happy fellow-travelers who vacationed together in such places as London, Moscow, San Juan, and closer to home, Long Boat Key. When celebrating the English edition of *The Book of Daniel* in London, we visited our mutual friend Sally Belfrage, on whose living room wall hung a painting by Michael Train, a realist who saw things through his own intellectual lens. At Edgar's urging, Annie and I made it our first joint art purchase, and it moved right from Sally's wall to our own living room wall, where it still hangs.

"Don't call the Doctorows before 6 a.m.," Jim Silberman, one of Edgar's friends and editors, once told me, not because you will wake them, but because Edgar writes for two hours each morning before he goes to work at the Dial Press. When we traveled together you could always hear his typewriter clacking in the wee hours. Where did he get his energy, his ideas? And what did we think about his books and his movies? We had numerous conversations on and off the record about writing and publishing—I can't remember which—so forgive me if I plagiarize myself in some of what follows.[2]

Welcome to Hard Times, he told me, was not so much a Western as "a play against the genre." And his second novel, *Big As Life*, played against the science fiction genre and lost. Subsequently he preferred to forget about it, saying, "There are some good things in that book, but it didn't work. Norman Mailer told me I didn't go far enough in that book and I think he's right. I overcontrolled it."

After six months writing 150 pages of the first version of what became *The Book of Daniel*, Edgar decided he didn't like what he had written, which was a straight chronological narrative, and even began to wonder whether he was a writer at all. "I was desolate. I was finished. I actually gave up," he said. "I sat down at the typewriter, recklessly and irresponsibly, full of rage and frustration and despair, and just to do something, almost in mockery of the pretense of writing, I began to type something. I didn't even know what it was. What it was of course was the book I had been looking for, struggling for. I was writing in a voice that I subsequently realized was the voice of Daniel, the couple's son. To do the book from his point of view rather than my own—that was the discovery that came out of my despair. Not I, but Daniel would write this book. And the act of writing would become part of the story."

After *Daniel* came *Ragtime* and again, to hear Edgar tell it, he was sitting at his typewriter in his home in New Rochelle, which was built in 1906, staring at the wall or the blank page when inspiration struck. "I live in a house built in 1906," he wrote, and while that did not stay the first line in the novel, he was off and typing.

Loon Lake? When interviewers asked Edgar where he got the idea for the novel, he would say with a straight face that he was driving one Sunday in the Adirondacks and saw a sign which said "Loon Lake," and that was it: "You've got to let things happen to you to write." When I asked, "What would have happened if instead of passing a sign which said 'Loon Lake,' you passed a sign which said 'Lake Placid'?" he responded: "I did pass that sign, but I didn't notice it."

One of Edgar's favorite stories was one he told to a group of librarians about an experience in his journalism class at Bronx Science High School that he claimed was "crucial" to his development as a writer:

> The journalism teacher gave us the assignment of doing an interview. I was a conscientious boy, so I turned in an interview with the stage doorman at Carnegie Hall. And he had a really interesting life story. He was a refugee, an old man who had gotten out of Germany just ahead of Hitler. And he wore this old blue serge jacket and brown baggy pants, and spoke with a strong accent. He lived alone on very little money, and he brought his lunch to work in a paper bag with a thermos of tea. His life had been shattered, but he had spirit, and as it turned out he was very knowledgeable about music. He knew the entire classical repertory. He knew all the musicians who had played at Carnegie and over the years had become a fixture in the place, and all the great recitalists, Horowitz, Rubinstein, Jascha Heifetz, knew him and called him by his first name, Carl. And the journalism teacher said, "This is the best interview I've read in all my years teaching this class. I want to run it in the school paper. What we'll do is send one of the photography kids downtown to take a picture of this guy." And I squirmed around a bit and finally had to confess that it couldn't be done. He wouldn't let his picture be taken. "What do you mean?" the teacher said. "I mean there is no Carl the doorman," I said. "I made him up."

I'm not sure if I believe Edgar's story: it's almost too good to be true. But his life as a journalism student sounds like a metaphor to me, whose truth, like much that he has to say about his own fiction, seems to me intended to be poetic rather than literal. Even his description of the genesis of his books has the sound of the apple which fell on Newton's head—nice mythology but of limited value as a guide to the complexities of the creative process, especially one which has yielded such carefully designed and structured works as *Ragtime* and *Daniel*.

Edgar was always modest when responding to questions about where he got his ideas for books, almost as if he had nothing to do with it. Just as the voice that turned out to be Daniel's emerged, unplanned, from his typewriter, as he tells it, one day he was sitting on his porch in New Rochelle, when what should come riding down the road but the idea for *Ragtime*, with Coalhouse Walker at the wheel. He once told an interviewer: "The fact of the matter is that for the fiction writer, once the book is composed, the fiction machinery keeps going—it doesn't turn off. Whatever you used to write the book, you're now using your memory to create a fiction about it."

Although Edgar was strategically evasive when discussing where his own ideas came from, he was nothing but eloquent and brilliant when sounding off on how The Writer's Mind works. Consider his testimony to Congress on behalf of the National Endowment for the Arts and why it was a mistake to condition grants on writers behaving themselves. Here is just some of what he said: "Any legislative condition put on artists' speech, no matter how intemperate or moderate, no matter how vague or specific, means you publish a dictionary with certain words deleted from the language, it means you lay out a palette with certain colors struck from the spectrum. Do you really want to do this? Does the Congress in its wisdom really believe that bleeping out words, blacking out images, erasing portions of the tape, is what is needed to save this Republic? It's bad not only for artists. It's bad for us all."[3]

Edgar talked about his own books the way he did partly to disabuse those who would praise or condemn his books for what he regarded as spurious reasons. When *Daniel* was celebrated for dramatizing the impact of a historically momentous episode, or when it was said that the distinctive contribution of *Ragtime* was to introduce historically verifiable characters into fiction, Edgar would say those were not his most important motives or interests. "The principle which interests me," he once told me, "is that reality isn't something outside. It's something we compose every moment. The presumption of the impenetration of fact and fiction is that it is what everybody does—lawyers, social scientists, policemen. So why should it be denied to novelists?"

My suspicion: when he gave interviews or lectures or when he talked about writing (even with friends, like me), he brought the same presumptions that he brought to his novels themselves—namely that a mix of fact and fiction, of objective and subjective, is the best way for us all to discover what we have to say. As he once put it, "I write the way other people read—to find out what I think."

Another clue to Doctorow's way of discussing his works may be found in his undergraduate years at Kenyon College, a bastion of the New Criticism (he studied with the poet/critic John Crowe Ransom), which holds that the text rather than the author's intention is the proper focus of the serious literary critic. Thus when he talks of the themes in his novels—whether *Billy Bathgate, The March, Loon Lake* or whatever—he was always careful to introduce or close his comments with such phrases like, "anyway, that's my theory," or "as I see it." In other words, he would always make it sound like he believed that his theories about his books deserved no more respect than anyone else's.

It is therefore ironic that unsympathetic critics have accused Doctorow of writing "political" novels. "It seems to me more of a comment on our time than on anything I have written," he once observed, "that a novel that contains concern for our society is seen to be unusual. *Moby-Dick* is a political novel. *The Scarlet Letter* is a political novel. Dostoyevsky and Conrad wrote political novels, although when they're taught little attention is paid to, say, Conrad's conservative politics. But to think that I'm writing to advance a political program misses the point. To call a novel political today is to label it, and to label it is to refuse to deal with what it does." His premise is that the language of politics can't accommodate the complexity of fiction, which is, as a mode of thought, intuitive, metaphysical, mythic. Elsewhere he observed that "[t]hose who would judge a novel by its alleged politics want to set up a Commissar in the Republic of Letters. They are members of what I call the love-it-or-leave-it school of criticism, making political judgments in the guise of aesthetic objectivity." "What was new about *Ragtime*," he would insist, "was not that it used historically verifiable people. To me the unusual thing was to have narrative distance. To create something not as intimate as fiction nor as remote as history, but a voice that was mock historically pedantic."

Once, when I interviewed Edgar for the *New York Times*, he told me, "In *Daniel* the narrator declares himself at the outset. In *Loon Lake* the narrator throws his voice, and the reader has to figure out who and what he is. The convention of the consistent, identifiable narrative is one of the last conventions that can be assaulted, and I think it has now been torpedoed. For the first time. I've made something work without the basic compact between the narrator and reader, and technically I'm pleased at being able to maintain a conventional story despite giving up that security."

When *Ragtime* first appeared, Doctorow was quoted as saying that he wanted his work to be accessible to all constituencies; he wanted gas station attendants to read it, which led one British journalist to dub him "the Balzac of the petrol tank."

How did Doctorow feel about his critics? "There's always someone around to tell you what you shouldn't be doing. You shouldn't be using historical characters. You shouldn't focus on the child labor laws. You shouldn't shift voices. In *Daniel* the narrator jumped around in time and tense. [In *Loon Lake*] you don't know who's talking so that's one more convention out the window. That gives me pleasure and I think it might give pleasure to readers, too. Don't underestimate them. People are smart, and are not strangers to discontinuity."

The bottom line: besides being fun to be with and some sort of literary genius, Edgar was an educator in the best sense of the term—not merely at the institutions where he taught, but by the books he wrote, the questions he asked (and sometimes answered), and the chances he took. His life and work were truly an inspiration to the rest of us.

Notes

1. Doctorow's contributions to *The Nation* have recently been collected in *Citizen Doctorow: Notes on Art & Politics. The Nation Essays 1978–2015*, ed. Richard Lingeman, afterword by Victor Navasky (New York: The Nation Co., 2015).—Editors.
2. Navasky is here drawing on his early important article and interview with Doctorow, "E. L. Doctorow: 'I Saw a Sign'," *New York Times*, September 28, 1980 <https://archive.nytimes.com/www.nytimes.com/books/00/03/05/specials/doctorow-sign.html?mcubz=1> (last accessed May 23, 2019). — Editors.
3. For a written, adapted version of Doctorow's testimony to the House Subcommittee on Government Activities and Transportation in a hearing on oversight of the National Endowment for the Arts, see his essay, "Art vs. the Uniculture" (1991) in *Citizen Doctorow*, 139–47. — Editors.

Index